I0787968

JUDGEMENT OF THE SIX

DUOLOGY

ALSO BY
MELISSA HAAG

THE JUDGEMENT OF THE SIX

Hope(less) *(Un)bidden*

(Mis)fortune *(Dis)content*

(Un)wise *(Sur)real*

JUDGEMENT OF THE SIX COMPANIONS

Clay's Hope *Luke's Dream*

Emmit's Treasure *Thomas's Heart*

Carlos's Peace

OF FATES AND FURIES

Fury Frayed *Fury Focused* *Fury Freed*

JUDGEMENT OF THE SIX

DUOLOGY

MELISSA HAAG

Shattered Glass
— PUBLISHING —

To my fans,
this book is not recommended as a pillow.

My place in pack society, forever the bachelorette, bothered me. My attitude toward finding a Mate hadn't changed. I didn't want one. I wanted out. No other female went through such a long Introduction period.

Two years of being the family disappointment was enough.

MELISSA HAAG
HOPELESS

HOPELESS

Chapter One

I KNEW THE LOCATIONS OF THE PEOPLE AROUND ME AS IF MY HEAD came equipped with a giant sonar. When I focused, a vast darkness opened in my mind. Instead of blips on a radar, tiny sparks of light shimmered, matching the location of people in the area immediately around me. The colors of the lights, always a yellow center and dark-green halo, never varied. Except for me. My spark had a vibrant orange halo, making me unique and alone. Always alone...

I STOOD at the entrance of the park while the bus pulled away with a screech of hydraulics. Dusk had already settled, casting shadows. Before walking my usual path through the park, I opened my senses to make sure it was as deserted as it seemed.

Though no sparks decorated the darkness in the area around

me, I kept my senses open. The void was endless, but my sight did have a maximum distance. So I monitored the area around me as I walked the path and started thinking of the homework I still needed to do.

Distracted, I didn't at first notice the pale blue light with a bright green halo lingering near the pond. There had never been a color variation before. My steps slowed. Perhaps this new color meant I could see something other than humans, maybe animals. As interesting as that would be, the idea of my sight suddenly changing worried me. What if it wasn't an animal? What if it was someone like me? I could keep walking, and whatever the spark was would never know I saw it. But, I was too curious and hungry for answers to walk away. I stepped off the path to investigate.

The lawn muffled the sound of my approach. Near the edge of the pond, I spotted a shadow moving. It was much too large for an animal. I moved closer. The shadow continued to move, and in an instant, I identified the shape. A man. I froze in shock. He stood close to the water's edge.

His presence didn't freak me out as much as the lack of the normal yellow-green life-spark. In its place shimmered the oddly tinted spark. I'd actually found someone like me–a person who had a uniquely colored life-spark. Excitement built even as caution reined me in. What could this odd coloring mean? I'd never run into any variations before. Stay or run? Investigating a color I thought could be an animal was one thing, but approaching a strange man in a dark park? Not the best idea...yet, my curiosity won.

As I edged closer to the grove of trees, I recognized the older man. I'd bumped into him, literally, a few days ago at the hospital. The man, who had kind brown eyes, a friendly smile, and grey hair, had apologized for bumping into me and continued on his way. That's why I remembered him.

Typically, men didn't just continue on their way after seeing me because, along with the ability to see those life-sparks, I also had a certain pull. Just on men. From adolescent to grandparent, I unwillingly drew them to me. The degree to which I affected them varied. Some just studied me like a puzzle that needed solving but forgot about me as soon as I disappeared from sight. For others, I became an obsession.

I crept forward as I watched the man sit and remove his shoes and socks. But, I stopped when he began unbuttoning his shirt. What was he doing stripping down in the park? Given his apparent age, perhaps he suffered from some type of dementia. Maybe he thought it a good place to take a swim.

When he stepped behind the trees for a moment and reemerged completely naked, I began to think he might have more serious issues than dementia.

Still debating whether I should call out to him, I gasped when his silhouette collapsed. I automatically moved forward, thinking he had fallen. My feet covered some of the distance between us before I saw he had dropped into a low crouch with his fingers touching the ground. I skidded to a stop so abruptly the grass tore up beneath my feet.

His skin rippled like sand in a current. Immobilized, I watched his body contort and fold in on itself in some places while it stretched in others. What would make him move like that? Was he sick? Something contagious? I couldn't make myself move away. If he was hurt or sick, he needed help.

Then the sounds started. His knuckles cracked and popped, and his thumbs shrank from the rest of his fingers. I took a step back and then another. Other joints began popping in earnest. It sounded painful. Through it all, he remained silent. My pulse pounded, and I eased another step back.

His skull grew larger, longer than it was high, and his nose and mouth extended with it. I forgot to keep moving. His ears shifted higher. A grey down emerged from his exposed skin and grew into thick fur. He shook it out when his slow transformation from human to large canine completed.

My mind screamed *werewolf* even as it denied the possibility. Werewolves were legend, myth.

His head swung in my direction. His eyes glowed eerily from the distant lights. My paralyzing shock left me, and I ran. The park entrance beckoned in the distance, but I knew I would never make it. Thanks to my second sight, I saw him rapidly closing in on me.

Rather than allow myself to be attacked from behind, I spun to confront the big, grey beast bearing down on me. One well-placed kick to its throat, that's all I needed to get in before it mauled me to death. Yeah, I was going to die. I braced myself.

As soon as I turned, the beast slowed to a trot. Within ten feet, it slowed to a walk. My breath still tore through my throat in ragged, terrified gasps.

A yard away, it sat on its haunches. I stared at the creature, poised to run again. Intelligent blue eyes watched me. For several long moments, neither of us moved, and a debate raged within me. What did it want? Should I run, or should I wait to find out?

Holding its gaze, I slid a foot back. It stood. I froze, heart hammering.

The creature began to circle me. I pivoted, following its progress. Finally, we stopped when it had positioned itself between me and the north side of the park—the way home. Then, it began to stalk forward, backing me toward the pond. My breathing spiked again. I didn't want to go back to the darker area of the park. Yet, I moved backward fearing what would happen if I didn't.

Just as I considered making another run for it, the creature sat down. What was he waiting for? Suddenly, it yipped. The sound scared the breath right out of me. As if that breath had been the signal he'd waited for, he trotted around me to his pile of clothes. There he morphed back to the man he'd been before; the transformation took less than two heartbeats.

Without perversion, I watched him dress, still too stunned and afraid to look away. I thought about running, but couldn't ignore the fact that he and I shared a connection. Unique life-sparks. I feared what that meant for me.

While buttoning his shirt slowly, he looked up and met my wide gaze. I tried to calm down. Was he like a real canine? If he smelled my fear, would he attack? I'd been afraid since he'd changed into his fur, and he hadn't attacked me then, so I supposed he wouldn't now either.

My rational thoughts fled when he paced toward me with his hands in the pockets of his khakis. I tensed to bolt.

He removed one hand from a pocket and held it up, palm out, signaling I should wait. Right...

"My name is Samuel Riedel, but calling me Sam suits me just fine. I'm sorry for the scare, but showing you was the only way for you to believe."

Believe I'm crazy? Done. I took a few steadying breaths before talking.

"Why did you show me? What do you want?" I fought hard to keep my breathing under control. My mind continued to race.

Sam smiled, turned, and walked toward a bench near the edge of the water. He sat and motioned for me to join him. A small noise of disbelief escaped me. He'd just changed into a dog large enough to pass for a pony. I stayed in the not yet dark shadows of the evergreens.

"You're different, but not as different as I am," he said, keeping himself turned so he could watch me.

He knew something about me? I fidgeted with the strap of my dark brown messenger bag. He could have the answers I needed to explain why I saw the lights in my head or why men acted so differently around me. The temptation of learning something, anything, rooted me. Yet there was also the possibility that he knew nothing of my gifts, that what he knew was something completely different from what I already knew.

"What do you mean I'm different?" I decided I had to be sure we were talking about the same thing before I could reveal anything more.

"You smell different. You're not exactly human, but you're not a werewolf either."

Having him say "werewolf" aloud made everything I'd just witnessed surreal. How could werewolves be possible? How could I be possible? At least, I now knew I wasn't a werewolf like him.

I still stood exactly where I'd been, yet I felt like the entire world had just changed while the crickets continued their night song.

"For clarification...no, I don't need a full moon. No, I don't eat raw meat, although I do enjoy medium-rare steak on occasion. And, no, silver bullets won't kill me any better than regular ones will." Sam chuckled while he moved over on the bench, making plenty of room, and patted the empty space invitingly. "You, dear, are not a werewolf," he repeated.

I blinked at the absurdity of his invitation to sit with him.

"What do you want from me?" I asked, not bothering to acknowledge his invitation. I still didn't understand why he'd shown me at all.

"You may not be a werewolf, but you are still special. How old are you?"

At five feet five inches, with a slight build and few curves to speak of, I looked young. The freckles sprinkling my nose didn't help me look any older either.

"Sixteen," I answered absently. "How exactly am I special?" I shifted my bag to the other shoulder.

"I was drawn to you. You have a certain scent that calls to my kind. I couldn't name the smell for you other than to say it's interesting, unlike anything else I've ever smelled."

"Is that why guys don't leave me alone?" What if I'd been born with more pheromones than the average person? I'd learned about them in biology. Pheromones attracted the opposite sex. It would explain the pull I had on men and why it'd grown stronger as I'd matured.

I couldn't pin it on anything about me physically. I had straight, shoulder-length, ash blonde hair, a medium complexion, and hazel eyes like a million other girls. My nose fit my face well enough, neither too wide nor too long, and my mouth wasn't so generous it'd give a guy dirty thoughts. No, it had nothing to do with my looks. Something else pulled them, and I wanted to understand what. Having extra pheromones didn't explain the lights though.

"What do you mean? What guys?" He sat forward too quickly for my comfort.

I flinched back a step and eyed him warily. When he moved like that, he looked a lot younger than his grey hair and weathered skin indicated. So, although he kept his tone light, I remained cautious.

"Guys under sixty and boys over ten."

"Well, you're young and pretty, so I'm sure it's not unusual for men to be attracted to you, dear." He settled back with a laugh.

He'd said it easily and without inflection as if he'd made an observation and stated a fact, reaffirming the pull I had on men didn't seem to affect him. Did that mean he didn't know about my gift and might not understand? Part of me deflated a little. Should I try to explain it? If I smelled different to his kind, it might still relate to my gifts. Confiding in him might be worth the risk. Besides, he could hardly run around telling people that I had special abilities when he'd just turned into a wolf in front of me.

I took a step closer, partially forgetting caution.

"No, it's more than that... A boy in school, extremely shy, picked on by jocks to the point of physical cruelty, nudged past those same jocks to wait by my locker to ask me on a date. A man shopping with two kids stopped me in the grocery store to ask if I'd consider dating an older man once I turned eighteen. The eighteen bit he threw in after my foster mom gasped in shock." I inched closer, becoming more animated as I spoke, trying to make him understand. "When I turned him down, he went back to his kids, red-faced, and told them that he'd just been asking for grandpa, who wanted to date again. I knew that wasn't true." I paused a moment, then added, "Those are just examples of what happens to me every day."

Sam studied me for a moment.

"What's your name, dear?"

"Gabrielle Winters. I prefer Gabby."

"Well, Gabby, I don't know why men act the way they do around you, but I'd like to help you figure it out. Few people would believe what I've shown you tonight, and I ask that you not try talking anyone into believing. I revealed myself to you because you're special and worth the risk."

He stood and approached me. With the pond reflecting dimly behind him and the warm breeze ruffling our hair, I knew that memories of this night would stay with me for a long time.

"There is so much about werewolves that you need to know. The first is that I'm not the only one."

My heart sank. I didn't like the sound of that.

"I'd like to meet your foster parents, and I'd like to get to know you better. I want to be there for you if you ever need anything." He stuffed his hands into his pockets and rocked back on the heels of his brown-laced shoes while I considered his words.

"You said that I smelled good to your kind. Does that mean I'm going to be run down by other werewolves?" The prospect scared me, but I managed to keep any tremor from my voice.

"It's unlikely, but precisely why I would like to be involved in your life. I can help guide your introduction to our world so it's not as scary as tonight."

He waited quietly while I thought it over. I watched him closely. I liked that he maintained eye contact. It was a refreshing change since the majority of conversations with men occurred while they tried to discover, visually, what about me attracted them.

He offered me an opportunity. With his help, maybe I could find out the reason behind my abilities. And given his condition, I felt certain he'd be able to keep my secret if I decided to tell him about the lights. Could I trust him? Not blindly, but I could start small.

"I'm willing to get to know you better, but I'm not ready for you to meet my foster parents." I wasn't sure if I ever would be.

I wanted to protect Tim and Barb Newton from what could be a monster. They were the first set of foster parents I actually liked. But, if I wasn't willing to bring him home, then just where would we get to know each other better? Dark nights in the park were out, and I had more brains than to suggest his place. He still scared me. Did I think he was going to hurt me? No, he had plenty of time to try to hurt me tonight and hadn't. But, I barely knew the man so anything was possible. Safety in numbers. Somewhere public. Then, I remembered he already knew I volunteered at the hospital, thanks to our run-in.

"Let's meet Wednesday nights at the hospital café. Around six?"

"That sounds good. I look forward to seeing you next week and am truly sorry for scaring you tonight." He held out his hand for a handshake.

I looked at him closely and ignored his hand. Instead, I decided to go for blunt. "You're not going to turn creepy uncle on me, are you, Sam?" I honestly didn't expect him to admit it if he did have that planned. I just wanted to see his reaction to the question.

He barked out a laugh and dropped his hand back to his side. When he saw I remained serious, he sobered.

"I suppose that's a fair question, given what you've just told me. With me, you're safe. Honey, I'm older than I look. Heck, I'm probably old enough to be your great grandfather." He looked at me for a moment. I mean really looked at me, studying my face as if he could read all of my secrets there.

"When I look at you, I see a young girl I want to help. I see a grandchild I could have had if only I'd met my one and only. And I see hope."

Fair enough. I'd wait until next week to pass any further judgments.

"All right, then. I've got to get home. See you next week."

He nodded his goodbye.

Reluctantly, I turned my back on him. Fear skittered along my spine as I walked away. My feet whispered through the grass until I reached the paved walk. When I looked back, he no longer stood by the pond, but I monitored his progress with my other sight as he left the park.

My already complicated life had just gotten more so. I took a huge risk, meeting with a complete stranger, but how could I refuse? Learning about him and his kind might give me more insight about my abilities, which had caused me so much grief over the years. I really wanted an explanation.

When I got home, it was later than I thought. Barb and Tim waited for me in the kitchen. They fed me dinner and sat with me at the table while I explained what kept me. I didn't mention a werewolf, just an old friend of my grandfather's I'd bumped into.

I mentioned my plans to meet up with him at the hospital next week, to talk some more. Barb looked at Tim with worry a moment before Tim asked when they'd get to meet him. I asked for their patience and said I wanted to get to know Sam—again—first.

THREE WEEKS LATER, I exited the sliding glass hospital doors with Sam. We both eyed the dark clouds. The imminent downpour had cleared the usually bustling sidewalks, but the charged air filled me with anticipation.

I turned to Sam. "What do you think? Still want to go? We will probably get wet."

Sam, dressed in his unusually trendy attire for an old guy, continued to study the sky as we walked toward the bus stop.

He had been kind and informative during the first two meetings, telling me as much as he could in such a public place about his "relatives" in the hour I allotted for our meetings. Wary of outsiders, many of his kind chose to live in a closed community across the Canadian border. It had plenty of land, and the rural population of the surrounding area allowed them more space to roam freely. It also had a few old buildings that, up until twenty years ago, had been more for show than living.

After the marriage of their leader, things changed. The leader's wife helped the community see they'd slipped too far from society and that their only chance to survive was to adapt.

A few people agreed and left to help reintegrate. A few more stayed in the buildings and started making small improvements. However, several of the structures needed larger-scale remodeling and, collectively, Sam's "relatives" just didn't have the money for it. Although remote, a few of the community's members ventured out to find work in nearby towns and supplemented the income needed to support their not yet fully self-sufficient way of life.

Gradually, those who'd denied the need for change started seeing the reality of what they'd become...a dying species...and more of the single men went out looking for work. When the leader's sons were old enough, they too left.

Sam had been sent even farther from the community to get the lay of the land in a more urban setting. Trying to blend, he'd decided he needed to dress more like the people of the area.

At that point in his narrative, I'd wondered what he'd been wearing. Furs?

When he'd gone shopping, he'd asked a sales clerk's advice regarding what to buy. The sales clerk had been about my age, which explained Sam's trendy choice of clothes.

It amazed me how much I'd learned about the man walking next to me. The compassion for his people's plight impressed upon me his selflessness, and watching him interact with other people around us, showed he had a sense of humor. Those defining characteristics had decided it for me—it was time to introduce him to Tim and Barb.

We'd reached the bus stop without a drop of rain.

"A little rain never hurt anyone," he said answering my earlier question.

Another thing I liked about Sam. He sensed when I was lost in my own thoughts and let me be.

"Okay, I'll text Barb and let her know you'll be coming over. They've been asking about you every week." He looked at me questioningly.

"I mentioned you that first night we met in the park. They wanted to know why I was late. I said I ran into an old acquaintance, a friend of my grandfather."

A city bus drew to a halt in front of the sheltered bus stop. Sam and I waited for the other passengers to board. He surprised me by pulling out his own city bus pass to pay. The familiar driver looked at me curiously when I took my normal place behind him and slid over on the worn, grey vinyl seat to make room for Sam.

Sam and I didn't talk much on the bus ride. Instead, I watched out the window, waiting expectantly for the rain.

At our stop, Sam stood and exited. He didn't offer me his hand. After only knowing me a short while, he knew I didn't want to be touched. I didn't like growing attached. When you touched people, you developed attachments. Then, when they left, it made it harder to say goodbye.

He waited for me to hop down from the last step, then fell in beside me as we made our way down the paved park path. Although we still had an hour of daylight left, the dark storm clouds writhing in the sky above cast the city into an early dusk. Ever since Sam had revealed himself to me, tension drove me to walk quickly through the park. Particularly in the dark. I liked having someone to walk home with me even if that someone had started the whole thing. In Sam's company, I didn't worry as much.

"You're certain I won't disrupt things at home just popping in like this?"

"I don't think you can disrupt it any more than it's been," I said. "Barb, my foster mom, is pregnant, which really is a good thing. Barb and Tim have been trying to get pregnant for years. Thinking they'd never have kids of their own, they decided to foster."

When we were halfway across the park, Sam slowed to give me more time to talk. I hadn't mentioned any of this to him before. The swings in the abandoned playground to our right started to sway in the increasing wind, their older chains squeaking slightly with each forward swing.

"They own a cute little two-bedroom house. If she carries the baby to term, there won't be enough room, you know?" I kept my eyes focused on the path, not wanting to see his expression. "Because she hasn't passed her first term yet, they haven't notified my social worker."

I had no regrets. I really did feel happy for Barb and Tim, and I'd moved around enough in foster care to know the drill. Plus, I counted down the days...months...until I turned eighteen and would be legally free from anyone's guardianship.

Sam remained silent beside me.

Leaving the park, we turned right on the sidewalk. The phone in my bag buzzed, and I quickly searched for it. The rain still held back, but the sky overhead rumbled ominously. I checked the message and smiled at Sam.

"Barb said she's very excited to meet you, and since you and I just ate, they'll have cake and coffee ready."

Sam nodded. A fat raindrop splattered on the sidewalk in front of us, and without a word, we both started walking faster. When we turned the last suburban corner, I pointed out the Newton's house to him, not pausing the brisk pace we'd set.

Barb and Tim both waited for us on the front stoop. Tim had his arm wrapped around Barb's shoulders as he peeked around the awning to look up at the clouds. When Barb nudged him to point us out, he looked our way and waved.

They greeted Sam enthusiastically and invited him in. I could see Barb sizing him up and finding him acceptable. In a rare twist, Tim did most of the talking that night and asked Sam about himself. When Sam said he originally hailed from Canada and managed the family business investments, I figured he stuck as close to the truth as possible. They did ask him about my grandpa, and he wove a beautiful tale about them growing up together. Since I never talked about my grandfather, the Newtons didn't know any differently. The skill with which Sam lied made me a little uncomfortable. If he could lie that easily to them, how easily could he lie to me?

The rain stopped before he finished his second cup of coffee. Sam stood and smiled at Barb.

"The cake and coffee were wonderful. Thank you for letting me drop in like this." He extended a hand to Tim. "I won't overstay my welcome or the coffee."

Tim clasped Sam's hand with a warm smile as the adults all laughed.

"It was a pleasure to meet both of you."

"We appreciate you stopping in," Barb said, already collecting the cups to bring to the sink. "When Gabby said she ran into you, we were both very curious."

"I can imagine. Now that I found her, I don't want to lose track of her. If it's all right, I'd like to stop by now and again to check in on her."

"We insist you do." Tim patted Sam's back in a manly display of affection as they walked to the front door. I quickly helped Barb put the dishes in the sink so she could follow them. Barb was a little compulsive and couldn't walk away from a dirty kitchen.

"What about dinner next Wednesday?" Barb asked, raising her voice from the kitchen as she washed and dried her hands at the sink. She hurried to the front door where Sam bent to put on his shoes.

"That sounds like a good idea." Sam finished tying his shoes and turned to me. "Is that okay, Gabby?"

Leaning against the arch dividing the living room and the kitchen, I watched the adults interact. In a way, it reminded me of the animal channel. I struggled not to crack a smile at the thought since Sam really did have one foot in the animal world.

"After I finish volunteering at the hospital, it should work for me."

Satisfied they would see each other soon, the adults said their goodbyes, and Sam left. Not bad for a first meeting.

SAM VISITED PERIODICALLY over the next two months, and life continued as normal for a while. Each time I met with Sam, I learned more about his world. Nothing that I could apply to myself, yet. I still had hope though.

Barb started to show, and the typically reserved Tim couldn't stop talking about it. My time with the Newtons ticked away like the seconds on a clock.

On one of our scheduled Wednesday nights, I opened the door for Sam as soon as he knocked. He didn't show any surprise when I swung the door open after just one knock, but then I didn't expect him to.

Despite meeting at my home where we couldn't speak freely, I'd managed to learn a little more about him and his kind. For example, he had exceptional hearing. He knew when I got nervous or upset by the change in my pulse. He could hear whispered conversations taking place in other rooms as long as the door remained partially open. He could even hear whispers through thin walls. In addition to keen hearing, he also had better eyesight. In the dark, his pupils expanded to a freakish dimension, allowing in as much light as possible and enabling him to see when a normal person couldn't. This explained the way his eyes reflected.

"Hi, Sam." I stopped him from taking off his shoes. "We're eating on the patio since it's nice out." He wiped his feet extra well on the rug before following me through the house to the back patio.

The solid concrete slab patio took up a fourth of their backyard space. The patio wasn't that big; the yard was just that small. Since it was surrounded by a classic wooden privacy fence, it would make a perfect play area.

We walked onto the patio, and Tim looked up from the grill to our left and nodded a greeting. Smoke drifted lazily upward as he flipped a burger.

"Sam, thanks for coming."

Barb stopped setting the table and moved to greet Sam with a hug. Sam gave one back with a smile. Barb had stopped trying to hug me a long time ago.

Tim brought the burgers from the grill, and we all sat to eat while Tim and Sam dominated the conversation with fishing stories.

When Sam asked if I'd ever been fishing, I nearly choked on my bite of burger.

"No," I said definitively.

He looked shocked, but I knew it wasn't real.

"How can it be that a girl your age has never been fishing?"

"Many have tried, and all have failed, Sam," I said, slightly amused. "I'm not an outdoorsy type."

His next comment wiped the smile from Barb's face.

"You should come with me for the weekend. I'll take you to the cabin your grandpa and I went to before you were even born. It has indoor plumbing now, so I bet you could talk a friend into coming with."

I glanced at all the faces at the table. Though Sam still smiled, Barb focused on me with an alarmed expression, and Tim glanced between me, Barb, and Sam. I took another bite of burger to stall.

In private, Sam had asked about my plans for the future. Barb's baby bump was hard to miss now. He had mentioned he had a spare room at his place if I ever needed it. He'd also mentioned he would like to take me on a trip to meet others of his kind. I felt fairly certain that's what he meant now. Having him ask tonight without any warning caught me off guard. I could have done some prep work like dropping hints that I had an interest in spending more time with him or something. But it did make sense that he asked now. Why try to delay the inevitable? The doctors saw no reason Barb's pregnancy wouldn't go full-term this time. School would let out soon, and I had no summer job.

Setting down my fork, I picked up my glass and took a long drink of water. They all waited. I decided to save the adults the long dance around a subject none of them wanted to face full-on. I turned toward Barb and Tim.

"I've spent a lot of time getting to know Sam over the last two months and told him about the baby on the way." I looked at Barb, meeting her beautiful, dark brown eyes. "We all know that I won't be able to stay once the baby's here." Barb started to tear up and speak, but I stopped her with a raised hand. "I also know that you want me to stay. I don't doubt that for a minute. You've both been so great to me, and I thank you."

I turned to Sam. "You said that you live in a three-bedroom house and that I was welcome to visit anytime. What about visiting until I graduate?" I didn't want to go back into foster care.

Sam continued to smile at me and nodded.

Barb started to sniffle, and Tim reached over the table to pat her hand.

Friday night, Barb and Tim dropped me off at Sam's. Though it was only for a weekend, they knew what it would mean if everything went well. So I willfully squashed my discomfort and endured Barb's hug. Tim, thankfully, settled on a nod and a wave as I climbed into Sam's truck.

I used the eight-hour drive to ask Sam direct questions about werewolf life, and I tried to soak up everything he said. I stopped talking when we turned off the blacktopped road onto a deeply rutted dirt lane I doubted saw much use. For a mile, I braced myself against the rough ride. Finally, we emerged from the tree-lined path into a wide clearing.

A large, two-story log cabin style structure dominated the space, its wings branching out to connect to outlying buildings. Sam parked on the combination of old gravel, stubborn grass, and plain dirt in front of the buildings.

The werewolf community reminded me of an old wilderness resort, one that had been closed for a few years. If not for the lights pouring from several of the windows, I would have locked the truck door instead of getting out.

I shouldered my bag and trailed Sam onto the covered porch. Sam pulled the solid wood door open without knocking. Inside, an eclectic array of rugs along the perimeter of the large main entry accommodated numerous sets of shoes. Hooks on the walls held a bounty of coats, jackets, and overalls.

"We don't have to worry about stealing here," Sam said when he caught me looking at the mass of shoes. "And it keeps the rest of the place cleaner if we leave our outside things here." He started taking off his shoes, and I bent to remove mine.

"You would not believe how messy this place was thirty years ago," a voice called from the hall.

I looked up from untying my shoes. A tall woman with blonde hair and a gentle smile walked into the entry. I estimated her to be in her late twenties.

"Hello, Gabby," she said, coming to stand next to me. "I'm Charlene. Sam's told me about you. I'm so thrilled to meet another person like me." She held out her hand in greeting as I stepped out of my shoes.

Excitement coursed through me. Finally! Sam had mentioned Charlene, another human among the werewolves, during one of our many talks. The possibility that I wasn't as alone as I thought obliterated any hesitation I might have had, and I reached out and clasped her hand.

Charlene's grip was firm and sure, but I barely noticed it. The darkness of my other sight had burst open, and the brilliance of the sparks surprised me; their normal soft glow amplified so much that the blinding light obscured their gentle colors. I let go of her hand while maintaining my focus. The lights dimmed considerably so I could, again, discern their soft colors.

Sam's spark glowed blue with a green halo, and hers, while still containing the yellow center as with any human, had a red halo. I'd considered the possibility that my orange halo was because I couldn't see myself correctly using my other sight. But seeing Charlene's assured me our uniqueness was real.

Beyond our sparks, I noticed other blue-green lights. Not in the immediate area but spread throughout my area of awareness. The coloring of those lights matched Sam's. Werewolves then were blue-green, I thought. Color by species made sense, but Charlene and I didn't match. Why?

"Like me?" Her words suddenly penetrated my study of the sparks. Could she see lights too?

"So far, we are the only two humans who seem to be compatible with werewolves," she said, still smiling in welcome.

My hope sank. So we were human and...wait, what?

"Compatible?" I looked at Sam in confusion. I knew that I smelled differently to werewolves, but he hadn't mentioned anything about compatibility. Charlene answered before he could.

"Yes, werewolves choose their Mate—husband or wife—instinctually. They have no history of ever before selecting from humans for their Mates, but here we are. Whatever it takes to become a Mate, we apparently have it, too."

My mouth popped open in shock as I understood. I turned on Sam.

"You brought me here to hook up with a werewolf?"

"No, Gabby. I apologize for upsetting you," Charlene said from behind me. I turned to look at her. "Yes, we're different in that a werewolf might choose us, but that doesn't mean that they must choose us or that we have to choose them. At your age, there will be no hooking up."

She looped her arm through mine and gave me a motherly pat. As soon as she touched me, all the sparks around us brightened again. I didn't even need to focus. The lights just flared and continued to glow brightly without effort. Weird.

She led me toward the hall from which she'd entered. After a few steps, she stumbled and pulled her arm from mine. With relief, the lights in my mind dimmed, and I concentrated on her words.

"I asked Sam to bring you so you and I can talk. As I said, there is no one else like us that we've found. I came here when I was younger than you—long story—and met Thomas, the pack's leader. It was a very hard adjustment with a huge learning curve on both of our sides. I don't want you to have to face any of that on your own. We'll introduce you slowly to this new world you're now a part of. If you have any questions, don't be afraid to ask them."

She led us down a second hallway and stopped in front of a closed door. When she opened it, I saw that it led into a very small apartment.

"This is still a work in progress. Let me know if you need anything," she said, looking at Sam. He nodded.

I took a moment to take in my surroundings as Charlene walked away. The small, main room had only a few mismatched pieces of furniture. The bedroom, which I suspected had once been a walk-in closet, barely held a twin-sized bed, nightstand, and lamp. Sam insisted I take that room as he set his bag on the foldout couch. I didn't complain. I figured sleeping in a half-sized bed ranked higher than Sam's sleeper sofa.

A tiny bathroom right off the main living area completed the suite. The apartment definitely qualified as rustic, but I didn't mind.

SAM WOKE me after a few hours of sleep.

Despite Charlene's assurances that my stay didn't include finding a boyfriend, I still felt leery over Sam not telling me about the compatibility thing. I'd thought I could trust him, and his omission stung a little.

I wanted to excuse it—maybe it'd slipped his mind—but it'd taken eight hours to get here. Granted, most of that time, we'd talked about the progress the community had made and the customs, like pack hunts, that they no longer followed. Still, he could have mentioned that doozy. *By the way, Gabby, werewolves will want you as their Mate.* I paused, then shook my head at the thought. Yeah, I would have reached for the door handle and tried to jump from the moving truck. Maybe he'd made an okay call. Only time would tell.

I got out of bed and dressed. Sam already had his bed made when I opened my door.

We left the apartment, and he led me to a large room, which he referred to as the commons, to get a bite to eat. The space served as a cafeteria and an entertainment area with seating arrangements scattered around the room. It even had a pool table set in the back corner.

Charlene saw us and came over to our table. Two young men followed in her wake. She introduced them as Paul and Henry. She thought I might like the opportunity to talk to people my own age. She even suggested that we go into the woods so they could show me more about the werewolf way of life. Sam heard my panicked heartbeat, and before I could refuse, he suggested we use the lounge in the commons to get to know each other, instead.

Paul and Henry didn't treat me the same as human boys did. As curious about me as I was about them, they asked a myriad of questions.

"What's school like?" Paul, the boy with dark hair and a carefree smile, asked while sitting on a padded dish-chair close to me.

"You don't go to school?" I couldn't believe it.

"Nah," said Henry, a short stocky kid with bright blue eyes. "We're home schooled here. It's way quicker to graduate since we can study at an accelerated pace because we don't have to break for holidays or anything."

"That actually sounds pretty great...what school should be, minus the no breaks part." I cringed inwardly at the thought of school year-round then answered his original question. "The majority of the teachers spend their time hating their jobs and finding ways to be as disagreeable as possible while the students look at it as a popularity contest and spend more time worrying about who's dating who than studying," I explained.

"Dating?" Paul glanced at Henry, who wore an equally puzzled expression. "I heard Charlene talking about that once. Sounds weird."

"Really? You guys don't date?" I didn't ask what they did to get to know a girl instead of dating.

"No, we get invited to Introductions," Paul said as if reading my mind.

"What's that?" Sam hadn't mentioned anything like that to me, and I wondered if I should add it to his list of omissions.

"When a female comes of age, she's brought to the Introduction room where she can meet werewolves she has never met before. The Elders are there to make sure the girl is safe and to give the guys a few minutes to talk to her. You know, to really get her scent. When there's a connection, a guy just knows and Claims her. If not, the next group comes in for their chance."

I started to sweat as I sat there. First, what did he mean by Claim? Second, they kept a girl in a room while guys came in to look her over and smell her? I reached for my water that sat on the coffee table in the center of our seating arrangement. My hands shook a little, and I tried really hard to calm down and not let my imagination run away with me.

"Hey, Gabby, you okay? Did Paul say something wrong? Charlene said we could ask any questions we wanted..."

They had no idea how foreign what they'd just said sounded to me.

"You don't have to worry about Introductions if that's what's scaring you." Paul looked at me with concern. "For you and Charlene, the attraction works differently. She explained it to us when she said that you were coming. You guys have a level of appeal, or chemistry, with just about all werewolves."

He is not helping, I thought while he continued.

"Because the level of attraction to you varies, it wouldn't be safe to put you in an Introduction room."

"Yeah," Henry agreed and, with a spark of excitement in his eyes, leaned forward in his chair. "That's when the mating duels happen. It's rare with a werewolf couple, but when Charlene was first brought here, I heard the guys went crazy because they didn't know what was happening. They fought over who had the strongest tie to her. But you don't have to worry about that with us. Paul and I think you're okay, and you smell good and everything, but we knew when we met you that you're not right for either of us. That's why Charlene left you alone with us."

My stomach churned. Werewolves were going to start fighting each other for me? No thanks. They both smiled at me encouragingly. They probably thought their explanations helpful, but the information they threw at me stunned me.

"What did you mean by 'Claim'?" My voice came out light and airy with anxiety, but I needed to know.

"It's when we bite our Mate. The bite draws blood but doesn't hurt," Paul explained reassuringly.

"What?" I nearly shouted. My freak-o-meter bypassed meltdown. My head spun dizzily, and no doubt, all the color had drained from my face.

"Oh, not for you, Gabby," Paul said, quickly leaning forward. He made shushing motions with his hands. "We can't Claim humans like that. When your Mate finds you, it's up to you to Claim him."

So, I would need to bite someone? Not going to happen. It was easier to calm down now that I knew I had control. I didn't want to be "the right one" for anyone at this point in my life. I hoped that the rest of the werewolves, like these two, would correctly use their keen sense of smell to determine my unsuitability.

I heard the main door swing open and saw Sam walk in with an older woman and another older man. Sam nodded to me and then moved with his group to another area of the room. They sat down and started talking. Paul and Henry shifted their attention to the new people, listening. I couldn't hear the conversation but had no doubt they could. Just as I knew Sam would hear if I asked either Paul or Henry to tell me what the group said. I decided to change the subject.

"What about sports? I noticed there are no TVs. Do you guys play or go watch any sports?"

"Nah, we don't get good reception out here, and the television tends to hurt our ears, but we do like to play football. There aren't enough of us for a team, though."

The door behind us opened again, and I watched two younger men, about our age, enter. They glanced our way but headed toward the group with Sam. I turned around and took another drink of water while thinking about this Mate business. According to these two, I needed to watch for a werewolf who acted as most human men would toward me, intense and weird.

Sam startled me out of my thoughts when he spoke next to me.

"Gabby, I'd like you to meet Eric and Derrick. They are the twin sons of a couple who lives here. They're home from college and have to leave again tomorrow."

I smiled and said hello. They both nodded to me but didn't speak. Awkward.

Feeling uncomfortable, I looked back at Sam, who nodded at the two. They turned and left. If they represented the normal reaction to me, I needed to watch out for someone even more intense and weird. Maybe I just needed a plan to avoid them all.

Sam waited until they'd walked out of the room to explain.

"I want you to get to know the people who live here. In summer, we'll spend a lot of our weekends here." He looked at Paul and Henry. "You two keep an eye on her. I'm counting on you to help explain our ways."

Sam walked back to the group, and I looked from Paul to Henry with an arched eyebrow. Was it just me, or did that feel weird? I wanted to ask but remained quiet. There were still too many ears to overhear. They seemed to understand my unspoken question and both shrugged in return.

Sam interrupted our conversation twice more, each time bringing someone to introduce to me. My mind caught on the word "introduce."

Paul and Henry's assurance that I would never face the Introduction room clicked everything into place. Sam had started slowly introducing me to the eligible male population of this little community right here, right now—in this room. After the third set left, I caught Sam's eye.

"Sam, would you mind showing me around outside for a bit?" I stood and made my way to the main door, not waiting to see if Sam followed.

After our time together, I'd felt sure enough of Sam that I'd risked a trip to an unknown destination with him, alone. I'd been willing to explain away the little doozy he didn't mention on the way here; but now, his actions and omissions devastated my confidence in him.

Already familiar with the layout of the Compound, I didn't hesitate to walk out the front door and stride purposefully toward the dirt lane. Sam didn't take long to catch up to me. If I told him I wanted to go back to the Newton's now, would he take me? If he did, then what? I couldn't stay there forever.

"Sam," I said when we walked side by side. "I don't want to be on the streets, but that's where I'll go if you think you can pull this crap if I move in with you." I didn't look at him; I was too angry. And scared. "I understand the condition of living at your place is that we come up here. But my condition is that you have to be completely honest about our purpose in coming up here. Each time," I stressed. "I don't know if I can trust you."

"I'm sorry, Gabby. You can trust me. I have your best interests in mind. This is another one of those things that is easier to believe when you experience it firsthand." He kept pace next to me as I led us farther from the Compound.

"No, Sam. You need to lay it out for me straight."

He stayed quiet for a few minutes, and I wasn't sure he had anything to say until he actually spoke.

"Well, I heard what Paul and Henry told you. That part's right. We do Introductions for our females in a controlled environment to keep them safe until they find their Mate.

"We learned from Charlene's time here that you'd need to be handled differently. I told you that werewolves would find your scent interesting. Since we're branching out into more urban areas, it would only be a matter of time before you attracted attention. So, we wanted to control your Introduction. A formal Introduction without mass challenges was out of the question.

"This is the compromise; they come into the commons, say 'hello' to you, then talk to the Elders. Because the level of attraction varies, we interview them. They must formally request permission from me to come see you again if they think of you as more than just interesting. They are not allowed to approach you while you are on your own. If they were to approach me for a second meeting, I would speak with you first before approving or denying their request."

The light filtering through the canopy cast the road into dusky shadow. I stopped walking and turned to Sam.

"What you're saying is, eventually, werewolves would find me, but if I stay with you, you'd be my buffer?" He nodded. I studied him. "And I'd only have to say hi to these guys. It'd be up to me if I wanted to spend any additional time with them?" He nodded again.

I liked Paul and Henry. They oozed useful information and didn't react to me at all. The others I'd already met hadn't seemed too interested, either.

When Paul and Henry had mentioned mating duels, I imagined

drowning in a writhing mass of hostile bodies, all in various stages of transformation. I still dreamt about Sam shifting. The dreams and my fueled imagination bothered me. But since arriving, everyone had remained in human form, and nothing freaky had happened. The general population of werewolves couldn't be all bad. I just didn't like the way I had to meet them. Yet, now that the werewolves knew I existed, trying to live on my own didn't sound like a good idea. I'd be better off with Sam. He'd keep the others away.

"Fine, let's go back."

Paul and Henry were playing cards while they ate their way through a stack of sandwiches set out on the coffee table. They waved me over, and I gladly joined their game and grabbed a sandwich for myself.

Several more werewolves came in throughout the day. Sam led each one to me. Most left after a polite nod of hello. A few asked for a second meeting. Each time, Sam would look at me and, at the shake of my head, reject the request. It relieved me to see him keep his word and restored some of my shaken confidence in him.

We packed up and left Sunday morning. I mostly paid attention to the scenery since I'd missed the majority of it on the way there. While I watched the trees flash by, I thought about the weekend. None of the guys I'd met seemed too upset over any type of rejection. For as much emphasis as they'd put on my smelling good to just about all werewolves, their laid-back attitude didn't make much sense to me.

"Why did the guys seem okay with their second request being rejected?"

"Although you smelled good to them, they knew it wasn't just right. When it is, they won't give up, which is why staying with me is so important. We have laws that control certain aspects of the social side of the pack. One is that unMated human females, like you, cannot be approached without the approval of the nearest Elder."

"Then, why can't you just tell them all 'no' for me in advance so we don't have to mess with this whole Introduction thing?"

"Because I have to give them the chance to see for themselves that it's not right. Was it that bad? Meeting people? No one treated you the way some human men have treated you."

I couldn't disagree. "How often is this going to happen?"

"Once a month."

I sat up straighter. "No way." I shook my head for emphasis. It was a cool enough place, but sixteen hours of driving in a single weekend every month would get boring. "Once every two months."

"Every five weeks, with flexibility to switch weeks if needed," he said.

"Seven weeks."

"Six," he said with a sideways glance at me.

"Fine, every six weeks," I compromised. Then I threw in another condition. "Until I graduate. Then, I'm going to college and won't be obligated to take time out of studying for dating—or whatever you want to call this—if I don't want to."

"Deal," he agreed.

I stared at him. He'd agreed too easily. Was that a hint of a smile on his mouth? Why did I feel like I just got the raw end of the deal? I'd have to play my cards carefully so I didn't find myself hitched in some weird backwoods werewolf custom.

SAM SAT AT THE WORN, OAK TABLE IN THE MIDDLE OF THE SUNLIT kitchen. He scowled at its dull surface, and when I walked into the room, he transferred the glum look to me. I shook my head at him and went to make his morning coffee.

Sam and mornings didn't mesh well. I'd realized that as soon as I'd moved in. How a werewolf, usually graceful and strong, could stumble and mumble until he had his caffeine still confused me. With his werewolf metabolism, I doubted it really did anything for him. Regardless, I still took pity on him and tried to wake up first to start a pot—even though it wasn't my drink of preference in the morning.

Today, however, his familiar morning scowl didn't solely relate to his need for coffee. After two years of almost monthly visits to the Canadian werewolf community, this weekend would be my last, and he didn't like it. Happily, I hadn't met a single werewolf who had any type of pull on me.

The way I figured it, I'd fulfilled my end of our deal. Though school had scheduled graduation for Sunday, I'd opted not to attend. I had no desire to put this visit off for another week. The faculty could mail my diploma. After this weekend, I planned to work as much as possible to save up what I could before going off to college.

I measured out the coffee grounds and reflected back on my time with Sam. I'd kept him company, and his mere presence had kept me safe while he'd provided me with the information I needed about the werewolves and the pack community. Although Sam had shared so much of the werewolves' life and culture, I acknowledged I still didn't know everything. It didn't matter, though. I'd learned enough...and not just about werewolves.

Sam was a great role model for responsibility and planning. It's what he did for the pack. Because of him, I already worked as much as I could after school. But, it wasn't just his example that pushed me to become so dedicated to work and financial responsibility. Shortly after I moved in with Sam, I'd discovered that work commitments ensured he couldn't talk me into going to the Compound more than we'd bargained. He knew I'd need the means to get an education and support myself and never tried to talk me out of working. So, I worked, and I tried to bank enough money to hold me over while I went to school.

As an Elder of the pack, Sam was extremely down to earth and wise. He carefully thought through all decisions with a deliberate calm that I admired. He didn't think of himself when making any decision, only of the pack. Their welfare ruled his life. Thankfully, even though he hadn't managed to tie me to anyone, he considered me part of the pack. That meant when I talked, he listened with his full attention, which I really did like.

Coffee brewing, I leaned against the counter and openly smirked at Sam.

"Come on, don't be pouty about this. We made a deal, and I stuck to it. I've met more man-dogs than I can remember. Some even twice." My made-up term seemed to amuse him.

I pushed away from the counter and walked behind his chair. Resting my forearms on his shoulders, I rolled them outward and pressed down with my full weight. The tension slowly left his shoulders, and I rested my chin on his head. Yeah, I was that short compared to him.

"Tell me you're going to be okay without me here." I couldn't remember my real grandpa, but over the last two years, Sam had filled that role well despite our rough start. I knew he had managed his own coffee in the morning for years before I'd moved in with him, but I still wondered what he'd do without me here to keep him company.

He sighed gustily and reached back to pat my cheek, the extent of affection I allowed with him. It had been a gradual progress to work up to it. He knew most physical contact made me uncomfortable. He understood it and never seemed offended by it. I'd held myself away from people for so long, I wasn't sure I'd ever be completely comfortable with casually touching anyone.

"You know I will," he said, sounding tired. "I don't understand why you won't go to the community college here. Out of state is so expensive."

"No, it won't be," I said, pulling away from him. "I have scholarships and aid because of being a foster." I made my way to the coffee. A warm breeze brushed past the kitchen curtains to swirl around the room. As I poured him a cup, I continued defending my choice.

"Besides, you know very well why I'm going out of state." It was an old argument. My place in pack society, forever the bachelorette, bothered me. I wanted out. No other female went through such a long Introduction period. Over the last two years, I'd become the one all the guys wanted to meet and hoped to Claim by the end of the weekend. Though they treated me with kind hopefulness, my attitude toward finding a Mate hadn't changed. I didn't want one. Besides, two years of being the family disappointment was enough.

"I want my own life before someone else tries to take it over. Sam, I've always had to follow other people's rules. I want to live by my own rules for a while."

Sam harrumphed. "What rules have I ever enforced on you?"

I gave him a steady look as I handed him the steaming cup.

"Besides insisting on the Introductions..." He dropped his gaze to the proffered cup and accepted it with a lack of enthusiasm. Not meeting my eyes, he blew on the brew and turned the cup in a circle on the table before he began to sip it slowly.

Suspicious, I continued to study his face as I waited for him to look up again. He seemed unexpectedly guilty for such an innocent remark.

Though I chafed at his rules, they were simple enough. Go to the Introductions. Spend the weekends getting to know the pack and the pack laws. Never stay out past dark without a way to get home, which meant a ride from Sam since owning my own car made him uncomfortable. How could he not see he completely controlled my life with those rules?

Though I understood the reason for the restriction, it didn't make them more palatable. The very real draw men felt when near me had only grown stronger as I'd matured. It made time alone risky. Sam had insisted I take self-defense classes. Those had been great until the instructor suggested one on one training sessions a bit too loudly in class. Before I bailed on the course, I'd learned enough to keep men at bay...but not werewolves. Despite knowing I had no protection against them other than Sam, I still wanted to try it out on my own. Sam's rules were simple; however, they weren't mine.

"It won't be safe," Sam said, interrupting my thoughts. He looked up from his half-empty cup. "You know it won't be safe."

"Sam, I'll get a dog." I could see by his expression that he was gearing up for another round in an old debate. Why couldn't he understand that I'd rather get a dog than be Mated to a werewolf? I hurried around him for the bathroom down the hall.

"I better go shower. We don't want to keep the wolves waiting." I spun into the bathroom and shut the door with a snick to stop any further objections.

JUST BEFORE DINNERTIME, I pushed open the door of Sam's old pickup and, ignoring its groan of protest, climbed out. My feet crunched on the gravel parking area. Not much had changed. Though still rundown and in need of repairs, to me the familiar buildings exuded welcome. With a twinge, I realized I'd probably miss these frequent visits. I pushed the door closed, reached around to the bed of the truck, and grabbed my canvas bag.

"There's a pack meeting tonight?" I asked Sam, looking at the other vehicles.

I couldn't remember ever seeing so many cars before. Yet, for the number parked in the yard, the Compound was unusually quiet. Typically, before a meeting, groups of people stood outside to talk and renew acquaintances. I glanced at the buildings again. Though quiet outside, thin lines of light escaped from behind thick curtains in many of the windows on the main house. Definitely a full house tonight. But why stay inside?

Sam just grunted in response to my question, shouldered his own bag, and headed toward the main building.

I studied Sam's back. He certainly seemed rushed. He'd even sped so we arrived in just over seven hours. We'd only stopped once for a five-minute gas-up, eat, and pee break. I hadn't questioned why, but it was unusual.

He'd stayed abnormally silent and pensive the entire trip, too. I didn't mind the quiet, but he generally updated me on current pack activity during the drive. Bored, I'd alternated between listening to my music and watching the country pass in silence.

I turned a slow circle, studying the area while I breathed deeply, and began to focus. In two years, the area of my sight had expanded so I could see much farther in the vast darkness of my mind. It didn't exhaust me as quickly as it used to.

I closed my eyes and continued to turn a slow circle. At the Compound, focusing was harder. Typically, for humans, some sparks came in strong and glowed bright like a newly replaced light bulb while others were weak, more like a lightning bug's glow. I didn't know why; it just was. The lights of the werewolves were different. Their sparks tended to flash in and out of focus regardless of how bright or dim I perceived them. I considered the flashing a false perception. Instead, I believed I was watching the amazing speed at which they moved—there one second, gone the next, then back again. Since I hadn't yet shared my ability with Sam, I couldn't confirm my suspicion.

In the darkness behind my closed eyes, I saw the usual flashes of light, but they jumped around in a pattern that made me dizzy. I could see flashes in the Compound and many more in the surrounding woods and beyond.

I stopped turning before I made myself lightheaded. When I opened my eyes, I faced the woods to the right of the Compound just inside the gate. I felt watched. Not moving, I listened. Nothing but silence and my own breathing. I mentally shrugged and turned away from the trees to walk toward the main building. If any werewolves lingered out there, they would show themselves, or not, depending on their nature and whether we'd already been introduced.

Several men exited through the main entrance as I stepped onto the porch. Two gave me kind but dispassionate—perhaps even indifferent—nods of greeting. Mated. The other two watched me alertly and nodded politely. UnMated. I nodded a greeting in return and walked past them, safe with the Mated males nearby.

Pack law: Protect unMated females from unMated males. Another pack law: Don't place yourself in a situation where you'll be alone with an unMated male or it could be seen as acceptance of his suit.

Inside, farther down the long hall that branched from the main entry, more men headed my way. I kicked off my shoes, nodded, and walked past them. Again, a Mated male amidst the unMated.

"You're early."

I smiled at Charlene, who walked briskly toward me.

"He drove fast. Are Paul and Henry around?"

"I haven't seen them, but I'm sure they're around somewhere. I'll see you at breakfast." Charlene didn't slow. She had a pile of clothes in her arms.

She seemed more hurried than normal. As a Mate to the leader, she tended to be busy, but she usually made time to talk to me.

With a tingle of apprehension, I hurried toward our assigned apartment. The same one we'd first stayed in but with big improvements. The once sparsely furnished apartment now made a cozy weekend getaway. A plush rug protected the refinished hardwood floors. Pictures decorated the walls, and various knickknacks adorned the room, just a few of Charlene's efforts to make it homier for those staying here. It also now had a small kitchen, which included a sink, dishes, and mini-fridge. It still lacked appliances for cooking since we all ate meals with the rest of the pack in the commons. The kitchenettes in the apartments were there for private convenience. Sam and I never used ours, but we weren't the only ones who stayed here. Though we had priority on the apartment, I knew visiting Mated werewolves used it on our off weekends.

Sam had already thrown his bag on the foldout couch in the living room when I walked through the apartment door. I walked past him, tossed my bag on my own bed, and returned to the living room to watch him and to try to puzzle out his mood. The last few informal Introductions had been less than typical with an unusually high number of unMated males coming to the

Compound from greater distances. I figured this one would be no different. Maybe he was worried about the number attending.

"So, when do we get started?" I paced around the room to stretch my legs after the long drive.

"Soon as you're ready, I guess." Sam riffled through his bag, searching for something.

"How many this weekend?"

He didn't look at me. In fact, he seemed to be avoiding eye contact, which he'd been doing that since breakfast. My stomach wanted to do a flip, but I firmly smashed down my emotions. I needed to figure out what was going on before I reacted. Emotions around werewolves gave a person away. They could smell some and hear others.

"I'm not sure. All of the Elders put a call out since it's your last one. Ready?" He straightened, with pencil and paper in his hand, and still did not meet my gaze. He kept himself busy by tucking the pencil into the spiral of the notebook as he moved toward the door.

"Yep." I fell into step behind him. "So, what does that mean?"

"That there are more ears than usual." He opened the door for me.

A werewolf fun fact to keep in mind at all times: They have excellent hearing. I didn't say anything more. Sam typically stayed very open with me, but something definitely felt different about tonight. I followed him down the hall. Our footfalls echoed softly on the hardwood floor.

Despite my effort to not react in any way to the oddities I kept noticing, a tension built inside of me. Not about the Introductions. I'd grown used to those. They could throw as many unMated at me as they wanted. I knew it wouldn't work.

In the past two years, not once had I felt any physical interest in any werewolf. There'd been some nice ones I'd enjoyed talking to, but nothing more. No spark that Sam had insisted I would feel. He'd stressed that whatever I felt, the male would feel infinitely stronger, a compulsion that they wouldn't be able to deny.

No, the tension wasn't about meeting more werewolves. It was Sam. The tension continued to grow as I puzzled over whatever Sam hid, whatever made him act so nervous and guilty at the same time.

When we didn't turn to go to the commons but instead, went down the hall I knew housed the infamous Introduction room, his odd behavior suddenly made sense. They planned to go old school for my last Introduction. Since Sam had stressed a formal Introduction could be dangerous to me, his nervousness and guilt were understandable. But I didn't understand why they thought a formal Introduction necessary. Did they really think the results would be different?

"Sam...you should have told me first."

He said nothing as he stopped and opened the door at the end of the hall. He motioned me inside. Resigned, I entered.

The windowless room had the same comfortable log cabin design as the rest of the Compound. However, near the center of the room, ten worn X's taped to the floor formed a gentle arch. A few feet away, a solid line ran from one side of the room to the other, separating the front and back halves of the room. On my half of the room, folding chairs waited along the wall, a place for Elders to wait and observe. Having Elders present meant disputes were resolved quickly and without bloodshed. It also meant better protection for the female. Each side of the room had a door.

According to tradition, five men would enter from the opposite door, which led outside, and remain in the room for five minutes. The Elders present would watch my reaction to these men and their reactions to me. Five minutes gave enough time for me to introduce myself to each of them. It seemed pointless to me, though. Through their own admission, true Mates would know within a minute of meeting each other.

All ten marks came into play during Introductions for older, unMated were-females. Once Introductions started, unMated males traveled from distant states until the Elder network announced a Claim.

The males competed aggressively for a Mate since fewer females were available to men. Sam had told me, statistically, the birth rate was about three to one. Some thought it nature's way to keep the werewolf population low. Others disagreed. They argued that it didn't make sense when human females appeared to be evolving to fill in the need.

I understood the seriousness of this Introduction and stood near the door I'd entered. If trouble broke out, I would step through the sturdy, thick door, lock it behind me, and run like hell. The locked door wouldn't slow a determined werewolf. Without an Elder standing between an oncoming werewolf and me, I wouldn't stand a chance. Still, locking it would make me feel better once I stood on the other side. Declared a safety zone, I was supposed to remain in the hall beyond to wait until the Elders calmed whatever disruption might occur.

Although the setting had changed, the rules hadn't. They couldn't force a Mate on me. It was up to Nature. One more weekend to play it cool, then...done.

The Elders began to enter behind me. During the informal Introductions in the commons, an Elder always remained nearby. If informal Introductions called for an Elder, I knew to expect more for a formal Introduction.

Sam already sat on a folding chair to my left. Two more joined him. I'd met Nana Wini two years ago while still learning about Introductions. A kind and patient teacher, she'd explained so much to me. Having her here comforted me, and I looked forward to talking to her afterward.

Once the last Elder sat, the outer door opened and ten men stalked in. Ten? I successfully kept my feelings from my face, but I knew they would smell my confusion. Ten explained the presence of three Elders. Werewolves in their fur were all-powerful and vicious, Elders more so because of their position in the pack.

In addition to the increased number of Elders, the ages of the werewolves who stood on the X's ranged from young to old without restriction. Screw Nature. No way would I be even remotely interested in someone old enough to be my father. Especially when I had no clue who my father might be.

Wanting to get the Introduction over with, I stepped forward so the toes of my socks rested just behind my safety line and met the eyes of the first man. I nodded a greeting, turned with military precision, and paced to the next taped X to meet the second man's eyes. I slowly walked down the line and met the eyes of each man I passed. At the last man, I turned around to face all of them.

"Thank you for coming."

They all stepped back from the tape and turned to leave.

I stayed on my side of the tape and watched their retreating forms. The door on their side of the room opened so they could file out. It felt weird not learning their names as I usually did in an informal Introduction. But I knew this was typical of a formal Introduction. Any man interested in me would remain on his taped mark while allowing the others to step back to leave. This would give Sam a moment to note the interested party. Anyone on Sam's list would have an opportunity for a second Introduction where I would actually converse with him. The second round had more danger.

Movement in the recently vacated doorway broke my chain of thought. The doorway had barely cleared before the next set of ten entered. Was it always this rushed?

Breaking protocol, I glanced at Sam. He watched the men, still not looking at me. Without frowning at him like I really wanted to, I turned back to focus on the men who now stood on their marks. In this group, all of them were over forty. I repeated the same process as I had for the first group, acknowledging each of them as I walked past. One appeared to have the start of a black eye.

I thanked them for meeting me and watched one remain on his

mark while the rest marched out. The remaining man waited for Sam to make a note then nodded at me before he turned to leave.

Again, ten more filed in as soon as the room emptied. This felt wrong. Too rushed. They weren't even waiting a full five minutes once the men stood on their marks.

Instead of moving forward toward my line, I put my hands behind my back and kept my eyes on the ground. The rules said that the Elders would not interfere unless they perceived danger. They would not speak unless it was imperative to my wellbeing. It ensured no outside influence to any decision I might make regarding my choice of Mate. That rule made it impossible to ask Sam for an explanation and actually get an answer.

Why did they change to a formal Introduction now? Why on the last visit? What were they trying to accomplish?

I stared at the line on the floor. The crisp tape looked new even though I'd heard from Henry and Paul, still my best sources of information, that it hadn't been replaced in years. It appeared new because it had never been walked on, never crossed. You leave by the door you enter. That's the rule.

I looked up. Rules are meant to be broken. Answers waited beyond the opposite door.

Stepping to the line, I met each of the unMated males' eyes. While doing so, I noted dried blood under one man's nose.

"It's nice to meet you," I said and waited, saying no more.

They all stepped back to leave, and the door swung open.

"A moment, please."

As one, they stopped before any of them reached the door, and turned to look back at me. I could feel the Elders watching me but didn't look at them.

I broke protocol, crossed the line, and walked toward the door. Since none of the men acknowledged any interest in me, I hoped I'd be safe enough.

"Gabby, wait," Sam called.

Hearing him stand and follow me caused my stomach to dip.

My steps slowed for a heartbeat. Stepping through the door could compromise my wellbeing...but staying inside wouldn't get me answers. The door beckoned. I stepped through onto a packed dirt path and looked around.

The light that spilled from the door illuminated a small area. The trees that crowded the building left only a small gap of about twenty feet between the treeline and the roofline, which cast the area in an early dusk. In the cleared space near the back door, twenty men waited quietly. I frowned, puzzled. Something still felt off. I'd expected to see many more given the rushed Introductions.

Closing my eyes, I breathed deeply and focused. Tiny sparks flashed around me in the darkness. Sam, I saw, stood to my right. His spark glowed steadily, not blinking at all. The group of twenty was different.

Some of the werewolves' lights blinked like strobes. Some faster, some slower. Some so slow that at first, I thought they might have left. As I studied them, it began to make sense. I wasn't seeing werewolves quickly running all over the place, rather an arrhythmic indication of a werewolf's location. I focused beyond the twenty. Lights too numerous to count stood out in the darkness. It would take hours to meet them all.

Had all the prior Introductions been a farce, a game to keep me from running until Sam could arrange the real thing? How strongly were the Elders determined to see me Mated? Would they let me leave unMated? Had my thoughts of college been a dream? I struggled with my growing frustration and panic. No. Not a dream. I wouldn't give up.

I opened my eyes, already knowing that the group of twenty had doubled. I studied their faces and noted more bruising and blood. Some men dressed in jeans and shirts while others wore clothes too filthy from fighting to identify. Seeing the filth and blood, I understood why they wanted to rush the Introductions. Too many werewolves had arrived for this, and the Mating challenges the Elders feared had begun.

I didn't say anything. I couldn't. Anger churned in my stomach at Sam for not telling me. I felt tricked and yet sad for the men waiting.

"Sam," I said, turning my gaze on him. There was nothing playful in my look. I wanted to tell him that I would never forgive him for this but knew the werewolves listening would take my words as a rejection. It would take away what little hope they had facing these numbers. Instead, I let my look convey everything I felt.

He lowered his gaze and broke eye contact, something he never did first. Good. He knew.

I turned away and studied the growing crowd. I'd lived among them enough to know not to show intimidation. They respected strength. With their hearing, I didn't need to raise my voice. Even those still hidden within the trees would hear me.

"No more fighting. There's no need to wait and fight for your place in tonight's Introduction. I will meet you all. Start a line here, and I'll walk it. If I am not right for you, there is no need for you to remain after I've passed you. You may leave and know that I am honored by your presence here tonight."

MEN SILENTLY STEPPED FROM THE TREES AND MOVED TO CREATE A LINE as I'd asked. They continued to emerge from the woods even as the line extended around the corner. Because of that, new rows started behind the first line. The shuffling continued until roughly five hundred gathered. So many men focused on me, all at the same time, made my stomach churn. If they were human...I suppressed a shudder at the thought.

Ignoring the vast number, I moved toward the first man, nodded stoically, then turned to start the slow walk down the line. The Elders kept pace with me. I didn't bother pausing to meet anyone's eyes. Only my scent mattered.

As I'd asked, those without a strong interest stepped out of the line and walked back into the woods. It allowed those behind them to move forward and take their place. When I reached the end, I turned around to walk it again. I paced the line several times in silence so all would get their fair chance. As the number remaining decreased, my mood lightened. Sam made note of names as needed. Soon, only a handful of men remained.

While my future loomed brighter, theirs dimmed. I nodded solemnly to those remaining and watched them melt back into the trees. I truly felt for them, but I'd experienced no attraction to any of them—no pull that Sam and the other Elders and werewolves had assured me I would feel when—not if—I met *the one*. A triumphant smile wanted to break free, but I contained it, not wanting to offend anyone. Finally, my duty was complete. I breathed deeply of freedom, ready to go back to my room.

Behind me, the Elders moved, reminding me of their presence. My mood shifted. The anger and betrayal from their lack of warning resurfaced. With a stiff back and tight mouth, I made my way toward the door and the waiting Elders. I didn't meet any of their eyes.

Sam had hours during the drive to say something but hadn't, and now all of his secrecy had been for nothing. I hadn't found a Mate. Did he realize the pointlessness of his gesture? I seriously doubted telling me in advance would have changed the outcome other than to make me nervous during the drive up. That, however, would mean I shouldn't be mad at him, so I quickly disregarded the thought. Honesty was honesty. He should have told me.

Walking the dirt path, which I realized I'd tread over several times in my socks, I saw a peculiar shadow on the ground melding with the shadow of the still-open door.

I looked up at the space behind the door and saw the flash of eyes just before a man stepped into view. I froze. My stomach dropped, and my heart did a strange little flip. Before I could take my next breath, a shiver ran up my spine, and gooseflesh rose on my arms.

My anger spiked, uncontrolled.

"You have got to be kidding," I whispered to myself without thinking. I'd been so close to escaping.

His filthy, long, dark hair trailed in front of his eyes and shadowed his face into obscurity. An old, dull-green army jacket, just as filthy as his hair, hung from his frame while his bare feet shone pale against the black sweats he wore. I couldn't tell his age, the color of his hair, or the color of his eyes—because of the tangle of hair—but I could see the glint of them as he moved away from the door.

He stalked toward me. I remained frozen and tried to deny the significance of the encounter as my stomach continued to do crazy little flips. Just before he reached me, he turned away and walked around the corner of the building, heading not into the woods as the rest had but to the front of the building.

I stared after him, momentarily confused. He'd recognized me. Just as I had him. Why had he turned away? Did it matter? Move! Escape before he changed his mind!

Finally, my feet obeyed, and I lurched toward the door.

"Sam, I've more than fulfilled any obligation I had to you or the pack. I'd like to leave tonight." The Elders stepped aside before I could bowl them over.

I rushed past them and crossed the Introduction room. At the door, I paused to pull off my dirt-caked socks. Charlene would have me cleaning floors if I walked through the main building in my filthy socks.

Maneuvering through the fortuitously quiet and empty halls, I struggled to check my emotions. Over the years, I'd learned control, knowing those around me would be able to smell things like fear, anger, lust, or even sadness. But tonight, all that restraint evaporated. Anger and fear swamped me. Anger at Sam for arranging the whole damn thing and fear that the Elders knew what had just happened.

I'd been so close to freedom. Sam had set me up, stacking the odds against me with the sheer number of werewolves in attendance. Why would it have to be the very last one I saw that sent a bolt of lightning right into my stomach? Was it too much to ask for just one break in my life?

Self-pity began to flood me, but then a spark of hope surfaced. Could it be possible that no one noticed? Maybe they had attributed my reaction to the way he looked. I turned a corner, almost to our rooms. If I didn't acknowledge him in front of others, then it didn't count...right?

Once in the apartment, I headed straight to my room and grabbed my bag from the bed. Thankfully, I hadn't unpacked.

Moving quickly, I went to Sam's bed and zipped his bag closed just as he walked through the door. His slightly mussed, grey hair gave away his agitation. Good. He deserved a little bit of it to match my own.

He met my gaze. I resented that he did so now, after the Introduction was complete and he'd gotten his way.

"Now, Gabby," he started in his soothing tone.

"Stop." I held up a hand to forestall anything else he had to say and to keep my temper in check. He might not know he'd gotten his way. Even if he did know, he didn't deserve the pithy remarks running through my head. He deserved my respect for all he'd done for me in the past and for everything from which he'd shielded me. Still, I wasn't going to listen to any more tonight. Amazingly, he didn't try to continue.

"Are you driving me or not?" I asked as I picked up his bag.

He held out his hand. I surrendered the bag and wondered what I'd do once we got home. I still had a whole summer ahead of me. A summer filled with two jobs and roommate interviews. Would Sam still let me leave like I'd planned?

I followed him out the door and closed it softly behind me. I knew I couldn't escape this place permanently because of my ties to these people, but I hoped not to see it again for a long while.

Sam's easy stride annoyed me within two steps. Was he stalling? I took matters into my own hands and strode past him to get to the entrance.

The longer we stayed, the more likely I'd run into that guy

again. According to the information I'd gleaned over the years, he shouldn't have turned away in the first place. Maybe he hadn't been attracted to me.

In the entry, I stuck bare feet into my sneakers, which felt wrong, but I didn't want to waste time and put on socks. A part of the heel folded under and wedged itself behind my foot. I was taking too long. Scalp prickling with tension, I struggled to pull the crimped portion out. Why had I crammed my foot into the stupid thing? I took my shoe off, fixed it, and slipped it back on as my gaze darted around the room, searching for any sign of *him*.

Sam had continued his leisurely pace and just stepped into the entry as I tugged on the door.

Nerves strung tight, I almost screamed at the sight of someone standing there, illuminated by the yard light. Instead, I only stopped abruptly. Not someone. Many someones crowded the porch. A whole group of werewolves. For that split second when I'd opened the door, I thought that man had returned for me.

The men fortunately didn't notice my near heart attack or me. They were too busy watching something in the parking lot. Standing shoulder to shoulder, they blocked my view. I didn't really care what had them so engrossed; I wanted to go home.

I heard Sam mutter a quick "excuse us" and moved around the small group. It took me less than a second to spot the object of their attention. Once I did, I couldn't look away.

Sam's truck had exploded. Okay, maybe not literally, but that's what it looked like at first glance. The detached hood leaned against the right front fender. Dark shapes littered the ground directly in front of the truck. My mouth popped open when I realized I was looking at scattered pieces of the truck's guts. Little pieces, big pieces, some covered in sludge. Deep inside, I groaned a desperate denial. Not Sam's truck. I needed it.

A clanking sound drew my attention from the carnage to the form bent over the front grill. He did this, the last man I'd met. He studied the gaping hole that had once lovingly cradled an engine—one with enough life to drive me home.

"Gabby, honey," Sam said from behind me, causing me to jump. "I don't think he wants you to go just yet."

My heart sank. Not only did the man's actions scream loud and clear "she's mine," but Sam's calm statement confirmed my worst fear. The Elders had noticed. My stomach clenched with dread for a moment and I wrestled with my emotions. No, it didn't matter who noticed. I wasn't giving up or giving in. I'd told Sam I'd come to the Introductions. I had never agreed to follow their customs.

"There's more than one vehicle here," I said.

"If we go inside to ask anyone else, we'll come back to more vehicular murder."

I turned to look at Sam. He watched the man and his truck. He was right. I couldn't ask anyone else to deal with this guy's obvious mental disorder. As soon as that thought entered my mind, I felt a little guilty. I usually didn't judge people. I preferred to avoid them altogether. But this guy made himself hard to ignore.

"Fine." I shouldered my bag, turned, and walked toward the main gate, pretending I didn't hear Sam's warning.

"You won't get far," he said softly behind me.

The yard light's glow didn't extend under the branches canopied over the Compound's dirt road. Crickets sang, and night creatures distantly rustled in the undergrowth. With a hint of anxiety, I marched toward the distinct boundary between light and dark. The dark didn't concern me as much as the things hiding within it. But my fear of that grimy man overshadowed any concern I had about crossing over that boundary. Darkness blanketed me. I slowed while my eyes adjusted.

I used my other sight to watch for signs of pursuit. None of the sparks from the yard moved to follow me.

My fear kept me walking for miles. No werewolves ever entered within the perimeter of my sight though I thought I spotted a bear. Maybe a werewolf escort wouldn't have been so bad.

Hours later, tired beyond imagination and satisfied that Sam's dire predictions had turned out to be false, I spotted a motel ahead. The empty parking lot screamed vacancy better than the creepy, flickering red sign mounted in the office's window. My feet and legs hurt too much to ignore the opportunity to rest. Sighing, I pushed open the office door and rented a room for the night, using the emergency cash I always carried. My plan remained simple enough. In the morning, I would find the nearest bus station and buy a ticket home or as close to home as possible.

Key in hand, I walked to my door and let myself in. A damp, musty smell engulfed me. I stretched out a hand and patted the wall until I found the switch. I grimaced at the room. It didn't inspire any thoughts of recently washed sheets. I kicked off my shoes and set them near the door. About an hour into the walk, I'd stopped to put on socks, and as I padded across the dirty carpet toward the bathroom, I was thankful for their protection.

The shower curtain looked brand new, but the tub and floor hadn't seen a scrub brush in a long time. I used the toilet but didn't look at it closely before or after. Sometimes ignorance was bliss.

The water dripping from the faucet had stained the porcelain brown. So I let it run while I dug through my bag. My stomach rumbled, and I regretted not grabbing some food before leaving. Ignoring my protesting stomach, I scrubbed my teeth. When the water ran clear, I spit and rinsed, smelling the water too late. Rotten eggs. Instead of wishing for food, I wished I'd just left the toothpaste in my mouth.

I wanted to go home where a clean bed waited, where inadvertently swallowing water from the bathroom sink wouldn't put me in the hospital. Where I could pretend this weekend never happened.

Purposely not thinking of anything but the present, I left the bathroom light on and moved to the main room. I set my bag on a chair, turned off the light, collapsed fully dressed on the bed, and pleaded with the universe that nothing gross contaminated the coverlet.

The drama of my day had taken its toll. My eyelids refused to stay open. Grossed out and hungry, my last thoughts were of the creepy guy at the front desk and chaining the motel door.

I STRETCHED, only half awake, and fell off the bed. For a queen-size bed, I must have rolled around on it a lot to work myself so close to the edge. Laughing at myself in the darkness, I pulled myself back up on the mattress and winced at the soreness in my legs. I paused. Darkness? My stomach flipped in fear as I remembered the light I'd left on in the bathroom.

I blindly stretched out my arm. There should have been a wall near this side of the bed. The door to my room swung open. Light flooded in, blinding me.

A shadow moved to block the light, and I suffered a moment of disoriented panic. Was it the man from the front desk? By my third squinted blink, I saw Sam standing silhouetted by light. Behind him, I spotted his foldout bed.

"You okay?" he asked.

"What am I doing here?" I turned and looked at my familiar room at the Compound.

"Dunno," he mumbled. "He brought you back before dawn. Didn't say a word, just knocked on the door, carrying you. I let him in. He set you on your bed then left." Sam's hair stuck up in places, and he absently scratched the hair on his chest, wobbling a bit as he stood in his flannel house pants. He needed his coffee.

I looked down at myself. Dirt stained my clothes as if he'd dragged me all the way back here from the motel...by my feet...through mud. I reached up to comb my fingers through my hair, and a leaf fluttered to the floor. I stared at it in disbelief and let my hands drop back to my sides. He'd left me looking like a wreck. What was going on with this guy?

"What happened after I left? Did he follow me?" I watched Sam closely. If he didn't respond with complete honesty, I wouldn't be responsible for what I said next.

"Not right away. When you started walking, he looked up from the truck and watched down the road for a while. Long after you passed from sight anyway. Then, he just took to the woods, leaving my truck in a heap."

Apparently, he wouldn't let me go easily. Not that walking half the night had been easy. It also meant he'd left after I'd walked far enough that I could no longer see his spark. He'd probably tracked me by scent, keeping his distance. Clever. But why?

I needed to talk to him and figure out what he wanted. There were probably new rules—his rules—that I needed to learn, too. My impotent frustration grew. Better to get it done now so I could figure out a way out of this mess.

"Where is he?"

"Gabby. Before you do anything else, I'd like two minutes of your time. You need to hear what I have to say."

My anger at Sam still lay in a dark, dormant pool inside me. I didn't want to listen to anything he had to say. Some of my anger and frustration collapsed in on itself as I acknowledged the truth. Sam's dishonesty bothered me, but my brush with freedom, to have it so close and then ripped away in the last few seconds, hurt more. Besides, if I didn't hear him out, I'd wonder what he had wanted to tell me. Defeated, I agreed.

"Fine, but please hurry."

Sam turned and walked back to his bed. I followed.

"His name is Clay," Sam said, sitting on the lumpy mattress. "Clayton Michael Lawe." Sam looked up at me and eyed me from head to toe as I moved closer.

In the brighter light of the living area, I really did look like I'd been dragged, or at least rolled, in mud. How had I slept through someone carrying me for miles?

"He's twenty-five and completely alone. His mother died when he was young. An accident. Shot by a hunter while she was in her fur. His dad took him to the woods."

That meant he'd been raised more wolf than boy. Sam had explained much of the recent pack history to me when we'd first started coming to the Compound. They'd only maintained enough of the original buildings to keep up appearances and used the 360 acres that came with it to live as wolves. Charlene's arrival had brought about huge changes, mostly in the social aspect of the pack. Afterward, most pack members started acclimating to their skin. Only a few of the old school werewolves still preferred their fur.

"His father died a few years back," Sam continued, pulling me from my own thoughts. "Clay's been on his own ever since, still choosing to live in his fur more than his skin. He's quiet and has never been any trouble. He comes when an Elder calls for him but still claims no pack as his own. So, by pack law, he's considered Forlorn."

Forlorn. I closed my eyes tiredly and recalled my werewolf history.

Prior to Charlene, the decimated numbers had only supported one main pack in Canada and a few packs overseas. Over the last two decades, the Canadian pack had grown enough to consider splitting their numbers.

Because of the dangers of discovery, joining a pack ensured an individual's safety and continuity for the pack. Some, like Clay, stubbornly remained reclusive. The majority of those who stayed solitary did so because they disagreed with the changes Charlene had helped to establish. Many wolves felt the superiority of a true pack entitled them to an elitist isolation from humanity and the world.

By staying on his own, Clay had effectively stated his opinion of the pack's reentry into human society. However, Sam's comment about never causing trouble meant Clay had not yet actually sided with the other opinionated Forlorn.

Yet Forlorn, not having a link to a pack, still had the link to the Elders. A link all werewolves shared. Elders acted as the lawmakers and enforcers for all werewolves while the pack leader enforced the rules for the pack, settling disputes. Elders and pack leaders worked hand in hand to keep the pack healthy and growing. Though a pack leader did not control any Forlorn, the base society rules laid down by the Elders still bound them.

According to Sam, a werewolf could not break their society laws. Once an Elder declared a law, it became an ingrained piece of the werewolf. Sam had compared it to a hypnotist. The werewolves heard the law, could contemplate it, have opinions about it, but followed the law regardless of their thoughts and feelings. Most laws made sense, and werewolves didn't try to fight them, but even when a werewolf disagreed with a law, there was no choice other than to obey it.

At least, no one had proven otherwise. However, I'd overheard Sam speaking with another Elder about several instances where a Forlorn had ignored certain aspects of their laws, which made the relationship between the pack and Forlorn even more strained.

Sam sighed and rubbed a hand over his face.

"He was here last night to help keep the peace. He didn't come to be Introduced to you."

At least that explained his presence by the door and not in the line with the rest of them. My conspiracy theory that Sam had set me up shriveled.

"There are two things I can promise you. Though he is technically Forlorn, he's always followed pack rules. He has no issue with humans. With him, you are safe. His control over the change is unusually strong."

When overstimulated, the change could burst upon a werewolf with less than adequate control. Sam had drilled that into me when

I first started hanging out with Paul and Henry unsupervised. He didn't want me to freak out if one of them went wolf on me for no reason. He'd stressed that whether in their fur or in their skin, they had the same intelligence and instinct. The change was just a defense mechanism because in their fur, they had teeth and claws to fight. So, what he meant was Clay had control, and he kept his emotions in check.

"And he won't give up," Sam added.

Clay hadn't been looking for a Mate like most werewolves did once they reached puberty. Did that give me any advantage? I doubted it. Sam had repeatedly stressed that instinct ruled this business. And fighting instinct proved extremely difficult for werewolves. So Sam's final warning was a given. Once they scented their Mate, they couldn't turn back. I sighed. Why couldn't werewolves get strategically-timed head colds like the rest of us?

"All right, where is he?"

"I think he's still tinkering with my truck. Try there."

Sam slid back under his covers, and I turned off the lights for him before walking out the door. My sock-covered feet, the only thing on me that didn't seem too dirty, muffled the sound of my passing. By the front door, I found my mud-caked shoes and put them on. They hadn't been that dirty when I'd taken them off at the motel. I couldn't believe he'd put them back on me before abducting me. Had I really been that tired? Maybe there'd been something wrong with that water. But why were my shoes caked with mud if he'd carried me?

Chapter Five

WHEN I STEPPED OUT THE DOOR, THE SUN, ALREADY HIGH IN THE cloudless sky, shone brightly. Moving off the porch, I closed my eyes for a moment and tilted my head back to soak in the warmth. The sound of a ratchet drew me back to my purpose.

I found Clay right where Sam had said, his torso bent over the grill of the pickup. He looked closely at the engine. Purposefully relaxing my shoulders, I started toward the truck. The yard was empty compared to yesterday. It left Clay more room to spread out the pieces he continued to remove.

Slowing my approach, I studied him a bit. The mid-day sun didn't make him look any better than he had appeared in last night's shadows. He still wore that heavy jacket, despite the warm day, and some type of very dirty, baggy cargo pants. His bare feet looked surprisingly clean after walking miles last night then carrying or dragging me back.

I looked at his feet again then down at my shoes. No way! How were his feet cleaner than my shoes? He couldn't have worn my shoes; his feet were bigger than mine. Didn't Sam just tell me he had complete control over his change? Couldn't he have partially shifted his feet? Maybe. It still didn't explain how I slept through being carried.

He continued his examination of the truck. I knew he could hear me coming, but I waited to speak until I stood next to the detached hood.

"We weren't officially introduced last night. My name's Gabby. Gabrielle May Winters." I tucked my hands in my back pockets and hoped I wouldn't have to shake his hand or anything.

He straightened, turned toward me, and gave me his undivided attention. I didn't think it possible, but he was even dirtier than I'd first believed. Long hair hung in clotted strands obscuring his eyes while his unkempt facial hair covered the rest of his face.

I kept my thoughts about his hygiene to myself.

At no less than six feet to my five-five, he intimidated me, and I fought not to show it. His continued silence didn't help matters. It puzzled me until I remembered Sam's comments about his upbringing. Maybe he didn't even have the social skills to return a greeting.

There had to be a way out of this. Please let there be a way out of this.

"Sam said that your name is Clay." I waited for some type of acknowledgment but didn't get one. He just continued to look at me. At least, I assumed I had his attention. I couldn't really see his eyes to know for sure.

"Listen, Clay, I know you think I'm the one for you..."

I decided to change my approach. Choosing my words carefully, I started again.

"I don't have a sense of smell to depend on like you do. Although the Elders say to trust the instinct of werewolves, I don't trust blindly."

He didn't move. How was I supposed to know if he understood what I was saying? We stood maybe five feet apart with the front quarter panel of the truck separating us. I couldn't read his expression or anything in his body language that would hint at what he might be thinking. I decided just to say what I wanted.

"I really want to go home. If I asked to borrow someone else's car, would it live?"

He turned away and continued with his examination of the truck, his body language, finally, easy to translate.

"Okay. I'll take that as a no," I mumbled more to myself than him.

He surprised me by turning back toward me again. I struggled to decipher his mood from his face. His ridiculously long and shaggy facial hair obliterated any trace of a smile or frown.

"Clay, I'm not trying to be rude here, but I'm struggling to figure us out. What's the plan?"

No visible response.

"Am I just supposed to stay here until you decide I'm not really your Mate?" I hated saying that word.

Again, nothing.

"Would it help speed things along if we spent a little time together?"

This time, he gave me a shrug. One-way conversations rarely worked well when trying to get to know someone.

"Do you talk?"

And again, I lost his attention to the truck engine.

"Okay. No talking. Got it."

Did being raised in his fur mean he'd turned feral? The thought of spending time with a Tarzan-mentality werewolf worried me. Who knew what he might do? Only Sam's assurance of my safety eased my fear before it could fully take hold. No, Clay couldn't be feral. He appeared to understand everything I said. For whatever reason, it seemed that he had no intention of speaking to me.

I sighed, pulled my hands from my back pockets, and leaned

against the truck. Chin in my hands, I watched him check the different fluids.

"You seemed to like the idea of spending time to get to know each other," I said. He turned toward me again. "But what's the point in spending time together if you don't want to talk to me? Isn't the point to get to know one another?"

And he turned back to the truck. Good to know the windshield washer fluid was getting low.

Frustrated, I wanted to kick a truck tire but figured I'd just hurt my toes. Instead, I walked back to the main entrance. The one-sided conversation hadn't given me any useful information. Why keep me here if he didn't want to talk to me? And he obviously wanted me here. First, he'd killed Sam's truck. Then, he'd brought me back to the Compound in the middle of the night after letting me walk for hours. That reminded me...I needed a shower badly.

Inside, the hallways remained empty. I let myself into the quiet apartment. Sam was no longer curled under his covers. His bed was made, which meant he'd probably left in search of coffee.

I grabbed some clean clothes, headed to the bathroom, and cringed at the sight of myself in the mirror. Clay wouldn't speak and dragged me through mud and leaves. How exactly was that a good start to a relationship? I spent longer under the hot spray than I would have liked as I tried to work the leaf debris from my hair. Too late, I concluded brushing the leaves out first would have been better.

Someday, I'd have to get the full story about how I got so dirty. But how could I? He wouldn't speak to me. He seemed willing to listen though...until I said something he didn't like. When I talked about talking, he stopped listening. Did that mean he wanted me to do all the conversing? It made sense that he wouldn't really want to reveal anything about himself given what Sam had mentioned about his childhood. I could empathize. There wasn't much I wanted to share with a stranger about my childhood either.

I tugged on the last of my clean clothes, a pair of cotton shorts

(I'd been counting on a lounge day) and a tank top. Having planned a three-day weekend, I hadn't packed much. I balled up the dirty clothes, tossed them into a plastic bag, and set it by the bedroom door. Hopefully, Sam's washing machine could take the abuse.

I sat on the edge of my bed and, swinging my bare feet over the carpet, thought over my options. Stay and accept my fate or find a way back home to continue with the plans I'd made for my own future? Sure, I could stay and make an effort to understand and learn more about Clay. But I'd already made my plans. How fair was it to expect me to change them? If Clay truly lived in the wild, it wasn't as if he had any plans. Maybe he didn't even understand the concept of planning. Could I possibly talk Clay into letting me go? He didn't seem too fond of me.

Absently, I started to towel dry my hair. When I had hinted we might not be Mates, he hadn't turned away. Did that mean he had doubts too? If he did, maybe I had a chance.

Determined, I tossed the towel aside and stood. Due to the pull I had on human men, I'd honed my skills of reason and avoidance. If reasoning didn't work, I avoided them. This would be no different. Piece of cake.

I gave myself a pep talk as I hurried through the halls. A few of the men I passed gave me curious glances. I remained focused on finding Clay while thinking of, and rejecting, the possible reasons for his doubt.

The main door swung open with a nudge. I hopped off the porch into the sun and winced when my bare feet met with the sharp gravel. Too absorbed in my purpose, I hadn't thought of shoes. Resolute, I tiptoed across the parking area as quickly as possible.

Clay still tinkered with the truck. However, when he heard me, he turned to watch my approach. Other than a few quick glances at him to ensure he didn't leave, I focused on placing my feet in the smoother areas where tire treads had cleared the stone and left sand behind. My ill-timed, stiff steps made a prancing dance. I hoped no one had caught that on video.

As I neared, he took a shop rag from his pocket and set it on the ground near the truck. I paused mid-prance and looked down at the soiled rag. I'd just showered. What was with getting me dirty? Not a fair thought. My soles were probably already filthy. The insistent bite of the gravel decided it. I stepped onto the rag, wiping my feet on the grease and carbon stained surface to dislodge the piercing shards still stuck to them. The relief made it worthwhile.

"Thanks," I said, looking up at him.

Since he'd set the rag directly in front of the truck, I stood closer to him than I would have liked. I could see brown eyes staring at me from behind the stringy hair. He studied me intently, and I felt that strange pull in my stomach again. It reminded me of my problem. We had an obvious connection; one I didn't want and one he might not want. Maybe, instead of trying to figure out why he might doubt our connection, I needed to explain why I didn't want it in terms he could relate to as a Forlorn werewolf.

Taking a breath, I plunged into a lie. I knew I played with fire. Living with Sam had taught me werewolves could sense a lie through increased heart rate and the smell of fear or anxiety. But, the simple beauty of the situation—the dash across the gravel, which had elevated my pulse—made the lie hard to detect.

"Sam just told me that you're to be confined to a room for the remainder of the day. With me. They want to see how we react to each other so they can determine if you really do have a Claim to me."

A low growl rumbled from him before I finished speaking.

"What? You don't want to spend time with me?"

He stopped his growling and looked down at my feet on the rag. I glanced at them too and noted what the gravel hadn't done, the rag had. They were filthy again. If Charlene found me walking through the hallways with feet this dirty, she'd give me an earful.

I looked back up at him. "You do want to spend time with me, don't you?"

He shrugged, still looking down. Not staring at my feet, then, but thinking. I continued to press my point before he caught on.

"So, it's not me. Don't you like being indoors?" He shrugged again, this time looking up at me. "Okay. If it's not me, and not being indoors, then what?" I let the question hang briefly before I said what I already knew. Ultimately, Forlorn didn't join packs because...

"You don't want to be told when or how to spend time with me. You don't want someone telling you what to do. Is that right?"

He didn't look away. Didn't move at all.

"Yeah, me neither."

I watched him closely, waiting for some sign he understood I'd lied to him. His motionlessness felt like a standoff and temporarily shriveled my hope. Maybe there was no reasoning with Clay. No, I just chose the wrong track.

Ignoring the pain, I stepped off the rag and bent down to pick it up. I shook it out and handed it back to him.

"I'm sorry I lied to you, Clay. I thought maybe if you knew how it felt to have your choices taken from you, you'd understand why I want to leave. It's nothing personal."

He took the rag from me and turned back to the truck. Someone had brought him more tools, and he was in the process of taking something off of what I assumed was the engine. He picked up a ratchet and started to loosen a bolt.

His inattention didn't deter me. I had to keep trying.

"Your instincts say I'm the one. I don't have those instincts. Instead, I just keep thinking about the fact that I don't even know you. And the little bit Sam's told me...that you spend most of your time in your fur, doesn't help me understand how there can be an us. I have no fur. I can't just run off into the woods with you." The clicking of the ratchet began to slow. He listened.

"I've enrolled in college—one I chose—despite Sam's

opposition. Do you know why I picked it? Because it was far enough away that I knew it'd be harder for people to tell me what to do. Major decisions, up until this point, have been made by others based on what they thought would be best for me. Sure, they ask me what I think and try to consider my feelings, but not always. How do you think Sam got me to Introductions for the past two years? It wasn't by asking me each time if I felt like going."

The ratcheting stopped, but he remained facing the engine.

"I don't mean to sound heartless. I've been through enough Introductions to know what they mean to your kind. I'm not trying to throw your traditions back in your face. I'm just asking for some compromise. Don't ask me to forget the one thing I've chosen on my own."

My pleading didn't appear to sway him any further, so I switched tactics and offered him a little hope.

"If you're serious about me, then come to the city with me and learn while I learn. We can get to know each other. I need that in order to even consider there being an us." He still didn't move. Frustration crept into my words. "I know I'm asking a lot. You'd need to start talking, stop growling, and bathe. No offense meant, but you look like a crazy man the way you are."

He moved slightly as if I'd poked him in the ribs. So he did understand how bad he looked. Inside, I jumped up and down on the balls of my feet, clapping my hands excitedly. I leaned against the truck to take some weight off my bare feet and pressed my case further.

"I know it wouldn't be easy on you. You'll be surrounded by people. It'll probably be uncomfortable after you've been on your own for so long. But we'd be able to spend time together, to get to know each other—the normal, human way—and see how things go. We'd both be giving a little, then. Well, you'd be giving a little more, but...will you think about it?" I didn't wait for his reaction. I turned and walked back to the Compound. It had to work. Please let it work.

I spent about five minutes trying to wipe my feet clean on one of the entry rugs before I gave up and walked back to my room. My speech continued to run through my head. Either it would work or not. We both knew I couldn't live in the woods. He would need to rejoin society. He'd see I wasn't worth the effort.

With a mental sigh, I pushed it from my thoughts and focused on the present. I planned to lounge in the apartment and finish the novel I'd started over a month ago. My stomach rumbled loudly. And eat.

THE NEXT MORNING, I woke early. I'd grown so bored reading the day before that I'd gone to bed by eight. So it was no surprise when I opened my eyes and saw my phone flashed five a.m. Sam would kill me if I woke him up. I only hesitated a moment before I threw back the covers and got out of bed. In the pitch-black room, I managed to pull my zipper hoodie on over my tank top, tiptoe to my door, and open it without a sound.

I only managed three steps into the living room when the light near the sofa clicked on, blinding me for a moment.

"Doesn't anyone sleep around here?"

"Sorry. I should know better than to try not to wake you." His hearing made him a very light sleeper.

"What are you doing up already?" He sat up and ran his hands through his hair as if trying to wake himself up more.

I doubted it would work and didn't think he would appreciate an offer to make him coffee given the time. He'd rather just go back to bed.

"I was going to check on the truck. He had it mostly taken apart yesterday afternoon. I wanted to see if he'd started putting it back together."

"What did you say to him yesterday?" Sam surprised me by getting out of bed and stripping the sheets. We always changed the bedding just before we left so it was ready in case anyone else ever used the rooms. But it was five a.m....

"What do you mean?" I took a few steps backward to lean against my door and watched his progress. He almost tripped over his bag while pulling off the fitted sheet.

"Do you want me to start some coffee?" It wasn't normal for werewolves to be anything less than agile. Coffee couldn't be good for him.

"No, I'm fine," he said, answering my last question first. "I mean, he asked for the keys to the truck last night and brought them back earlier this morning. Truck's fixed. I checked myself. So, I'm wondering what you said to him."

My mouth popped open. I couldn't believe he'd actually listened to me. A silly smile tugged at my mouth. Did this really mean he'd let me go? My barely formed smile faded. Or would I just wake up back in this apartment tomorrow morning if I tried to leave?

Sam continued to remake the bed with the clean sheets from the hidden compartment in the matching sofa ottoman.

There had to be a catch. Sam had told me a tied pair didn't part until completing the Claim. When Clay had scented me, and I'd recognized him openly, the Elders saw us as a pair. They, in turn, announced it to everyone over their mental link. Every werewolf, whether in a pack or Forlorn, recognized our tie. If my words truly changed Clay's mind, great—but Sam's question caused me to begin to doubt that possibility, and I struggled to come up with what I'd overlooked.

"The truth," I said, answering Sam's question. "Let's say he is my Mate. He's an uneducated man from the backwoods. How are we going to live? I can't turn on the fur like you guys can and live as a wolf like he's done for most of his life. Where does that leave us? I just pointed out that I had to go to school to get the education I needed to land a good job to support myself because he can't."

Sam had stopped remaking the bed and looked at me in disbelief.

"Well, I said it nicer than that."

He gave me a disappointed look.

"You don't know anything about him, Gabby. He may have lived most of his life in his fur, but it doesn't mean he isn't intelligent or that he's more wolf than man. You may have caused yourself more trouble than you intended."

I shifted against the door. "Hold on, I didn't say either of those things to him." Granted, I did tell him he needed to bathe. "And what do you mean 'more trouble'?"

"He said that you suggested he live with you so you could get to know each other better."

I froze in disbelief. That is not what I said.

"Wait. Did he actually talk to you?"

"Yep."

"As in use his human voice?"

Sam's kind communicated in several ways. Claimed and Mated pairs shared a special bond using an intuitive, mental link. Once establishing a Claim, the pair could sense strong emotions as well as each other's location. Mated pairs had the same ability to communicate with each other as the Elders had with everyone in the pack.

"Yep," Sam answered.

I closed my eyes and thought back to my exact wording.

"I didn't say we should live together, but that he should come back with me to get an education." Fine, I hadn't worded it well, but how did he get "Hey, we should live together" out of that?

"Like I said, you've got trouble." He gave me another disappointed look, folded the bed back into the sofa, then picked up his bag from the floor. He strode to the bathroom and closed the door on any further conversation.

Crap. I needed to talk to Clay again and find out what he intended. I'd been counting on his feral upbringing and his need for freedom to cause him to reject my suggestion—a suggestion that hadn't included him living with me. I'd meant he should find a place nearby so we could go through the motions of human dating, which was the extent of my willingness to compromise. I hadn't thought he'd take any of it seriously but that, instead, he would just let me go.

I left the apartment and stole through the deserted hallways. At the main door, I paused to put on shoes then stepped out into the predawn darkness. The yard light cast shadows near the vehicles. I stood on the porch for a moment but heard nothing.

Cautiously walking across the empty expanse, I found the repaired truck but no Clay. My stomach knotted as I studied the truck. Sam's words about Clay's intelligence haunted me. A man raised in the wild knew how to dismantle and reassemble an engine. I'd underestimated him. No matter which way I looked at it, it all pointed back to the fact that I didn't know enough about Clay to try to guess what he'd do next.

Back in the apartment, Sam waited, ready to leave. I didn't bother with a shower but remade the bed and grabbed my own bag.

We made it back to the truck without any sign of Clay. Sensing my mood, Sam didn't say anything to me as I climbed in, and we started the long drive home.

It was several hours into the ride when I finally stopped looking behind us or stretching my second sight to search for werewolves. There'd been no sign of Clay following us, but there'd been no sign of Clay following me the night before last, either.

Chapter Six

I was on edge the first week back, unsure if, or when, Clay would show up.

Desperate for distraction, I plunged into my two part-time jobs and worked as much as possible. I woke up early each morning, showered, ate breakfast, and packed a lunch, all long before Sam got out of bed. And because I still cared, I started his coffee before I walked out the door. In the evenings, a dark house greeted me when I returned home, worn out from the long day. Usually, Sam had something set aside for my dinner. I'd eat, go to bed, then start the cycle again the next morning.

I could have asked Sam if he knew what Clay planned, but he hadn't mentioned Clay since we'd left the Compound. I feared if I brought it up, he would think I missed Clay or something. Since I didn't want Sam sending out a call that might cause Clay to show up when he otherwise wouldn't, I kept quiet. Worry ate at me; but, as time passed, and my hectic schedule successfully prevented thoughts of Clay, I started to feel safe again.

Three weeks before the start of school, I found the perfect roommate, Rachel. I'd been watching the papers near school when I came across her ad for a roommate. We hit it off the first time we spoke on the phone. She attended the same school in which I'd enrolled and was going into her third year in the nursing program. She rented a two-bedroom house. Her roommate from the prior year had moved out after graduation. Rachel had tried living on her own over the summer, but the bills grew too expensive and the house too quiet.

After our call, I did some research and found the house wasn't in the best part of town, but I couldn't find anything closer that I could still afford. Plus, the unoccupied bedroom she offered came furnished with a bed and a dresser; I didn't own the bed I slept on now and didn't feel right taking it with me when I left. So, I called Rachel back and let her know I wanted the room.

Sunday, the week before school started, I once again packed my possessions, an old familiar routine I'd forgotten while living with Sam. Sam pretended not to care that I was leaving, but I knew he did. I'd only stepped out of my room for a minute to grab my shampoo and brush from the bathroom, and when I walked back into the room, I caught him slipping some money into the emergency cash I kept hidden in a half-full tampon box in my dresser. He pretended to check the dresser as if ensuring I hadn't forgotten anything. I went along with it.

Packing didn't take long. Everything I owned fit into several messenger bags and an old suitcase I'd gotten at a secondhand store. By lunch, we had what I needed loaded into the back of Sam's truck. A passerby wouldn't have noticed the small pile.

After one last look around the house to make sure I had everything, we climbed into the truck and started the journey. Sam looked slightly depressed as he drove. Excitement filled me, but I fought hard to keep it from showing. I didn't think my joy would give him any comfort.

"You'll call me if you have any trouble?" Sam asked, yet again.

"Yes, Sam. But I'm over four hours from you. I'll need to face things on my own."

"Not on your own. Elder Joshua has moved nearby. I'll be able to contact him if you have a need."

Sam had mentioned Elder Joshua to me a few days after I'd found Rachel. I knew Elder Joshua's recent move was for me, but I didn't complain. As long as he stayed away until I needed something, we'd get along just fine.

When we arrived, Rachel sat waiting on the front step of the small ranch house. She'd described herself on the phone as just over average height with brown hair and eyes. She'd left out everything else. Her deep, brown hair hung silky-straight, and the beautifully bronzed tone of her skin had me wondering if she had any African-American heritage. Her perfectly arched brows didn't appear tweezed or penciled, and they highlighted her darkly lashed eyes.

At about five-foot-ten inches, she surpassed average height. Long, lean legs extended from her cutoffs, and her V-neck top showed sufficient cleavage to know she didn't need to stuff her bra, either. Overall, she was gorgeous enough to make a straight girl wonder if she should switch teams, and that worried the hell out of me. Oh, not that I'd switch teams. As annoying and obsessive as men were, I still preferred them. No, her attitude the first time a man overlooked her and focused on me, worried me. Let's face it. Pretty girls can be very mean.

I drew my brief gaze from her as she stood to watch Sam do a Y-turn to back into the driveway. Using the side mirror of the truck, I studied the house.

A cracked and uneven sidewalk led to the front steps. Faded yellow aluminum siding and brown trim gave the small house a slightly run-down look. Rachel had mentioned room dimensions to me to prepare me. After living at Sam's place, this house did appear small from the outside. Only two windows adorned the front of the house. There was a large picture window, which probably meant a living room, and on the side of the house close to the driveway, a much smaller window. With the shade half-drawn, I assumed it belonged to a bedroom. How many houses had just two windows on their front? At least, they looked new, as did the roof.

As Sam backed into the driveway, I smiled and waved to Rachel. She walked toward the truck while Sam parked.

"Hi! Gabby, right?" Rachel said with an excited smile.

"Yes." I opened my door and stepped out of the truck. She caught me off guard by pulling me into an embrace. With my arms pinned to my sides, I fought the urge to pull back. "I hope you're Rachel." With that, she let me escape from her exuberant hug.

"I'm so glad to see you look so normal," she said looking even happier than she had a moment ago. "I was worried I'd end up with someone weird when I put that ad in the paper." Ah, that explained the happiness. Too bad, she had no idea how "weird" I was.

Sam came around from his side of the truck.

"Rachel, this is my grandpa, Sam."

"Hi, Sam!"

He quickly extended his hand for a friendly handshake, and I hid my smile. He'd noticed her boisterous hug.

Rachel clasped his hand. "Would you like to come in and see the place before we carry everything in?" She darted a puzzled look at the back of the truck.

I smiled. "We'll be able to carry it in and take a tour at the same time. I don't have much."

We grabbed my bags and walked around to the front of the house. The door opened to a tiny entry with the vacant bedroom immediately to the right, a small hall closet straight ahead, and the living room to the left.

We all stepped into my room to set down my things. I'd been correct about the window being a bedroom window.

As Rachel had promised, my room came furnished with a full-sized bed. I had just enough space around it to walk. Accustomed to a twin, it seemed overly large. Thankfully, I had the correct bedding for it. A gift from Sam. The closet was a small rectangle but more than enough space for what I owned. The only other piece of furniture—a small, battered, wood dresser—leaned against the interior wall. Nothing decorated the walls, which Rachel said she'd done on purpose so I could add my own flair to the room.

Rachel gave us the grand tour of the five-room house. The living room was long, but not very deep, and occupied the rest of the front of the house. Rachel had it tastefully decorated. Two sets of curtains hung in the picture window. The soft, cream-colored ones faced the road while the inside set matched the color of the worn, brown leather couch centered in front of the window. Square, wooden end tables held cream-colored lamps with matching shades and crowded each end of the couch.

A chair, set at a sharp angle against the interior wall, used the remaining space in the living room. The TV wall she'd painted a medium brown while the standard off-white covered the rest of the walls, which included my bedroom and the entry. A large, dark-brown rug, a shade close to the color of the couch and the curtains, covered all but a small swath of the living room's beige carpet. Overall, the room looked comfortable.

Through the living room's arched doorway, on the same wall as the TV, a small hallway connected the living room, her bedroom, a tiny linen closet, the kitchen, the bathroom, and the door to the basement.

Rachel turned left and briefly showed her room, the larger of the two bedrooms. Then she turned us and opened the door between the living room arch and the bathroom. She flicked on the basement light and told me we had our own washer and dryer and plenty of room for storage.

She gave the bathroom, opposite her room, a quick wave. "It's small, but it could be worse."

I noted that although the bathroom measured half the size of the one at Sam's place, it didn't feel cramped. The pedestal sink, tub, and toilet abutted the wall shared with my bedroom. White tile covered the walls to about midway, except for the shower area where the tiles ran from tub to ceiling. Dark-blue paint coated the walls and offset the overabundance of white. She'd also defused the white of the plastic shower curtain by layering a dark-blue, cloth shower curtain over it and used a cute, white flower clip to swag it to the side. Everything looked neat and clean.

Finally, she led us to the kitchen. An addition there extended the room five feet into the backyard and brought it from worthless to functional. Just inside the kitchen arch, to the right, a table for four sat against the interior wall. Along the wall that faced the driveway, a wall-to-wall counter supported the sink and provided four cupboards. Two separate wall cupboards hung on either side of the sink, allowing light through the kitchen's only window. The refrigerator stood to the left of the arched kitchen entry, along with four more cupboards top and bottom. Standing free, the stove occupied the unclaimed space on the exterior wall. Just enough room separated the cabinetry from the stove to allow the bottom cabinet door to swing open. A garbage can hid between the stove and the door that led to the wooden deck and backyard.

Overall, the exterior condition of the house didn't match the inside. The exposed carpet in the living room looked worn but relatively stain-free. The walls and ceiling could use a fresh coat of paint, but with the string of switching roommates over the last five years, the landlord probably hadn't had a chance.

Rachel concluded the tour on the back deck.

"We'll take turns mowing the lawn and shoveling the snow, and since it's only a one-car garage, we'll switch parking, too. But we'll work that out when it starts snowing."

I nodded in agreement as I looked at our small backyard. A new looking, barn-red, wooden fence separated our yard from the neighbor's behind us while evergreen hedges barred the rest of the yard from the neighbors on each side. With the deck and garage, there really wasn't a lot of grass to mow in back, but the front yard made up for it a bit. It reminded me of the Newtons' place, and I suffered an uncomfortable moment of longing before I strangled the feeling.

During the tour, Sam had remained quiet as he followed us and scrutinized the house. Outside, he stood beside me, studying the backyard as well.

"Well, Gabby, looks like you'll be comfortable here. I'd better start heading back. You need anything, let me know." He patted my cheek and stepped off the deck, neither of us comfortable with drawn-out goodbyes.

I watched him climb into his truck and waved when he looked back. Again, my emotions ran amuck for a few moments as he pulled away, nostalgia robbing me of my moment. I'd been so ready to leave and start out on my own I'd not inspected my feelings for Sam too closely. Now I knew. I'd miss him. A lot.

Rachel seemed to understand my mood as we went back into the house.

"You have a nice grandpa," she said, sitting on my bed as I unpacked.

I agreed and tried to shake the unhappiness that lingered. Less than five hours ago, I had looked forward to making my own rules. Here, in this house, I had the freedom I'd wanted. No more obligatory weekends in Canada. No meeting men I didn't want to meet. My internal pep talk began to work, and I started to unpack with more enthusiasm.

Rachel took a few of the wire hangers from the closet and helped hang the t-shirts I'd crammed into a bag.

"Please tell me there is more in these bags than t-shirts," she said. "I don't mind them—they're comfy—but where's the clothes for going out?"

"Um, I really don't own any." Watching her while I said it, I didn't miss the shocked expression that briefly flitted over her features. I looked over my small pile of clothes, most of them already on hangers, thanks to her help. They lacked diversity. I'd never noticed before.

She changed the subject. "Got your bathing suit handy? With the backyard surrounded, the deck is perfect for working on a tan. Join me when you're done." Without waiting for my answer, she popped up from the bed and left the room.

Bathing suit? I didn't even own one. I finished unpacking and heard the back door a few minutes later.

Tucking my suitcase under the bed, I covered the mattress with the sheets from Sam. Instead of feeling sad, a new feeling bloomed. Resolve. I needed this, living here with Rachel, someone my own age. Well, close to it. And female. Normal things like lying out in the sun had escaped me over the years. She'd help me catch up. That she didn't seem adversely affected by me gave me hope. Granted, she hadn't yet faced rejection from a man because of me. Maybe we could work on becoming friends first. Who knew? It could help prevent the ugly hostility I'd grown accustomed to. I liked the idea of having a real friend. Sure, I had Paul and Henry, but I wanted a friend of the same gender.

I changed into the shortest shorts I owned and a strapless top that Barb had given me for my eighteenth birthday. I'd kept in touch with my foster parents because of their insistence. Even though they had a beautiful little girl of their own, they still thought of me, especially on my birthday. Feeling light at heart, I headed out to the deck.

Rachel turned her sunglassed-gaze my way when I closed the screen door.

"Where's your suit?" she asked curiously.

"I don't own one," I admitted, lying on my stomach on the cartoon beach towel she'd laid out for me. "Didn't want to embarrass my grandpa. He's a little old school." Honestly, I kept my wardrobe modest because it was safe...and I hadn't wanted him to suggest I bring a swimsuit with me to Canada.

"Really? You don't own one?" She propped herself up on her elbows and glanced at me over the top of her sunglasses. A wide smile spread over her lips. "Wanna go shopping? I'll use any excuse to go."

I hesitated. If I declined, we'd be starting out on a poor note. If I said yes, we'd most likely have an issue with guys somewhere along the way. But if I didn't say yes, how could I hope to win her over as a friend? Any normal girl probably wouldn't even stop to think about this. I really wanted to try for normal.

"Sure, let me go change," I agreed.

"Yay!" She jumped up, grabbed both towels, and danced into the house behind me.

Since she had the car, she drove us to an outlet mall that she promised was the best and cheapest place to shop. Stunning in a tank top, short shorts, and cute little sandals with a heel, she outshined my drab, worn t-shirt, jeans, and sneakers. Still, I twisted my fingers in my lap and tried to quell my worry.

"While we're here, we should look for some clubbing clothes for you." She pulled into an open space and parked the car. "And don't be afraid to tell me if I'm being too pushy. I love shopping but have too many clothes already. By shopping for someone else, I get my fix without adding to the mayhem in my closet."

"No, you're not being pushy. I could use a swimsuit and a few new tops. But, I have to be honest...I'm not really into the party scene. Guys act too weird around me, and it makes me uncomfortable."

"Weird how?" she asked as she reached for the door.

"Wait."

She paused, turning to look at me.

I'd rather tell her where no one else would overhear. I took a deep breath. Normal. I needed to sound normal.

"Every friendship I've ever had was ruined by competition over a guy. Only problem was, I was never competing. I wasn't interested in the guy my friend was attracted to. But the guy was interested in me."

Behind her sunglasses, her eyes searched my face. I struggled not to squirm or look away. Anxiety bloomed. I should have kept my mouth shut.

Her lips curved into an amused smile, and she laughed.

"You're a serious one. I can see that already. Don't worry, Gabby. If a guy doesn't trip over himself to get to me, I'm not interested. I don't want to waste my time chasing what doesn't want to be caught." She opened the door to the sunbaked parking lot, and I followed.

We'd just crossed the black expanse, stepping onto the sidewalk in front of the stores, when Rachel nudged me.

"Check out this hottie."

The man she'd spotted exited the same door we were headed for. As I expected, he first looked at Rachel then at me. I looked down and kept my eyes on the sidewalk as we strolled past him.

Rachel obviously didn't know about the "wait for the door to close" rule because she started laughing before I'd even made it over the threshold.

"He kept his eyes on you the entire time. I can't wait to see what happens the first time we go out."

I wanted to groan.

The clerk at the register glanced at us just then because of Rachel's laughter. His double-take at me caused her to start laughing even harder. I pulled her toward the back of the store before he decided he wanted to talk to us. Her carefree attitude about my effect on men did bring a smile to my face. Maybe things would work out.

After helping me pick out a swimsuit, a rather daring bikini that she insisted would not cause her the least bit of animosity no matter what attention it brought me, she talked me into a few more stores.

In three hours, I'd purchased two "clubbing" tops and a black mini skirt. I probably wouldn't wear any of it. Sexy was a dangerous look for me. Heck, mildly attractive was even dangerous. But I liked spending the time with her. My careful spending slowed the process down a bit, but she didn't seem to mind.

Back at the house, the pleasantly warm breeze and inviting deck beckoned us, and we decided to catch the dying rays before calling it a night. Really, I just wanted to try on my bikini.

I shook my head at the sound of the back door opening and closing five minutes after being home. How she managed to change so fast amazed me. My new clothes hung in my closet, except for the bikini. Since I was pale from spending most of my summer working, Rachel had insisted I purchase a bright pink number with vibrant yellow straps. She said it would give me a little more color. Normally, I'd be reluctant to wear anything that called attention to me, but Rachel had been adamant that people our age didn't wear one-pieces with built-in skirts, the style I'd deemed safer. The top with its strings and triangle coverage concerned me, but I'd given in because of the boy-shorts style bottoms. When she'd held up a different option with even less material, I'd quickly judged the pink and yellow suit the better option.

I pulled the tags off the bikini and slipped it on. Then, I twisted and turned in front of the mirror in my bedroom, worrying. The string top covered me decently. The boy-shorts bottoms hugged my backside. However, a lot of skin reflected back at me. I did like the suit...I just needed to get used to it.

Grabbing the sunglasses I'd bought, I left my room. When I reached the kitchen, I heard Rachel's crooning voice outside. I stopped. Was someone here? Did I want to go out there in this?

I looked down at myself. Hiding myself because of the pull hadn't made me self-conscious...more like extremely cautious. Men reacted less if I kept to myself, which included staying modestly covered. What would happen in a bikini? Better to find out now, at home, if I could wear it in front of someone else than to go to a beach wearing it. I straightened my shoulders and walked out onto the deck.

"Gabby, look," Rachel squealed as I pushed open the screen door. "A dog!"

On the deck, Rachel reclined on her side, stretched out on a beach towel. Between her towel and the one she'd set out for me lay a monster of a dog, relaxing in the sun. I stopped and stared. What was that thing? Although the size of a mastiff, it looked nothing like one. At least seven feet from nose to tail, the dog's shaggy brown coat gave it a wild look. Rachel didn't seem to mind, though. She continued to pet its head affectionately.

It turned its head, which moved it out of Rachel's reach. Its soft brown eyes met mine.

Rachel shifted to a sitting position to reach its head again.

"It just walked up the porch steps and lay right down. I nearly peed myself. Have you ever seen a dog this big before? What kind do you think it is?" She continued to pet it lovingly.

I remained glued in place, my stomach sinking. Any lingering homesickness died as my suspicion grew. What are the odds that an extremely large, random dog just appeared at my door scant hours after Sam dropped me off? Improbable odds. When I'd said I would get a dog, I'd meant it as a joke. I couldn't afford a dog.

"And you're not going to believe what its tag says," Rachel said, not seeming to care that I hadn't answered her questions. "'If found, please provide a good home.' Isn't that funny?" She ruffled his neck fur, which made his hidden tags jingle. The dog continued to watch me and ignore Rachel's ministrations.

"Yeah. Funny," I mumbled.

The size of the dog would ensure men didn't bother me. But a dog half its size would do the same. Why get one so big? Its size compared to Sam in his fur. Did Sam think some of his kind might bother me? If so, I didn't see how a plain old dog would help.

My eyes widened as my own idiocy dawned on me. Not a plain dog.

I needed to call Sam, find out what he'd been thinking, and then give him an earful for sending someone to the house to keep an eye on me. I was about to turn and go back into the house when Rachel said something that made my stomach drop to my toes.

"His tag also says his name is Clay. What do you think? Should we keep him?"

Chapter Seven

I turned to look at Rachel, eyes wide with shock.

"What?" I glanced down at *him*.

He continued to watch me, his eyes not wavering from mine. He'd left me alone the whole summer. I had truly thought he'd let me go, despite Sam's ominous warning, and had forgotten about him.

"Aw, you aren't allergic, are you?" Rachel asked with a small pout. "The lease says a single pet is allowed as long as it's licensed."

I doubted the lease had taken into consideration that Rachel would fall in love with a freakishly large monster bearing similarities to a dog.

"No, I'm not allergic," I said distractedly. Clay had all summer to make his move. Why now? And why when I wore a bikini for the first time ever? A bikini did not say "stay away." I considered grabbing the towel and wrapping myself in it, but I discarded the idea after thinking about how it would look to Rachel. Instead, I continued to stare at the frustrating dog until he huffed out a breath, turned away from me, and laid his head on his paws.

Clay had finally shown up and, apparently, he still didn't want to talk.

"Good. He's so cute!" Rachel reached over to scratch his ears, and he closed his eyes.

"I'm going back in," I said as I turned toward the door. Clay sprang to his feet before I reached it and crowded behind me. I looked down at him then back at Rachel, who watched us with an enormous grin.

"Looks like another guy who can't take his eyes off you. Living with you is going to be a riot." She laughed and picked up the towels. "Let's all go in. The neighbor's tree is going to shade the deck soon anyway."

Having little choice, I opened the door for Clay. His fur brushed my bare thighs as he moved past me into the house. His head came to about my sternum. He really was huge...a huge problem.

Sam had warned me Clay had taken my speech as an invitation to live together. At least Clay had shown up in his fur. However, any relief I might have felt went unnoticed as I contemplated how he'd found me in a completely different state. If Sam had told him, I'd have to kill Sam. Since I didn't have the stomach for outright murder, I'd break his coffee maker.

I took a deep breath to clear my hectic thoughts and followed Clay and Rachel inside. She patted him again, and I knew I wouldn't be able to tell him to leave. Especially with Rachel around as a witness. It'd make me look like a complete psycho if I started to speak to the dog, not only as if I knew him but also as if I was giving a breakup speech. I didn't really have much of a choice...for now.

"We can keep him. But he's going to shed everywhere," I predicted then walked away.

Wisely, Clay stayed in the kitchen with Rachel. She continued to talk to him. She told him how cute he was and asked him if he wanted anything to drink. I heard dishes clank as I closed my door.

Even knowing Clay could probably hear me, I grabbed my cell phone and called Sam. Sam answered before it rang on my end; he knew I wouldn't call so soon for just any reason.

"Gabby, what's wrong?"

"Clay is here. In fur," I said as quietly as possible.

After a brief pause, Sam chuckled. "What did you expect, hun? He scented you as his Mate. He's probably been following you since. Only, when you were with me, he trusted me to protect you and kept his distance. Moving away...well, you might have forced his hand a bit. Then again, I think he had planned on joining you from the start."

"Right..." I heard a creak of leather and knew Sam had sat in his office chair to get comfortable for a long conversation.

"Listen, this isn't so bad. With him there, you won't need to worry as much about other men, right?"

"Yeah, but what about him?" I went to my dresser to look for clothes.

"I told you...he has control. You won't have to worry about him becoming aggressive with you."

Before I could say anything, Rachel's muted voice called from the kitchen.

"Hey, Gabby?"

"I gotta go. Just wanted to tell you he was here. I'll call if anything stranger pops up." I didn't wait for his goodbye. I ended the call, tucked the phone into one of my messenger bags on my dresser, and hurried to change. After putting on lounge pants and a tank top, I headed toward the kitchen.

"What's up?"

"Do you think I can feed him leftover steak?" she said, sounding a bit muffled.

Bent at the waist, Rachel riffled through the fridge. Clay sat off to the side with a perfect view of her string-bikinied backside, only he wasn't looking. He faced the arched door, watching for me. Should I be happy that he'd ignored the perfect view or annoyed? Instead of thinking about it, I answered Rachel.

"I'm pretty sure people-food is bad for dogs." Yes, I knew it wasn't nice, but if he wanted to play the dog, I'd play along. "We can pick up some dog food for him in the morning. He'll be fine overnight."

I sat at the kitchen table, pulled my legs up, held my knees, and watched Rachel straighten from the fridge and let the door close. She turned to look at Clay with concern, but Clay ignored her and continued to watch me.

My stomach growled.

"But dinner does sound good," I said to Rachel, ignoring Clay. "I should have thought of groceries while we were shopping."

"No problem. I forgot to tell you during the grand tour that there's a cupboard over there that you can stock and call your own. The top shelf in the fridge is mine. But don't worry about it for tonight. I was lazy yesterday and ordered take-out pizza. There's still plenty if you don't mind leftovers."

"Leftovers are fine with me." My stomach rumbled in agreement.

"We've got cheap plastic plates in the cupboard to the left of the sink—inherited from a prior roommate. Grab two, will you?" she said as she re-opened the fridge.

I unfolded myself from the chair and grabbed the plates while Rachel pulled the pizza from the fridge. Clay lay down where he sat and put his massive head on his paws. I could see his eyes move to follow my progress.

Rachel chatted about our neighbors and the university while we warmed the pizza in the microwave. She was easy to be around and fun to listen to.

"What kind of movies do you like?" she asked, changing topics abruptly once both plates held several steaming slices.

I had to think about it for a moment. "Action-comedy, I guess. I don't watch movies often."

She handed me a plate. "Let's eat this in the living room and watch a movie."

Clay stood and walked toward the living room before either of us moved. When he passed through the arch, he only had two inches of clearance on each side. I wondered if his fur made up his bulk. Not that it mattered. Our tiny house didn't suit a dog his size.

Rachel laughed as she watched him. "I think he's going to fit right in."

She had no idea how much he didn't fit in. I turned off the light in the kitchen and followed them into the living room. Clay settled on the floor and stretched out in front of the couch, which forced us to step over him. Rachel sat on one side of the couch, and I took the other.

The movie Rachel selected not only held my interest, but it seemed to hold Clay's as well. I ate two of the three pieces of pizza Rachel had put on my plate and set the remaining piece aside. During a quiet moment, Clay stood, stretched, and turned to study my pizza. Rachel noticed.

"Just one bite?" Rachel begged.

"If he's never eaten it before, he might throw up. Are you willing to clean it up? I'm not." I wasn't about to make living with us easy for him.

She pouted prettily, not really upset. Her easy-going personality allowed me to speak without having to censor my words too much. A few minutes later, I saw her break off small pieces and set them on the edge of her plate. Clay innocently turned around and snatched the pieces.

"Fine," I said when the movie ended. "Give him the steak."

Rachel cheered, hopped off the couch, and called to Clay as she went to the kitchen. He looked at me dolefully and followed her.

"Your choice, bud. Not mine," I whispered, knowing he'd hear me over Rachel's puttering as she heated the steak for him.

I grabbed my plate and cup and made my way to the kitchen to quickly wash and dry them.

"Thanks for the shopping and movie, Rachel. And the leftovers. You've made this feel like home in less than a day." I quirked a half-smile at her. "But I'm beat and going to bed. See you in the morning."

Before I left the kitchen, I looked back to make sure Clay didn't follow. He sat near Rachel, watching me. Hastily looking away, I escaped to my room. The last thing I needed was for him to think that backward glance had been an invitation to join me.

Odd as it sounded, having Clay in the house made it easier for me to fall asleep. Although still a stranger to me, I knew his world and his rules. He'd keep me safe. Yet, regardless of Sam's assurance that I needn't worry about him, he remained a concern.

THE NEXT MORNING, I woke up feeling great. Sleeping on a full-size bed definitely beat sleeping on a twin. I didn't think I would ever be able to go back. The new comforter had done a better job keeping in the heat than my old one. My feet were nice and toasty.

I stretched my legs from their curled position and hit something warm and solid through the covers. No...he wouldn't. I sat up and glared at Clay, who was already awake and contentedly stretched out at the end of my bed. His eyes met mine.

"No," I whispered. "No dogs allowed on my bed."

He snorted out a sigh and laid his head down, closing his eyes.

"Seriously, Clay. Don't you think this is just a little inappropriate?"

He didn't move.

"Fine." I used my feet to try to push him off the bed, but he didn't budge. Leaning back, I braced my hands on the wall and pushed harder, straining to move his stubborn, irritating fur from my new comforter.

He still didn't move but did open one eye to look at me.

I gave up and glared back. "If you shed all over my comforter, I'm locking my door at night." I tossed back the covers and got out of bed. "With a hook and eye," I added for good measure.

He wisely didn't follow me as I made my way to the bathroom. Rachel already moved around in the kitchen.

"Are you a coffee drinker?" she called to me.

With a mouthful of toothpaste, I had to spit before I could answer.

"No. More of a milk or orange juice person." I finished up in the bathroom, joined her in the kitchen, and noticed her scrubs.

"Going to work?" I asked as I sat on a kitchen chair and pulled my feet up from the cool floor.

"Yep. Sorry to leave you on your own so soon. I'll be back around five. If you need anything, just call my cell. If I don't answer, leave a message, and I'll get back to you." She filled a travel mug with the coffee she had made and rinsed out the pot. "Oh, when I went to bed, Clay whined at your door, so I let him in. Hope that was okay..."

"Yeah, that's fine." What else was I supposed to say without sounding weird or bitchy? Inspiration to pay him back for his sneaky method struck.

"Have you thought of taking him to a vet?"

Rachel paused mid-rinse. "I hadn't, but you're right. He should probably go if we're going to have him in the house with us. I'll call around and make an appointment. I need to check into licensing him, too. Ugh. Shots are probably going to cost a fortune." She looked at me pleadingly.

Darn idea to get back at him would cost me money. "Yeah, I'll go in halves." I got up and started back toward my room.

"Great. Talk to you tonight," she called as she went out the back door.

Clay still sprawled on my bed. He took up the full width with his back paws folded in toward his stomach so they wouldn't fall off. I stood in the doorway and studied him while he, in turn, watched me. We were finally alone, and I was determined to set some rules.

"First, I'd like to clarify that this does not qualify as getting to know each other. Second, you smell like wet dog. If you want to continue to sleep in my room, on my bed, you'll let Rachel give you a bath when she gets home." He snorted at that but didn't get off the bed. "Third, once I'm awake, you get out. I know what you are, and I am not changing in front of you."

He outright harrumphed at that one, and I swore I saw a canine smile. But, he did hop down from the bed. He left the room with quiet dignity.

I closed the door behind him, remade the bed—thankfully, he didn't appear to shed—and grabbed some clothes. I had two goals for the day. First, I needed to figure out how long it would take me to walk to the campus from here. Then, I needed to learn the bus schedule for the days I ran late or the weather prevented walking. If worse came to worst, I'd buy a beater car to drive.

Opening the door, I was startled to see Clay sitting there patiently waiting for me.

"What are you doing?" I asked when he didn't move. Of course, he didn't answer.

I eyed him warily and walked past him. In the kitchen, I grabbed the house key from the counter then moved to the back door. Clay's nails clicked on the floor as he followed me.

"I'm going for a walk, and you're staying here," I said when he made to follow me outside.

Clay growled slightly in response.

His deep growl gave me pause. He sounded scary.

"Please don't do that. Unless you really *are* trying to scare me."

His fur continued to bristle, but his growl stopped. Our relationship wouldn't go anywhere if he thought he could bully and maneuver me to his way of thinking.

"And don't crab at me. I'm not the unlicensed dog without a leash. Do you want me to talk Rachel into buying a pink collar for you?"

He coughed out a strangled bark then turned and walked back to the living room.

"See you later," I said, feeling a little smug.

The walk to campus took about forty minutes. I didn't mind the time, but the distance and the number of catcalls I'd received made walking impractical and unsafe. After checking the bus schedule and stops, I knew I'd need to buy a car. A necessity that would put a significant dent in my savings.

On the way home, I stopped at a small grocery store to pick up some essentials. Browsing, I found a new bar of soap, an extra toothbrush, dog food, and groceries for the week.

Loaded down with the bags, it seemed to take forever to reach the house. When I finally got there, my arms ached. I would need to remember to bring one of my messenger bags if I ever walked there again. It made carrying things so much easier. I made my way to the back of the house and saw Clay sunning on the deck.

"Nice to know you can let yourself out," I said as I walked past him. I nudged open the door and kicked it closed behind me. With a sigh, I put the bags on the table and began to unpack.

After a sharp bark from outside, I grudgingly turned to let Clay in.

"What? Can't let yourself back in?" He didn't respond except to sit by the sink. I went back to the table and reached into one of the bags.

"Look what I got you." I pulled out a small bag of dog food.

Clay growled again, but it lacked any menace.

"You want to look like a normal dog, don't you? Well... as normal as a dog your size can look, anyway." I set the bag on the floor next to the bowl of water Rachel had set out for him and continued to unpack, saving the soap and toothbrush for last.

"These are for you. You have two choices. You can use them when Rachel's gone, or you can wait until she's back, and I'm sure she'd be happy to help you."

He studied me for a moment then walked out of the kitchen, turning toward the bathroom. I followed a few steps behind.

A startled yelp escaped me when I rounded the corner and caught sight of a naked backside. Without much thought, I tossed the soap and toothbrush in and slammed the door shut.

"You could have waited until I put the stuff in there," I said through the door as my heart thundered in my ears. I took a steadying breath and heard the water turn on, the clink of his dog tag hitting the sink, then the shower curtain moved.

Who would have thought he would even know how to use a shower? I hadn't. On the way home, I'd started to think of all the different things I would need to explain, like making sure to position the curtain inside the tub. Standing outside the door, still reeling from the view I'd gotten, I realized I might see the same thing again if I didn't get him a towel.

I'd packed two bath towels. Purchased from a discount store, they both sported gaudy floral designs. I grabbed one and waited outside the door again until I heard him splashing in the shower. Then, I knocked.

"I have a towel for you," I said through the door. "If you're still in the shower, I can open the door and toss it on the toilet seat. Okay?" I didn't hear anything. No surprise. "Okay, I'm coming in." I waited a moment for any indication that I shouldn't enter.

When the water continued to run, I cautiously opened the door. As soon as I saw a clear path to the toilet seat, I tossed the towel. Standing just inside the bathroom with my hand wrapped around the door handle for a quick exit, I paused. His new toothbrush rested on the sink.

"My toothpaste is the one marked with the pink nail polish on the cap. I'll let you use it as long as you promise not to squeeze the tube from the middle."

His answer took the form of an accurately aimed splash of water over the top of the shower curtain. I barely dodged it.

"You're cleaning that up."

I closed the door, grabbed a book, and went to the couch to wait. I hoped he would use the towel before he turned back into a dog. He'd make a mess if he shook out in there. After a minute, I actually opened the book and started to read.

Several minutes later, the water turned off. With my attention divided between listening and trying to associate an action to each sound I heard, I couldn't concentrate on my book. A moment of silence. Then running water. It sounded like the sink. Brushing his teeth? Then silence again. It remained quiet until I heard the doorknob turn. Quickly, I held the book higher to block my view, just in case he chose not to wear his fur...or the towel. A chuffing bark, apparently his dog version of a laugh, had me lowering my comically high book.

He strolled over by me and hopped up on the couch. Incredibly, his fur looked even fluffier.

"Don't get too comfortable. I don't know Rachel's rules about pets on the furniture." I curled my legs under me to give him more room.

Forgetting myself, I leaned over to smell him.

"Much better," I said, straightening. At his intense look, I went back to reading my book and pretended I hadn't just leaned over and smelled a man. We stayed like that, side by side in companionable silence, until lunch when both our stomachs rumbled.

On the way to the kitchen, I noticed his wet towel on the bathroom floor.

"Next time, fold it over the edge of the tub," I said. The bathroom lacked any other available space to hang a towel, and I didn't want his towel hung in my room, either. That seemed a little too domestic.

I made us both dry ham sandwiches. Dry because I'd refused to pay six dollars for a miniature jar of mayo.

"I'm guessing your bowl of dog food will always be full," I said as I set his plated sandwich on the floor. Sitting at the table, I started to eat my own sandwich. He finished his in two bites.

"So, we have a week before my classes start up. What's your plan?"

He cocked his head at me.

"Did you want to try to enroll in any classes? Study anything?"

He lay down on the floor next to his empty plate, eyeing it sadly.

"Okay...well, if you change your mind, let me know."

I washed our dishes and went back to reading. Eventually, he joined me on the couch.

Later that night, Rachel breezed into the house and tossed her keys and purse on the table. She had a manly spiked collar in her hand along with a leash.

From my position on the couch, I watched her kneel down next to Clay, who stood near his bowl of water. I wasn't sure, but she appeared to have interrupted his contemplation of drinking from the bowl. The thought made me smile.

Trying to ignore the pair, I focused on my book. Shuffling movements sounded from the kitchen. Rachel mumbled something that was too quiet to hear. When the noises didn't stop, I went to investigate.

"This is a joke," she said. She knelt in front of Clay, face to muzzle, trying to get the collar on him.

I laughed from the doorway as I watched them struggle. She would wrap her arms around his neck to buckle the collar, and he would duck or shift to avoid her, but he never got up and walked away. I caught a twinkle of amusement in his canine eyes.

I knew Rachel wouldn't give up on getting a real collar on him.

He needed proof of license. Yet, he appeared very determined to avoid the collar. It served him right. He was the one who chose to be a dog.

Rachel mumbled again, and I decided to take pity on her. I knew how to reason with him. If Clay ever wanted to leave the house with me, he had to have a collar. I just needed to point that out.

"Here." I held out my hand. "I'll try."

"Good luck," she said with a laugh as she got off her knees and handed me the collar. She took my position in the doorway.

"It was the biggest collar they had. I don't even know if it fits, he won't let me get close enough."

With a half-smile on my face, I knelt in front of Clay. I liked that he had a sense of humor when he interacted with Rachel. It made having him in the house tolerable...almost. I looked him in the eye.

"Clay, if you want to be able to go anywhere with us, you need a collar we can clip a leash on. Not just the twine you have holding your tag around your neck."

He didn't move, so I leaned forward and reached for the string that held his current joke of a tag. He held still for me while I removed the twine and replaced it with the real collar.

"At least it's not pink," I said and patted him before I realized what I was doing. I'd forgotten myself again and treated him like a dog.

I quickly stood and avoided Clay's direct gaze.

Rachel laughed. "Hey, I wouldn't do that to him. No pink for our man. I don't know why he sat still for you and not me."

I'd forgotten about Rachel. She moved to pet and praise him for his good behavior. If I wanted a chance of having a friend as a roommate, I knew I needed to deal with Clay as a pet. But, I needed to watch myself. The direction of my thoughts—his assumed permanent residency in the house—troubled me. Making him comfortable and buying him a license wouldn't help me get rid of him.

Rachel gave him a kiss, and he sighed. Maybe he'd grow tired of her affection and run back to Canada. I held onto that happy thought.

"He's moody," I said, looking into his eyes. Moody and stubborn with a quirky sense of humor. Not a good combination.

Chapter Eight

As soon as Rachel sufficiently praised Clay for wearing the collar, she went to her room to change. From her room, she asked if I wanted to join her for a girl's night out. She explained she typically didn't stay in too much; when not busy working, her social life called. Still too unsure of our relationship—I didn't want to risk having someone Rachel might be interested in hitting on me—I declined. Thankfully, turning down her invitation didn't seem to bother her.

While Rachel exceeded my expectations as a roommate, adjusting to Clay's presence was something else entirely. When I woke Tuesday, Rachel was already gone. Clay still lingered at the foot of my bed.

"Get out," I said as soon as I opened my eyes. He left without complaint.

I took my time to dress, then went downstairs to check out the basement. Clay followed me. I tried to ignore him as I looked around. There wasn't much to see. The washer and the dryer were right by the steps, and there were a few utility shelves against the walls for storage.

With nothing else to do, I decided to take advantage of my idle time by sunbathing. I walked back upstairs and went to my room to change. After our talk the day before, Clay didn't attempt to follow me.

The second time wearing the suit was a little less nerve-racking. I didn't stare nervously in the mirror and eye all the pale skin glaring back at me. Instead, I appreciated the vivid coloring on the suit. Rachel had good taste.

Intent on finding the beach towels Rachel had used, I opened the door and stopped short at the sight of Clay. His huge dog head moved up, then down, as his eyes traveled the length of my body. I flushed, slammed the door, and changed back into shorts and a tank top. I opted to cut the grass, instead.

Clay sat on the porch and watched me push the mower back and forth. When I moved to the front, he followed. He was never in the way, just always there. After I went back inside to read, he did disappear for a bit. He had apparently taken my complaint about his hygiene seriously and had chosen to shower again. I hoped he would make it a daily routine.

Since he'd bathed and given me privacy as I'd asked, I had no reason to complain when I went to my room that night and saw him lying on the foot of the bed. However, when I woke Wednesday morning with him lying next to me, I did complain. Lividly.

"Now, just hold on," I whispered with a scowl. "You're a dog. Act like one. Fur stays at the foot of the bed."

He grudgingly moved to his place at the foot of the bed, watching me the whole time.

"Don't give me your doleful eyes. This is your choice, not mine."
As soon as I said that, I recalled his talent for misinterpretation, which
had caused this co-ed housing in the first place. "Not that you'd get
to sleep next to me in your skin either. So, don't even think about it. If
you don't like the end of the bed, you can always sleep on the floor."

AFTER GETTING THE PAPER, I scoured the classifieds for a beater car
and found two promising ads. Both required a long walk. I fetched
my bag, tucked the folded newspaper inside, and grabbed the
house keys.

Clay beat me to the door. I scowled down at him. He stared
back at me. After a moment, he shook his neck, jangling his tags.
Defeated, I clipped on his leash. He negotiated well without using a
single word.

I used my cell to call the number for the first ad. The man
sounded a bit brusque as if my planned visit inconvenienced him.
Shrugging it off, I led Clay to the address. A rusty car parked on the
front lawn with a "for sale" sign affirmed I had the right place. Clay
and I walked toward the car.

A man called hello from the open garage and made his way
toward us. As he neared, his demeanor changed, and I inwardly
groaned. He introduced himself as Howard and looked me over
with interest. Clay moved to stand between us, his stoic presence a
good deterrent.

Howard talked about the car for a bit, going through the
laundry list of its deficiencies. Then he popped the hood so I could
look at the engine. In the middle of Howard's attempt to impress
me with his vast mechanical knowledge, Clay sprang up between
us. Howard yelped at Clay's sudden move and edged away as Clay
placed his paws on the front of the car to get a good look at the
engine, too. I fought not to smile at the man's stunned expression.

At Clay's discreet nod, I bought the car, not bothering with the second ad.

No matter what errand I wanted to run during the week before classes started, Clay insisted on tagging along. On Friday, when I drove to the bookstore, Clay rode a very cramped shotgun and waited in the car while I made my purchases. Later, he sat in the hot car again while I bought some basic school supplies.

However, Monday, when I tried leaving for my first class, I put my foot down. He bristled and growled and tried to follow me.

"Your license only wins you so much freedom. Dogs aren't allowed on campus and definitely not in the classroom."

Thankfully, Rachel had left first and didn't hear me scold him.

I tried to leave again, but he stubbornly persisted. Finally, exasperated, I reminded him that he slept on my bed because of my good grace. He resentfully stepped away from the door.

AFTER THE FIRST week of classes, I didn't have time to mind Clay's constant attention. Maxing out at eighteen credits, desperate to get the general requirements out of the way so I could delve into clinicals sooner, I spent much of my day on campus in a classroom or in the library. When I actually found myself at home, I spent my time studying. I'd known when signing up for the courses that they would occupy all of my time and prevent me from having much of a life. Other than the fact that I couldn't get a part-time job while taking the overload, I hadn't minded the commitment.

Even though I ignored him, Clay still stayed close to me. I realized how bored he'd grown when I came home and found one of my books on the couch, the bookmark on the wrong page. The next day, I took pity on him and brought back some books I thought might interest him. The one I thought particularly clever, about flora and fauna of North America, I included to remind him of home. He eyed the titles dispassionately. The day after, a bookmark nestled between the pages of two of the books.

I woke up one morning with a single-word note on my dresser. It simply said "mechanics." The first stack of books lay next to the note.

I turned to glare at Clay, who still lounged on the end of the bed.

"So you can write words to me, just not speak them?"

He blinked at me.

"Whatever. You're going to get caught creeping around the house at night."

Later that day, I returned the books on forestry and wildlife and checked out several books on mechanics. For fun, I threw in a do-it-yourself book for home repairs.

THE SECOND FRIDAY after school began, I sat on my bed with the door to my room closed. Clay lay in his usual spot beside me, his eyes devouring the words of his current book. He'd spent enough time reading next to me that I'd grown used to our system, a nudge when he needed a page turned. Trying to turn the page with his nose hadn't worked out well for him or the first book.

When he nudged me, I turned his page without looking up from my own book. When he did it again, I lifted my head. He read fast, but not that fast. He briefly met my eyes then turned toward the door. Just then, I heard the front door open, and I froze at the sound of Rachel's voice.

"...and this is where I live. Please have a seat, and I'll change quickly. My roommate and our dog should be around here somewhere."

"No rush," a man answered. "Our reservations aren't until six."

I turned wide eyes to Clay. Rachel had brought a man home? I didn't have time to think about it further because she knocked on my door. I wanted to ignore it, but instead, quickly closed the book in front of Clay.

"Come in."

Rachel walked in still wearing her scrubs. Her smile and flushed cheeks spoke volumes, as did the way she tactfully closed the door behind her.

"There you are. Come meet Peter." She walked close and leaned in so she could whisper more. "Don't kill me, but he has a friend without a date tonight, and I said I had a friend without a date tonight...please come with."

I groaned quietly. "Don't do this to me, Rachel. This won't end well, and you'll probably never forgive me."

"Come on...please?" she said, sitting on the bed next to me. "I really like this one."

"That's the problem. Remember what I said? It's always a guy that ruins a friendship. I don't want to go out tonight." I looked at Clay from the corner of my eye. He glared at Rachel. Not good. Too human. I nudged him with my foot while keeping my focus on Rachel.

"I like having a friend," I said.

She smiled at me. "If he hits on you, then it wasn't meant to be. Don't worry so much." She pulled me off the bed, and I reluctantly followed her out the door. Clay was close behind.

Peter, a pleasant-looking man with light blonde hair and blue eyes, stood when we walked into the living room. He was an inch shorter than Rachel and, with his coloring, seemed her polar opposite. He immediately smiled at Rachel, and I could tell he had eyes only for her. I sagged with relief. His kind were rare.

"Peter, this is Gabby. Gabby, this is Peter. He's going to med school. I bumped into him at the library last week. Peter, why don't you tell her about Scott while I go get dressed?"

Rachel left the room in a rush, probably so I couldn't retreat. I smothered a grin as I watched Peter's gaze follow her. It took him a moment to collect himself.

"Nice to meet you, Gabby."

"You too. Want to sit?" I motioned him back to the couch and took the chair for myself. Clay settled on the floor between us. "This is Clay."

"He's huge," Peter said, appearing to notice Clay for the first time.

A huge pain in the butt, I thought without any malice.

"Yeah," I said instead. "So, who's Scott?"

"Oh, a friend of mine," he said, looking up from Clay. "He's also in med school. We had plans to go to O'Donell's tonight for dinner and a drink or two. Then, I ran into Rachel and invited her to join us. We thought it'd be more fun if you could come, too."

Rachel waltzed back into the room at that moment. Amazingly, she had already changed into a skirt and complementing silky top. She'd heard Peter's last comment.

"Of course you will, won't you, Gabby?"

Two love-struck fools, who wouldn't even consider my presence if it weren't for Scott, had me cornered. Rachel really didn't know what she was asking of me. A public restaurant wouldn't be enjoyable. Yet, as she watched me hopefully, I knew my answer.

"Okay...but I need to be home early enough to let Clay out." A lame excuse, but I needed to prep the idea now so I would have an out later.

"I'm sure he'll be fine for that little while." Rachel waved her hand dismissively at Clay. Clay huffed, but she didn't notice. Instead, she shooed me toward my room.

"Go get dressed."

I stood to go to my room, but Clay leapt to his feet in front of me. I stepped to the right to go around him, but he mirrored my move, blocking me.

Rachel laughed. "Come here, Clay. Come here and let Gabby get ready." She squatted down and patted her leg.

I'd seen her do this a few times before. Usually, Clay grudgingly responded. Not this time though. He kept his gaze focused on me and copied my feinted attempts to get around him.

"I've never seen him act like this," Rachel said to Peter.

I kept my narrowed gaze on Clay.

"I'm surprised you have such a wild-looking dog. It seems too big compared to the house...and the two of you." Peter eyed Clay, too.

Giving up, I dropped to my knees and wrapped my arms around his thick neck, pretending to hug him so I could whisper in his ear.

"I'm not crazy about the idea either, but you have to let me go and stop acting weird." I pulled back. "Ready to be good, Clay?" I said as I stood and scratched him behind the ear just as a pet owner would do.

He turned and trotted into my room. Nope, not ready to be good.

Rachel laughed again. She knew I usually kicked him out when I wanted to change and had already teased me about it. I'd pointed out she wouldn't know how awkward it felt because he never tried to watch her change.

Resolutely, I followed Clay into my room and closed the door. I could just barely hear Peter and Rachel talking as they waited for me. Clay sat on my bed, watching me.

I folded my arms and kept my voice low. "I am not changing in front of you."

My words evoked an eerie canine smile from him, and he settled down onto my comforter and continued to watch me.

"Fine. I'll change in the bathroom."

I went to my closet and started looking at my clothes, already knowing very few things in there compared to the style Rachel wore. The skirt I'd bought a few weeks ago would look nice, but added to my pull, it would scream, "Hit on me." Biting my lip, I reached for the skirt. Clay began to growl fiercely.

"Zip it," I mumbled and grabbed one of the dressier tops I owned, a fitted cowl neck top with three-quarter sleeves.

Clay started barking, a deep menacing sound that raised the little hairs on the back of my neck. I spun toward him.

"What the hell, Clay? Cut it out." I knew he didn't like that because he got louder.

Rachel burst in without knocking, and Peter followed right behind her. Clay, who had been sitting at the end of my bed, sprang to his feet as soon as they entered.

"What's wrong?" Rachel looked at Clay, who continued to bark at me.

If possible, his volume increased, and I had to yell over him.

"Nothing. Just give me a few minutes to calm him down, okay?" I walked to Clay with the clothes still under one arm, and he growled at me. I faltered and eyed him with a hint of fear.

"Uh, I'm not so sure you should do that right now," Peter said.

Clay turned and started barking at Peter.

"Enough." My voice echoed in the small room. It apparently took Clay by surprise because the noise stopped. However, his attitude hadn't changed. Teeth still exposed in a fierce snarl, he glared at all of us. At least he'd finished barking and growling. For the moment. I turned toward Peter and Rachel.

"I'm fine. Thank you. Just give me a few minutes to change."

They shared a glance then left the room and shut the door behind them.

Closing my eyes, I took a deep breath. Without trying, I could "see" Clay in a painful burst of light. A first. My other vision usually required an amount of focus.

With a sigh, I opened my eyes and turned to him. He looked seriously pissed. My stomach churned. Sam had promised he could control himself.

"Will you bite me if I sit next to you, Clay?"

He snorted, and I watched the silent snarl ease from his muzzle.

His hackles slowly laid flat. When he settled onto his haunches, I knew he'd calmed down, and I sat next to him.

"You know I don't understand dog, right? It'd be so much easier if you just told me what was wrong."

I turned my head to meet his gaze. Our faces were close together. Because of his height, he was looking down at me. He let out a gusty sigh and bent his head to nudge the clothes I still held.

"You don't like the clothes or that I'm going out?" I watched his face, trying to figure out what he was getting at. He actually bobbed his head yes.

"You don't like both?"

He lowered himself down onto the mattress and watched me with his sad puppy eyes, not trying to communicate further.

"You're really frustrating me, Clay." I moved to get up, and he growled again.

"Now, hold on..." I did get up but spun with my hands on my hips to look him in the eye. Aware that only a door separated us from the suspiciously silent couple in the living room, I kept quiet despite my anger.

"I'm trying here, Clay, and you're not. So stop growling at me. Got it? And so what if I go out? Do you trust me so little? Have you not been paying attention? I'm not comfortable around guys. It's not as if I'm going to go out tonight and come back with a boyfriend or something. So, just chill out about your Claim, all right?"

He continued to growl at me and gave me a dog-eyed glare. In his mind, he and I shared a tie. I knew that. I also knew, from a werewolf standpoint, in a strongly tied pair, the male often acted in an extremely possessive manner. If other unMated males came near before the Claim was completed, a fight typically broke out. Sometimes to the death.

"But we're not talking unMated males," I whispered to him, thinking aloud. "They're just men."

He chuffed out his canine laugh and hopped from the bed to

walk toward me. I couldn't help it; after all that barking and growling, I stepped back from him. His sides heaved as he sighed and stopped advancing. I knew my fear disappointed him.

"Sorry," I mumbled automatically. Although he'd done nothing but try to communicate why he didn't want me to go out tonight, I didn't appreciate his chosen methods of communication. They could use improvement.

"Let me think, Clay." I sat on the edge of the bed while he stood on the floor and watched me. I still didn't understand what continued to bother him. The date wasn't with a werewolf. I had no interest in Scott. I only wanted to go as a favor to Rachel. And the clothes were the only going out clothes I had.

"Can we compromise? I don't want to spend the entire year sitting at home with a possessive dog who won't talk to me." Yeah, that sounded weird. "What if we went somewhere dog friendly? There's a bar Rachel knows with cute little bistro tables on the sidewalk. If you're on your leash, you could come."

He stood, turned around so he faced away from me, and sat again.

"Is that a yes?" I leaned to the side in an attempt to see his face. He didn't move.

"I'm taking that as a yes. If you turn around while I'm changing, I'm going to have you neutered."

He just laughed again, so I hurried into my skirt and switched my t-shirt for the fitted top. As my head cleared the neckline, I met his eyes in the mirror. Thank the stars I hadn't changed any underthings.

"Hope it was worth it," I said. "You're on the couch tonight."

Rachel and Peter sat talking on the couch when I walked out of my room.

"All set, but can we change our plans? I think Clay was freaking out because he knows we're leaving. He's been left alone so much this week..."

Predictably, Rachel made soothing noises and went to cuddle

Clay. He tolerated it with as much dignity as a man in fur and a collar could muster.

"What if we went to that bar with the bistro tables that you were telling me about?" I said to Rachel.

Rachel leapt at the idea. "That'd be perfect. It's still nice enough out. Besides, I think this is the last week they do the outdoor dining. We should go before it's closed for the season."

Peter stalled. "Are you sure he will be okay? He looked pretty aggressive in there."

Rachel stopped petting Clay to look back at Peter. "He's never done that before. I think Gabby might be right. We've been leaving him alone a lot. I even forgot to let him out this morning before I left."

Peter looked adoringly at Rachel, and I knew we'd be going to the bistro bar.

"Let me grab my shoes. I'll follow you guys in my car just in case I need to leave early."

"I'll let Scott know about the change in plans." Peter pulled out his cell and started tapping the screen.

"I'll let Clay out." Rachel got up, walked to the back door, and called to Clay. Clay looked at me imploringly, but after what he'd just pulled, I had no pity.

"You know the drill. Go do dog business."

He left the room without a backward look. I went to the hall closet to search for my black flip-flops, the best footwear I had to offer the outfit, and grabbed a light jacket.

"You talk to him like he's a person," Peter said.

"I tease her for it all the time," Rachel said with a smile as she rejoined us. "You should hear her scolding him at night for taking up too much room on the bed."

Annoyingly, I started to blush. "Well, he's huge. Most of the time I have to sleep curled up. But, I'm sure I'll appreciate him more in winter." I slipped my feet into the plain flip-flops and made my way into the kitchen where I grabbed my keys.

I locked the back door while Rachel and Peter left via the front.

Clay already sat in the passenger seat when I turned toward the car. It meant he'd switched into his skin to open the door. I shook my head, got in, and started to buckle up.

"You're going to be seen doing stuff a dog shouldn't do. That or someone's going to call the cops because a naked man keeps popping up in my backyard." He didn't laugh this time. I turned to look at him while I started the car.

"You okay?"

Clay met my eyes, but I couldn't tell what bothered him now. I wished I could read him better.

"Fine. No growling, no biting, no barking. Pretty much no anything but acting like a passive, well-behaved dog," I said, laying down the rules as I backed out of the driveway.

I followed Peter's red compact through traffic with ease.

"I'm really nervous about this and don't want to worry about you, too." I sighed and started to doubt my decision. Although Clay had witnessed how the man who'd sold me the car had acted, he didn't know how guys acted around me in general. Maybe this wasn't a good idea. He would flip out when someone started to hit on me.

"Clay, you should know...men make me uncomfortable because of the way they act around me. They usually start flirting or ask me on a date. Most girls would be flattered, but if you really pay attention, there's something unnatural about it. It's like they can't help themselves. And sometimes, after I tell them no enough, they walk away with..."

I groped for the right word but came up blank.

"I don't know...a look. Like they've been caught doing something they're ashamed of. I just want to try for normal tonight, okay? It'll be hard enough being in a public place. You'll see. I just need to know you're not going to make it any harder on me."

Out of the corner of my eye, I saw him turn to look out the window and reached over to ruffle his fur gently.

With increasing frequency, I caught myself touching him as if he were a dog. If I didn't think about him as a guy, petting him comforted me.

"Does it bother you when I pet you?" I asked, keeping my eyes on the road. I knew his answer when he contorted his large body to lay down with his head against my leg so I could reach him better. I laughed, feeling lighter than I had in a long while.

"Okay. If I start annoying you with it, just move away. I promise I won't pester you."

Peter considerately picked a parking spot with a free space next to it for me. Clay unwedged himself as I parked. I grabbed the leash and snapped it on. He watched me exit, hopped out after me, and stayed close to my side as we walked.

Rachel and Peter politely included me in their conversation. It helped distract me from my nervousness about meeting Peter's friend. I knew what to expect even if neither Rachel nor Clay fully understood. Peter's lack of reaction had pleasantly surprised me. But, his response wasn't the norm. I just hoped Clay would behave.

Scott waited for us at one of the outside tables. He stood and flashed a welcoming smile when he saw Peter. From a distance, I saw several female patrons at nearby tables cast speculative glances Scott's way. Fit and tall, with light brown hair and a carefree smile, no doubt his good looks warranted it. But, something about the way he held himself bothered me. It sent off an insincere vibe as if he'd practiced his pose.

His smile turned secretive and cunning as his pale blue eyes fixated on me. The subtle change probably escaped everyone else's notice, but not mine. Depressed, but hiding it well, I rested a hand on Clay's back. Whether in comfort or restraint, I couldn't be sure.

"Scott, this is Gabby," Peter said when we stood next to the table.

I smiled a tentative greeting but didn't offer my hand.

"A pretty name you don't hear often," Scott murmured, pulling out a chair for me.

Taking the chair he offered would put me across from Rachel and force me to sit between the two guys. Clay wouldn't like that. He didn't like the comment about my name either, but other than a twitch I'd felt with my hand on his back, he behaved.

"Would you mind if we switched spots, Scott? That way our dog won't be so close to people walking by. He's very friendly but big. I don't want anyone to be intimidated by him."

"No problem." He gave me a reassuring smile and pulled out his own chair for me.

Loosely holding Clay's leash, I moved to the chair next to Rachel. Scott politely pushed the chair back in as I sat. Then he leaned close to move his drink. Clay quickly went to lie between my chair and Scott's. He nudged Scott's chair farther away before Scott could sit. I pretended not to notice.

We made small talk while we perused the menus. I felt Scott's gaze continually return to me but refused to look up.

After we ordered, each of the more experienced students shared their knowledge of the university. Scott offered—twice—to take me on an official tour when I admitted I didn't know many of the campus locations they mentioned. As soon as I declined the second time, he looked less like the nice guy I'd met and more like a guy who would give me problems. I looked down at Clay. He still lay next to me, head on his paws. Only the twitch of his ears indicated his attention to the conversation.

"Why not have a drink with us, Gabby?" Scott asked, pointing at my water.

He hadn't worried about what I drank until I'd turned down his invitations for a tour.

"I'm a bit younger than the rest of you." I glanced at Rachel and saw her studying me. Crap! Was she noticing? Was she getting mad? I should have stayed home. Folding my hands in my lap, I tried to play it cool.

"Really? How old are you?"

"Eighteen. I'm not much of a soda drinker either, so water

works." I tried to turn the conversation off myself. "How much longer until you graduate?"

"It depends on how far I want to go," Scott said, his intense smile relaxing a little. He nodded toward Peter. "Peter told me he declared his major freshman year and has never changed. I, on the other hand, have changed twice. I like what I'm learning now, so I hope I won't change it again, but you never know. What about you?"

"I'm going for massage therapy. So, I won't be here as long as the rest of you."

"Massage therapy? I hear they ask for volunteers to come in for those classes." He leaned closer with a fascinated smile on his face. "If you ever need someone to practice on, let me know. I'd be happy to come in." He reached over to pat my hand. The timely arrival of our food saved me from having to avoid his touch.

Clay nudged my leg with his surprisingly warm and dry nose, and I glanced down. He stared at me a moment then shifted his gaze to Scott, who was moving his drink for the waitress. Clay returned his glance to me and pulled his lips back in a silent snarl. Without the growl, it looked more like a scary, crazy wolf smile, but I got his meaning. Scott was getting on Clay's nerves, and Clay wouldn't put up with too much more.

Peter spoke up while Scott was distracted. "I think you'll both be in some of the anatomy classes next semester, Gabby. If you want a study group, you should let Rachel and me know. I've already been through them." He gazed admiringly at Rachel. "And since you're graduating in spring, I know you have, too."

"Thank you, Peter, but I really do study best on my—"

"That's a great idea," Scott said. "We should start now so the class won't be so hard later. What do you think about Tuesday nights?"

"It's a good idea to get a head start," I said, ignoring Clay's insistent bump against my leg. "But I'm so swamped with classes and homework now that I don't even have time to take poor Clay for walks."

I reached over to pat Clay reassuringly but stopped when I noticed Scott's gaze drop to my chest. The cowl neck had dipped away and revealed a little glimpse of the shadows within. Scott's eyes went from glassy fixation to glazed obsession. This was getting ridiculous.

Turning back to my dinner, I stuffed a few bites into my mouth to prevent me from needing to converse. Unfortunately, Scott took the opportunity to try to slide his chair a little closer. Thankfully, Clay didn't give an inch.

"What's your dog's name?" Scott asked, looking down at Clay.

"Clay," Rachel answered after seeing my mouth full.

Clay, I noticed, didn't look up at the sound of his name. Instead, he tensed and laid his ears back. Time to go.

"Nice name," Scott said, but I could tell he didn't care. "Let's bring him home after this and go out to a new club that opened downtown."

"Rachel?" I looked at her pleadingly, hoping she'd know that I wasn't begging to go out dancing. Her perceptive gaze locked on Scott.

"I see it," she said with a serious expression.

"See what?" Peter said. His gaze bounced between the three of us.

"Exhaustion. She's been studying like crazy." She waved over the waitress and asked for boxes and the check for the two of us.

"And she needs rest, not a night out. Although, I am really glad we came." She looked at Peter with a smile.

My weak smile didn't cover my gratitude at her diplomacy.

I reached for my purse, which I'd hung on the back of the chair. Desperate, Scott moved to grab my hand. Clay stood abruptly. He successfully knocked Scott's hand out of the way but also bumped the table in the process. Peter reached out to steady his and Rachel's drinks, and I hurried to pull a twenty from my purse.

The waitress returned with the bill and the wrapped-up leftovers. Since Rachel was still digging in her purse, I just handed the waitress the twenty after a quick glance at the bill. I was willing to pay for Rachel if it helped us leave faster.

"I better drive her home," Rachel said to Peter. "You have my number. Give me a call if you want to do something next weekend."

I stood, and Rachel shadowed me, ready to go. Clay bumped into me, knocking me off balance so I had to grab Rachel for support. I looked down at him and noticed Scott stand and hand the waitress his portion of the bill.

"Rachel, you can stay with Peter. I don't mind taking Gabby home," Scott said. Oily enthusiasm dripped with each word, and I didn't even need to look at Rachel for her to decline.

"No, Scott, I think we're done for tonight." She waved to Peter and grabbed my hand.

Poor Peter looked at us all, bewildered. His night out with Rachel had fallen apart fast, and I truly felt bad about it.

I went with Rachel, relieved to escape before Scott's recklessness grew. An "oof" sounded behind us, and I panicked, realizing I'd forgotten Clay. I spun around in time to see Scott hit the ground. He'd tripped over Clay in his hurry to catch me. I suspected Clay had done it purposely to slow Scott down.

Clay wasted no time. He ran to me and bumped his head against my back to get me moving before Scott could pick himself up again. There wasn't yet enough distance between the table and us to mute Peter's next words.

"What the hell is wrong with you, man? You come on too..." What he still had to say faded as we quickly walked away.

"I'm sorry," Rachel said. "You told me, but I didn't really get it. Even the men sitting around us were eyeing you."

I'd been too busy keeping an eye on Scott and Clay to notice. We continued to speed walk to the car.

"No big deal. You should see me in some of my classes. 'No' is the most common word in my vocabulary. Scott's reaction was worse than most because he already considered me his date. If you say 'no' consistently and to everyone, it doesn't get so bad." I handed Rachel the keys when we reached the car. "You really can drive."

She nodded, and we got in. Clay climbed into the back and stretched out so his head lay on the console between the two front seats. Rachel wasted no time backing out and leaving.

Halfway home, she pulled into a gas station. "Tonight's an ice cream night. Be right back." She jumped out and strode into the convenience station with the determination of a girl on a shopping spree.

Laying my head back, I sighed, and my hand found its way to Clay's soft fur. I pet his head and ears. He exhaled loudly but stayed still, so I figured he didn't mind. I was just glad he wasn't rubbing in that it'd been a disaster of a night out.

I looked out the window, watched traffic zip past, and allowed myself just a small amount of self-pity. I'd wanted normal so badly. No werewolves. No second sight. No weird pull on men. Yet, I *knew* I would never be normal. I would never have a normal date. I kept trying to mold myself into something I could never be. Why?

Clay lifted his head under my hand, and I reined in my emotions, knowing he could sense my melancholy.

"I'm fine," I said as I met his gaze. "How are you doing?" He scooted forward to lay his head on my lap in response. Yeah, that was pretty much how I felt.

The door opened, startling us both.

"I got double fudge brownie for each of us," Rachel said as she slid in behind the wheel and handed me the bag. "Sorry, Clay. Chocolate's poison for dogs. None for you."

She made me smile.

When we got home, I went straight to my room to change. Clay stayed with Rachel as she praised his good behavior and good sense to trip Scott when he'd started to follow us. No doubt, he'd get the other half of her burger before I finished. Tossing the shirt into the closet, I vowed never to wear it again and pulled on the comfortable clothes I slept in.

Shaking off my mood, I walked into the kitchen.

"Where's my chocolate?"

Clay moved to my side, and I patted him again. I'd asked a lot of him tonight, and he deserved a real reward. He'd been surviving on sandwiches and leftovers from Rachel. Tomorrow, we'd go to the store, and I'd buy him a big steak.

Rachel handed me my pint with a spoon standing in it. She'd already dug into hers. After eating another spoonful with a blissful groan, she set her container of ice cream on the table.

"I'm going to go change. Want to watch a movie or something?" Rachel stripped out of her shirt on her way to her bedroom.

I looked at the wall clock and savored another spoonful of ice cream. It was only seven, but I was tired. I put the lid back on and tucked my container in the near-empty freezer.

"What do you think?" I asked Clay, noting he watched me and not the striptease Rachel had unknowingly put on or the chocolate ice cream she'd left unguarded. "Stay up and watch a movie or go to bed early? Lead the way." I waved him forward, and he trotted through the living room to my room.

"Rach, we're just going to go to bed early. 'K?" I leaned against the wall in the living room, waiting for her answer.

"It's okay. Go ahead," she said, appearing again. She wore short shorts and a tank top for bed. "I won't keep you up with a movie, will I?" She glided past me and flopped on the couch.

"I'm so tired I doubt anything will keep me from sleeping."

"'K. Night, Hun. Thanks for going with me even if it did suck," she said, giving me a smile.

"Don't worry about it. Night." I walked into my room and closed the door behind me as she turned on the TV.

Clay lay on the end of the bed, his usual spot. His head rested on his paws. He still had his eyes open.

"Thanks, Clay." As I passed him, I stopped to kiss the top of his furry head. He made a funny grunt noise that made me smile. Probably his wolf version of "no problem." I crawled under the covers and wiggled my feet under his body to the spot he'd already warmed.

I felt Clay relax a moment before he let out a gusty breath. He started to breathe deeply, and I tried to unwind as well. Going on a double date hadn't turned out as badly as it could have.

It was still dark when I woke. Not only dark but also colder. The mild weather we'd enjoyed last night while eating outside had apparently fled with the sun. I nestled under the covers, trying to avoid the chill in the air. When I stretched my legs searching for Clay's weighted warmth, I felt nothing. His spot was cool.

"Clay?"

My bedroom door creaked open, and he jumped up on the mattress, causing it to bounce. He settled on my feet, and his heat immediately warmed me.

"Thanks."

Laying my head back down on the pillow, I burrowed deeper. The warm nights of summer, of sleeping with the window open, had retired for the year. Soon, going outside during the day would require a jacket. The thought was a little depressing. I didn't really care for the cold.

I wanted to sleep a little longer and tried to close my eyes again, but they popped back open on their own. Clearly awake, I knew I should really get out of bed and do something. Yet, the thought made me cringe...until I remembered I owed Clay for last night. This early, there'd be no one around outside, especially with this first cold snap. We needed to take advantage of the still above freezing weather and do something together. He'd like that.

"Hey, Clay. Wanna go get breakfast with me?"

With a sigh, he jumped back down off the bed.

"You could have said no," I said with a soft laugh as I rolled out from under the covers.

Grabbing my clothes, I tiptoed to the bathroom. When I reemerged, Clay sat next to the back door, waiting patiently. I glanced at the car keys. Drive or walk? Walking would save money, and I enjoyed it.

"You up for a walk?" I kept my voice low since I didn't want to wake Rachel.

The idea of walking outside with Clay before dawn made me smile. He looked like a beast. Any sane man would keep his distance. It would be vastly different from the heckling first walk I had taken to campus.

When he didn't move away, I took that as affirmation and clipped on his leash, loosely looping it around his collar so I wouldn't need to hold it. He turned to me with a questioning look.

"What? I'm following the law...you're on a leash. Let's go."

I opened the door, and we soundlessly slipped outside. As expected, crisp air engulfed us, but the lack of wind made it tolerable. After pulling the hood up over my loose hair, I tucked my hands into the pockets of my hoodie and stepped off the porch, suspiciously testing the air to see if my breath clouded. Clay trudged next to me, still looking a little tired.

We walked in the direction of the campus, toward a small diner that was open all day, six days a week, closed Sundays. Well-known on campus, Ma's Kitchen served good, cheap food for the perpetually broke college kid. With ten dollars in my pocket, I figured we could stuff ourselves before walking back home.

The sidewalks remained empty. Streetlights buzzed overhead. The soft scrape of Clay's nails on the pavement comforted me, and I filled my lungs, relaxing. Very few cars passed us as we made our way from one pool of light to the next.

The walk to campus offered an eclectic array of buildings. Businesses jumbled in with residences, some so close together their shadows merged, creating perfect places for hiding. But Clay's calm presence allowed me to enjoy the walk without using my sight.

We strolled in companionable silence for a few minutes before I spoke up.

"So what do you like for breakfast? Oatmeal?" He laughed, and I smiled back. "Yeah, I was thinking you're more a steak and eggs kinda guy."

"Who you talking to darlin'?" a man called as he stepped out from the shadows across the narrow street. His sudden appearance made my heart race.

"My dog." Even though I considered this area safe, it paid to be smart. So I whispered to Clay, asking him to bark. He obliged with a deep "woof" that almost scared me. The sound bounced off the surrounding buildings. I hoped it wouldn't wake anyone.

"Damn," the man called back, keeping pace with us on the opposite sidewalk. "That thing on a leash?"

"Yep, but there's no holding him back. I'm safer letting him go or he'd just drag me along."

The man laughed. "I bet. Have a good morning," he called before turning at the next corner to walk around the block.

"You trust that?" I asked Clay, watching the man's retreating form. Clay harrumphed.

"Me neither. And thanks for warning me there was someone close by," I said. He made a noise I interpreted between a snort and a laugh.

"Brat." I smiled down at him.

Night sounds began to fade, and I heard the occasional bird call out though dawn was still an hour away. Clay continued to pace alertly by my side until we reached the diner. Judging from the empty parking lot, they didn't get much business this early. Still, the air outside smelled like frying breakfast sausage. Delicious. Beside me, Clay's stomach rumbled.

"Since they don't allow dogs, I'll go in and get our food for carryout," I said, pulling open the door. He obediently sat just outside, the position enabling him to watch me through the glass.

When I entered, the waitress set down the basket of jellies she'd been using to refill the jelly holders on the tables and moved to the register.

"Good morning," she said with a chipper smile. "How are you this morning?"

Wow. A people-person and a morning-person. I weakly smiled back and ordered.

As soon as I had our breakfast, I brought it out to Clay. We sat together on one of the cement parking blocks in front of the building. The early-morning traffic crept along quietly, keeping the illusion of solitude.

I opened his container and started to cut up his steak. He laughed at me again, and I shushed him. He could laugh all he wanted. He usually ate so fast I worried he'd choke. I set his container on the ground for him when I finished. He dug in, making it hard to think of him as a man.

"I hope you're a slower eater when you're in your skin," I commented.

He stopped eating and looked at me. Too late, I realized how critical my comment had sounded. I tried to soften it.

"It's just that you eat faster than me. That's all." It sounded lame.

I felt worse when he made an effort to eat slower. He still finished first. In an attempt to make up for my thoughtless comment, I offered him the rest of my breakfast, too. When he finished, I threw our containers away in the parking lot trash can.

We began the long walk back with each of us lost in our own thoughts. Well, I was lost in mine, anyway. I didn't know what to say to take away the sting from my words. Why didn't I think before I spoke to him? I sometimes forgot about the man beneath the fur and tended just to talk, letting anything flow from my mouth without much thought. Sure, I may have meant what I said, but I could have found a better, nicer way to say it. Maybe.

Distracted and dwelling on my own thoughts, I paid no attention to my surroundings until Clay began to growl. My head snapped up in surprise at the soft, menacing sound. Clay stopped walking. His head turned so he watched the space between two houses on our left. Dawn still hadn't lightened the sky, so I saw nothing but shadows.

I closed my eyes and focused, depending on my other sight—something I'd mostly ignored since coming to school—to see what my eyes couldn't. The yellow-green sparks of the people in the houses around us glowed softly. To the left, closing in fast, a blue-grey light surged. Stunned, I blinked at it and glanced at Clay's spark. Blue-grey compared to his blue-green. Another color variation?

"What is it, Clay?" I whispered, taking a cautious step back. The colors I saw classified into werewolves, humans, and anomalies like Charlene and me. This new color moved too fast for a human.

Clay remained alert to the other werewolf's advance.

"What should I do, Clay?" I tried not to panic, but I could think of only one reason a werewolf would run at us like that. It wanted to challenge Clay.

If I walked away, it would think I was rejecting Clay's Claim. As much as I didn't want to Claim Clay, I didn't want a tie to anyone else.

Clay's growl increased in volume. I looked at the darkened houses around us. Perhaps I could use them to our advantage.

Clay tensed in front of me. I retreated a few more paces until I stepped into the road, no more than five feet from Clay. The faint, rapid thud of the werewolf's paws hitting the ground resonated from the darkness ahead. I tracked its spark. It sped forward. Suddenly, the rhythmic sound of its approach stopped even though its spark continued toward us.

Clay braced himself. In that moment, an enormous object soared at us from the darkness. I scrambled back. Its large body rivaled Clay for size. But, it was the newcomer's dark grey fur and bright blue eyes that forever burned into my memory.

The flying mass hit Clay hard. Clay let loose an aggressive snarl as he twisted, and worked to keep his back legs under him. His claws dug into the asphalt, scraping and scrabbling to slow the skid toward me. The two werewolves grappled, swiping claws and snapping jaws.

Eyes wide, I continued to maintain my view of the human sparks while watching the fight before me. Focused on each other, neither looked my way.

The challenger scuttled out of Clay's reach and regained his own footing. Clay lunged forward and snapped down on the other's muzzle. His sharp teeth ripped into tender flesh. I wanted to cheer when the other werewolf yelped in pain. They broke apart. Clay continued to growl. The low rumble made my heart beat even faster. The challenger responded with his own snarl but didn't attempt another attack. Instead, he sidestepped, looking for an opening.

I moved with them and maintained a small distance from both.

The noise escalated as they stalked each other. The challenger feinted toward Clay, lips drawn back and teeth parted. My heart beat harder with fear. Clay gave no ground, carefully keeping himself between the newcomer and me while I tried to stay out of the way. The dogs in the neighborhood started to bark. The continued use of my sight began to strain me, but I saw a spark moving in a nearby house.

Time to take the offensive.

"Hey!" I yelled loudly.

Clay didn't jump, but the other werewolf did. His bright blue gaze flicked to me. A light turned on in the house.

"Whose dog is this? Someone help me get him off my dog!" Another light went on in the house.

Clay took advantage of his opponent's momentary distraction and went for its throat. The other wolf dodged the attack but just barely. Bleeding freely from Clay's first strike, red began to color its muzzle.

With a deep-throated bark, it lunged again at Clay, refocusing its efforts. The lunge caught Clay in the shoulders and almost knocked him off balance. I forgot to breathe for a moment. Clay exposed his neck in an attempt to bite his opponent's front leg rather than spin away and leave me unprotected.

The other wolf grunted in pain as Clay's teeth clamped down. Still, he went for the opening. His teeth clicked against the metal that studded Clay's collar. The wolf growled, pulled back, and made to try again. Clay quickly released his hold on the wolf's leg and backed away as did his limping adversary.

Clay's leash unraveled from its coiled pile under his collar and trailed in his wake. The other werewolf noticed it, moved forward, and attempted to step on it. Brown fur ruffled as Clay twisted sharply to flip the leash out of the way.

I looked around, trying to figure out how to stop this. In the houses closest to the fight, more lights burst on. In the house across the street, someone pushed back a curtain to peer out.

Behind me, I heard a shrill whistle. "Duke! Come here, Duke."

The neighborhood was waking.

This time, the sudden interruption didn't distract either of them. Both maintained focus on their opponent. This had to stop now before Clay got hurt.

"The noise has everyone waking up, whoever you are," I said. "You don't have enough time to finish this. It'd be better to leave now when Clay won't be able to chase you. Someone's going to call the police, and when they get here, they'll see a dog that's neither licensed or leashed. You'll either have to change and expose yourself or let them take you away, thinking you're a dog."

The challenger continued his circling attack as if I hadn't spoken.

The front door of the house closest to us opened, and a man shined a flashlight at the fighting dogs then at me.

"Can you help me?" I called, my voice purposely coming out high-pitched and fearful. "Do you know whose dog this is? It came running at my dog from the direction of your backyard."

"It's not ours. Want me to call the police?" he yelled over the snarls and growls.

I didn't get a chance to answer. The grey werewolf broke away from the fight and bolted back into the darkness from where he'd come. Apparently, he had heard my warning.

Clay, panting heavily, stayed close to me and watched the other wolf retreat. The challenger conceded with his withdrawal. For now.

"Did you see what kind of dog it was?" the man called as he left the safety of his house to look at his side yard where the wolf had disappeared. He cautiously shined his flashlight to search for it.

I let out a shaky, thankful laugh, knelt beside Clay, and wrapped my arms around his neck. My hands shook, the strain and fear taking their toll, as I ran my hands over the area around his collar. I didn't find any injuries. Relieved, I leaned against him. He really was growing on me.

"Ma'am? You okay?"

The man pointed his flashlight at us but stayed near his house. Any closer, and he'd feel the pull. I didn't need to deal with any more problems. Across the street, a door opened, distracting the man.

"They okay, Mike?"

I lifted my head from Clay. "You okay?" I whispered.

He turned his head and licked my cheek, reassuring me.

"Next time, I'll just carry the leash," I promised. My eyes watered. It had been too close. It would have only been a matter of time before the other wolf would have pinned him because of it.

"We're okay," I said as I stood. I kept a hand on Clay's head. "The dog was as big as Clay here but had dark grey fur."

"Doesn't sound like any dog from this neighborhood, but I know there are some big dogs a few blocks away. Do you want me to call the cops?" The man started toward us.

I picked up Clay's loose leash and nudged him to get him moving.

"Nah. I think we're fine," I said, taking a step back. Too late. The man had gotten close enough that the pull had him. I saw the interest in his eyes.

After a few moments reassuring him that neither of us had suffered injuries and that police involvement was no longer necessary, I grudgingly gave him my phone number just in case anyone had called the cops and they showed up. Clay remained quiet and unusually calm throughout the conversation.

Crisis averted, we hurried home. I didn't talk. Instead, I concentrated on scanning with my second sight. I pushed to see farther than ever before, and it drained me. My legs grew heavier with each step. I tried not to let it show.

While I scanned, so did Clay. His eyes missed nothing, and he constantly scented the air.

The sun cleared the surrounding rooftops, and its bright rays lit the sidewalk. My hurried walk degraded to a plodding step somewhere along the way, and it took us much longer to get home. No further sign of that weird light reappeared during the rest of the walk.

Because I watched my shuffling feet as we retraced our steps to the back door, I didn't see Rachel standing on the porch.

"There you are!"

My hand flew to Clay's thick mane at the same time as my heart skipped a beat. The scare distracted me from my second sight, and it snapped closed at my loss of focus. I struggled to reopen it, but a sudden pain in my head stopped my attempt. I'd done too much.

"Nice morning for a walk," she said, moving toward us to pet Clay.

I unclenched my fingers from his fur, not wanting her to notice my death grip. She fingered one of his ears. He shook off her touch. She laughed and bent to kiss the top of his head. He endured the kiss but rolled his eyes at me. Some of my tension melted at their antics. He appeared more relaxed, too.

"I made a call this morning and can get him into the vet for his shots," she said as she tugged the leash from my loose grasp. "I figured after the way he acted last night, we should have him current...just in case."

It took a moment for what she said to click. My stunned gaze dropped to Clay. He calmly met my eyes, not giving any indication what he thought of her announcement. I looked back at Rachel. I didn't know what to say.

"You okay, Gabby?" She looked at me with concern.

No. Not okay. What had started as a nice thank you breakfast for Clay had turned into a dog fight. And now she wanted to take him to the vet? He didn't deserve that. Besides, after the attack, would he be willing to leave me? Wait. Could a vet figure out he wasn't really a dog? I tried to contain my panic.

"Uh, I didn't budget for it," I blurted, hoping at the very least to put the visit off until I talked to Sam about the risks.

"Don't worry." Rachel untangled his leash. "I can cover it for now, and you can pay me back."

"Let's all go." The words popped out of my mouth before I thought about it. What good would that do? Did I think I could block the vet from touching Clay? Rachel would definitely know something was up, then.

"No offense, Gabby, but you look like hell. I think you'd be better off with some quiet time. Don't worry; we'll be fine." She tried to pull Clay toward the garage again, but he didn't move with her.

Instead, he nudged me toward the back door, almost knocking me off-balance. Rachel tugged on his leash and scolded him, but he ignored her and stayed focused on me.

"Would you mind giving him your standard pep talk? I don't know why he only listens to you. I'm the one that feeds him treats." She handed the leash over to me. I rubbed my forehead, still unsure what he wanted me to do.

"Is it safe for you?" I breathed in his ear as I bent to give him a hug.

He snorted, which I took as a yes. Did he want me to stay here, then?

"I'm so sorry about this. I'll need to call Sam and let him know what happened."

I straightened, looked him in the eye, and smoothed the fur on his head. "It's your choice." I dropped the leash and stepped back.

He gave me a long look as Rachel moved to open the car door. He sighed then followed her.

"The control you have over him is weird but cool," Rachel said as he jumped into the back seat.

Control? I didn't have any control over him. He only listened when I threatened to kick him out of my room or leave him behind.

"Yeah. Just don't be gone too long. He'll get upset."

"The vet's just a few minutes from here. We should be back soon." She climbed behind the wheel, closed the door, and rolled down her window.

I couldn't believe we were actually doing this. What did a vet usually check for? Shots...Age...Neuter... Crap, crap, crap! The engine roared to life.

"Just don't have him neutered! Or anything that involves blood or blood work. It's expensive, and I promised him he'd keep his jewels." Oh, how I wished those words back when Clay started to make an odd coughing noise. I could only assume it was his version of laughter. I really needed to start filtering what I said.

Rachel swiveled to check on Clay. "Maybe we should have the vet check his lungs."

"He's fine. Think cost," I said from the deck as she backed out of the driveway.

I went inside and immediately called Sam to let him know about the attack. He assured me of my safety, but I wasn't worried about that. Paul and Henry had long ago educated me in regard to challenge etiquette. A challenge questioned Clay's right to me. If present, I needed to stay near him to show my support of his right. Fleeing rejected him. Though rejecting him sounded tempting on the surface, doing so would put me back into the eligible pool. I didn't want that.

Sam said he would let Elder Joshua know about the attack, too. He also felt certain the challenger wouldn't try again anytime soon, given the extent of his injuries.

A werewolf's tough hide deflected many things that could damage human skin. What it couldn't deflect, it reduced in severity. A knife could still cut a werewolf, for example, but not lethally like it could me. On top of the nearly impenetrable skin, nature also threw in a phenomenally fast healing process. A shallow cut would knit together in less than an hour and heal with no scar visible in less than a day. However, injuries from another werewolf tended to take twice as long to heal. Still faster than a human's, however.

Talking to Sam helped settle my nerves. Though the werewolf's odd light still bothered me, I couldn't bring it up. I'd never shared the details of my ability with Sam. However, I did almost bring up the vet visit. Only Clay's willingness to go had me keeping it to myself at the last minute. I felt guilty enough and didn't need to add a lecture to it.

Before I hung up, Sam reminded me that challenges weren't unheard of and that I had no reason to worry, yet. I agreed, and neither of us said what I already knew. Challenges occurred when more than one werewolf became interested in the same potential Mate and the potential in question didn't have a preference. So, the challenge was my fault.

AN HOUR AND A HALF LATER, I had showered, scrubbed the kitchen floor, and vacuumed every room in the house in an effort to keep myself awake.

At the sound of Rachel's car in the driveway, I ran through the house and out the back door. Rachel parked the car in front of the garage and smiled at me. I leaned over the porch railing, trying to see into the back of the car. I spotted Clay lying on the back seat with his head down. He didn't look up at me.

Rachel opened her door.

"How'd it go?" I said, trying to sound indifferent.

"He took it like a champ." She opened the back car door for Clay. He lifted his head and stood with obvious effort. Then he hopped down with care and pathetically climbed the deck steps to my side. I stared at him for a moment.

"What'd they do to him?"

Rachel shook her head and closed the door.

"He wasn't acting like this when we left. I swear. I think he's hamming it up for you." She patted Clay's head with a laugh.

He accepted the pat with a defeated grunt, stopped hobbling, and started to walk with his usual gait. I heaved a relieved sigh. He looked up at me and winked. I quickly checked to see if Rachel had noticed, but she had already walked away from us and into the house. I shook my head at him before we followed Rachel in.

"So what shots did he get?" I poured some orange juice from the refrigerator and took a drink to keep myself busy. Clay's eyes never left me.

"Just rabies. The vet had a hard time determining his age by his teeth but thought him to be in his prime."

I choked on my juice.

"That's great," I managed to gasp out as I glanced at Clay.

A small, smug smile curled his lips. I needed to find a nice way to tell him his wolfie smile looked creepy.

"Hey, while I was waiting for him, Peter called. He said he had a good time last night and hoped Scott hadn't ruined his chance by coming on too strong. He's never seen Scott act in any way but smooth. He naturally thinks Scott's falling hard for you."

Both Clay and I gawked at her. I knew my jaw had dropped a little and wondered if Clay's had done the same.

"I'm just repeating." She held up her hands with a laugh at my expression. "Anyway, Peter said Scott's already been bugging him about getting your number to set up another date. Given what you told me, I said no, that last night was just a friendly get together and that you were seeing someone else."

Clay's gusty sigh of relief competed with mine. We'd been through enough today. Okay, fine, he'd had to go through all of it while I just stood by. But still...the stress of it, along with the overuse of my sight, wore me out.

Looking down at him, I realized how much I didn't mind having him there. We'd at least become friends of sorts. But I worried I treated him unfairly by allowing him to hang around. Would that mislead him to think our relationship might grow to more than friendship? I hoped not. If he ever thought I asked too much, he could always walk away.

"You know, sometimes that dog creeps me out with how human he acts," Rachel said, shaking her head. "Anyway, I'm going to meet up with Peter for another try at a date. We're going to see a movie, and this time, I'm not asking you to come with." She had a huge smile on her face as she walked past us toward her room.

"Thank you!" I called to her retreating form.

<h1 style="text-align:center">Chapter Ten</h1>

THE REST OF THE WEEKEND PASSED IN A BLUR OF STUDYING. WHENEVER Rachel left to meet Peter, Clay and I would sprawl on the living room floor. I would read my books while he read his, and I turned his pages. I didn't talk much. He seemed content just to lie by me.

Because of Clay's sensitive hearing, we always moved back into my room before Rachel could get from the car to the door.

"I bet I'm looking for a new roommate before the next semester starts," I said to Clay when I heard Rachel come through the door late Sunday night. He didn't seem to have much opinion one way or the other.

On Wednesday, I realized I hadn't done my laundry in days. My meager wardrobe lay in a mashed pile in the corner of my closet. With a sigh, I plucked out a semi-clean shirt and the jeans from the day before. After I dressed, I grabbed what I could from the remaining heap and ran downstairs to cram it into the washer. Clay watched me from the top of the stairs. If I didn't leave now, I'd arrive late for class. I threw in the detergent, ran up the stairs, and nearly plowed Clay over on my way out the door.

When I pulled into the driveway that evening, there was a service truck parked in front of the house, and Rachel's car already sat in the garage. Baffled, I watched her hurry out the back door. She wore a wide grin.

"You are brilliant!" she said as soon as I opened my car door.

"What'd I do?" I took my bag loaded with library books out of the front seat and closed the door.

"There's a hot repairman working on the washer in the basement. Thank you for breaking it." She linked her arm through mine and walked me to the house.

"I didn't do anything but throw in a load of laundry before I left," I said quietly as I glanced at the open basement door.

Clay sat in the hallway, staring down the stairs. When he heard me, he turned his head to watch us.

"Hey," Rachel said. "I'm not blaming...I'm just thanking." She continued to grin.

"I thought you were into Peter," I whispered.

"I am. It doesn't mean I don't window-shop. Go down there and flirt with him and see if we can get twenty percent off our bill."

"I will not," I huffed with a laugh. I moved away from her and got myself a drink of water. "It'd be safer to send Clay down there to learn how to fix it than me trying to get us a price break."

"If our dog starts fixing things, we're hitting the road and making some money," said Rachel.

We both heard the heavy tread on the basement stairs at the same time. Rachel's face lit with anticipation while I eyed the door with dread. Was it too late to run past and hide in my room? With Clay so close to the door, I'd probably trip on him, and the repairman would find me lying at his feet.

Then, I saw the guy. Denim hugged his long, lean legs, and a snug shirt displayed his biceps and abs to perfection. I knew better than to stare; he would take my attention as a come-get-me signal for sure. But with a body like that, a girl had to look her fill. When my eyes finally met his, he smiled broadly and flexed.

Well, that just ruined the whole window-shopping experience. A conceited hottie. Their vocabularies didn't include the word no, which made it difficult to fight them off. The situation called for a retreat. I turned to Rachel.

"I have to go pick up my ring before Clay gets here. He'd be heartbroken if he found out I bent a prong on the setting already. Plus, my hand feels naked without it." While I spoke, I held out my left hand dramatically and gave it a wistful look. Maybe I was overdoing it, but I wasn't sure he'd get the point otherwise.

"The dog?" the man asked with a puzzled look at Rachel.

A nervous laugh escaped before I could stop it. "We named the dog after my fiancé. He has a good sense of humor and likes the dog, too."

I bolted out the door and got back into my car. Clay hadn't been fast enough for a change, and I had to leave him behind.

Not knowing what else to do, I went grocery shopping and took my time to read the labels of the different orange juices the store offered. Even after the drawn-out shopping trip, I had to drive past the house three times before the truck finally disappeared.

When I staggered in through the back door, laden with groceries, Clay sat waiting for me in the kitchen. I set down the bags and peeked around the corner to look for Rachel. When I didn't see or hear her, I spoke to Clay in a whisper.

"You better keep reading the books I bring home. You can be our repair guy. It gives me the willies that he knows where I live."

Clay nodded his head in agreement...which Rachel saw as she walked into the kitchen. She paused mid-stride, her eyes wide.

"Did he just nod?" she demanded.

I acted natural. "Yep. I've been working on it with him. He caught on really fast. The nodding isn't bad, but his smile can be a little scary."

Rachel stared at us for a moment then shook her head.

"You're weird, Gabby, but in a good way. Anyway, it was one hundred and twenty-five dollars to fix the washer. I covered your half. With the vet bill, you're up to one hundred, minus the burger and drink from disaster night."

Ouch. "Okay. I'll run to the bank after class tomorrow." I chewed my lip for a moment. My pathetic savings couldn't take these kinds of unexpected hits. Life was more expensive than I'd anticipated.

I turned to unpack the rest of my groceries and noticed Clay watching me closely. Not wanting to draw Rachel's attention to him again, I ignored his look and finished up so I could go study.

ON FRIDAY AFTERNOON, Rachel rushed in through the back door while calling my name in a panicked tone.

"In here!" I said as I jumped up from the bed.

We nearly collided as she flew through my bedroom door at the same time I tried to leave it. I caught her by the arms.

"What's going on?"

"Peter broke and told Scott he had plans to go to dinner with me tonight," she panted.

I stared at her. She ran through the house to tell me she had a date? I really didn't see how I qualified as the weird one sometimes.

"So...?"

"Peter's coming here to pick me up, and Scott's coming with. Gabby, I don't think he's going to take no for an answer tonight. Peter can't shake him." Her emphatic expression told me the degree of insistence Scott had used to accompany Peter.

I groaned, flopped back on my bed, and forgetting about Clay, landed on him. He didn't even twitch, but I still reached back to pat him.

"Sorry, Clay." I froze mid-pat then bolted upright. "I've got an idea! Rachel, if you have any clothes that would say I've been dating a guy for a while, can I borrow them?" I didn't want to spend any money unnecessarily.

"Sure, but who are you dating?"

Rachel moved out of the way as I rushed from my room. I heard Clay hop down from the bed to follow me. I grabbed shoes from the closet. My plan could work. I just needed to convince Clay. They both trailed behind me as I struggled to slip on some shoes while I walked to the kitchen. It wasn't easy. I almost tripped twice and covered most of the distance hopping instead of walking. I grabbed my car keys.

"I'll let you know when I bring him home. Come on, Clay," I called, holding the door open for him. With a baffled glint in his eyes, he followed me.

I rushed to the car and waved for him to hurry. I had the doors slammed closed and the engine rumbling seconds later. Clay studied me as I careened out of the driveway and took off in the direction of the shopping district.

"You're here to keep me safe, right?" I took his grunt as a yes. "Then, I need you to be more than my dog." I risked a glance at him. He tilted his head at me, clearly confused. "I need you to put on your skin. Be my date tonight. Please?"

I sounded desperate, but I didn't really care. The thought of Scott cornering me gave me shivers. His normal personality probably qualified as nice, but I'd seen how the obsession had worked on others. Scott's fascination with me had obviously advanced. Yet, if Clay were to run interference as my date, it could permanently dissolve.

"You took a shower today, right?" I expected the harrumph he let out. "Do you know what size you wear? Shirt, pants, shoes?" Unhelpful, he continued to stare at me.

Given what he'd worn when I first saw him, he probably didn't know. It made my work a little bit more difficult, but I would manage.

I found an open spot and careened into it, slamming on the brakes at the last second. Only Clay's good balance kept him from falling out of the seat.

"I'll be back in a few minutes," I said as I rushed out the door.

Inside the store, I tried to remember how he'd looked as a man. Hairy. Dirty. Tall. Well, taller than me. Had he seemed thin or chubby? I couldn't remember. His jacket had obscured most of his shape, and I'd been distracted by the whole "Hey, I'm your Mate" thing.

Usually, when I shopped on my own, it didn't turn out well. However, my crazed sprints from rack to rack held most of the men I encountered at bay. So, I scoured the clearance racks and guessed at sizes while trying to stick with safe styles.

Panting for breath, I raced to a register. I bought Clay a linen pant and shirt set, the largest brown foam bottomed sandals I could find—I could always cut the foam down to size—and a few other essentials.

Then, I ran out of the store. Clay was standing on the seat. He just stared at me as I opened the car door and tossed the bags at him. They landed at his feet.

I started the engine and tried to think where I could take him to get dressed. Somewhere he could walk in as a dog and out as a man. I couldn't think of a single place that allowed dogs in changing areas. I'd just have to try to pull a fast one on Rachel. I put the car in gear and drove it as if I'd stolen it. I made it to the house in record time.

Rachel was already dressed and standing outside by the back door when we got home. She had a stack of clothes in her arms.

"Where's the date?" she said as her eyes searched the empty car. "They are going to be here in fifteen minutes."

I waved her back into the house. "He'll be here in a few minutes. I hope."

We followed her in, and I paused to toss the bag of new clothes in the bathroom for Clay. I really hoped he'd help me.

"Let's go in my room, and you can help me pick what to wear," I said to Rachel.

"Really?" she said with an excited smile. She'd already noticed I liked my privacy and usually left me alone. But, I expected the opportunity to dress me would distract her from noticing that Clay hadn't followed us from the kitchen or, later, his absence.

"I need something a little tropical or hippie-ish," I said as I closed the door and started to undress.

Rachel set the clothes on the bed, her expression filled with suspicion.

"Who is this guy? Why do you need to dress like a hippie?"

"He's a good friend, and he didn't have much notice to go home to change. Because I'm cheap, I got him some clean clothes from the summer closeout racks." I spoke a little louder for Clay's benefit. I wanted him to know why I purchased what I had.

Rachel looked up at my sudden surge in volume. Clearly, my weirdness had just increased a level. I motioned to the pile of clothes to distract her. She began to riffle through them, searching for something to fit my requirements.

"He's got longish hair, so I think he might look like a hippie in what I bought." At least, I thought he might still have longish hair. It'd been months since I'd last seen him. "He was just behind me. I told him he could use our bathroom to change."

"How good of a friend is he?" she asked.

I smiled. "Well, we've slept together."

She surprised me by not saying anything. Instead, she held up a few options. I picked a flowing, knee-length, cream skirt with a light yellow, scoop-necked top and hurried to get dressed.

"You do know that the best way to appear like you've been dating a long time would be to look like you don't care how you look, right?" she asked.

I rolled my eyes at her, gave the skirt one last tug to straighten it, and studied myself in the mirror. Dressing up was a gamble. It might send the wrong message to Scott even with Clay present. Maybe I should follow Rachel's advice and dress down. But then Clay would look out of place in his clothes.

"That looks great on you," Rachel complimented as she scooped up the rejects.

Worried Clay might need more time, I stalled by asking her how I should fix my hair. I didn't own any make-up to apply.

"So what's the guy's name?" Rachel watched me closely.

"Clay," I admitted reluctantly. Since I'd asked a huge favor of him, I couldn't lie about his name.

"Shut up," she said with a laugh of disbelief.

"Not lying," I said, holding up my hands in the mirror. "He talks as much as the dog, too. So don't bother trying to make conversation."

I figured I'd pushed our time limit and turned to let Rachel inspect me. She smiled her approval then dashed to her room to ditch the extra clothes. We crossed paths in the living room as she went to look out the picture window, and I went to find Clay.

The door to the bathroom remained firmly closed. I tapped on it.

"Do you need help?" I whispered.

Unfortunately, Rachel overheard and started sniggering behind me. Apparently, there was nothing to see out the window. I tried to shoo her away with a wave, but she shook her head and leaned against the hallway wall to watch.

"Please hurry, Clay," I begged.

The door opened. I took a step back to avoid the cloud of steam that rolled out. Clay stepped out with it. Stunned, I stared at him. I hadn't seen him since the beginning of the summer. Well, excluding that brief look at his backside. I'd been too shocked to notice the rest of him, then.

He still looked scruffy. Between the beard that concealed his cheeks and entire neck and the full mouth-covering mustache, I still couldn't see much of him. His damp hair hung in limp, wavy strands in front of his eyes and covered the top portion of his face almost down to his nose. Yet, clean and dressed in the clothes I'd forced onto him, he looked amazing.

His shoulders filled the short-sleeved shirt, and although snug on his chest, it fell loosely to his waist. He put his hands in his pockets as he waited for my inspection to finish. Embarrassed, I tore my gaze away, but not before I noted he'd left himself barefoot.

"Brat," I muttered. Then, I cleared my throat and added, "You'll do."

I turned and caught Rachel's smirk. "Quiet from the peanut gallery."

Mercifully, the doorbell rang then so she just laughed and rushed to answer it. Their arrival spared me from having to look at Clay again. In a way, I'd forgotten the man under the fur.

I followed Rachel slowly, feeling curiously lost. Clay walked softly behind me.

"Come on in," Rachel said to Peter. Peter stepped in, and Scott followed inches behind. Peter gave me an apologetic look as he moved aside. Scott's eyes found mine, and he smiled widely. I flashed a politely cool smile in return.

I could see the moment Scott spotted Clay. His face first fell then firmed in tense appraisal.

"Hi, Peter," I said. "Nice to see you again, Scott." His face lit at my statement, and I felt bad that I needed to hurt him in order to end his fixation. "We were going to join you guys, but Clay just got off of work a little while ago and suggested he and I take advantage of the empty house tonight." My heart skipped a beat or two at my bold words, and I struggled to control the blush that wanted to paint my face. Thankfully, Clay stood behind me so I didn't need to witness his reaction to my words.

Scott's face was a different story. I watched it turn red.

"Isn't Clay your dog?" he asked suspiciously.

"We named the dog after my boyfriend. It's a bit of a joke. Clay, meet Peter and Scott, Rachel's friends." My disassociation of Scott broke him. His shoulders slumped, and the familiar look of shame stole over his face. Why did this happen? I hated it. Pity and remorse swamped me.

Clay lightly set his hand at the small of my back. A casual touch. His palm slowly warmed a large area. Even in man form, he could sense some of my anxiety.

Scott noted Clay's hand on my back, glanced between us, then turned to his friend.

"Peter, Rachel, I'm sorry to back out on you, too, but I think I'm going to head home. I've been fighting a cold all week." Without waiting for acknowledgment, he turned and left.

Peter, who'd looked apologetically anxious when he entered, watched his friend leave with a concerned frown. Rachel murmured something to him. He nodded and went to the closet to retrieve her jacket. Rachel looked back at me as Peter held out her jacket to assist her.

"Are you sure you want to stay in?"

Rachel accepted Peter's help with an ease that usually came after being together for years. I doubted they even realized how in tune they were with each other. That often happened when people found their perfect match. Their lives blended in a seamless perfection they simply called love. It was more than that, though. Their deep connection put them in tune with each other's needs and wants. It kept them open to suggestion and reason so they would always listen to each other. Yep, I'd need to look for a new roommate soon.

"We're sure," I said with a smile and waved them out the door. "Don't come home early."

When the door closed behind Peter and Rachel, I exhaled slowly and turned to Clay, breaking our connection. I smiled at him.

"Home free. Thank you, Clay."

The subtle difference between living with Clay-the-dog and

standing in a room alone with Clay-the-man tickled the nerves in my stomach. I refused to show it.

He simply watched me as he placed his now empty hand back into the front pocket of his pants. The air cooled the spot on my back that he'd warmed.

"Um..." I wasn't sure what to do. I hadn't thought past getting rid of Scott.

Clay's calm gaze made the nervous butterflies in my stomach worse. Silly, really, considering he watched me all the time as a dog. I took a breath and tried again.

"Did you want to do something since we're both dressed up?"

He shrugged.

"You can talk to me, Clay," I said with a little hope. I really began to wonder if he could speak. When he didn't respond, I spoke again. "Okay, do you want to go out or stay in?"

He moved to the couch and sat in the middle, his choice clear. Stay in tonight.

I hesitated. The chair, set at an odd angle to the TV, gave you a sore neck if you tried to watch a movie from there. That meant I'd need to sit next to him to watch a movie. But I felt so exposed in a skirt and sleeveless shirt. I wasn't sure if I could sit next to him for a full movie.

While I debated my options, he watched me closely.

"I'm going to go change," I stammered. "I'll be right back."

I turned and made it one step before the back of my shirt snagged on something. Surprised, I looked over my shoulder and found Clay standing right behind me. He held a fold of my shirt between his thumb and forefinger. I could see the glint of his brown eyes behind the still damp strands of his hair. He tilted his head back toward the couch and gave a slight tug on my shirt. My stomach dropped, and I couldn't tell if it was in a good way or a bad one.

When I hesitated, he gave another tug. I surrendered, turned back, and sat on the couch.

He padded over to the movies, made a selection I couldn't see, and crouched to start it. It amazed me that he knew how to do that. Then again, he watched everything Rachel and I did. I wondered if anything escaped his notice.

He pressed play, stood, and walked toward me with fluid strides. I felt graceless in comparison. He settled next to me and watched the previews. I tried to focus on them, too, but couldn't. Instead, I noticed our bare feet, the scratch on the wall next to the TV, his leg lightly pressed against mine, the sound of the water as it slowly dripped from the showerhead in the bathroom, his hands loosely resting on his lap. The long list of unimportant details would not let my mind settle.

It was midway through the movie when my mind calmed enough to notice we watched an action-comedy I'd wanted to see. I'd just mentioned it to Rachel this past week. She must have gotten it after that.

Slowly, I began to relax and enjoy the movie. I even laughed aloud at one point. Clay's echoing chuckle startled me but in a good way. So, he *could* do more than growl as a dog. His deep laugh sounded pleasant.

When the movie ended, I stood and went to put it away. It was still early, just about six.

"Do you want to watch another one?" I asked as I knelt to look at the movie selection. "I can throw in a pizza for us."

When I heard nothing, which wasn't unusual, I turned and saw a pile of folded clothes on the couch. But no Clay.

"Clay?"

I went in search of him, but he wasn't in the house. In the living room, I glanced at the pile of clothes again. He had been so quiet I hadn't heard a thing.

It took me a moment to think about using my second sight. Because of school and Clay's presence at home, I'd fallen into patterns where I didn't use it often. I felt safe enough that I didn't *need* to use it. Still, I checked. He wasn't anywhere in the immediate area, but I wasn't too worried about it. He did occasionally leave my side, but he never stayed away for very long.

With a smile, I picked up his clothes and headed to my room. Good thing I took forever to pick a movie.

Since I had nothing else to do, I decided to watch the movie I had spotted just before Clay disappeared. I changed into some sweats and a tank top then scrounged around in the kitchen and found what I needed to make a big bowl of buttered popcorn.

Popcorn in hand, I headed for the TV. When I walked into the living room, Clay once again lay on the couch. I smiled at his familiar furry presence.

"There you are. Want some popcorn?"

I didn't wait for an answer but went to the kitchen to get him his own bowl and split the popcorn between the two. In the living room, I set his bowl on the floor within his reach. Then, I curled into my end of the couch and tucked my feet under him. With my bowl balanced at my side, I reached for the remote.

I'd barely started the movie when he sighed gustily, repositioned himself, and laid his head on my curled legs. The heat of him relaxed me, and I settled in comfortably, content not to move him. I ate a piece of popcorn as I watched the intro. His head shifted on my leg, following the piece of popcorn. I absently took another piece and offered it to him. He gently ate it from my fingers. I offered him a few more pieces, not fully paying attention when he licked the back of my hand.

The second movie was more an action-suspense than comedy. Halfway through the movie, I'd abandoned my bowl of popcorn to the floor. One of my hands burrowed in the thick fur at Clay's neck, and the other lightly worried his fuzzy ear. He didn't seem to mind my grip as I stared at the screen. At a particularly suspenseful part, the front door opened. It scared me so badly that a strangled scream tore through the air. My scream. My heart pounded as both Rachel and Clay stared at me.

"And that's why I don't watch suspense movies," I said to both of them once I could breathe again. Clay didn't stop laughing for two minutes. Rachel laughed just as hard and thankfully didn't notice Clay's reaction.

Clay licked my exposed midriff then, finally, settled down.

I gently tugged on his ear. "Cut it out," I scolded softly.

"So when did Clay leave? I thought he'd still be here after you said I shouldn't hurry home." Rachel kicked off her shoes and flopped sideways on the chair.

I turned off the movie to give her my full attention. "Nah, I turned my back, and he took off on me." I patted Clay on the head, and he snorted. "It's okay, though. I have my favorite guy here." And I realized it was true. I liked no man better than I liked Clay in his fur. Sam used to take first place, but I still felt disappointed in him for not warning me about the last Introduction and about the possibility of Clay showing up at the back door.

"He was a little scary looking if you ask me," Rachel said as she reached over to pet Clay. Turned away from her, he took the opportunity to arch a brow at me. I fought to keep my face straight.

"When I first met him, I told him he looked like a crazy man. I still think he's crazy, but he's also nice and dependable." Clay heaved a sigh. It seemed werewolves didn't like to be described as nice either.

"So does he ever act like Scott?"

"No way." It came out so fast I had to pause and rethink it. Nope, I definitely spoke the truth. "Most guys talk about themselves to try to impress me, or they just act scary obsessive. Clay's different. I don't think I affect him like I do other guys."

I looked away from both of them, thinking. At times, he showed his possessive streak—like when I'd gone on the double date—but he didn't act obsessive. According to my reliable sources of werewolf lore, Clay did feel a strong pull for me, but it was dissimilar to what human men felt. His pull, the werewolf version, should make him territorial and controlling, but he never seemed affected by any of that. Yet, for some reason, he stayed.

"I think he just likes being with me," I said. I noticed Clay looking up at me and met his gaze. Even when he wrecked the truck back at the Compound, he didn't creep on me like most guys had. "And I'm grateful that I get to be normal around him."

Rachel laughed at me. "You sound like you're really serious about him. Why didn't you talk about him before this? And why didn't you say the dog had the same name? We could have changed it."

I decided to ignore the part about being serious. "I wasn't sure if or when he'd make an appearance. And I like the name Clay. Besides, he doesn't mind." I wasn't sure if I was talking about Clay-the-dog or Clay-the-man anymore.

Rachel switched topics. "We should probably talk about overnight visitors. What rules do we want to set?"

"Um...no loud noises?"

"Come on!" Rachel laughed louder. "I meant weekends only? Maybe guests till midnight on weekdays? Notice needed? You know, that kind of stuff."

She grinned at me, still lounged sideways on the chair. I really didn't want to have this conversation with Clay present. He lay quietly, head on my lap, considerately pretending to sleep.

"I don't know. I trust you and your judgment, and you can trust my lack of a social life. I really don't think I'll see Clay very often, so you don't need to worry."

"Oh, he'll be back. I saw the way he watched you. Are you sure the only rule you can come up with is no loud noises?"

I thought of adding that she should warn me when we had a visitor, but I looked down at Clay and figured we had it covered.

"Yeah, I think we're fine."

"Great!" she said with a huge grin. Then she cupped her hands and yelled, "Peter!"

The front door immediately opened and a sheepish looking Peter entered.

"You were supposed to text me," he muttered uncomfortably.

I laughed. "Come on in, Peter. Clay and I were just going to bed." Clay jumped off the couch first, and I got up to follow him into my room. "Night, guys."

"Another early Friday night for us," I whispered to Clay after I closed the door.

I pulled back the covers and slid between the sheets. Clay settled in his usual spot and began to breathe deeply while I lay awake thinking about the conversation with Rachel.

As she'd pointed out, Clay wasn't like the other guys. At the Compound, when I'd felt the pull Sam had warned me about, I'd panicked. I'd thought Clay would be just like the rest and that I would spend the rest of my life trying to avoid him.

When he'd shown up at the door as a dog, and not as a man, he'd thrown me off guard. Now, I realized he'd been pretty smart about it. Somehow, he'd known I would be more likely to give him a chance as a dog than as a man. Again, I'd underestimated his intelligence.

Rachel was also right about Clay watching me. He followed me everywhere. I assumed his attentiveness was to observe and learn. What if it wasn't? His quiet presence had already lulled me into indifference over his company. I needed to be more careful.

THE NEXT MORNING, I TIREDLY WENT TO THE KITCHEN AND OPENED THE fridge. My deep thoughts had kept me awake longer than I'd intended, and I felt like Sam looked most mornings. Instead of coffee, I wanted my OJ.

I squinted against the harsh light and scanned the sparse contents of my designated shelf for the orange liquid of life. No orange juice. Shuffling the contents around didn't change the answer. Nope, not there. Straightening, I surveyed the kitchen and spotted its remains in the recycling.

The shower turned on in the bathroom, and I remembered Peter had stayed over. I looked down at Clay, who silently accompanied me, as usual.

"Great. Another non-coffee person," I complained to him.

Since I drank the last of the milk yesterday, I went for a glass of water instead. The faucet handle jiggled loosely in my hand, and only a trickle came out.

"Seriously?" I mumbled as Rachel glided into the kitchen.

"Looks like I'll have to call the hottie plumber back."

"No, thanks. And no big guy showing two inches of crack, either." I settled for a third of a glass of water and turned off the faucet.

Rachel might have thought the plumber hot, but he'd been big-headed about it. I knew I wouldn't be able to get rid of him so easily a second time. Having narrowly avoided one potential stalker, there was no way I would invite another one in.

"I was going to go pick up Clay later, anyway," I lied. "I'll have him look at it." I smiled at Rachel as Clay's head whipped up at me. I'd beg him again if I had to.

"Really? No-talk, leave-early, Clay?"

"Yeah, that one. Not the dog."

"I believe you said you didn't think he'd be around much." She smirked at me while she measured the coffee. I stuck my tongue out at her, but she just laughed.

"Don't remind me. I'm probably going to need to beg."

"Does he know much about plumbing?" Rachel asked as she moved to the sink to fill the coffee pot.

"Don't know...we don't talk much." I laughed while she groaned.

WITH NOTHING TO DRINK, I dressed to go shopping. Clay waited for me just outside my door.

"Wanna come shopping with me or stay here?" I knew he'd want to go even if he did have to stay in the car. He moved to stand by the back door.

We drove to one of those discount supercenters. I left Clay in the car with the windows cracked—it was more for show than actual airflow. If he got hot, he'd just let himself out.

It worried me a bit that I needed to shop several days sooner than planned. In order to feed Clay and myself, I had already made compromises in my original budget. Yet, at this rate, I would surpass even my revised spending allowance for groceries. That meant I needed to change my shopping habits, not just to save money but to fill the pantry with more food. I didn't mind eating light, but looking back, since Clay didn't eat his dog food—not that I blamed him—he ate light, too. A little too light when I recalled how much Sam could consume.

The orange juice I liked cost more than a five-pound bag of potatoes. I put the potatoes in the cart and walked past the fresh juice. Maybe I could buy a decent concentrate. I went to the freezer section, found some cheap veggies, and ignored the speculative look from a man a few yards away.

Everyone found shopping a pain at some point. I found it a pain all the time.

In the next case, I studied the meat options. The flash-frozen chicken breasts were cheaper than the steaks per pound so I went with those. The man moved from the veggies to the meats as I eyed the cart and tried to envision our meals. Meat, potato, and veggie.

Before the man tried to start a conversation, I moved on to dry goods. A large tub of generic peanut butter and another of grape jelly joined the growing heap in the cart. I used my other vision to check for and skillfully avoid as many men as possible while I wove through the aisles. Not for the first time, I wished I could tell men and women apart.

Always on the lookout for deals, I spotted the day-old bakery rack and found two loaves of bread for a dollar. The cart held more than it usually did when I went shopping. Although it lacked variety, it had quantity; and I'd managed to keep it under twenty dollars. My smug happiness lasted until I recalled I needed something to drink in the morning. Dang. And cereal. Oh, well. Under thirty still helped the budget.

When I thought back to what Clay had already done for me, like putting on clothes last night, I couldn't regret spending more to feed him. And there was still the faucet that awaited him. I frowned as I realized all he had to wear was the linen getup. Surely, I could spare enough to buy Clay a decent set of clothes.

I turned the cart around and hunted the store for the best bargains. The store had off-brand denims on sale. I guessed at his size and tossed a pair in the cart. Next, I stumbled upon a returned three pack of t-shirts that looked poorly repackaged. I saw nothing wrong with the shirts and figured the low price correlated with the packaging. Whatever dropped the price down by three dollars worked for me.

A flannel shirt, hidden within the mass of other shirts on the clearance rack, caught my eye. I looked it over closely. The shirt lacked most of the middle buttons. An easy enough fix. I put it in the cart. It would get chilly soon, and he'd need it. I paused. Would he stay that long? Probably. He showed no sign of wanting to leave. I went to find some warm socks then looked for shoes. I had to guess the size based on the feet that I'd seen last night.

Waiting in the checkout line proved painfully annoying. I couldn't avoid men while standing still. However, I did manage to find an open lane with a female cashier. Two men lined up behind me and persistently tried to start up a conversation with me before I unloaded the cart. The woman gave me a look. Whatever.

I left the store in a hurry. Usually, if I put enough distance between us, my admirers forgot about me.

The cart clattered over the blacktop as I made my way to the car. Clay watched for me from the back seat. His steady gaze tracked my progress. I looked forward to showing him what I'd managed to purchase and smiled at him.

Unfortunately, the man who'd just pulled into the space beyond my car thought I'd meant the smile for him. I mentally groaned as I kept pushing the cart toward my car. The man climbed down from his truck. Like Clay, he didn't stop watching me as he stepped out from between the vehicles to wait for me. Clay tensed inside the car.

"Hi, there. Need a hand?" the man asked.

I stopped near the trunk.

"No, thanks. I got it."

He didn't leave.

"My name's Dale. I own Dale's Auto Body on South Mitchell. You should bring your car by. It looks like it might be due for an oil change."

Did I really look dumb enough to believe he could determine the car needed an oil change just by looking at the exterior? It certainly wasn't leaking oil as a giveaway.

"That's a nice offer, but my boyfriend does the oil changes." I unlocked the trunk and started to load groceries.

Dale didn't take the hint and go away.

"He's a handy guy, then?" He grabbed the potatoes and set them in the trunk for me. Unfortunately, it brought him closer.

"Yes, very." A brief conversation sometimes worked to get rid of a pest.

"I'm sorry, I didn't catch your name," he said.

I could see Clay through the back window. Crouched down, he watched the man through the small gap between the trunk lid and the trunk. I bent forward and set a bag in the trunk so Dale wouldn't see me as I rolled my eyes at Clay. Clay's gaze briefly flicked to me before returning to Dale with serious intent.

"Gabby," I said as I closed the trunk. "Thanks for helping me with the groceries, but I need to get going. My dog's been in the car for a while already."

Not waiting for his reply, I moved the cart to the empty spot next to my car.

"We have an opening at the shop. If your boyfriend's looking for work, send him by. We'll see how good he is," Dale said, opening the driver-side door for me.

Clay hopped from the back seat to the driver's seat. With bristling fur, he growled at Dale, who backed away a step.

I nodded to Dale and nudged Clay over so I could slide in behind the wheel. Braving Clay's wrath, Dale closed the door for me. I started the car and pulled through the empty spot in front of me.

"Well, that was a challenge if I ever heard one." I reached over to pet Clay's head. "But no challenges until you fix the sink." He looked up at me, and I smiled.

When we got back to the house, both Rachel and Peter were gone. That seemed to make Clay happy. It definitely made me happy. I hadn't been sure how Clay would get dressed with Rachel around.

"You go shower while I unpack. Then you can look at the sink and see if we have to call that big-headed plumber back."

He willingly trotted to the bathroom. After that first time, I'd learned to let him close the door on his own.

It didn't take long for me to put the groceries away. When I finished unpacking, I picked up the pile of things I'd bought for Clay and went to my room. The stuff from yesterday already hung neatly in my closet except for some underclothes which I'd hidden in my bottom drawer. I grabbed an item from his drawer—it made it less personal if I didn't overthink it—then moved to the bathroom. I could hear the shower running and tapped on the door.

"I'm coming in, so please stay behind the curtain." I waited a moment then entered. Steam already filled the room. "I have some clothes for you. Better stuff for looking at a sink than what I bought yesterday." I realized then that I'd never actually asked him if he would help.

"Clay, I'm so sorry," I apologized sincerely. "I'm being rude and making assumptions. Will you look at the sink? Please?" I asked using my syrupy voice.

He splashed me over the top of the curtain...again.

"Okay, okay. I'll just leave the stuff here on the floor. If something doesn't fit or you don't like it, leave the tags on it, and we'll take it back. I guessed on the shoes. Some of the stuff isn't for now, but I figured you could try it on." I realized I was rambling at the same time I remembered the missing buttons on the shirt. I closed my mouth and quickly grabbed the flannel from the pile.

The water turned off just then, and I rushed from the bathroom.

In my room, I pulled out my travel sewing kit and got to work moving buttons around. The two spares on the inside seam remained intact. With those and a close match I found in the sewing kit, I solved the missing button problem.

While I stitched, I listened for Clay to leave the bathroom. By the time I finished, I still hadn't heard anything. I set the repaired shirt aside and went to look for him.

I found him in the kitchen. He already had his head bent over the faucet. The jeans hung loosely from his hips. The white shirt clung lightly to his back, outlining the curve of each muscle and his broad, firm shoulders. I blinked twice, swallowed hard, and caught myself a moment before I tried clearing my throat to swallow again. The clothes I'd picked out looked good. A little too good. And looking at him in them did funny things to my stomach.

Thankfully, he didn't look up and notice my gawking. I pulled myself together and moved to the refrigerator. Opening it, I studied the contents then grabbed what I needed to make him a big breakfast: eggs, bacon, potatoes, and yes, orange juice...from concentrate. I set everything on the table.

When I first stayed with Sam, he'd amazed me with the amount of food he'd consumed on a daily basis. He'd explained that the werewolf's metabolism ran a bit higher than the average person's did. So, I planned to make enough breakfast for three and only serve myself one portion, leaving the rest for Clay.

While he ran down to the basement, I washed the potatoes under the pathetic trickle of water. When he came back, I noticed he still had bare feet.

"The shoes didn't fit?" I moved to the table to peel the potatoes and stay out of his way.

He shrugged in response. I tried to guess what that might mean.

"So they fit, but you didn't want to wear them?"

No response. He continued to tinker with the sink. I started to cut the potatoes.

"Did you like them, or should we bring them back? I wasn't sure what style you liked. There were several different colors. They're cheap shoes, but I figured it was better than walking around barefoot in the snow. That's got to be cold even for you."

Halfway through my one-sided conversation, he'd turned to look at me. I knew I'd rambled a little...again. Then I realized I'd just referred to him still living here in winter. I had really grown used to having him around. Kind of. I hoped he wasn't looking at me because of that.

"I just don't want you to think you have to keep them if you don't like them. It won't hurt my feelings if we take them back. Just wear the flip flops for now, and you can come in with me next time and pick out what you like." The plain, grey and blue running shoes were muted enough that I'd thought they'd look okay with whatever he wore in the future. I hadn't given the style more thought than that.

I got up from the table and put some butter in the pan on the stove. When I turned to get the diced potatoes, he was sitting on a chair at the table. He already had his socks on and was bent forward to slide his feet into the shoes.

"No, no, no, Clay." I hurried over, reached out, and almost touched his back before I caught myself and pulled my hand away. "I wasn't saying you *had* to wear them." He continued to tie the shoes. "It's okay to bring them back if you don't like them."

When he finished tying, he stood and looked down at his feet. I could see him wiggle his toes through the canvas and mesh tops. The length seemed to fit well enough. The loose lacing told me they ran a little snug in the width. He moved past me and walked to the sink then back to try out the shoes. What little I could see of his expression appeared relaxed as did his stride.

"You like shoes, but you don't wear them much, do you?"

He answered with his typical passive shrug as he moved back to the sink.

The sizzle of the potatoes called my attention, and I got another pan out to start the bacon. He used the tools he'd brought up from the basement to try to fix the sink while I cooked. The sound of water running at full pressure heralded breakfast.

"Good to have a handyman," I commented, setting our plates on the table.

Clay cleaned up the tools and disappeared downstairs. I wondered if he would come back in his fur and eyed the plate I'd set on the table for him. We had eaten together before but always with him in his fur. Before I could stop it, an image of him trying to use a fork for the first time popped into my head. I quickly squashed the picture and sat down to wait for him in whatever form he chose. I would not underestimate him again. Nor would I thoughtlessly remark on his table manners no matter how poor they might be.

The soft tread on the stairs warned me that he remained a man. He sat across from me and dug in. He didn't eat like Clay-the-dog or use his hands. Instead, he had perfectly normal table manners. Though his beard shredded it, he even used his paper napkin in an effort to keep himself neat.

"What are the chances of trimming that beard?"

He used his napkin while he finished chewing and then flashed me a full view of his teeth. His canines remained completely elongated as if he still wore his fur. I froze briefly with my fork suspended midair. Then I gave myself a mental shake. The view scared me, but I reminded myself of Sam's words. I had nothing to fear.

"Do they stay like that all the time?"

He didn't answer but continued to eat, slowly clearing his plate. I waited patiently, hoping he'd give me some type of response. This was the second occasion we'd spent time together without his fur since he'd arrived. I knew so little about him and wondered if this was a sign he was ready to start talking to me.

When he finished, he moved to the sink and ran the water. I wasn't ready to give up. I followed him, leaned against the counter, and studied the little bit of his face I could see.

"Is this something you don't want to talk about?"

He shrugged. Okay, not a closed topic...and apparently he wasn't yet ready to speak.

"Is it something I need to guess, or can you explain it to me?" I felt like I was playing twenty questions.

He turned to consider me for a moment then went back to washing his plate and fork. Taking the hint, I cleaned up my place while he moved to wipe the stove. I washed and dried my plate and tried to figure out what to ask next. Obviously, only yes and no questions even though he hadn't answered when I asked whether his teeth stayed like that all the time. Perhaps asking about them embarrassed him.

When he returned to the sink, I briefly thought of letting the subject drop, but then he dropped the washcloth into the sink and turned to me. He crossed his arms, leaned against the counter, and watched me. Not just looking at me but studying me...all of me...as if he weighed a decision. I couldn't help but return his stare.

We stood just a few inches apart. The close proximity brought the corded muscles under his snug t-shirt to my attention. I tried not to notice. He was downright drool-worthy. I considered reaching out to touch him, just to see how he felt without fur. But his possible reaction stopped me. Would he take it as a sign of acceptance? Of interest? I'd meant what I'd said to Rachel. Clay didn't act like other guys. I didn't want to push my luck.

With a sigh, he uncrossed his arms and leaned forward. His movement shot a wave of panic straight through me, and I froze. Had he caught me eyeing him? Did he think that meant I wanted him to try to kiss me? I didn't know what to do.

His nostrils flared. He slowly shook his head and pulled back, and I knew he had smelled my fear. He didn't completely move away, just distanced himself enough so that I could breathe and think and not freak out. I caught the glint of his eyes behind his long hair. Calm. Patient. So this wasn't about a kiss. But then, what was he trying to do?

"You're trying to explain the teeth, right?" I sounded pathetic, like a child who needed reassurance. I tried not to fidget on top of that.

He gave me the reassurance I needed in one of his rare nods.

Okay. No kissing. Just him moving closer. He slept at the foot of my bed every night. That was pretty close—right on my feet—and no big deal. But he had fur on when he did that. Now he looked...

I eyed him again. My stomach did a funny flip. Maybe my fear wasn't about his reaction but mine. I was afraid I'd forget myself. I needed his control. I took a deep breath.

"It's okay then. Go ahead, explain. I'll behave," I promised quietly. I saw his mustache twitch with a quick smile. The canines explained some of the facial hair, but the full-bearded, crazy-man look seemed overkill.

After a slight hesitation, he leaned forward again while keeping his hands loose at his sides. I pushed back the fear and held still. He didn't stop his slow approach until his whiskers tickled the side of my neck and collarbone. There he paused and inhaled deeply.

As soon as he inhaled, I knew what he was doing, and although I didn't move, fear blossomed. Heart pounding, eyes wide, I waited for him to finish scenting me as a werewolf would a potential Mate, not a distant inhale but an up-close sample of my scent, infinitely more potent. His warm exhale sent goosebumps skittering over my arms. I braced myself, anticipating some type of slip in his highly-praised control. He leisurely inhaled once more then lifted his head, exhaling as he went.

With his face only inches from mine, he opened his mouth to display his teeth again. The canines had grown even more pronounced, the surrounding gums swollen from their thickness.

I didn't know what to say. He had canines when in his human form because of me.

"So, when you're around me, they're worse? I guess that means they're like that all the time."

He shrugged and casually took a step back. I was unsure what the shrug meant.

We both heard a car pull into the driveway, and I knew questioning him further would have to wait. I remembered the new clothes still on the bathroom floor and moved away from him.

"I gotta move your clothes. I'll be right back."

When I returned, Rachel was kneeling, petting Clay-the-dog. She asked me why we had a man's clothes on the kitchen chair. Clay impassively met my gaze. Darn him. Why hadn't he just stayed Clay-the-man?

"Clay stopped by and fixed the sink. He figured he would leave a change of clothes because of last night," I lied. Thankfully, Rachel focused on the fixed plumbing rather than the fact that I had a man leaving clothes behind at our house.

"The sink's working? And for free?"

I shrugged, feeling very Clayish, and grabbed the clothes. As I walked from the room to put them away, she continued to talk to Clay, using her normal nonsense babble. He was such a good boy and so handsome. Did I treat him well while she was gone? Did he want a treat? I sniggered, put the clothes away, then sat on the couch and left Clay to his torture.

Done with her affectionate praise, she released him. He trotted from the kitchen and sat on the floor near me. She went to her room to change, leaving her door open so she could talk.

"I just heard the weather report, and we're going to get a cold snap this week. Frost. With past roommates, we always tried to make it to November first before turning on the heat."

"That's fine by me," I answered.

"Even though the landlord replaced the windows, air still somehow gets in. They're better than they were and seemed to help the AC run less. But if Clay knows anything about weatherproofing, maybe that'll help us save even more on the heating bill."

I looked at Clay. "Know how to weatherproof a house?" I whispered.

"What?" Rachel asked from her room.

"Nothing, just talking to Clay."

THE REST of the weekend passed like the one before with studying and turning pages for Clay-the-dog. Although I still wanted to know about his pronounced teeth in man-form, I couldn't come up with any reason to ask him to shift again. When I tried asking him about his teeth while he wore his fur, he just walked away from me. I couldn't tell if he did that because he was moody or just bored with my conversation.

Monday night, I got home, and Clay stood in the kitchen cooking dinner for two. I had to suppress the happy-dance I wanted to do and, instead, nonchalantly walked by him. A note on the table from Rachel explained she had gone out with Peter and would be back late. The note stressed *alone*.

Since Clay's last appearance, I'd thought of several questions to ask him—starting with his teeth—and hoped he wouldn't get annoyed and go fur on me again. I decided to ease him into my agenda.

"Wow, I didn't know you cooked. It smells great." I set my messenger bag on a chair and hovered behind him, watching him work.

He pulled baked potatoes from the oven. To the side, two plates waited with steaming chicken breasts. Seeing dinner almost ready, I grabbed flatware for us and sat down.

"So, other than cooking, how did you keep yourself busy today?"

He set a plate in front of me and sat down. He pointed to the last batch of books I'd brought home that he had piled neatly on the table between us.

"You read them all already?"

He nodded.

"That's a lot to read in just five days. Are you skipping chapters?" I teased.

He glanced up at me then back down at his food. Maybe I needed to work on my teasing. I supposed smiling would have helped.

"So, about the beard...are your teeth ready to play nice?" That got an actual laugh from him. A short one but still very nice.

"Does that mean we can trim your beard?" I asked, excited by the prospect. The scissors would also make a beeline for his hair. How could I read his face when he kept it so hidden? Since he didn't actually speak, it hindered our communication even further.

He shook his head, and my face fell. I looked back down at my plate, feeling silly for the stab of disappointment because I wouldn't get to see more of his face tonight. Lost in my own thoughts, it took me a second to realize he'd stopped eating. He leaned back in his chair and studied me.

Pretending not to notice, I gave him a slight smile, and for a change, I kept my thoughts to myself.

"This tastes great. Thank you for cooking. Do you have a favorite food? I can put it on the next shopping list."

He watched me for another minute as I ate. I tucked away my

disappointment and annoyance and tried not to let my face show anything I felt. I knew neither emotion did me any good, and both made it hard to enjoy the food. I pushed a few bites around on my plate before he finally uncrossed his arms and picked his fork back up to start eating again.

"Actually, let's keep a shopping list on my dresser. When you think of something, you can add to it so I know what to get without guessing." Maybe writing fell into the talking category, and I'd be out of luck there, too.

I ate the majority of the food on my plate then brought it to the sink. Not wanting to risk him going back to his fur just yet, I grabbed my messenger bag and sat at the table to work on homework while he finished his meal. I usually did homework the same day and left the bigger projects and in-depth studying for the weekend if needed.

"If you want, when you're done, we can watch a movie," I said.

He shrugged and moved to clean up his plate. I hopped up to help, but he motioned me back to the table, pointing to the open book. I sat and read while listening to him move about the kitchen.

As soon as he washed the stove, I packed up my homework for the night. He wiped down the table, and I hovered with my bag over my shoulder. I did not want to put it away and give him the opportunity to change again. When he had everything clean and the dishrag rinsed, he walked into the living room. I followed him and sat on the couch.

He bent to the cabinet below the TV and picked the movie for the night. A suspense.

"If I scream again when Rachel comes home, no laughing," I said as I curled on the couch and waited for him to start the movie.

A strong wind blew outside, and the curtains moved slightly. Considering where I lived, it seemed pointless to dread the cold, but I did. Soon I would probably start to consider wearing snow pants just to walk to the car. I gave the fluttering curtain one last glare and turned my attention to the movie as Clay settled next to me.

This time, I didn't feel so nervous and actually concentrated on the movie. Clay never twitched, but I jumped twice within the first ten minutes.

The temperature in the room dropped to the point that I ran to get a hoodie during a suspenseful scene. Thankfully, Clay didn't pause the movie for me.

By the time the movie ended, the wind really howled outside. I sat on my fingers in an effort to warm them and knew it would be a long wait until the first of November.

"Hey, Clay. Do you like cookies?" I sprang from the couch and moved toward the kitchen. I could bake cookies to heat the house, and Rachel couldn't scold me for turning on the heat.

I rummaged through the cupboard, and I saw we didn't have any of the main ingredients. No sugar of any kind or flour.

"Shoot," I grumbled.

I had splurged and bought Clay clothes, something I considered a necessity. Along with many of the other unplanned expenses, it set me behind in my budget. Keeping the heat off longer would help make some of it up. But that meant no frivolous spending, not even for ingredients to bake cookies to warm the house.

I closed the doors and turned to tell Clay the disappointing news. Instead of staying in the living room as I'd thought, he stood right behind me. All that came out was a strangled "gah." He flashed a smile so wide that I saw teeth and couldn't help but smile back.

"Har-har. I told you no suspense movies. Life is scary enough without them. Oh, and false alarm on the cookies. We're missing some main ingredients."

He picked up my car keys and dangled them in front of me.

"It's tempting, but unless I want to get a part-time job, I can't afford to keep spending the money I've saved. I've got to stick to the budget so it lasts through till spring. If we can manage to keep the heat off until November, I should have cookie money for Christmas. That's when cookies are best, anyhow. I'll just need to start wearing more clothes inside."

I took the keys from him and put them back in the dish on the counter. When I turned, Clay wasn't looking at me but off to the side. I tried to follow his gaze, but he didn't seem to be looking at anything. Shrugging, I left him to his own thoughts.

"I think I'm going to bed." I almost asked if he would come with but didn't know how to word it so I would be asking Clay-the-dog, not Clay-the-man. As a result, I went to my room alone.

Not long after, I heard him enter, and I wondered what I'd do if he tried to climb into bed with me as a man. I anxiously listened to the rustle of his clothes as he removed them. The quick pounce on the end of the bed told me Clay had once again become my personal foot warmer.

Chapter Twelve

On Tuesdays, my first class started later. It gave me time to catch up on things around the house. After falling behind on laundry once, I made a point to wash at least one load each Tuesday.

Clay padded softly behind me, following me down into the basement as I carried a basket of our combined clothes. I teased him that the discount detergent I'd purchased smelled like babies—not very manly. He chuffed out a laugh and watched me fill the machine. Nothing I did seemed very exciting to me, but he followed me as faithfully as a real dog would.

After I finished, he trailed behind me as I skipped back up the stairs. The closed basement door silenced the whir of the washer.

I moved to the bedroom and pulled the sheets from my bed to start making a pile for the next load. While I worked, I told Clay about what we'd covered in my classes so far. He sat off to the side, out of the way, but I could tell he listened by the tilt of his head. Glancing at the clock, I groaned at the time, called goodbye to Clay with a promise to see him at dinner, and ran out the door.

Not only did I like Tuesdays because of the delayed start but also because Tuesday nights, Rachel spent time with Peter. It gave me the house to myself. Well, and Clay, too, but she didn't know that. I looked forward to dinners with Clay since it meant spending time with him as a man.

I rushed to the car. The door protested loudly when I yanked it open. I tossed my bag in, closed the door, started the engine, and thought of Rachel as I backed out of the driveway.

Rachel and Peter's growing relationship made the increasingly frequent dinners with Clay possible. She hadn't come home last night and probably wouldn't come home tonight as well. It amazed me to see two people so meant for each other. When I focused on them, their lights, the essence of who they were, pulsed in harmony.

Although I'd never stopped wondering why I saw the lights, learning werewolves existed had tempered my need for answers. After all, if a completely different species could evolve unknown to the rest of the world, why couldn't one girl develop a uniquely strange ability? Oh, I still believed my ability to see the sparks served some purpose I hadn't yet identified, but I no longer actively searched for answers.

Before meeting Sam, I'd volunteered at the hospital, thinking I'd learn to use my ability to identify different illnesses. But no matter the patient or their illness, I always saw the same yellow-green color. However, because of my time at the hospital, I'd found what I wanted to do with my life. Massage therapy had benefited some of the elderly patients with whom I really liked working.

With a few minutes to spare, I pulled into the student parking lot, grabbed my things, and started the walk across campus. Students milled around outside a few of the buildings or purposefully strode the sidewalks, like me, to get to their next class.

Someone called my name. I stopped and saw Scott cutting across the dying grass. He jogged to meet me on the sidewalk.

"I think we should start drawing straws or something," he said when he reached me.

"What do you mean?" I shifted my messenger bag, eager to get to my class. Telling someone no only worked as long as I didn't send any mixed signals, and a long conversation definitely qualified as a mixed signal.

"Peter and Rachel. We should draw straws to see who has to put up with the lovebirds. I didn't get much sleep last night." He rolled his eyes, and I noted the dark circles under them.

"Ah. I didn't know you and Peter were roommates. I usually don't have a problem sleeping when he comes over, so if you want them to stay at our place, just tell Rachel. I certainly don't mind." He opened his mouth to say more, but I cut him off. "Sorry, I have to get going. I'm going to be late for class."

He nodded, and I walked away without a goodbye. I hoped that counted as a short conversation. I knew Rachel had been staying at Peter's place because she felt guilty if he stayed at ours more than twice a week. I'd never stopped to consider Peter might have a roommate, too. Maybe I should say something to Rachel. They never kept me up when Peter stayed over. I wondered, belatedly, if they kept Clay up.

Realizing I'd slowed a little, I picked up the pace. I wanted to arrive early enough to talk to Nicole, the shy girl in my basic massage class. Today we would start doing more hands-on practice to try the few techniques already described to us along with muscle identification, and she'd agreed to work with me.

Last week, the instructor had warned us we would work in pairs and would be switching partners over the next few weeks. The announcement had given me a mild panic attack. Although the majority of the students were female, the few men had glanced my way. So, I'd carefully prearranged partners.

On the positive side, the instructor had also stressed we

wouldn't need volunteers from outside the classroom this term. It was a relief to know I wouldn't need to fend off Scott as a volunteer.

AN UNUSUALLY QUIET house greeted me. The brisk wind rattled the kitchen window as I set my keys down and searched the house for Clay.

I didn't find him but did see evidence of his busy day. The neatly folded items from the laundry I'd put in, and the load I'd set aside before leaving, filled my dresser drawers. Clean shirts hung in my closet. Clay had even remade the bed with the fresh sheets. The baby powder smell of the detergent permeated the room. I grinned, thinking of him wearing his clean clothes.

A knock sounded at the front door. Still smiling to myself, I turned and answered it.

An older gentleman stood on the stoop. Dressed in a smart grey suit that complemented his dark grey hair, he reminded me of Sam, and I felt a moment of guilt. Sam had called several times to check on me, but I hadn't returned any of his calls.

A smile lined his face, reaching his warm hazel eyes. "Gabby? I'm Joshua."

My polite smile froze in place. This was Elder Joshua? I'd pictured a younger man. Doubt crept in, and I did a quick scan. His bright blue-grey spark glowed before me. That color...my stomach dipped in fear. Joshua had the same color light as the werewolf that had attacked Clay. Coincidence? I doubted it. So far, only Charlene and I had unique sparks. A knot formed in my throat.

In the distance, a child squealed in laughter. The sound snapped me out of my other world. I held myself still, clutching the edge of the door while I fought hard to push back the sudden burst of fear.

His nostrils flared slightly, and I knew my efforts were too late. I wanted to slam the door and run but knew it wouldn't work.

"I apologize for startling you, Gabby. Sam was concerned when he didn't hear back from you after the confrontation. He asked me to stop by and check on you."

"Confrontation?" My voice sounded dry and strained.

"Yes, we heard there'd been a failed challenge. Is everything okay here?"

I swallowed hard. "Yes, thank you."

Think, Gabby! Why would the werewolf launch itself at Clay from out of the darkness only to politely knock on my door? And why the front door? The neighbors could see him.

Staring at his puzzled face, his hazel eyes called my attention. The other wolf's eyes had been blue. What did it mean that he had the same color light as the werewolf that'd challenged Clay? I really wanted to believe it was just a coincidence. I had to call Sam and get a description of Elder Joshua to be sure the man before me was who he said.

"How are things going with Clay? Any other problems? Is he becoming too aggressive?"

"Everything is fine. He's very polite." But missing when I really need him, I thought. Convenient that Elder Joshua just happened to show up when Clay wasn't home.

"We were surprised to hear of a challenge. Usually, strong ties aren't challenged," he commented.

I didn't know how to respond, so I remained quiet.

He reached into his pocket and withdrew a business card. "Well, if you need anything, give me a call, or call Sam. We're here for you." He handed the card to me.

The card simply had his name and number printed on it, no title or business name. I nodded, hoping he would leave so I could give in to the panic attack I barely held back. He smiled, bobbed his head in farewell, and turned to leave.

I closed the door and tucked the card into the front pocket of my jeans. This time, I watched through the peephole as he got into the car he'd parked in front of the house. The door muffled the sound of the engine as he started it.

When he drove out of my line of sight, I closed my eyes and leaned my forehead on the cool wood of the door. First, a wolf with a uniquely colored spark challenged Clay. Then, Elder Joshua appeared with the same color. For more than two years...through every visit to the Compound...not once did I ever see a variance in the color of a werewolf spark. Just like humans, they remained consistent.

If not for the challenge, I wouldn't have worried about it. But I knew, without a doubt, I'd never met Clay's challenger before. And if I'd never met him, why would he dispute Clay's tie with me? I needed to know who the challenger was and why Elder Joshua had an identically colored spark. Yet, no one knew about my ability to see the sparks. I could ask Sam outright if Joshua was different from their kind in some way. The best I could do was verify Elder Joshua's identity without raising too many unwanted questions. I needed to calm down and call Sam. If I called sounding freaked out, he would probably send Joshua right back over.

I pushed away from the door and turned to go into my room. Someone stood right behind me. I produced a full-throated, someone's-sawing-off-my-arm scream before I realized it was Clay dressed in jeans, t-shirt, and running shoes. By his shocked expression, I'd just scared him as badly as he'd scared me.

Heart stuttering, I clapped a hand over my mouth. No way would I call Sam now. I wasn't even sure I could speak. The hand over my mouth shook from the adrenaline rush.

Clay tilted his head, studied me, then reached into my pocket to pull out the card. He glanced at it, shrugged, and shook his head, clearly puzzled. How did he even know it was in there? Had he been watching me?

I dropped my hand and did another round of deep breaths to try to calm down.

"Did you see who was here?" I asked. My voice wavered, so I cleared it.

He shook his head.

"How did you know that was in my pocket?"

He briefly lifted the card to his nose. So, he could smell the other werewolf? That was good.

"Have you ever met Elder Joshua before?"

He shook his head.

"Have you ever smelled him before?"

Again, he shook his head.

I closed my eyes briefly and let out a relieved sigh that sounded a bit like a sob. Joshua wasn't the werewolf Clay had fought. Even though I remembered blue eyes, I'd still worried.

The new color variation bothered me, though, and I wished I had someone to talk to. Now that Clay had confirmed Joshua wasn't the same werewolf from the challenge, I didn't see much point in calling Sam other than to yell at him for sending Joshua over.

Lost in my own thoughts, I jumped when Clay lightly tapped my forehead with his index finger.

I gave him a weak smile. "You want to know what's going on in my head?" I guessed.

He nodded, and I finally recognized that my someone-to-talk-to stood right in front of me.

"I'd like to know what's going on in my head sometimes, too." If only I could figure out those lights. "Let's make dinner while I talk. Let me know if you hear Rachel or anyone else."

He nodded, kicked off his shoes, and put them in my room before joining me in the kitchen. He took the lead on dinner prep and gave me busy work so I could talk. I started to peel a potato while he clanked pans on the stove.

"That was Elder Joshua at the door. He stopped by because I haven't talked to Sam lately, and Sam asked him to check up on me.

I guess he was worried after that challenge." I picked up a second potato. "Something was odd about him, Clay."

When I was quiet for too long, Clay nudged my chair on his way to the sink with the potatoes I'd peeled. His way of saying I should keep talking, but I struggled with how to tell him everything.

"I'm different," I said abruptly.

He turned from the sink, looked at me, and shrugged as if to say it didn't matter.

"No. Really different. It's kind of hard to explain. Sam told me I was different when he met me, but he doesn't know all of it. He said that I was rare because I was one of only a few humans compatible with werewolves, just me and Charlene."

I sighed and ran my hands through my hair. Based on my mom's reaction when I'd told her the truth, the idea of telling someone everything scared me.

He picked up two more potatoes and handed them to me. I started peeling again as he went to the stove. I spoke slow, essentially thinking aloud.

"Since as long as I can remember, I've seen lights. Not with my eyes but in my mind. When I was younger, I had to close my eyes and concentrate to see a relatively small area around me. As I got older, I didn't need to concentrate as hard and could see a much larger area. Now, I can see these lights at will, briefly, with little effort, and over a longer distance. And I don't need to close my eyes.

"These lights are people, Clay. I can see the neighbors moving around in their houses right now. It's not an aura I'm seeing.

"To put it into perspective, I can see a square mile around us, but in my mind, the area looks like an inch. The lights within that area are small pinpricks, but I can see them so clearly that they could be the size of quarters, three inches from my face. And all those dots are the same color. Every human around us has the same yellow light with a green halo."

Clay handed me a glass of water, breaking my train of thought. He rescued the potatoes I'd cubed into tiny pieces.

"Thanks." I took a drink and studied the glass for a moment before continuing. "You and I, in the middle of those dots, stand out. I have the same yellow light as everyone else, but my halo is orange. I'm different from the people around us. Even from you. Werewolves have a blue core with a green halo. At least, that's all I ever saw in the past two years, until the night you were challenged. That werewolf had a blue-grey light. Now, imagine my shock when I opened the door and saw a man, who introduced himself as Elder Joshua, with the same color light. Only the difference in the color of their eyes kept me breathing.

"I've been like this my entire life, and I have more questions than answers about this second sight. Why are all humans green and yellow except Charlene and me? We're human. Why does Charlene have a red halo? Or me an orange halo? The only similarities are the yellow cores. I've been thinking it means human but don't know what the halos mean.

"And I'm sure that you've caught on to the whole guy situation. I call to them somehow as if I'm a beacon or something. Do I really send out some kind of signal?" I looked up at him questioningly.

He held a plate in each hand. Both loaded with some kind of chicken skillet dinner. He handed me a plate and studied me for a moment before shrugging and shaking his head.

"So, nothing as far as you can tell. There's got to be a reason, a connection to it all." I sighed and played with the food on my plate for a minute, thinking.

"I've never told anyone all of this. People figure out there's something different about me if they're around me long enough. But no one knows about the lights. I'm torn. Do I call Sam and tell him everything? Do I tell him the light of the guy who challenged you is the same light as Joshua? There's nothing concrete I can offer about the coloring or why I'm so worried about it.

"Why would a werewolf I've never met challenge you? And

why does he share the same coloring as Joshua? So far, the lights have had a category: humans, werewolves, and compatible Mates. I don't think the challenger and Joshua can be compatible Mates because Charlene and I are uniquely colored from each other." I shook my head to try to clear away my frustration at my inability to solve the puzzle.

Taking my first bite, I struggled to swallow the cold food. I looked up at Clay in surprise and saw his empty plate.

"Bet you're wishing you hadn't asked."

He shook his head slowly, still watching me. I started to doubt the wisdom of sharing so much with him. What if he started to treat me differently? I didn't want to lose his friendship. It devastated me to think I could lose the one person with whom I might have had a chance to be myself. When he didn't say anything, I forced myself to eat.

He waited until I finished eating, took both our plates, and cleaned up the kitchen while I sat at the table and did my homework. The spatter of running water, the soft clinking of dishes, none of it distracted me as much as my own doubts. Uncertainty over what I'd just shared and his lack of response ate at me. Granted, he hadn't spoken to me at all *before* my announcement, but still.

When he finished, he left the room for a few minutes. His nails clicked on the kitchen floor as he padded back in. I didn't have time to wonder why he'd changed to fur. He nudged my arm with his head and looked toward the living room. The tightness in my chest, which I hadn't even noticed, loosened slightly. He watched me expectantly, and I ran my fingers through the fur at his neck, hoping he wouldn't ever act like a real dog and run away from home.

Deciding I'd done enough, I packed up my homework and followed him. We watched some sitcoms then called it a night.

When he curled up on his usual spot at the foot of my bed, I sighed and closed my eyes. He hadn't seemed to treat me any differently after I'd told him everything. I hoped it would stay that way.

Rachel came home after a very late evening shift at the hospital. I knew she was alone because Clay only shifted on the bed to acknowledge he'd heard something. The nights Peter stayed, Clay grumbled a bit. They probably did keep him awake. Poor Clay.

Chapter Thirteen

SEPTEMBER PASSED IN A BLUR, TAKING MOST OF OCTOBER WITH IT.

While on campus, I still struggled to fend off a few stragglers who hadn't yet grasped the concept of no. Thankfully, those stragglers didn't include Scott.

At home, Rachel and Peter were inseparable even though they made a big fuss about giving each other their own time. It just meant they only did overnights three times a week. It limited my quiet time with Clay, but we managed.

On Rachel nights, Clay-the-dog usually waited for me by the back door. Occasionally, I came home to an empty house. Those absences explained why he no longer consumed five books a week, but they did make me wonder how he spent his time when we weren't together. When I tried to ask where he went, he never answered.

I began to notice things, though, like he now owned more jeans

—I'd only bought him one pair—and had a few new shirts. Despite the extra clothes, he still seemed to favor the ones I'd gotten him, especially the flannel shirt.

On nights we didn't expect Rachel home, Clay-the-man waited for me. He was never missing for those nights. Tuesdays, still one of the nights Rachel stayed over at Peter's, Clay did laundry for me if I forgot to do it before then, and he always had dinner ready when I came home.

He still didn't talk when he was in man-form, but I gradually learned more about him through many well-phrased questions. I guessed at his favorite color for over a minute. Pink...naturally. What guy wouldn't have a feminine stereotypical color as a favorite? I gave up trying to guess *why* it was his favorite after twenty minutes.

I also found out he liked to try new foods and made it a point to bring home one unique food item each week. Fruits like pineapple and kiwi disappeared quickly. Vegetables like okra and Brussels sprouts...well, I laughed long and hard when I watched him eat those.

Besides the new clothes that he'd mysteriously acquired, I also came across his wallet on my dresser. Since he'd been crouched right behind me when I spotted it, I'd peeked inside. He could have barked or something to tell me to stop, but he didn't.

The contents of his wallet had been informative. On his driver's license, he looked just as scruffy—except with a clearer view of his eyes. I'd stared at that photo until his laughing penetrated my fascination.

Behind the license, I found a folded copy of his GED transcript. With a few questions, I discovered that his dad, now deceased, had taught him how to read at an early age. The education he'd received was essentially comprised of homeschooling. When I asked him how he managed to get his GED and a driver's license without speaking, he stopped communicating with me for the night. Moody.

The glimpse at his eyes in the photo started me back on the "off with the beard" kick. His standard response was to bare his teeth. Darn canines. But, in a way, his consistent answer proved to me that telling him about my abilities had no noticeable effect on our relationship, other than to open a floodgate in me. I couldn't seem to stop myself from sharing all the weird or exciting things that happened to me on campus—the only time he couldn't shadow me.

When I talked, he sat and listened, always giving me his full attention. I'd grown so used to his attentiveness that he confused me one day when he abruptly walked away after I told him I'd been invited to a Halloween party.

I'd wanted to tell him more like it was Nicole from my basic massage class who had asked me. Her reason for the invitation was pretty simple. A guy from our class, who she really liked, planned on attending, and she didn't want to go alone. Everything in me had cringed at the idea of a party, so I'd told her I'd never been to one because of the way guys acted around me. She'd admitted to noticing, but that didn't change her insistence that I attend. Her acceptance of me felt good. Yet I had to point out the obvious. Having me along could backfire. The guy she liked could start bugging me again. He'd tried for the first two weeks of class before giving up. She didn't care. She wanted the support.

However, after Clay walked away from me, I didn't mention it again.

THE LAST SATURDAY IN OCTOBER, I found myself getting ready for a party instead of studying.

Clay grumbled, making it pretty clear what he thought of me going. I'd borrowed some of his clothes, the stuff that would fit without falling off, and slicked back my hair under a ball cap. Then, I used some funky hair gel from Rachel to comb a portion of my hair to look like pork chop sideburns. While that dried, I began the process of penciling in some thick, manly eyebrows. Clay stood on the bed behind me so he could watch my progress in the mirror.

"What do you think?" I asked, turning to Clay.

He grumped again then jumped off the bed to leave. Obviously not a fan.

"Rach?" I called to let her know I'd finished. She'd started as my costume consultant until she presented me with a skimpy dress from her closest and suggested that I go as a call girl. I'd kicked her out then. Clay had looked ready to rip apart the dress.

The door flew open, and only Clay's agile reflexes saved him from a concussion.

"What the hell did you do?" she said after she took one look at me. Her shocked expression was priceless.

"I'm going for dude. It's safe, right? What guy is going to want to hit on a guy even if he knows that underneath, it's a girl? Guys get weird about that stuff." I thought I looked pretty authentic. My layered clothes safely hid any curves I had.

"You know what's going to happen?" She sat in the middle of my bed. "All the guys are still going to be attracted to you. Only they're going to freak out because you're going to make them think they're gay, and you're going to get your ass kicked tonight."

Clay let out a yowl that sounded like "that's it" and ran from the room.

Rachel stared after him. "I love that dog, but he creeps me out sometimes."

"Yeah, I guess I shouldn't be trying to teach him to say 'No way'. I thought it'd be cool to train him to say it to guys, but I guess it's encouraging him to make other sounds, too." I hated lying, but Clay had just acted much too human.

"Oh, I didn't know you were doing that. Still...weird." She smiled and got up from the bed.

She'd told me earlier that she planned to stay in. I had a feeling Peter would arrive soon. Like magic, someone knocked on the back door.

"I got it," Rachel said as she bounded out of the room.

Shaking my head, I checked myself one last time. I didn't think I'd get my butt kicked...I hoped not anyway. I looked at the clock, expecting Nicole shortly. Nicole wasn't as close to me as Rachel, but she still seemed to genuinely like me despite the attention I usually received.

We'd decided I would drive in case fate smiled upon her and she managed to hook up with the guy she liked. To make it easier to keep an eye on her, I'd suggested she drive here. That way I could see when she came home like a nosey friend should do.

"It's for you, Gabby!" Rachel called from the kitchen. A hint of laughter laced her voice.

I moved toward the kitchen, wondering why Nicole had gone to the back door. When I saw who stood just outside, I stopped abruptly.

He stood motionless in the yellow glow of the porch light. The blue coveralls he wore had the name Clay sewn on the right pocket. Spattered patterns of grease stained the material, and one arm had a tear, making the getup look far from new. I'd never seen the coveralls before but didn't give it much thought as I stared at his face. I could actually see it. Well, sort of.

Our eyes met, and I couldn't look away. He'd pulled his hair back into a ponytail, fully exposing a broad forehead, nicely shaped eyebrows, and thickly lashed brown eyes, for the first time. His beard covered most of his cheekbones, but everything above his upper lip, he had trimmed shorter.

Stunned, I said nothing in greeting. I could feel Rachel's curious gaze flicking between the two of us. His eyes crinkled at the corners, and I knew he smiled at my reaction. It warmed my stomach and set my heart fluttering.

Thankfully, Nicole chose that moment to knock on the front door.

"I got it," Rachel said, breaking the spell Clay's sudden appearance had cast. She rushed from the room.

Breaking eye contact, I looked at his uniform. "You have some explaining to do, I think." My heart still fluttered as I turned away from him.

"I love your costume," Rachel gushed from the other room.

I turned the corner then smiled in awe of Nicole, who was dressed as a mermaid in all its shimmering beauty. The modified, silky green, body-hugging evening gown included a tail-like train. I anticipated people would repeatedly step on the end of her dress the whole night. A heart-shaped neckline adorned the sleeveless top. She'd altered it to make it appear as if she wore a bikini top. When she turned to give Rachel the requested full view, I also saw a cute fin strategically placed on the back just above her butt. A tasteful dusting of glitter decorated her sleek, straight hair.

"You're gorgeous, Nicole," I said. "Are you going to be warm enough?" Both she and Rachel laughed at me. "Hey, it's a valid question. It's the end of October, for Pete's sake."

"I'll be fine." She looked at Clay and smiled warmly. "Hi, I'm Nicole."

Clay nodded and stuck out a hand. She clasped it.

"Uh, this is Clay," I said for him. "He doesn't talk much. And this is Rachel, my roommate. Are we ready?" I didn't want to give Nicole or Rachel a chance to comment on Clay's quiet presence.

"Sure. I parked on the street."

"Great. Let me grab my keys." I turned in time to see Clay already walking into the kitchen.

Because of his head start and longer stride, the storm door was just closing behind him when I reached the kitchen. The car keys I'd wanted to grab no longer rested on the counter. Outside, an engine started. I peeked out the window and saw him sitting behind the wheel of my idling car.

He stunned me with his sudden appearance, distracted me from a vital question—how did he have coveralls with his name on them?—with the first real look at his face, and now sat in my car, ready to play chauffeur.

Slowly retracing my steps, I listened to Nicole explain how she'd made the costume herself.

"Nicole, if it's all right with you, I think Clay wants to come with. The way he's acting, I don't think he's ever been to a Halloween party and is curious."

"It's fine with me," she said with a smile as she moved to follow me to the kitchen. "Are you two dating?"

"Don't you dare say you are," Rachel said from behind her. "He's almost never here, and when he is, he doesn't talk and he leaves early. That's not dating."

Since I hadn't told Rachel that Clay appeared most Tuesday nights, I kept quiet. Better to just leave her with the impression she had than to try to explain our odd relationship.

"So, he's available then?" Nicole said.

"If you're asking my permission to make a move, go for it. Just don't be disappointed. I don't think it will go far," I said as I walked out the door. Giving her permission to hit on Clay didn't sit well, yet how could I not give it when I wasn't interested in making a move...right?

We hurried to the car. I sat up front with Clay, and Nicole shimmied into the back seat alone. I turned in my seat to look at her as Clay put the car in reverse.

"I don't know where we're going. Just tell Clay where to turn and be sure to give plenty of warning. This is the only car I have for the winter." I was nervous about Clay's driving experience. He had never answered how he'd gotten his license.

Clay expertly backed out of the driveway. Listening to Nicole's directions, he got us to the party in less than fifteen minutes. We couldn't park within a block of the address, therefore Nicole shivered as we walked. Within two blocks, I spotted the obvious party house. Music blared, ghosts hung from every tree in the yard, and I thought I saw a keg on the porch. So this was a college party? It looked interesting. People crowded the front lawn in groups that overflowed into the neighbor's yard.

As we neared, predictably, men turned to stare. Their eyes drifted to me, their expressions turning to confusion before they looked at Nicole.

I wasn't the only one to notice.

"I knew you would make this fun," Nicole said with a laugh. "Oh, I see him on the porch. Do you think I should say hi?" Her teeth chattered though she maintained a brilliant smile.

"Let's push our way through the crowd and get inside. We can warm up for a minute. It'll be more attractive if you're not stuttering with cold."

Clay didn't wait but took my hand and guided me through the crowd. Nicole followed in our wake. People moved for Clay, and it didn't take us long to reach the door where a man stood selling cups for three dollars. We declined and went to find a place inside.

The bass of the music echoed in my ribcage. Good thing Clay wasn't a talker. I would never hear him, even though he could probably hear me. I wondered how his sensitive ears handled the volume.

He kept hold of my hand and pulled us through the crowded entry into an equally crowded living room. He forced his way between people to reach the small couch then paused in front of it to glare at the two male occupants. They uneasily stood and left, making room for us to sit. Nicole and I sat while Clay perched on the arm right next to me.

Nicole warmed up as I looked around. From the decimated state of the snack table, the party had started a while ago. That also meant the majority of partygoers were drunk. One guy caught me looking around and made his way over.

The man stopped right in front of me and swayed slightly on his feet. I didn't look at him, but watched Nicole's face as her eyes darted to the man.

The music decreased in volume as a ballad came on.

"Hey...wash shore name?" he asked, his articulation long gone.

"Go away." I spoke clearly and rudely, knowing he wouldn't

even remember in the morning. It didn't seem to faze him in the least.

"Wanna go up shtairs? They have a pool table," he said, drawing out the L's in pool table just a tad too long.

Nicole coughed discreetly next to me to cover her giggle at the drunk's poor attempts at a pickup.

"No. Go away." This time, I added a glare to go with the words.

He looked beyond me with a startled expression, which quickly relaxed into a smile.

"Oh, god it man. Sheesh yours."

He ambled away, and Nicole and I turned to look at Clay.

"What did you do?" I said. Maybe some secret man-sign for "not interested." Whatever he'd done had worked well. I hoped I could learn it.

Clay flashed his teeth, showing elongated canines.

I heard Nicole's whispered "whoa," and I glared at him. If he kept flashing his teeth, people would start panicking.

"If you keep those in all night, you're going to have sore gums tomorrow," I said thinking fast.

"Those are so real looking. You have to tell me where you got those." Nicole looked at him in fascination.

"He won't say," I said then changed the subject. "Warm enough? Are you going solo or do you want backup?"

She hesitated. She looked uncomfortable and nervous. Honestly, I felt nervous, too.

A group of guys across the room had started watching us once the drunk walked away. Their gazes pivoted between Nicole and me. Most of them just looked confused. One focused on me with a frown. Maybe this was a bad idea after all. Rachel's prediction of a butt whooping appeared likely. Since Clay had already flashed his teeth once with minor provocation, I didn't want to think what he'd do if the frowny man approached me.

Nicole's bright gaze flitted around the room, oblivious to the tension I created. Normally an introvert, she seemed to bask in the attention we received, and I understood why she wanted me to come with. Without me, she would have been a wallflower. With me, she shared some of the notice I pulled in. I didn't feel used but did feel a little sorry for her. I wished I could help her get the man she so obviously wanted.

Deciding to speed things up, I reached out to pat Nicole's shoulder. She needed confidence.

When my hand touched her shoulder, a shock ran from my hand to her skin, the sting of it strong enough that we both yelped. I saw an actual spark.

"I'm so sorry, Nicole. I was just going to tell you that we should say hi now, and I go and scare you, instead." That's what I got for getting all touchy-feely.

"No, I know what that was. It was a jump start." She smiled at me, and I noticed the group of guys across the room had completely shifted their focus to her. The face of the man who'd frowned at me cleared as he watched Nicole.

"I'm going to go out there, now. If I can't get his attention, we can go." She got up and made her way to the door.

The group started to follow her while others in the room viewed her appreciatively as she passed. Girls who had previously smiled a greeting now frowned or outright glared at Nicole.

Too busy observing, I let Nicole's lead grow. Something was wrong. This was what typically happened to me. Granted, dressed as a man, the attention I normally drew had flagged a bit when we'd arrived, but if I'd worn something like Nicole wore...they would be eyeing me as they were her. Their behavior was so odd for me to see as a bystander and not a participant.

Automatically, I got up to follow at a distance. A sudden, dizzy spell sapped the strength from my legs, and I wilted a bit.

Clay had his arm around me instantly. I didn't look up at him but, instead, tried to keep my eyes on Nicole as I waited for the spell to pass. Maybe I'd gotten up too fast or skipped lunch a few too many days this week. Whatever its cause, it passed, and I did my best to follow Nicole despite the crush of bodies.

Clay had to physically shove a few people out of the way since they were too busy staring after Nicole to pay attention to my attempts to squeeze past. When they did see me, they barely spared me a glance. They just moved out of the way while trying to crane their necks to see Nicole. I didn't like their reactions to Nicole. Not out of jealousy but out of concern. If all of these guys didn't snap out of it soon, Nicole would be in trouble. She was too introverted to deal with all of this attention.

I made it to the porch in time to see Nicole say hi. She shimmered beautifully in the light. Randy, the guy from our class who she spoke to, appeared captivated. He'd dressed as the man from the Old Spice commercial, with a towel wrapped around his waist and nothing else. I figured it was a frat house thing because I'd spotted several others dressed similarly. As the only Old Spice-guy willing to brave the temperature outside, I guessed keeping the keg company also kept him warm.

He laughed at something Nicole said and offered her a beer. His own. He didn't seem willing to look away from her long enough to fill a new cup. I couldn't believe this was the same Randy. Since school started, he hadn't noticed Nicole once. What was going on here?

As unobtrusively as possible, I moved so Clay and I stood close to a railing where we had a better line of sight. The crowd continued to shift around us as people moved from group to group to talk.

After ten minutes of watching, I didn't know how she could stand the cold. Shivers shook me so badly my head ached. Naturally, I leaned back against Clay and wrapped my arms around myself. The heat of him penetrated through the back of my borrowed flannel and warmed me fractionally, but not enough to stop the shaking.

Giving up on the attempt to warm myself, I reached back,

grabbed both of his arms, and pulled them around me. He willingly wrapped me in his arms and tried to warm me. His chin rested on the top of my head. I could feel his heat, but the tremors continued.

"I don't feel good," I said with chattering teeth.

When he placed a hand briefly against my forehead a few minutes later, I knew he'd heard my complaint.

"Do I feel warm?" I turned my head to look at him.

He met my eyes and shook his head. I lost my train of thought for a moment. I'd forgotten he'd pulled his hair back so I could see more of his face, and I smiled absently. He had nice eyes. Expressive. My brain began to feel foggy, and I knew he could tell when his brows drew down in concern. I didn't like his frown. It detracted from his lovely brown eyes. Chocolate. That'd taste good.

I realized my mind had wandered and reined it in.

"I think I'm ready to go, but I don't want to leave Nicole here. What are my chances of getting her away from him, you think?"

He shifted his regard to the couple on the other side of the porch. I followed his gaze.

A few of Randy's towel-wearing friends had joined them, and their quiet talk had grown into an animated conversation. Nicole still smiled, but I could read a new tension in her stance. I'd been right. She wasn't ready for all the male attention she was receiving.

"I think now's a good time to s-see." The chatter at the end slipped out despite my Herculean effort to keep it in.

Clay loosened his hold on me and let me lead the way while he kept a hand on the small of my back. Whenever someone moved in my way, an arm snaked out from behind me and jostled them aside. There would be a few hung-over people tomorrow, wondering how they bruised their shoulders. But I wasn't going to complain. It felt like a plague had struck me, and I really wanted to get to Nicole so we could leave.

The men in the group saw our approach and bristled. I tried on a rare smile but knew it lacked wattage because I felt like crap.

"Hi, guys. Sorry to interrupt, but we need to pull Nicole away for just a minute."

"I'll be back in just a bit," Nicole said to them. "Can someone get me a soda?"

She took me by the arm and turned me around so fast that Clay had to step aside for us. We didn't look back but walked right off the porch and cut across the yard in the general direction of my car. Her arm linked through mine propelled me along more than she realized.

"Thank you for that. It was really weird the way they were acting tonight. I guess mermaid sends off the wrong vibes. I hope he remembers talking to me, though. I liked it until his friends showed up."

Her astute observations brought a trembling smile to my lips.

"Yeah," I agreed, "He s-seemed okay. D-don't trust his friends."

"Are you okay?" Concern laced her voice.

Behind us, I could hear Clay's soft footfalls.

"I think I'm getting sick or s-s-something." I felt colder without Clay's borrowed warmth. "Clay felt my head, but s-said I didn't feel warm."

"Is Rachel going to be home tonight? You said she's going to school for nursing, right? She'll probably know if there's something going around on campus. The nursing students doing clinicals always seem to know." Nicole switched position so her arm wrapped around me, chafing me in an attempt to warm me. I thought it funny since I wore flannel and she had a strapless dress on.

"Good idea." The sounds of the party slowly faded to a normal decibel. I tried using my sight to make sure none of the men followed us and felt a sharp pain in my head, instead. I flinched and immediately stopped. Nothing had appeared in my brief peek. No lights at all. That had never happened before.

When I spotted the car down the block, I sighed in relief. All I could think about was getting home, taking a hot shower, and going to bed. Clay surprised me by jogging ahead to the car. I heard the engine start a moment before he was back on the sidewalk, opening the door for me. He looked worried as Nicole helped me into the front.

"Do I look as b-bad as I f-feel?" I tried to joke.

Nicole looked at Clay, but he kept his eyes on me, so she answered.

"Well, you do look like you're coming down with something. I'm so sorry I begged you to come out tonight."

"Don't w-worry about it. It w-was r-really interesting," I said, forcing the words through my tensed jaw.

Very interesting. The sudden interest of the men...the animosity of the woman...I was certain I'd somehow passed my pull onto Nicole. And broke my mental fish finder in the process, too.

Clay drove fast, dividing his attention between the road and me. I continued to shiver despite the heat pouring from the vents. Minutes later, Clay smoothly pulled into the driveway. The house was dark.

"I hope you feel better," Nicole said. "I'll see you on Tuesday."

I nodded, unable to speak. My clenched jaw ached from shivering so much.

Clay was out as soon as he parked by the porch. He stalked around the hood. His eyes never wavered from me as Nicole slid from the back seat and left. I blinked tiredly and wondered how I'd get into the house.

He opened the door, and his eyes traced my face a moment before he wrapped an arm around my shoulders to help me out. Between the shaking, the headache, and the stiffness I felt from shaking, I had all of the symptoms of the common flu. And I wanted it to go away.

With his arm supporting me, we made it around the car and to the porch. My shivers increased to spasmodic, and he still easily managed to unlock the door without dropping me. I figured unlocking the door as a dog made this kind of move child's play.

The quiet house told me Peter and Rachel must have gone out after all, and I was glad. I would rather not have an audience to whatever had decided to plague me. I slipped from Clay's helpful embrace and started to tug off the flannel on my way to the shower.

"Clay c-can you get my towel?" I asked, dropping the shirt on the carpet outside the bathroom.

Had I felt better, I might have worried about how that sounded. But, really, I just wanted to stop shivering.

He moved past me and strode to the bedroom. His coveralls caught my eye again. I had to remember to ask him about those later.

I closed the door, struggled out of my t-shirt, and lost my balance as it cleared my head. I bumped into the sink. The chilly porcelain along with the cool air prickled over my skin and caused more gooseflesh. Curling the fingers of one hand on the sink for support, I lowered myself to sit on the toilet seat.

Tired and cold, I weakly kicked off my shoes then began to remove my socks. Without meaning to, I started whimpering like a little kid. I needed to warm up. Shivering sucked. The more clothes I took off, the worse it grew. It messed with my finger coordination.

I stood and tried to manipulate the button on my jeans but couldn't get it. I'd just begun to debate whether a hot shower was worth the effort when Clay tapped on the door.

"J-just a s-sec," I said in a panic. "I'm not ready, y-yet." I desperately yanked at the button, and it sprang free a moment before Clay opened the door.

"Hey!" I crossed my arms over my chest even though I still wore my bra. Sick and outraged, I glared at him for a moment. It cost too much energy to maintain.

He tossed the towel on the toilet lid and moved past me without a glance. Nudging the shower curtain back slightly, he turned on the water. I wanted to groan and smack my forehead. I hadn't thought to turn it on so it would warm up.

He turned from the shower, bent, and had my pants unzipped

and around my feet before I could move. I stared down at him in complete shock.

"Clay, g-get out!" Had I not stuttered, it would have been an impressive shriek. Instead, it came across weak, and he ignored it. Embarrassment flooded me. "Really, I c-can do the rest."

He stayed crouched, kept his eyes averted, and indicated I should step out of the pants. Of course, he wouldn't listen to me when I sounded ready to have a seizure. I looked down at his turned head so close to my belly, and wanted to push him over. But my legs quivered, and I knew I'd just end up falling over, too. Obstinate man.

Sacrificing my pride and my coverage, I placed a hand on his shoulder to steady myself and stepped out of the pants.

"N-now out, Clay," I said, crossing my arms again.

He picked up my pants and stood. Then, still turned away, he shook his head.

"The h-hell you s-say!" Oh, if my grandma had heard that, I would have gotten an earful; and then she would have laughed because I'd learned it from her at a tender age.

Clay reached around me and set the pants on the towel. His sleeve brushed my waist, and his hair tickled my arm. When he straightened, he pulled back the curtain and held out a hand for me. Steam started to fill the air as I stared at him belligerently. Did he really think I'd undress all the way in front of him?

He continued to look at the wall, patiently waiting for me. The shivers grew worse, and I debated my stubbornness. With his hair pulled back, I could clearly see his eyes and knew he wasn't peeking. Yet, I didn't understand why he continued with his own pigheadedness and wouldn't just leave to let me do the rest.

As if he'd read my mind, he nodded his head toward the shower and tapped the tub with his booted foot.

I looked down at the high ledge. The shivers prevented any coordinated movement. If not for Clay's support, I would have fallen when stepping out of my pants. Suddenly, he made sense.

"You're s-staying until I'm in? So I don't fall?" I guessed.

He shrugged, and I knew I'd guessed right.

With a defeated sigh, I uncrossed my arms and clasped his hand. The showerhead angled toward the front of the tub so I could step in without getting my remaining clothes wet. He closed the curtain behind me, and I waited to hear the click of the door.

Once I knew he had left, I finished undressing. I tossed my things on the bathroom floor and stepped into the hot spray.

It felt so good that I stayed there, just standing under the spray for several long minutes. My only movement was a slight side-to-side rocking motion to keep all of me as warm as possible. The shivers lessened but didn't disappear. I began to worry they weren't really due to the cold. My energy continued to drain, and my headache progressed to a steady thump. When I heard the click of the door again, I knew I'd pushed it.

"Clay?"

I heard a grunt but peeked around the curtain to be sure. He held out a towel with his eyes closed. I turned off the water and grabbed the towel.

It took a moment to wrap the towel securely around me. Covered, I peeked out again. Clay faced the door but had a hand extended to help me. Clasping it again, I stepped from the shower. I was warmer but more exhausted than when I'd gotten in.

I hustled as best I could to my room. Clay remained outside the door as I threw on the warmest pajamas I owned and did my best to blot the water that dripped from my hair. My arms quickly grew too tired, and all the heat I'd gained from the shower left me. Giving up, I tossed the towel to the floor, crawled between the covers, and curled into a ball. I couldn't even rub my feet together to try to generate more heat.

Clay walked in and turned off the lights. I listened to the familiar rustle of clothes. Instead of the usual bounce of him jumping up on the end of the bed, he peeled back the covers, and the bed dipped as he slid in next to me.

I didn't bother to pretend I wasn't interested in what he offered. Heat radiated from him, chasing the chill from the sheets.

"I really hope you're wearing shorts or something," I said with a slight slur. I stuck my cold feet right on his legs and shimmied over to his side to huddle against his warmth. Boy, was he warm. It didn't matter, though. The shaking didn't stop, but I was too exhausted to worry about it.

Sighing, I immediately fell asleep.

BRIGHT LIGHT FILLED the room when I peeled my eyes open, still barely conscious. I lay against Clay, basking in his warmth. My headache had faded from a steady thump to an annoying dull ache. I felt drained and very tired.

I tilted my head and met Clay's observant gaze. Worry glazed the chocolate brown depths. I tried to swallow, but the muscles didn't want to work.

"I'm thirsty," I rasped.

He gently moved me and got out of bed. I closed my eyes; I didn't want him to prove me wrong about the shorts. After a few seconds of silence, I forced my eyes back open. He stood next to the bed, holding out a full glass of water.

Shakily, I leveraged myself up on an elbow and grasped the glass. The cool water felt good going down. I drank it all and handed him the empty glass. He watched me curl up with my pillow.

I closed my eyes.

THE NEXT TIME I WOKE, I checked my alarm clock. The red digits showed two in the afternoon. Turning my head on the pillow, I happily noted the absence of weakness and pain. Whatever I'd done to cause my sudden illness, over sixteen hours of sleep appeared to have helped.

Gingerly, so as not to bring my symptoms back, I boosted myself into a sitting position. Clay no longer lay beside me. I glanced at my closed bedroom door. He must have gotten bored watching me sleep. I didn't blame him.

Although I could have slept longer, I pulled myself from bed. I grabbed my books then hopped back into my warm nest of blankets. Pillows stacked up behind me, I spread the work out. I'd lost a night and most of today because of the party. I couldn't afford to lose more time. I still had a few assignments from Friday to finish. In addition, I needed to review the prior week's materials to make sure I didn't miss anything.

After about fifteen minutes, I smelled bacon. My stomach growled loudly. The aroma tempted me to leave my warm bed. As I sat thinking about closing my book, the door opened fractionally, and Clay peered in. When he saw me sitting up, he nudged the door further to show a plate of food and a glass of juice. His appearance ended my internal debate and saved me from exposure to the cold.

"Thank you. I'm starving." I moved the book to the side, and he handed me the plate with a fork and set the orange juice on the dresser. I dug in right away, not realizing the extent of my hunger until the first bite touched my tongue. Eggs, bacon, potatoes, and toast vanished in minutes.

Without a word, Clay handed me the glass of juice.

I drank it slowly, starting to feel the pull of sleep. Resisting it would prove difficult. I patted the bed next to me.

"Want to read by me?" Maybe his company would help keep me awake.

He flashed me a smile, collected the dishes, and left the room. I heard him move around in the kitchen. The sound of running water had me wrinkling my nose; I knew I'd need to risk the cool air once again for a quick visit to the bathroom.

When I dashed back into my room eager for the warm bed, I saw Clay already lounging on the covers. He was reading a book.

We spent the rest of the day together in my room. Clay read next to me while I paged through notes and completed assignments. Each of the few times he left my side, he returned with a drink for me.

Near dinnertime, Clay closed his book with a snap and left the room. I heard Rachel's car pull into the driveway a few moments later. Before I heard her car door close, he returned wearing his fur again. Somewhere in the house, Rachel would see a pile of clothes.

I grinned at him as he jumped up on the end of the bed. He settled with a sigh, and I stretched out to tuck my feet under his warm body.

MONDAY MORNING, I FELT BETTER AND GOT READY FOR CLASS UNDER Clay's scrutiny. He didn't voice any complaint when I left, but I knew he worried that a full day so soon after recovering would overtax me. And he was right. By the last class of the day, I wanted to go to bed.

Dinner waited when I got home; two steaming bowls sat on the table. I dropped my bag next to the back door and flopped into the closest kitchen chair. Soup. Perfect. Clay picked up my bag and carried it into my room while I started to eat. After the first bite, I eyed the contents. I couldn't remember buying it and guessed he'd somehow managed to go grocery shopping.

He rejoined me and sat across the table. We ate in silence for a few minutes.

"Are you going to tell me about the coveralls or where you got the money for groceries?"

He shrugged in response.

Sighing, I pushed my bowl away. "I know I'm supposed to start asking you a bunch of questions, but I'm still too tired. Just don't be doing anything illegal, 'kay? It would be hard to visit you in jail on top of school."

I used a battered plastic container to put the rest of my dinner in the refrigerator and quickly washed the dishes despite his silent protests. He dried. Skipping homework, I changed and went straight to bed.

AFTER ANOTHER NIGHT'S SLEEP, I felt more energetic and noticed more than I had the day before. The people I encountered during the day treated me indifferently. The continuation of the phenomenon I'd experienced at the party surprised me.

I saw Scott crossing the campus again. He only waved when he saw me and continued to his destination. A friendly wave from one acquaintance to another. Confused, I made an effort to interact more. I smiled at the people I passed. I'd grown so used to the pull I had on men that it felt odd when they didn't turn to look. Eventually, someone did stop me, another freshman, but he only wanted recommendations for a nice place to take a date. Why he stopped me out of all the other people drifting around on the campus grounds, I had no idea. However, it was the most normal, random conversation I'd had in my life, and I loved it.

Nicole caught up with me after our basic massage class and gave me the details of her weekend. Randy hadn't forgotten her and had called her on Saturday to ask her out on a date for Sunday night. She'd excitedly accepted.

"He was nice and everything, just not the way he normally is in class. He seemed a little more intense on the date. I talked to him before class today, and he seemed more like his old self. We're going to go out again tonight."

Then she told me about her walk across campus that morning. She'd turned down no less than eleven date requests and two, blunt one-night stands. She giggled as she related the details, but the humor didn't reach her eyes. I gave her a few pointers about keeping her physical distance if she didn't want someone to bother her and to say no bluntly. She nodded her thanks.

I wished her luck and hurried home to tell Clay my suspicions. I felt sure that something had happened to make Nicole the magnet for unwanted male attention instead of me. The shock we'd felt seemed to have been the turning point. I wondered how long the effect would last.

RUSHING through the back door with a smile on my face, I felt a stab of disappointment at the greeting I received from the dark and empty kitchen. I set my bag on the table and dug the leftover soup out of the fridge.

While I leaned against the counter, waiting for it to warm, I wondered again about Clay's coveralls. I'd never gotten an answer about them. He probably worked somewhere, which would explain the wallet with the GED and the driver's license. But where? I could drive around and look for him, but I had no idea where to even start.

I sighed and settled at the table to eat and study. That he might have a job didn't bother me. That he bailed on what I considered our dinner night without a note or warning did.

When he wasn't home by six, I decided to head to the library to work on my speech. I needed the reference materials for research.

Studying at the library without my pull thoroughly increased my efficiency. Thanks to the uninterrupted work, I finished my speech by eight and headed home.

The windows glowed with light, and I felt a spark of excitement. I really wanted to share my unusual experience at the library. However, when I pulled into the driveway, I saw Rachel's car already in the garage. It meant I couldn't talk to Clay freely, but maybe I could still manage to whisper to him when we went to bed.

Inside, Rachel sat on the couch alone. There was no sign of Clay. She said she'd just gotten home and asked if I wanted to watch a movie with her. She didn't mention Clay-the-dog, so I told her I felt a little tired and went to bed early. I had no explanation for his disappearance and didn't want her to worry. I hoped that she thought he was already on my bed.

THE NEXT MORNING, I woke snuggled up against Clay, who must have snuck in at some point during the night. Though Rachel had technically turned on the heat, she kept it low. It made Clay's extra warmth nice.

When the sleep cleared enough from my head, I realized he lay next to me on his back...in man-form. I held still, trying to decide how I felt about it. When I'd been sick, he'd done it to help me. There hadn't really been a choice. I wasn't sick now. But he wasn't being weird about it. So, should I really make a big deal out of it? I decided not to. Warm feet felt nice; a warm all-of-me felt better.

Considerately, he wore a shirt, and although I wasn't going to check, I felt sure he'd included shorts. I shifted my head from against his side to look up at him.

He lay with both arms behind his head. His hair again covered the majority of his face. I thought he'd gotten over that phase. Since the party, he had kept it pulled back whenever he was Clay-the-man.

"It's annoying not being able to see you," I said in place of a good morning. I flipped to my stomach and propped myself up with my elbows to get a better look at him.

"If you don't talk, and I can't see your face, how am I ever supposed to figure out what you're thinking?"

I reached out to move some hair out of the way, but he stopped me in a blurred move, catching my wrist gently in his hand. He didn't let me any closer. First, he ditched me on dinner night, then he wouldn't let me touch him? The thought stopped me. I really hadn't touched him before either, at least not as a man. Maybe he was like me, a little standoffish. I could understand that.

"Seriously, Clay, what kind of bribe is it going to take for you to get rid of some of that hair?"

He flashed his elongated canines at me again in explanation.

"Can't we at least trim it back some?" Okay, maybe a lot, but I knew to start with baby steps.

He tugged my hand to his chest, laying it flat. So much for my theory about not wanting to be touched. I patiently allowed it because, with him, everything was guessing or pantomime. His chest warmed my palm.

Using his free hand, he tapped my mouth. I frowned, perplexed.

"What, you want me to be mute like you?" Was he hinting I talked too much?

He shook his head and reached out again. This time, he cupped my jaw and lightly ran his thumb over my bottom lip. The gentle touch caused the pull in my stomach to intensify. Though I couldn't see his eyes, I read his intent.

"Whoa!" I scrambled out of the bed as if it had caught fire.

He stayed where I left him and turned his head to study me as I stood trembling beside the bed. I nervously rubbed a sweaty palm, the one that had moments before rested on his chest, against my leg. His whiskers twitched down. I couldn't recall him frowning at me before.

I almost asked where that idea suddenly came from, but guessed it was long overdue. According to the Elders, when an unMated male finds his female, he begins a courtship of sorts. The end goal is to Claim his Mate.

But Clay hadn't courted me. He just lived here in his fur. And sometimes cooked for me. And sometimes helped me with chores...and when he wasn't around, I felt disappointed and missed him. My fearful expression slackened to one of stunned amazement. He *had* been courting me these last few months. Clever dog.

Not comfortable with simple contact to begin with, I naturally balked at his request. Then I paused, reconsidering my hesitancy. Yes, I'd held myself back from everyone. Contact meant an emotional connection, either for me or for the other person. But Clay didn't act like the rest. He wasn't compulsively drawn to me.

Maybe I needed to stop treating him like the rest. Hadn't I already started doing that? I'd sat next to him to watch movies, ate dinner with him, and, yes, technically snuggled with him at night. At least, my feet did regularly. And I had to admit, I liked looking at him—the parts I could see. Thinking of that caused a blush. I sent another panicked look in his direction, but he remained motionless.

But he didn't ask for just a simple kiss. Our current relationship placed so many strings on it. Strings I'd never before had to deal with. It definitely took us one step closer to Claiming in his book. As I thought of it, I realized my stance on Claiming had subtly shifted. I wouldn't mind having Clay around indefinitely. We meshed well together. But there still existed aspects of a werewolf relationship I wasn't ready for. Like biting his neck hard enough to break the skin and establish my Claim. My eyes drifted to his throat. That didn't sound like something nice to do to someone you cared about.

Clay waited patiently for me to consider his request. Would it really hurt to give in to just one little kiss? I wiped my hands on my pants again.

The male's drive to Claim his Mate increased with each passing day, building to a compulsive need. There'd never been a courtship that lasted more than six months. Paul and Henry shared that tidbit with me long ago.

I calculated back and cringed. We'd just passed six months. He hadn't pressed for anything from me in that entire time. I'd been so focused on school that I hadn't given any thought to the Claiming stuff I'd learned other than to be glad he wasn't pressing me.

I edged closer to the bed and touched my bottom lip, thinking. Was he struggling to hold back his aggressive side? Could that be why his canines were elongated more often than not? Had I put too much faith in his control? But the toughest question was whether I trusted Clay. If I did give him what he asked for, would it be enough to satisfy him, or would he want more and then become unbearable to live with?

Glancing up at him, I considered my options while he continued to watch me in silence. I really wanted to see his eyes again.

"I have some questions before we talk about my bribe and your price." I crawled back up on the bed and sat on my heels once I reached his side. "Will you try to answer my questions?"

He continued to watch me without answering.

"Are you able to physically speak?"

After a brief hesitation, he nodded.

"Are you ever planning on talking to me?"

He smiled wide and nodded again.

I nervously noted his teeth were bigger than they'd been a minute ago. My stomach did a flip, and I could feel the fading blush rekindle and spread across my face.

"Clay, were you asking for a kiss?" I had to know for sure.

He nodded slowly and reached out to twine his free right hand with mine. His thumb soothed the outside of my hand while he waited for me to decide what to do.

"Clay, I can't even see your mouth to know where to kiss. I hope this bargain includes a shave."

His whiskers twitched, and I guessed he smiled. He appeared

laidback, completely calm as if my answer didn't affect him at all. It bolstered my courage.

I let go of his hand and leaned forward, bracing myself on his shoulders. I could see the glint of his eyes as he watched my slow descent. My stomach churned with nerves and anticipation. Despite my teasing comment, I found his lips without any problem and lightly touched mine to them. His warm breath fanned my face, and I pressed closer. Something inside me melted a little.

Closing my eyes, I reached a hand up to gently brush against his face, exploring his brow, ear, and jaw. He changed the kiss by tilting his head slightly. His lips began to nibble at mine, slow and easy. My stomach dipped, and my heart started to flutter with desire.

When I realized how easy it would be to keep kissing him, desire changed to panic. I pulled away then gasped at the sight of the black eye I'd exposed.

"What happened?" I said, forgetting desire and panic. Then, thinking of Rachel, I dropped my voice to a whisper. "I thought werewolves weren't supposed to get hurt like this."

Seeing his eyes again gave me a nice advantage. I easily read the frustration in them. Before he could try something else, I bounded off the bed again.

"A deal's a deal. Go shower and shave. After you're done, we can play charades until I have the story behind the black eye." The stubborn look in his eyes had me adding, "That or I call Sam."

I stayed well back while he ran his hand through his hair in agitation. Then, he sighed and sat up. The flex of his abdomen under his snug shirt dreamily distracted me. When he swung his feet over the edge of the bed, he turned his back to me. Part of his shirt had ridden up, exposing more bruises on his back.

Forgetting to stay away, I rushed around the bed. He heard me and stayed where he was. He didn't fight me when I started tugging his shirt over his head, either. Numerous bruises covered his torso.

"What happened?" I demanded again. I nudged his right arm away from his side, saw a huge, ugly purple mark, and lightly ran my fingers over it. He held perfectly still for me.

"This is really scaring me, Clay. I thought werewolves were supposed to be this tough, nearly indestructible, race."

I'd lost my mom to a car accident and my grandma to cancer. With no other family, I had endured as an orphan, truly alone in the world. Then, when I'd realized Sam's plan to pair me with one of his kind, a single thought had resonated with me: If I found a werewolf Mate, he would never die on me and leave me alone.

"Is this why you were gone last night when I came home?"

He didn't move at all.

"Fine." I turned to leave him, but he caught my wrist again and gently tugged me to his side. He brought my hand to his mouth, kissed the back of it, then my knuckles. I felt a tug in my stomach. That stupid, annoying, kinda-growing-on-me-a-lot pull which tied us together. My annoyance at him evaporated. Unable to help myself, I brushed my fingers through his hair. I liked the feel of it.

"I've lost everyone that's ever really mattered to me. I thought caring about a werewolf would be safer," I admitted softly.

He raised his head to look at me for a long moment then pulled me into his arms.

Normally, I wouldn't like someone hugging me like that. But with Clay, it felt safe. I hugged him back gently, not wanting to hurt him more, and hoped the safety I felt wasn't because I'd already lost too much of my heart to him. I'd never fully recovered from losing my mom or grandma. I doubted I could lose much more and remain the same person. Losing Clay, even now, might break me.

Eventually, I pulled away first. His stomach began to rumble, and mine answered. I tiptoed out of my room and moved my car, knowing Rachel would need to leave soon. Then, while Clay waited in my room, I made him breakfast. I didn't want Rachel to see him when she woke. We ate together on my bed. Before we finished, I heard Rachel leave.

While I washed dishes, he slipped into the bathroom with scissors and a razor.

It would be an understatement to say I was a little curious about what he really looked like under all the fur, er, whiskers. The anticipation built while I put away the dishes.

I walked by the bathroom door but couldn't hear anything. Trying to keep busy, I went back to my room and sorted laundry before deciding what to wear. It didn't take me long to dress. I paced around the house listening to the shower run.

Chapter Fifteen

THE ANTICIPATION HAD ME SO DISTRACTED THAT I JUMPED WHEN someone knocked at the front door. Of course, the shower turned off at that moment. Bad timing. I scowled, took a breath, then walked to the front door. Smarter this time, I checked the peephole.

Sam stood on the doorstep, and he looked very serious. He must have left in the middle of the night in order to get here first thing in the morning. I frowned. The surprises just kept coming, and it wasn't even eight.

Fixing a welcoming smile on my face, I pulled open the door.

"Morning, Sam. This is a surprise." I wanted to see Clay freshly shaven without an audience, but I motioned Sam in anyway. If he took the time to drive here, I would take the time to listen to whatever he had to say. Maybe it would be a short visit.

He stepped inside.

"Um, don't get me wrong, I like seeing you, but is there a reason you're here?" I asked, trying to hurry him along.

"We'll wait for Clay."

His cryptic answer caught me off guard. It'd been more than two months since we'd seen each other. Sure, we had talked, but it wasn't the same as seeing someone face to face. I'd expected him to look at least slightly happy to see me.

Just then, the bathroom door opened. I excitedly turned to look for Clay. Dressed in a t-shirt and jeans, he stepped into the living room. But I didn't waste my time ogling him. My eyes honed in on his face. Only Sam's observant presence kept me from wrinkling my nose.

Clay still sported his beard, but he had trimmed it back. The neat length continued to obscure his teeth while revealing a hint of his lips. At least now, I'd be able to see when he smiled. The whiskers that had covered his neck were gone, leaving the clean-shaven column of his throat exposed. My eyes lingered on that skin for a moment before moving on. He'd also run his fingers through his hair so it lay back out of his face. The deep purple of his black eye had already faded to an ugly green-yellow. Even with his bruising, he looked really good. Just not shaven all the way.

I smiled warmly at Clay, wishing we were alone so I could tell him what I thought.

"You know why I'm here, Clay," Sam said from behind me.

My smile fell as I turned to look at him. What was he talking about?

"I'm told you didn't take the news well."

I turned back to Clay in time to see him shrug and cross his arms.

"What's going on? What news?" I said, glancing between the two.

Sam gave Clay a sharp look. "You didn't tell her?"

"He's not talking to me, yet," I said, wondering what bad news Sam had to share.

Sam shook his head at Clay. "You've dug your own hole then, son." He focused on me. "A group of Forlorn have asked Elder Joshua to approach you for an unofficial kind of Introduction. Joshua approved, but he made it clear they were to keep it brief and then leave unless any of them had a further request of him."

The meaning of Sam's words sunk in deep like a vicious bite. It also explained his less than warm greeting. He stood in my living room as an Elder on pack business, not as family or a friend. I struggled to contain my anger.

"I thought I was done with that. We had a deal." I crossed my arms and coldly regarded Sam. "I know I said I was done."

The carefully composed expression on Sam's face faltered a bit. "Honey, there are rules we must follow to keep peace in the pack. Clay had six months to convince you of his suit. That time has passed. That means unMated can once again approach you, with permission."

My mouth popped open. Six months. Permission from an Elder. That's why they'd stationed Joshua here. A backup plan because they knew I didn't want to Claim Clay. They failed to understand I didn't want to Claim anyone. I'd never been free. I clenched my fists. My temper boiled.

"That's complete crap," I gritted out. "First of all, I didn't reject anyone. Second, no one ever told me about this stupid rule." My voice rose to a yell, and I took a deep breath and closed my eyes briefly to restrain myself. When I reopened them, I felt more in control and able to speak calmly. "You know what? I don't care what the pack rules are. I gave you my word and my time. Now, I expect you to keep yours. I worked hard to get here, Sam. I won't let anyone take this away from me." My hands shook. That Sam had cared for me in the past and given me a place to call home for two years kept my tongue marginally civil.

"By not completing the Claim, you've become eligible again. Charlene was granted a special consideration because, at that time, we weren't even sure a Claiming would be possible between a human and a werewolf. Now that we know it is, you fall under the same rules," Sam explained calmly, his face again carefully devoid of emotion.

"No, I don't." I knew I could stand there and argue all day with Sam and he wouldn't budge. It would always be whatever's best for the pack with him. "Is this why Clay was beat up?"

Clay made a noise—like a snort of disagreement—behind me.

"Feel free to jump in at any time," I said, turning to arch an eyebrow at him. He remained mute, but his eyes softened when he looked at me.

Sam spoke up from behind me, but I didn't turn to look at him.

"Gabby, it's the reason he's been fighting. He's not relinquishing his tie to you. Every time an unMated shows up here, he will challenge that man for his right for an Introduction. Did Clay get beat up? Only as a byproduct of handing out beatings."

Clay steadily met my gaze the entire time. It broke my heart a little to know he was fighting so hard to keep me, and all I'd given him in those six months was a kiss. Not even spontaneously given but relinquished as part of a bribe. I hadn't rejected him. I just didn't want to be forced into a choice. If I chose to be with Clay, I wanted it to be on our terms.

"Why is two years of school too much to ask for?" I said to Sam, tearing my guilty gaze from Clay.

"And after that? Then you'll want time to establish your career. Let's face it. There will never be a perfect time for this in your life. You just need to make the best with what you have."

As in, suck it up? My temper boiled over. Screw respect. He just crossed a line. I walked right up to him and poked him in the shoulder.

"No, Sam, you do. I'm not your pawn in this game you play with women's lives. I went to your Introductions and fulfilled any obligation I felt I owed you for the roof over my head. You have no say in who I see..." Poke. "...or what I do, unless you intend to drag me back to the Compound and physically force me to bite someone."

Clay growled slightly behind me, obviously sharing my sentiment. I stepped back from Sam and moved closer to Clay.

"It's time for you to leave, Sam. Don't come back." Saying those words hurt just as much as knowing I only mattered to him because of what I meant to the pack, rather than what I meant to him.

"You were never an obligation to me, Gabby." When I looked away, he tried to persuade Clay. "You know it'd be safer for both of you if the Introductions continued at the Compound. If you keep going like this, there might be someone you won't beat. Are you willing to risk leaving her alone, then?"

What did he mean by that? Clay could get hurt even worse? I thought they were nearly invincible. Glancing at Clay, I looked at each bruise and saw the real answer. They were hard to beat but made to break just like the rest of us.

I walked to the door and opened it for Sam, signaling the end of the conversation.

"All right, then." He walked to the door and turned toward me. "Gabby, call me anytime. I'm here to help you, no matter what you might think right now."

I nodded stiffly and closed the door behind him. His help would only extend as far as it could help the pack. He'd just proven I meant less to him than they did, but I'd always known that. Why, then, did I let it hurt me?

For a few seconds, I just stared at the door's surface and tried to let go of my anger. Sam made his choice. I needed to make my own.

I turned to look at Clay. He'd moved closer to me, probably waiting for my reaction to everything Sam had just said. I didn't want to deal with it yet. Instead, I reached up and teased my fingers through the whiskers along his jaw.

"Much better, but I'm going to keep at you until it's all shaved off, and maybe a haircut, too."

He briefly bared his teeth, re-explaining the reason for the beard.

I spent a moment studying his face. I ran my fingers over his forehead and traced his black eye. He held still, patiently letting me look my fill. Would things have progressed differently if I'd known about a timeframe? I doubted I'd have even let him in the door if I'd known he only had six months to try to convince me.

With a sigh, I stepped away. "I need to get ready for class. Before I go, would you show me where you got the coveralls from?"

He nodded, and his lips curled in a slight, secretive smile. I definitely liked seeing his lips.

My hunch had been right. He pulled into a small auto body shop on South Mitchell. The street name tickled a memory. I couldn't place it until the mechanic currently working looked up at our approach. Cleaning his hands on a rag, he smiled at us.

"Dale from the parking lot?" I whispered, looking at Clay questioningly. He just nodded. It explained his secret smile and his interest in books about auto mechanics.

Clay exited the car and moved to open my door. I'd thought I would get a drive-by tour, not a walking one. Wide-eyed, I stepped out.

Dale walked toward us. "Hi there, Gabby. Glad Clay finally brought you around." He held out his freshly wiped hand. I clasped it briefly. "I have to tell you that I was surprised when Clay showed up and was as good as you boasted." I didn't recall actually boasting. "Although, it doesn't look like he's been taking care of your car."

Clay said nothing in his defense—of course—leaving the talking to me.

"I'm always running back and forth to my classes. It's hard to give it up for any amount of time." I shrugged away his question. "Speaking of which..." I looked at Clay. "I really need to get going, or I'll be late." I turned back to Dale. "It was nice seeing you again, Dale. I hope stopping in was okay. I really wanted to see where Clay was working."

"Stop by anytime." He waved as we walked out and got back in our car.

"I'm sure there was some type of logic to picking that place," I said to Clay as he drove us home. "Someday you'll have to tell me about it."

BY FRIDAY, everything seemed back to normal with my pull. Men once again noticed me. Their eyes followed me around campus. Thankfully, they seemed to remember my repeated rejections from the beginning of the semester and didn't approach me anew.

I did wonder what exactly had happened, though. The suspicions that floated around in my head needed further examination, but I wanted to talk through them while Clay listened.

When I walked through the door just before five, an empty house greeted me. I really needed to find out his work schedule.

Rachel got home a little after five. As soon as she walked in the door, she announced she'd decided to go out to a dance club. She continued to her room without waiting for a response from me. I followed her, needing the company. Life had just been a little too weird for me over the past week.

"Don't suppose you'd like to come with?" she asked, looking at the options in her closet.

I sat in the middle of her bed, safely out of the way of any clothing options she tossed behind her.

"You know how it is," I said as I plucked at a string in her quilt. "It's just worse if they're drinking."

"Which one do you like better?" Rachel asked, demanding my attention. She'd pulled two dresses from her closet. "This one?" She held up a red dress with a tuck that crossed the middle to accentuate the wearer's curves. "Or this one?" She indicated a standard black dress with a twist. The real hemline was shorter than the red's, but a secondary hemline, comprised of strands of beads, hung from the first hemline, giving the illusion of another six inches.

"I think the black one would be more fun to dance in."

"I think you're right." She set both on the bed and rummaged in her jewelry box. "I have an idea. Peter can't go out tonight. I think we should make it a girl's night out." She turned with something in her hand and arched a brow at me. "Unless you have plans with Sir Talks-A-Lot?"

"No, but—"

She tossed what she held in my direction. By reflex, I caught it.

"Have you ever tried wearing a ring? Some friends of mine do it when they want to go out to have fun and not be bothered by anyone." She grabbed the black dress, handed it to me, then begged. "Let's just try. It's a club with extremely expensive drinks. The prices discourage an all-out drunk, and it has great music."

I hesitated, thinking of Clay. Did I really want to sit here, waiting? It wouldn't help him get home faster. The niggling concern that his delay related to another challenge reared its head. But Sam had assured me that the challenger would want to heal between fights. If Clay dished out more than he got, the other guy wouldn't be ready yet, anyway.

She pounced on my hesitation. "You know I'll leave anytime you say you're ready to go. You never seem to let your hair down and just have fun. With that kind of constant tension, you're going to end up with heart disease or something."

Her comment about never having fun hit home. I did tend toward the more serious course. When was the last time I did something just for the fun of it? For myself? The double date with

Scott had been for Rachel. The party last weekend had been for Nicole. The Introductions for the last two years had been for Sam.

Pathetically, I hadn't done anything just for fun since before I went to live with Sam. Even going to school and getting an education was more for my grandma than me. Before she died, I'd made her a promise to get an education and find something that made me happy.

But would going out dancing really be something I would find fun? I toyed with the fringe on the dress. Yes, dancing would be fun. The men who I'd rather avoid made it a less than fun idea. I looked at the ring in my palm. The large stone sparkled brightly. It was meant to be noticed, but not gaudy. Would it work?

"We'd leave at the first sign the ring doesn't work? Even if we never make it into the club?" I glanced up at her and caught her hopeful expression.

"I've got your back," she promised. "First sign, and we're home, curled on the couch, watching a chick flick."

"All right," I sighed and grabbed the black dress. "I've got nothing better to do."

"Gee, thanks," Rachel said with a laugh as I left to change.

RACHEL and I had to stand in a long line. It seemed the college crowd favored the downtown club despite the overpriced drinks. We shuffled forward every few seconds while listening to the muted music that thumped from within. Each time the bouncer opened the door it briefly grew louder. The door didn't open frequently enough.

I shivered as we inched forward and tried not to move too much so the cold beads wouldn't touch my legs. Eventually we grew close enough that I could watch the man at the door methodically check everyone's ID. I wasn't worried. I knew I wouldn't have a problem getting in.

"Finally," Rachel said with a smile as she stepped up to the man. She showed her ID.

The bouncer barely looked at her. He eyed me closely, not even glancing at the ID I held out. I withstood his scrutiny, wishing he'd hurry so we could warm up inside. I'd pulled my hair back into a messy knot and added a touch of eyeliner and mascara. It wasn't much of a change, but between the makeup and the dress, he looked at me as if I were a goddess. Maybe this wasn't such a good idea.

Then his eyes settled on the ring I wore.

"You come get me if anyone inside gives you any problems," he said. I nodded. He opened the door for us, and I stepped inside after Rachel.

The music's bass reverberated through the floor and my body. I wouldn't be able to hear anything else but didn't care. The club's warm air enveloped me.

Rachel pointed toward the bar. A long blackboard above the bar, filled with neon-colored chalk, listed their specialty drinks and prices. As promised, the drinks were expensive. Good thing we wanted to dance, not drink.

Grabbing my hand, she pulled me to the edge of the swaying crowd and started to dance. I did a little twist in the dress and smiled to myself as the beaded hemline flared out. The dress was as fun to wear as I'd thought. Then the beads slapped my legs on the backswing. The sting of it made me rethink the fun factor. If anyone got out of line, maybe I could use it as a weapon.

The music freed me from worry about male attention, about Clay, and about Sam and his stupid rules. I danced with Rachel and truly had fun.

Eventually, reality invaded in the form of our own all-male crowd, and our dancing became a game of evasion. Rachel arched a brow at me. I shook my head, not yet ready to call it quits. The deafening music made it impossible for them to talk to me, and its fast, heavy beat didn't inspire a slow, close dance. As long as I evaded the bump and grind, I could still enjoy myself.

After a few songs, I signaled to Rachel because a persistent member of the group kept rubbing up against my backside. She grabbed my hand, and we both ignored the protests of the men around us as she led the way to the bar. A few of the men followed. One of them managed to pull out his wallet and order drinks for both of us before we could stop him. Rachel took hers, but I shook my head and shouted to the bartender that I just wanted water. The generous buyer sulked a bit, but I ignored him and his shouted attempts at conversation.

Sipping my water, I looked around, feeling watched—by someone not in the immediate group of men who surrounded us.

I spotted two women further down the bar. They weren't exactly watching me. They were eyeing the crowd of men around us. Neither looked angry, but both looked a little envious. Dressed very similar to Rachel and me, they stood isolated at the bar. The way they kept glancing at me, they probably wondered what I had that they didn't. I couldn't blame them. I looked a bit frumpier than they did.

I motioned to Rachel, and we moved down the bar so our group would spread out to include the two women as well. I shouted my name over the music and pointed to myself by way of introduction. The women smiled and seemed friendly. They tried to make conversation with a few of the men.

I didn't notice someone leaning close to me until his breath tickled my neck and his unfamiliar voice spoke smoothly in my ear.

"About time you left your guard dog at home." He was just loud enough so I could hear him over the music.

Curious, I turned. He stood several inches taller than I did. No surprise since just about everyone towered over me. He looked even taller than Clay, but not as wide-shouldered. He had copper brown hair and hazel eyes. A humor-filled smile flashed at me as I studied him.

"Excuse me, do I know you?"

He leaned in and spoke in my ear. "No need to shout, love. You know I can hear you just fine." His lips touched the curve of my ear, and I shivered as he inhaled deeply. "Mm, you smell good."

I pulled back, leaned against the bar to put some space between us, and really looked at him. In the background, the bodies on the dance floor moved in rhythm to the steady beat of the music. I opened myself to my other sight and wasn't surprised to see his blue-green spark or several other matching sparks in the crowd behind him. Blue-green I could deal with. The other color I didn't want to face until I knew what it meant.

"What do you want?" I said.

With humans, the "safety in numbers" rule worked. Not necessarily so with werewolves. But they did have their own non-human set of rules they still needed to follow unless they were Forlorn. I'd be okay as long as I followed the rules Sam taught me.

He leaned in again. "Just to say hi, love. You're hard to catch by yourself. Did you know your dog follows you to school?"

"Hi, then," I said, refusing to respond to his last question. If Clay followed me to school, how did he ever find the time to work? Again, I wished he'd just start talking to me.

The man beside me remained close. I didn't like that his breath continued to tickle my ear. Clay would smell him on me.

Rachel noticed us and sent me a questioning look. I gave her a half-smile to reassure her that I didn't mind—even though I really did.

"I was hoping we'd be able to go somewhere quieter to talk."

"Really? Just us? Or those other guys in the crowd, too?" I took a sip of my water and glanced at him.

His smile stretched wider. "And I thought we were blending in well."

None of their kind could ever blend into a human crowd. At least, not for me.

I decided to be blunt. "Do you have permission to be here?"

"We have permission to approach you and request a second meeting."

"Second?"

"This would count as the first," he clarified helpfully.

"Ah." So talking me into leaving with him would probably be the second meeting that he had permission to request. However, I bet he didn't have permission to have the second meeting without Elder supervision. Typical Forlorn rule-breaking. His eyes never left my face, and the longer I remained silent, the more his humor slipped. I didn't think he would accept no to his request. It might even result in my immediate, forceful removal from this bar. Could nothing in my life ever go easy?

"I can't go with you tonight. I'm with a friend. But I plan to be at the Compound for an Introduction tomorrow night."

"Really? It's odd that no call's gone out for it." He tilted his head and studied me, probably trying to sense a lie. Didn't matter. He wouldn't sense one as I'd just made up my mind.

"That's because I haven't told my guardian yet. We had a fight, and I'm still pretty pissed at him." Pretty pissed at him, and pretty pissed at you. Why couldn't everyone just leave me alone? "I'm tired of being told what to do and want the Introductions on my terms. I didn't think about the call. Sorry."

He looked at me closely for several moments. "I can understand not wanting to be told what to do. That's why we left our packs."

Forlorn. My stomach dropped, and my hand tightened on my glass. Bad grew worse the moment he smelled my fear. His nostrils flared minutely, and his grin widened.

"Don't worry, little one. We're not going to cause you any trouble tonight. We will see you tomorrow night."

Yep, that sounded like a threat. If I didn't go to the Compound, they would be coming to get me either way.

He nodded to me, turned, and disappeared into the crowd. I used my sight and monitored his progress as he and his group left the club. Once they cleared the building, I grabbed Rachel's hand to distract her from her shouted conversation and motioned for the exit. A true friend, she immediately set her barely touched drink on the bar and moved to follow me.

One of the women noticed and snagged my arm.

"Please stay!" she shouted.

I smiled regretfully at her and her friend. Both pleaded with their eyes as did the men behind them. But the men begged for a different reason—they were only feeling the effects of the pull I had. I felt a moment of pity for the women. At some point in our lives, we all looked for that one being to connect with. These two just wanted a chance to find their special someone.

Though I understood, Rachel and I needed to leave in case the Forlorn changed their minds about waiting until tomorrow. I reached out to the women, ready to apologize.

As soon as my fingers made contact with their arms, a large shock took the three of us by surprise. I knew immediately what I'd done. It hadn't stung as bad as it had when I'd zapped Nicole, but the drain of it was worse. Now Rachel and I had even more reason to leave quickly.

The women looked stunned. I just laughed it away and patted their arms.

"Sorry," I shouted over the music and waved goodbye.

This time when I moved to go, no one paid me any attention. One of the men behind the girls had already called the bartender over to order more drinks for the group. I hoped the women would stick together and be smart about the attention soon to be showered on them.

The first wave of dizziness washed over me as Rachel and I pushed our way through the crowd toward the door. The bouncer didn't even give me a second glance as we left. No man did. It confirmed what I had already guessed.

Our heels tapped out a rapid cadence on the sidewalk, but the clipped sound seemed like it came from under water. I wondered how long it would take my ears to recover from the loud music.

"We need to get home," I said as soon as we were far enough away from the club that I could hear.

"Why? Is someone following us?" She turned to look behind us.

I hadn't thought of that. I hoped the Forlorn would keep their word because I couldn't look for them with my sight. I didn't want to drain myself further.

"No, I'm just really not feeling well."

We reached Rachel's car, and I slid into my seat. By the time Rachel eased into the driveway, I shivered uncontrollably. She had cranked the heat in the car, but it hadn't helped. After all, the shivering wasn't because of a chill or a fever. I didn't argue when she parked and told me to stay sitting. She came to my side of the car to help me out.

"Why didn't you tell me sooner that you weren't feeling well?" Rachel said with one arm wrapped securely around my waist as she helped me into the house. The cold beads of the dress tickled the backs of my legs.

"I d-didn't know. It c-came on f-fast."

Rachel unlocked the door. We'd stayed at the club an hour, at least, but the house remained quiet and dark.

"Clay?" I called from the kitchen. No answer. How long did Dale keep him on a Friday night? Rachel helped me to my room and frowned at the empty bed.

"I wonder where he is," she murmured.

Too late, I realized my mistake. When I'd called for Clay, I'd wanted the man, forgetting all about Clay-the-dog. Thankfully, I hadn't said anything more.

She unzipped the back of my dress, because I shook too badly to reach it, then left my room to search the rest of the house for Clay. I let the dress fall to the floor and struggled to put on my warm pajamas. Rachel came back a few moments after I'd managed to pull up the pants. She looked even more worried.

"I can't find him anywhere."

"M-maybe he got out. I'm going to bed. I'm sure he'll sh-show up tomorrow," I said, crawling under the covers.

Rachel got me a glass of water, set it on the dresser, then felt my forehead.

"Doesn't feel like a fever. Maybe it's low-grade."

"I'll be fine. Don't worry about me. I've had this before and just need sleep." I burrowed deeper under the covers and tried to curl up to stop shaking. I wished for Clay again. I needed him. He warmed me, comforted me, and I needed to tell him about my promise to go to another Introduction. That wouldn't go over well.

Rachel continued to watch me—nurse Rachel, not friend Rachel. I needed to distract her before she insisted I go see someone.

"I forgot to tell you. I have plans to leave tomorrow to see Sam. If Clay's back, I want to take him with me."

"You sure you'll be up for it?"

"Yeah, it's not something I have a choice about."

"All right. Wake me up if you need anything." She left the room but kept the door ajar. It made my heart ache as I recalled how, first my mother, and then my grandmother, had done the same for me whenever I'd been ill.

I felt Clay hop up on my bed and forced my eyes open. Tremors still shook me, and the mid-morning light sent shafts of pain into my aching head. The last time this had happened, it had taken close to twenty-four hours of sleep before I woke up without a headache. Unfortunately, I didn't have time to sleep this one off. If I didn't show up at the Compound on time, those Forlorn would come looking for me, and Clay would get hurt again.

My mind worked sluggishly as I stared at the time. The clock displayed nine. It would take a little over eight hours to get to the Compound. We'd arrive around dinner.

"C-Clay, we need to get to the Compound. Can you drive?" I struggled to sit up. He cocked his fuzzy head at me. "A lot happened last night while you were gone. I'll tell you about it on the way."

I tried to stand, but a wave of dizziness knocked me back onto the bed. Blood rushed to my head and pulsed in my ears. I almost didn't hear Clay move while I sat there panting. I waited a moment, took a deep breath, then tried to stand again.

This time, Clay wrapped an arm around me to help. He'd shifted. I glanced at the door. It stood ajar. Was Rachel still home? He needed to be more careful. My wandering eyes caught our reflection in the mirror.

He stood beside me, looking down at me with concern. No wonder. I had my arm curled around his bare waist in a death grip, just to stay standing. My pale face enhanced the dark circles under my eyes. A frizzy mass of hair haloed my head. I looked like hell.

He, however, looked—I stopped gazing at his naked chest long enough to see his eyes narrow—pissed. He'd just figured out what I'd done again, and for the first time, I experienced a sense of appreciation over the fact that he didn't talk. Not wanting to meet his gaze, I decided to go back to enjoying the view. He wore jeans, unbuttoned and low on his hips. One arm wrapped around my shaking shoulders. He started to rub little circles on my skin with his thumb. He reached up with his other hand and lightly touched my forehead. Though he was upset with me, his concern was plain as was...I squinted in an attempt to see clearly and then scowled.

He once again sported bruises and what looked like a bite mark. How many challengers were out there? I'd thought just a couple. He came home with bruises too often for it to be the same few. And a bite? I frowned at the mark on his shoulder, but my fuzzy brain distracted itself again. I lost my scowl. Even with his bruises and bite mark, Clay looked incredible. I would have drooled at the view he gave if I weren't so sick.

"I need to use the bathroom then start packing."

He nodded and helped me through the door. My head throbbed with each step. I leaned against him, let my head hang a little, and trusted him to guide me. Because of my position, I saw Rachel's feet as she intercepted us.

"Hi, Clay. How'd you get here?"

I forced myself to look up. Still in her pajamas and sleep rumpled, she looked gorgeous. How she pulled that off, I had no idea. Concern filled her eyes when she took in the sight of me.

"I called him. Sorry, Rachel. I didn't want to bug you."

Her gaze drifted to Clay. "It's okay. I get it." She eyed Clay's bare chest and his face as he continued to support me.

I'd forgotten she hadn't seen him cleaned up like I had. Although bruised and bitten probably wasn't the best first impression, being shirtless kind of made up for it. She certainly wasn't looking at him in a clinically concerned way, and it made me smile. Rachel was a free spirit and loved life. She didn't mean anything when she looked, but I could sense it made Clay a little uncomfortable. I shivered again. Perfect timing.

"Are you sure you should be going?" she asked, managing to look away from Clay.

"Yeah, Clay's going to pack for me, and then we'll go. Oh, and he came by last night, saw the dog out, and took him home. We'll take him with, so don't worry."

I closed the bathroom door on both of them and focused on pulling myself together. I splashed some water on my face, leaned heavily on the sink, and ran my fingers through the snarls. It didn't help much, but I didn't think it would matter anyway with a long drive ahead of us. I took care of business and shuffled out of the bathroom to look for shoes, not concerned about changing.

Clay came in from the back door before I could make it to the hall closet. He took one look at my chattering teeth and scooped me up in his arms.

My squeal brought Rachel from her room before Clay could make it out the door.

"When you're feeling better, let's talk about rental rates," she called after us with a snicker. "And I'm not talking about the house!"

A blanket waited for me in the front seat of the warmed car. My bulging messenger bag, packed to the point of bursting, sat on the back seat. I twisted, grabbed the cell phone from it while Clay closed my door, then I buckled up. My fuzzy slippers were on the floor, but I curled my legs under me instead and pulled the blanket snuggly around me.

He slid in behind the wheel and took some time to better tuck the blanket around me. His hand smoothed over mine briefly before he pulled away and backed out of the driveway. I struggled to keep my eyes open. Sleep pulled at me.

"I don't want to keep going on like this," I said once we cleared town.

His hands noticeably tightened on the steering wheel, and I could have smacked my forehead if it wasn't already hurting so badly.

"I don't mean being with you. I like that. But I don't like seeing you bruised."

He loosened his tight hold on the wheel and glanced at me. A smile twitched his lips. I scowled at him.

"There's nothing amusing about it. I don't like worrying."

I lifted my cell, dialed Sam's number, and struggled to hold the phone to my ear. My arm trembled from the effort. Sam picked up during the first ring. I didn't wait for his greeting.

"I'm on my way. Put out a call for tonight only." I hung up before he could speak. I wasn't ready to talk to him. He'd hurt me too much with his last appearance.

I tossed the phone on the back seat and ignored it when it started to vibrate again. My gaze drifted to Clay. He looked outright pissed now. He knew who I'd called and what I intended. I hurried to explain.

"It's not what you think, Clay. I don't want to do another Introduction, but something happened last night. I went out with Rachel to a club downtown, not my best decision, but I think I've figured out what's going on with me." I shivered and pulled the blanket tighter around me. Sleep continued to tug at me.

"Remember the party with Nicole? When I touched her, I gave

her a huge shock. That happened again last night. I think I can transfer my gift, that thing with guys, to other people. I didn't know how it happened the first time. But I think I've figured it out.

"Last night, these two women at the club had been on their own until Rachel and I—and the groupies I'd collected—joined them. When we made to leave, the women had been so disappointed. They knew the guys would walk away when we did. I felt so bad for them that I went to...I don't know...pat them, I guess. I'd just meant it as an 'I'm sorry' gesture, but then it happened again just like before. A huge shock." My words started to slur, and I had a hard time keeping my thoughts coherent.

"Both times I was thinking about how I wished I could help find the person they were meant to be with. And I think that's the key." I noticed the speedometer hovered ten miles over what I considered a safe speed, but I didn't comment on it. "I don't understand why I can see the lights, but I know it must be all tied together because when I try to use my sight, it hurts. Really bad." Clay's expression hadn't changed, and I realized I'd skipped the explanation of why I'd agreed to an Introduction.

"Oh, yeah. Before I shocked those two, a Forlorn came up behind me and started a conversation. My fish finder still worked then. There were more of them in the crowd, Clay. The one talking to me said he just wanted a chance to say hi. He was very persistent, so I told him I would see them at the Compound for an official Introduction. They left right after but gave me the impression that if I didn't show up, they'd come looking for me. I got the feeling they'd been pushed too far." I watched his face. "Has it been the same werewolves trying to see me, or is it always different?"

He didn't answer, but I didn't really expect him to. I sighed and snaked a hand out from under the blanket to touch his leg.

"It hurts to see you like this, Clay. If I have to put up with an Introduction to keep you safe, then that's what I'll do." My lids refused to cooperate any longer and drifted shut.

"I'm sorry, Clay," I mumbled sleepily. "I wish I could just get over my need for freedom and Claim you. We both know you're the one. I just don't want to lose myself."

I fell asleep without looking at him to see his reaction.

I WAS SURROUNDED by darkness and in a bed. Clay had carried me around while I slept again.

"Clay?" I whispered, reaching out to feel the mattress beside me. Empty.

Sam's voice came from nearby. "You're safe, Gabby. At the Compound."

"Where's Clay?" I asked, trying to wake fully.

"In the unMated's wing. I was surprised he chose to stay there. After I kicked him out of here, I thought he'd go to the woods."

Sam's words annoyed me. How dare he kick Clay out. He had no right.

Still tired, I could have easily fallen back asleep. Instead, I struggled into a sitting position to keep myself awake.

"You don't know anything about him," I muttered, using Sam's own words. "Can you turn on a light, please? I can't see."

The lamp next to the bed clicked on. Sam sat in a chair near the bed. He looked worn, but I didn't feel very sympathetic. I looked around. I wasn't in the same room I usually occupied, but I didn't bother asking why.

"What time is it?"

He glanced at his watch then met my eyes again.

"Just after seven. You look worse than sick. Charlene came in to look at you. You have us all worried. Are you going to tell me what's happened to you?"

Of course, they were worried. They'd promised their horde an Introduction.

"Nope, I won't. Did you put out the call? Did anyone respond?"

He didn't care for my answer, but let it go. "Yes, there's about fifty or so. There were more, but we explained that you were ill and wouldn't be able to—"

"Put the call out again." Why did he choose now to care about my wellbeing? "They have an hour to get here. Get Clay for me, please." I swung my legs out from under the blankets and started to get up.

Sam moved in a blur of speed and pushed me back down, his hand on my collarbone. He didn't have to use much force. I flopped back onto the pillow and glared at him. He kept his hand on me for a moment, probably waiting for me to try again. As if I could move a werewolf.

"I get it, Gabby. I disappointed you and lost your trust, but you're sick. This isn't what I asked for when I said you'd be better off doing Introductions at the Compound." His voice turned gruff. "Please, don't push yourself like this. You'll get worse."

His expression and pleading tone swayed me enough to take pity on him. I patted his cheek sadly and half-smiled.

"Not everything is about you, Sam. Yes, I'm still mad at you, but this is about Clay and me. I don't want to see him hurt because he's trying to fight other werewolves away from me. Now, help me up, and go get Clay." I held out my hands, and he reluctantly helped pull me to my feet.

Wobbling a bit, I made my way to my bag that lay at the foot of the bed. Sam shook his head as he watched my determined, but slow, progress. I sat on the mattress and pulled the bag toward me. With a sigh, he left to go get Clay while I rummaged through my messenger bag.

I was still digging in the bag when Clay walked in without knocking. He didn't walk past the threshold, though. Concern filled his expression when I looked up. I lifted my hand from the bag and let the bikini I'd found dangle from one finger.

"Really, Clay? You're killing me. Where are my jeans?"

His lips twitched with a smile as he leaned against the frame, content to watch me dig through the bag some more.

Despite my playful greeting, I felt winded and dizzy again. Shocking both of those girls took more out of me than I'd anticipated. I'd expected to feel much better by now like I had the last time. The shocks hadn't seemed as strong as Nicole's had, but perhaps because it had split between the two of them, it drained me more.

At least my head didn't hurt. I took a break from my search to look up at the fading bruises on Clay's face. He still wore his hair back. I loved seeing his face.

He must have seen something in my gaze because he pushed away from the door and moved closer. He stopped in front of me and, without breaking eye contact, reached into my bag and pulled out a pair of jeans. He held them out to me and tapped his lips.

I smiled widely. "A kiss for the jeans?"

He nodded. I grabbed the jeans from his loose grasp and tossed them on the bed.

He watched me, curious, as I stood and placed my hands on his chest for balance.

"I don't need bribes to kiss you, Clay. Come here."

His lips covered mine in a move so fast my head spun even more. I clutched his shirt in my fists, not sure if it was his kiss or my condition that caused the current wave of dizziness. His arms circled around me. I felt safe. And so desired. I pressed myself closer, and he increased the pressure on my lips. His warm breath fanned my face. One of his hands roamed up to curve around the back of my neck.

My heart skipped a beat, and my breathing became more erratic. I knew he'd hear, but I didn't care. Standing on my tiptoes, I loosened my hold on his shirt and slid my hands up and around his neck. I didn't want him to let go just yet.

Tentatively, I opened my mouth and ran my tongue across his bottom lip. He growled, and his hold tightened fractionally. A thrill shot through me, heating my limbs and tickling my stomach. I used my tongue again. His mouth opened in response. He took control of the kiss and turned it from tender-sweet to passionately melting. Our tongues touched. I stopped breathing. My world tilted then steadied. He anchored me. How could I doubt this? Us?

My lungs burned for air, and he gently pulled away even though I whined in protest. He kissed my cheek then my forehead.

It took a minute for the world to right itself again while I caught my breath. Clay placed his chin on my head and held me tight. My head rested on his chest over his thundering heart. The kiss had affected him as much as it had me. It made me smile because now I knew, without a doubt, *I* attracted him, not my strange pull.

I heard the apartment door open and figured it was Sam. With regret, I pulled back, and Clay let me go. I looked up at Clay.

"Can you come with me for this, or will that cause more problems?"

"It would be best if he stayed away, Gabby," Sam answered from the doorway behind Clay.

I moved around Clay to look at Sam. "I didn't ask what was best. Best went out the window years ago, Sam, when 'making do' moved in. Is he allowed?"

Sam flinched when I repeated his words then ran his hand over his face. The move muffled his sigh.

"It's allowed. He's unMated, but he's considered rejected. He'll be challenged by everyone for his place in the Introduction order."

I made a non-committal noise and looked at Clay. "Do you want to be there?"

He nodded sharply.

"All right then. Sam, please head over and get things ready. Clay will walk me there. Clay, I just need to change then I'm ready."

Both men stared at me as if I'd grown horns. I knew I looked like hell. I was probably still pale and definitely had a worse tangled mass of hair than I had that morning. But, it didn't matter.

Sam wanted an Introduction, and I wanted peace for Clay. I arched a brow at both of them.

Sam grumbled to himself as he left. Clay followed and closed the door softly behind him, leaving me to dress. I smoothed down my hair, not really caring, and changed into a shirt and jeans. My legs shook by the time I finished, and I had to sit on the bed for a minute.

I took a fortifying breath, stood, and made my way out to the living room. Clay waited for me by the kitchenette. He had a glass of orange juice ready for me. He knew me well. I smiled my thanks and gulped it down. It felt good and gave me a tiny energy boost.

"I need just a minute in the bathroom. Can you find my shoes for me?" I held the wall as I made my way there and leaned on the sink while I brushed my teeth. As I brushed, I dwelled on the fact that Sam had kicked Clay out of my room. If it weren't for the long drive, I'd insist we leave right after the Introduction. But I knew Clay needed sleep soon, too. I wondered what Sam would do when I insisted that Clay sleep next to me later. He was warm and comforting, and I needed both desperately.

Clay stood right outside the door when I opened it. My slippers waited on the floor by his feet.

"Where are my shoes?"

He shrugged and pointed to the slippers. Hey, he'd packed for me and remembered the jeans. He'd even packed underclothes and a toothbrush. If he forgot the shoes, I really had no complaint. I stepped into the slippers then squeaked when my world spun, and I suddenly found myself in his arms.

"I can walk, Clay."

He shook his head and carried me to the door. There, he repositioned me to one arm and opened the door while I clung tightly to his neck. I rather liked the feeling. With an arm wrapped around him, I leaned my head against his shoulder and ran my fingers through his hair.

The few people in the hallways stopped and stared as we

passed. At the intersection of halls, which led to the Introduction room, I stopped Clay.

"No, go outside and around back. I won't go into that room ever again." As childish as it might be, I wanted something about the impending Introduction to be on my own terms.

He grunted in acknowledgment. But, instead of turning to go out the nearby back door, he backtracked to the main entrance. He set me on my feet, snagged a spare jacket from one of the hooks, and carefully buttoned me in. I studied his face as he concentrated on each snap. Always thinking of me. When he finished, he scooped me back into his arms. I didn't protest.

Bundled warmly in a thick coat, I didn't cringe when he carried me out into the cold. The sky was dark, and the yard light didn't reach very far. Clay carried me toward the back of the building. I couldn't hear the werewolves as we approached but saw their sparks briefly before a sharp pain not so gently reminded me not to look. I guessed close to seventy-five waited out there. It meant some of them had returned.

"Put me down, Clay," I said before we rounded the corner of the building. "I'll walk now." I didn't want to give the waiting unMated any reason to believe this wasn't a fair Introduction, even though it really wasn't. I still felt the pull for Clay.

Clay hesitated. It'd be safer for both of us if I stayed in his arms. He wouldn't fight, and I wouldn't fall. Yet, despite my anger over another forced Introduction, I truly felt sorry for the men who waited. The Introduction was just a false hope. One I couldn't take away from them.

"It'll be okay Clay. There are a lot of fast people here. I won't fall on my face." I spoke normally so everyone could hear. I really didn't want to fall on my face.

As soon as he set me on my feet, I walked around the corner with my shoulders back and head held high, determined to look strong. The slippers probably ruined the image, but I pretended otherwise.

The Elders stood by the back door.

"I'm Gabby. There will be no Introduction order. I won't have anyone left out or leaving without a fair chance. So, instead of the stuffy cabin, let's just do this out here." The warmth of the jacket when not supplemented by Clay wasn't adequate, and I started to shiver slightly. "I believe the Elders mentioned I was ill, so if I start to stammer, bear with me."

The men began to line up. So many looking for a Mate, and this was just a fraction of what was really out there. Some were too far away to answer such a short notice call. I wondered how many of their kind I still hadn't met.

I met the eyes of several as I walked slowly down the not yet fully formed, long line. As I'd anticipated, the shivers grew more noticeable. This time the tremors were due to the cold, not my fatigue, and I fought not to duck further into my jacket. They needed to smell me. I kept walking and listened to Clay keep pace with me, just a few steps behind. Several of those I passed glanced at Clay, but no one actually commented on his presence.

Walking helped warm me a little. While the shivering didn't go away, it at least didn't increase.

A few exceptionally young werewolves stood mixed in the line. I smiled kindly at each of them. For the most part, I paced in front of the line as if I performed a quiet military inspection. The males scented me as discreetly as possible, so hopeful for some type of connection. Many walked away after I passed.

About halfway down the line, I noticed a man step back and retreat into the woods. No unMated male walked away from an Introduction before being Introduced. It just wasn't done. The possibility of meeting a Mate was too important to them. Suspicious, I used my other sight despite the knowledge it would hurt. I pushed myself to look as far as I was able and gasped. A jolt of pain pierced my temple and forced me to close my other sight. My hand flew to my head, cradling it.

Clay moved so quickly my hair lifted in his breeze. He stood close enough that I felt his heat at my back. I forced myself to straighten. The werewolf I faced looked confused. His eyes moved to the Elders standing several steps behind us.

"Gabby," Sam began, but I held up a hand.

"A moment, please," I managed to say.

Although it'd been a brief glimpse, I had seen a blue-grey spark moving away from our group. In the distance, three other blue-grey sparks waited. I couldn't say anything to Clay since I held everyone's attention, but I glanced at him. He studied the worry on my face for a moment then looked around. I felt safer because of it but still wished I could reach out to take his hand.

Instead, I turned to the men in front of me.

"I'm sorry. Like I said, I'm not feeling well. The pain in my head just took me by surprise." I took a steadying breath and continued my slow progress. The werewolves I passed watched me with concern. I probably looked even worse than I had just a moment ago.

More than halfway down the line, I came across a face I knew. He studied me, his playful smile from our last meeting absent. I used him as an excuse to stop and rest for a minute. I'd started shaking again, not from the cold.

"A f-face I know. I'm here as p-promised."

His eyes turned slightly remorseful at my words.

"I see that, little one. Although, it looks like you should be in bed instead."

"I would b-be if people would j-just leave me alone." I felt bad for saying it as soon as it left my mouth. How many times had these men stood in line, hoping to meet some faceless girl? "B-but it's not meant t-to be. So, you know my name, but I d-don't know yours." I made conversation to make up for my harsh comment.

"Luke Taylor, love." He offered his hand, politely. A human custom, not a werewolf one. With my pull gone, could I safely touch him without causing some type of obsession? I hesitated and studied his face. He'd been desperate at the club, but now he looked resigned. He knew I wasn't the one for him.

Feeling sorry for him, I accepted his hand. A mild shock went through me to him.

Time stopped as my vision tunneled. The world around me disappeared, swallowed by darkness until only a pinprick of light remained. Then the darkness exploded into a spark-filled view of the world in its entirety. The tiny lights dazzled me. The yellow-green of humanity almost consumed the world. However, diversity persisted, though small.

Slowly, the sparks of each human, werewolf, and the yet unexplained blue-grey winked out of existence until a single, faint spark tinted with a violet halo remained on the east coast. My focus changed, honing in on that light. Like reading a map, I saw its exact location. My eyes swam in the yellow-violet light for a moment. Then, with a snap like an elastic band breaking, I returned to myself.

My lungs sucked in a breath with a loud whoosh, and my heart hammered in my chest. I ached all over and felt like vomiting. Only Luke's steady, warm hand, desperately clutched in my own, anchored me and kept me from falling apart.

Clay paced directly behind me. I vaguely imagined he wouldn't like me holding another man's hand for so long. I met Luke's gaze and swallowed down my bile before attempting to speak. He eyed me warily.

"I need to talk to you. Don't leave until I do."

His brow rose in surprise at my heavily slurred words.

"Clay," I whispered. My head lolled to the side as I tried to catch his eye. "Catch me." I let go of Luke's hand, and the world disappeared.

MY POUNDING HEAD WOKE ME. I couldn't tell if I lay in a dark room or just had my eyes closed. It didn't really matter. My skull would certainly shatter if I had to deal with light, too. I tried to whisper for water but only managed a faint croak. When I attempted to clear my throat, the pain in my head brought tears to my eyes. I was dying. I had to be to feel this way.

An arm gently slid under my neck and lifted my head a bit. A cool glass pressed to my lips, and I slowly sipped the contents. I stopped when the darkness began to pull me down again.

I WOKE SEVERAL MORE TIMES, only drinking a bit of water before passing out again. Each time the pain in my head decreased a little until, finally, I woke with more clarity.

"Water," I whispered into the darkness.

Again, an arm snaked under me and lifted me for a cool drink. I drained the cup. The arm lowered me, and I settled back onto the pillow. My ears rang in the silence.

"How long have I been sleeping?" I asked just to hear something.

Instead of an answer, I got a tight hug.

"I really hope you're Clay," I whispered breathlessly.

His gruff laugh wrapped around me just as comforting as his hug.

"Can we turn on a light?"

He moved away from me, and I took the opportunity to sit up a bit and lean against the headboard. My legs still felt shaky.

The bedside lamp clicked on. I squinted against the light and regretted my request. My head ached slightly. I rubbed a hand over my face as my eyes watered. A tangle of my hair got in my way. I brushed it aside and felt the knots in it.

Blinking several times, I finally focused on Clay. He was dressed in the same clothes he'd worn outside. Maybe I hadn't been out that long after all. He stood near the bed and watched me with a tender, relieved expression.

"Clay, I think I know what's going on. Can you help me up? I really need a shower." And a toothbrush.

He shook his head.

"Clay, now's not the time to put your foot down. This is really important." I tried to sit all the way up but couldn't. My head started to throb again. "Okay. Maybe you're right," I mumbled as I rubbed my forehead. "Can you get me something for my head, please? It feels like it's going to explode all over the walls."

Clay leaned over me, smoothed back my hair, kissed my forehead, then left the room. The guest apartments didn't have any type of medicine in them because the werewolves typically didn't need it.

I waited until I heard the outside door close then struggled up again. My comment about my head was absolutely true. Therefore, I stayed in a sitting position for a minute before attempting to swing my legs off the bed. However, headache or not, I needed to speak to Luke.

Reaching for my bag, I smiled again at Clay's attempt at packing for me. Flannel pants and a t-shirt were perfect, after all.

I USED THE PANELED WALL FOR SUPPORT AS I MADE MY WAY TO THE bathroom. Sweat beaded my forehead when I finally stepped onto the cold, tiled floor. I flicked on the light and fan then set my clothes on the toilet tank.

Knowing I had limited time, I immediately turned the shower on to let the water warm. I moved to the sink, caught my reflection in the mirror, and cringed. Sunken eyes, hollow cheeks, and hair that stuck out at varying angles reflected back at me. Without a doubt, Clay really did care about me. I shook my head then brushed my teeth, giving the water an extra minute to heat.

When I finished, I struggled out of my clothes and further depleted my waning energy. I eyed the high edge of the tub and thought back to when Clay had insisted on helping me. If I fell, I'd never hear the end of it. Bracing myself, I successfully stepped over the edge and tugged the curtain closed.

The hot spray felt great, but I didn't pause to warm up. If I stayed too long, I'd lose what little energy I had or Clay would discover me. I grabbed the all-in-one hair wash and lathered my natty head. My arms grew heavy as I rinsed, and with relief, I turned off the water. Navigating the high edge proved more difficult the second time, and I clutched at the wall after a near fall.

The fan worked to suck the built-up heat and steam from the room as I hurried to dry off. My unsteady legs forced me to sit down to finish dressing. The cold helped hurry the process.

I used my towel to bundle my dirty clothes then moved to the door. Though it felt like the process took forever, I knew only a few minutes had passed since Clay left. If I could get to my room and dry my hair, I'd be home free. I pulled open the door and yelped. The steady thump in my head increased its tempo.

Clay stood just outside the door, leaning against the wall. He held a glass of water in one hand and two pills in the other. I tried to read his face, but he kept it perfectly blank. I hoped that meant he wasn't angry with me. Desperate to relieve the pain in my head, I released my death grip on the door and gulped down the pills.

When I tried handing him the empty glass, he shook his head and picked me up again. My feet had been getting cold, anyway. Holding the empty glass, I sighed and rested my head against his chest.

He went toward my room, and I almost complained until I saw what he'd done. He'd changed the sheets and remade the bed. Socks, slippers, and my hairbrush lay on the quilt, waiting. He'd known I would go for the shower and had given me privacy even though he hadn't wanted me to get out of bed. Not only that, but he'd gotten everything ready for when I finished.

I looked at him. He studied me, his arms still securely around me. I leaned in, kissed his cheek tenderly, and hesitated there. He smelled so good. I just wanted to curl back up with him. But I couldn't. I pulled back and looked at him again.

"You are so sweet, and I truly appreciate this, but I'm not going back to bed, Clay. I need to see Luke."

The muscles in his jaw clenched as he stepped into the room and carefully set me on the bed. He left without a backward glance.

I stared at the empty doorway, puzzled, until the outer door slammed hard enough that I heard the wood crack. I flinched.

"I shouldn't have said I needed to see Luke."

I hurried to put on my socks and slippers while hoping Clay wouldn't go too far. The movement made my head feel like it would fall off at any moment. The pills needed to kick in soon. I rubbed my brow again, but it didn't relieve the pain at all. This wasn't a normal headache. I just needed to deal with it. With a sigh, I stood.

I'd only made it to the living room when the door burst open again. I stared at Clay as he dragged Luke in by the cuff of one pant leg. Luke didn't appear to mind. Instead, he was laughing. His hands clutched the waistband of his pants to keep Clay from pulling them off entirely. After they cleared the threshold, I saw a crowd watching from the hallway. Not good. News of this would get back to the Elders. No doubt Sam would want to talk to me as soon as he found out I was awake. I moved from the couch to the door and slammed it closed. The poor door would need some repair work.

Clay reached the middle of the room, dropped Luke's leg, and without pause, turned back to the door. I didn't move away from the exit. He reached for the knob without meeting my gaze, but I stopped him with a hand held up.

"Clay, I need you to stay and listen. Please."

He still didn't look at me, and I knew asking to speak with Luke had hurt him. Why wouldn't it? Had I really ever given him much hope we had a future together? Sam showed up at our door just days ago, saying I'd rejected Clay and needed to do the Introductions again. Instead of putting my foot down, we went back. Granted, I'd told Clay I didn't like to see him hurt and admitted we both knew he was the one for me, but we hadn't talked about what we'd do about it.

"Please," I said again when he hadn't moved. "Give me a chance." I touched his face and forced him to meet my gaze. "I've asked so much of you already and know it's not fair to ask again, but I am." I chose my words carefully aware of our audience inside the apartment and in the hall.

He sighed, reached up to cup my face, and gently smoothed his thumb over my cheek. A tender look crept into his eyes before he abruptly dropped his hands, turned, and headed toward the still laughing Luke. Clay dragged his feet as he stepped over Luke. Luke grunted when a foot connected with his ribs, and his laughter started to quiet.

As Clay settled on the chair against the wall, Luke sat up.

"Most people wouldn't laugh while being dragged through the Compound like that." I stayed by the door because I didn't want either of them leaving. I knew I couldn't stop them physically even on my best day, but I'd cry if I had to.

Luke stood and turned toward Clay with a grin, ignoring me to taunt Clay.

"I've never seen anyone hold a transformation like that. He was man, but the fangs, ears, fur...it was amazing and hilarious, mate," he said as he settled himself on the couch.

"Um, isn't that a sign that he's in an extreme emotional state?" I asked Luke. He didn't appear to hear me.

I walked behind Luke and smacked him hard on the back of the head. It really hurt my hand, but it got his attention.

"Meaning, you should stop trying to annoy him."

Since Clay sat across from Luke, I moved to Clay and gingerly perched on one of his knees. He held still for a moment then his hands gripped my hips. He pulled back so I fully sat on his lap and turned me so we could both see Luke. Much better than sitting in my own chair. Warmer, too.

Having successfully gained both their attentions, I decided to get to the point.

"Luke, what happened when I touched you? What did you feel?"

"One hell of a shock. Listen, did you bring me here for a reason, or was it just to rub your relationship with him in my face?" Luke nodded at Clay, and though Luke's usual smile still curved his lips, his words conveyed the agitation he tried to hide.

"It's for a reason." I tried to lean forward, but Clay wrapped his arms loosely around my waist. He didn't give an inch, and I didn't fight it. I'd pushed him enough for the night...or day. I still didn't know how long I'd been out.

"How long have I been sleeping?"

"Two days, love. Everyone's been pretty worried, and the Elders are waiting to talk to you."

"I bet." My eyes drifted to the door. I focused and immediately cradled my throbbing head. My eyes watered as I tried to breathe through the pain. "Crap."

Behind me, Clay grunted in annoyance.

Luke's smile slipped. "Listen, I think you should still be in bed, little one. No disrespect intended, but you don't look well."

My hair hung wet and uncombed around me. I could imagine what I looked like. I pressed my cool fingertips to one temple and wished I hadn't been so stupid. Clay started to rub my back soothingly, working his way up to my neck and then lightly stroking my hair. It helped.

"I know you're right, but I can't go back to sleep yet. I need you to tell me what happened."

Nicole told me that she'd really connected with Randy. Even after my pull wore off, they had continued to date. I couldn't go back to the two women at the club to find out what they'd experienced. I needed to get more information from Luke.

"I don't know what happened, love. You shocked me, told me not to leave, then fainted. After that, Clay picked you up and ran inside with you. He hasn't let anyone near you for two days. We only knew you were still alive because he didn't take off into the woods."

Clay's tight hug when I woke up made more sense. He'd been worried about me, taking care of me and keeping the Elders away.

I forced myself to stay focused on Luke.

"And after Clay left, what about you? What did you do?"

Luke began to look uncomfortable. "Uh, I went out for a bit then came back here."

"The constant attention probably went to your head," I muttered. Luke was too sure of himself for any woman to have a chance.

His startled expression told me I was right.

"Did you meet anyone special while I was out?" I asked, glancing at the door again and wishing we didn't have an audience.

I looked back in time to catch Luke shaking his head. Still unMated. I'd thought as much but had to be sure. Normal humans wouldn't tempt him, and there were too few unMated females at the Compound. I had an idea but needed sleep and time to think through everything.

"Luke, there is so much I don't understand, and I really need your help." I nodded toward the door and hoped he'd know I meant with the Elders who probably waited outside. "I need some time to myself to understand what I'm feeling." This is why Clay had to be in the room with me. Anyone standing in the hall would probably think I felt torn between Clay and Luke.

Luke looked from me to Clay then back again. He started to ask a question, hesitated, then gazed at the door once more. Finally, he stood.

"I'll be around," he said.

I hoped he'd understood I wanted his help to get us out of here. The door had barely closed behind him when a knock sounded.

Still sitting on Clay's lap, I turned to him. He met my gaze. I shook my head and wrapped my arms around his neck. His arms cradled me as he stood and carried me to the bedroom. He set me on the bed, covered me, then closed the door. I listened to him answer the apartment door.

I heard Sam's voice but didn't bother trying to hear what Sam had to say. The Elders would come to get me soon enough. My exhaustion didn't wait for them. I fell asleep again.

MY STOMACH GROWLED SO LOUDLY it woke me. I listened for a minute before opening my eyes. Clay had left the lamp on so I could see. I turned my head. He lay next to me, on top of the covers. Given the steady cadence of his breathing, he still slept. I let my mind drift, content to think and let him get the rest he needed.

Whatever ability I had was something I could temporarily pass to people via a shock, but the effect only lasted until I recovered. I could also zap more than one person at a time, and I felt certain now that my emotions, in addition to my touch, triggered the transfer. The drain I experienced afterward varied. It felt like the flu the first time, but when I passed it to the two women, the symptoms intensified.

Shocking Luke had been different. I couldn't say if the drain had been worse since I'd started out drained. However, focusing on a specific person's spark was new.

Based on the yellow-violet coloring, I guessed it belonged to another compatible, like me. Could it mean my ability was to find Mates for the people I touched? But then, why hadn't I zoomed in on a single person when touching the others? Maybe a werewolf amplified my ability, and the view appeared whether I wanted it or not. Or maybe one spark had stood out when I'd touched the rest, but I hadn't focused on my spark-sight to check.

But what about my pull? Where did that play into this? There were still too many possibilities. I needed a test group. Immediately, I thought of Rachel and Peter. When I sensed them without touching Rachel, I knew they were a perfect match. If I tried to pass my pull to Rachel and saw Peter's spark, I'd have my answer. If it didn't work on them, I wouldn't rule out my theory completely. The difference between human and werewolf might be the key to the results. I could experiment on Clay. He knew I was his match.

In addition to figuring out why I had the ability to pass on my gift, I needed to understand why I saw different werewolf colors. The one who'd left the line and the others waiting for him worried me.

Regardless of my anger at Sam, if trouble stalked the pack, he needed to know. But I needed to talk to Clay about it before I could talk to anyone else. He would help me figure out how it all tied together. However, I couldn't talk to Clay here. There were too many ears, and I was still uncertain if I could trust Sam with everything.

I needed to leave before the Elders started pushing me for answers I didn't have. What reason could I give Sam for my sudden faint during the Introduction? He'd know any lie before I told it. And if I gave him the truth, would he then share it with all the Elders? After seeing those werewolves leave the Introduction, I couldn't blindly trust Elder Joshua. Too many werewolves of that same color acted unusually.

Feeling a light caress on my hair, I turned to look at Clay, who watched me again.

"Do I say good morning, or is it close to goodnight again?"

He smiled at me, reached down to twine his fingers through mine, and brought my hand to his mouth. Instead of kissing it, he whipped his head toward the door. A silent snarl pulled back his lips. The bedroom door opened, and Luke poked his head in.

"Better hurry. You carry her, and I'll grab her things," he said, speaking directly to Clay.

I let out a relieved breath. Luke had understood and come through. I opened my mouth to thank him, but Clay leapt off the bed and quickly scooped me into his arms, covers and all. With the blankets twisted around me and partially covering my face, I felt a moment of disoriented panic as he lifted me.

I shook my head to dislodge the blanket and sent Clay a quick scowl. His lips twitched.

Over his shoulder, I saw Luke cramming my things into my ragged messenger bag. My bag wouldn't last through another werewolf packing.

Clay left the room. Just in case anyone else roamed the halls, I laid my head on Clay's shoulder. He held me close and walked quickly. We quietly made it out the main entrance with Luke following us.

The black sky twinkled with stars, and crickets conversed with their night song as the two werewolves stealthily moved over the graveled parking area. It had to be Monday night. I regretted missing a day's worth of classes, but there'd been no way to help it.

The car faced the gate. Luke must have moved it. The door's loud creaking groan made us all cringe. Clay quickly settled me inside, reached across me to secure the seat belt, then silently jogged around the hood to get in behind the wheel.

Luke handed me my bag then moved to close the door. I motioned for him to wait and dug in a side pocket of my bag for a pencil stub and paper. In those few moments after I shocked him and before I passed out, I'd gleaned some information about the person I saw. Whoever she was, Luke needed to find her and help me understand if some of my suspicions were right. Was she like me? Was she his Mate?

I jotted him a hasty note and handed it to him with a wave. He quickly closed the door. I hoped giving him the information was the right thing to do. I barely knew him. Would he even try to find her or just hand the information over to an Elder? Worried, I looked at him through the window. He didn't see me. His eyes scanned my note. He crumpled it in his hand and spun toward a waiting motorcycle.

Clay pulled away from the Compound, spitting gravel with the tires. The motorcycle roared to life and quickly zipped past us. Luke saluted me with a wicked grin then disappeared from sight. I peeked in the side mirror and caught the reason for their loud exit. Sam stood on the porch, his gaze locked on us. He grew smaller as we sped away. I wished I knew whom to trust.

I laid my head back and closed my eyes. What a crappy Introduction weekend. The worst yet. I hoped there were no more in my future.

The drone of the engine and the soothing vibrations of the tires put me right to sleep. I dozed the whole way home, waking when Clay lifted me from the car. With blankets still twisted around me, he carried me to my room and gently set me on the bed.

A few minutes later, he settled next to me. It didn't matter anymore if he wore his fur or stayed as a man. He remained with me. It was enough.

CLAY TRIED to keep me home Tuesday. First, he planted himself, in his fur, in front of my door so I couldn't get out of the bedroom. Then, when I pleaded to use the bathroom, he allowed me out and took the opportunity to hide my keys.

My suspicion rose when he calmly watched me get ready. I discovered that the keys were missing and resorted to further pleading. I explained my need to talk to Nicole in hopes of piecing together the puzzle of my abilities. The one-sided conversation reminded me of the first time I'd reasoned with him.

Of course, Rachel caught part of my serious chat with our dog and did a double-take on her way to the bathroom. I laughed and waved her away then gave Clay a look. Grudgingly, Clay led me to my keys, and I made it to campus on time.

I parked and took a minute to lean my forehead against the steering wheel, still recovering from sharing my ability with three people in one weekend. Clay had obviously sensed it. If Tuesday hadn't been the only day I saw Nicole, I would have stayed in bed. Steeling myself, I got out of the car and trudged across campus.

For the first time ever, I didn't pay much attention to the instructor. Instead, I sat by Nicole and whispered questions freely but failed to uncover anything more than what she'd already shared. Men had hit on her quite a bit after the Halloween party. She attributed the attention to the costume, which she planned to reuse. Since it wasn't a bad costume, I didn't dissuade her from the idea. Better to think it was the costume than a freak friend passing some kind of power to her.

I smiled and waved goodbye to her at the end of the class. People pushed past me to leave. I watched them go and dreaded the long walk back to the car. With my pull gone, thanks to Luke and two strangers, I could safely ask someone for a piggyback ride. I'd seen it happen before. Yet, I couldn't picture explaining to Clay why I smelled like another guy.

RACHEL AND CLAY-THE-MAN stood in the kitchen together making an early dinner. Surprised, I hesitated in the doorway. Rachel typically spent her free time with Peter or at work. And Clay tended to stay in his fur when she was home.

Rachel paused her one-sided conversation to wink at me. I glanced at Clay, stepped farther into the room, and slowly closed the door behind me. Clay remained focused on the food he stirred in the pan. Rachel walked past me on her way to get silverware.

"You didn't tell me he could *cook*," Rachel stage whispered.

Giving her a crooked smile, I made my way to a kitchen chair. I was exhausted.

"He cooks, he cleans, he warms up my feet at night, and he keeps the toilet seat down...so hands off. He's mine."

Rachel laughed, and Clay turned to give me an undecipherable look. I had a feeling he liked the "mine" part.

"How you feeling?" Rachel said, coming over to touch my forehead. "I asked Clay, but he didn't say." Rachel gave Clay a pointed look. Clay shrugged and went back to cooking at the stove.

"Not the best, but it's getting better. I think it's mental exhaustion, nothing contagious."

"Mm," she said in a noncommittal way as she eyed me speculatively. "I still think you should go to the doctor. Could it be something you didn't think of yet?" She casually leaned close to me. "Pregnant?" she whispered.

Clay dropped the spoon. It hit the stove and bounced back at him. He caught it tight after a close fumble. Both Rachel and I stared at his back, but with dignity, he stayed facing the stove and kept cooking.

I turned back to Rachel with a wide smile. "No. Now, behave."

We ate dinner companionably. After we finished, they shoved me out of the kitchen with orders to rest while they cleaned up. I went to my room and changed into my lounge clothes while listening to Rachel tell Clay about a cute pair of shoes she'd found. It made me smile. She would never break him. He'd never talk.

Dinner, though delicious and entertaining, had drained my reserves. I lay on top of the comforter, thinking I'd rest for a bit before I tackled that day's homework. I still needed to talk to Clay about what I'd seen in the woods at the Introduction.

SUNLIGHT PENETRATED the darkness behind my eyelids. I no longer sprawled sideways on the bed on top of the comforter but underneath it, snugly tucked in. Clay sat up in the space next to me, pillows stacked behind him as he read a book. His posture didn't fool me. He really sat there to watch over me while I slept. I knew with an unexplainable certainty that he would never leave me again.

"Good morning," I said, pulling the covers up to my chin. Thanks to Rachel-the-heat-miser, the room felt cool, but I enjoyed lower rent.

Clay closed his book as soon as I woke and turned to examine me.

"I want to talk to you but keep falling asleep. If I do it again, wake me up." I smiled at him when he pulled me close to snuggle against him. It was much warmer that way.

"During the Introduction when I said my head hurt, I saw a man step away from the line. I know how your kind view Introductions. It didn't seem right, so I peeked at his spark. It hurt like hell, but I saw he had the same color light as Elder Joshua and the wolf that'd attacked us. I thought maybe it could be the same guy, that he needed to leave because you'd recognize his scent. Then I saw three more, farther away. Something's going on, but I can't figure out what.

"I know you didn't stay with the pack full-time, but did you ever notice any of them acting different?"

He shook his head, actually giving me a direct answer. It should have made me happy. Instead, I sighed. I still didn't have a clue.

He gently stroked my hair as I thought it through. "If only I could trust Sam. If I could ask him questions about Elder Joshua without him repeating them, I might be able to figure this thing out."

My head started to hurt again. Maybe if I stopped thinking about it so much, the answer would just come to me.

SAM CALLED my cell the following weekend. I'd expected to hear from him much sooner. He surprised me by asking if I'd come back to the Compound over the long holiday weekend. I hedged. Did he want me to return so he could arrange another Introduction?

When I didn't give a definitive answer, he launched into a long speech about how he knew he'd disappointed me and how he really did worry about me, not just the pack. I tried to be understanding but didn't bend much.

Finally, he came right out and asked what had happened to me during the last visit. I answered vaguely, claiming ignorance. Werewolves couldn't recognize lies as well over the phone. A long moment of silence passed. When he spoke, he didn't comment on my answer but again asked that I consider coming home over the holiday break. I knew he meant the Compound and told him I'd think about it.

After that, he continued to call me daily just to talk. Most of our brief conversations touched on the weather, school, or investments. Anything pack related stayed off-limits. I could tell he was concerned, but trust, once lost, took longer to earn back. I wouldn't tell him any of my suspicions until I could confirm some of them.

FOR THE NEXT FEW WEEKS, the challenges stopped, and I pushed the pack, strange colored sparks, and my pull from my head. Instead, I focused on my studies.

Clay worked at Dale's while I stayed on campus. I hadn't given up trying to figure out why he'd picked Dale to be his employer. However, whenever I asked, he responded with a shrug. I never asked him if he followed me to school as Luke had suggested. Some things I preferred to remain a mystery.

I thought Clay's expectations would change after our kiss, but he never pushed for more. He continued to stay in his fur most of the time except for Tuesday nights when he had dinner waiting for me. I looked forward to our nights together, and not just because he cooked exceptionally well.

Rachel knew I was spending more time with him, and on one of our quiet nights together, she asked about Clay-the-man while Clay-the-dog lay curled on the floor next to me.

"You are so weird about him. What is it about the guy that keeps you coming back?" She sat on the couch, folding her summer clothes and packing them into a tote.

Smiling slightly, I turned the page of the book in my lap before I answered.

"You don't know him like I do."

"How can you know him at all when you two don't talk?"

"You don't need to talk to get to know someone. You just need to listen," I said absently, trying to concentrate on my reading. My words rattled in my head for a moment before what I said clicked into place. I froze and looked at Clay. His brown eyes met mine steadily.

Damn the patient, clever dog. A smile twitched my lips. I never had a chance...and I didn't mind.

"But that's what I'm saying. He doesn't talk. What are you listening to?"

I laughed at her and myself. "Actions speak louder than words," I quoted, finally looking up at Rachel. "He's there when I need him. He's kind and caring. He keeps me safe, and as you've seen, he cooks and cleans. What's not to like, Rachel?"

She grumbled under her breath but didn't have anything else to add.

Clay walked over to her and lay on some of her dresses, ending her mutterings that I should get out and meet other people. She laughed at him then tried to move him. He laid his head on his paws and winked at me. He wasn't mad but enjoyed giving Rachel some grief.

Shaking my head, I went to the fridge and left Rachel to tug her dresses out from under his bulk on her own. In the fridge, I saw a new carton of orange juice along with a double-chocolate cake. Two layers of chocolate-frosted goodness. My mouth watered. I usually ignored the food Rachel bought, but that one begged my attention.

"Can I have a piece of your cake?"

"I thought it was yours. It was here when I got home," she

called back.

I stood staring at the cake for a long time. How could I be so blind? He'd shrugged when I'd asked why he'd gotten his job, but the answer, wrapped in layers of sinful chocolate mousse frosting, sat before my eyes.

Thinking back, I identified several of the little things I'd previously overlooked. Things I'd assumed Rachel had purchased, like movies I'd mentioned I wanted to see. He'd gotten his job for *me* because of my speech the day after we'd met. My heart melted a little as I thought of all the effort he'd put into trying to be what I needed, and I knew I fought a losing battle.

THE AIR GREW COLDER, and snow started to fall the week before Thanksgiving. The wind howled outside, still finding a way past the new windows. Despite the low-set thermostat, the heat kicked in often, and I worried about the bill. Even with Clay warming my feet, I'd added another quilt to the bed.

Broke and out of quilts, I lay under the covers, shivering. I wore two pairs of lounge pants, a t-shirt, and a sweatshirt. If I could just fall asleep, I knew I'd warm up eventually. During the night, I usually stripped to one layer. But warming the bed took forever...on my own.

"Screw this," I said, sitting up. I started pulling off my sweatshirt. The streetlight filtered through the curtains, so I could make out the shapes in my room. I tossed the sweatshirt toward the closet.

Clay lifted his head, tilting it just so.

I ignored him for the moment and shimmied out of my second layer of pants while trying to stay under the covers. The pants soared through the air and landed next to the shirt.

"Clay, will you keep me warm tonight?" I'd barely whispered the words when he jumped off the bed.

A moment later, he pulled back the covers and joined me. He wrapped his arms around me and pulled me to his chest. Bare chest. I sighed, pressed my face against his skin, warming my cold nose, and wrapped my free arm around his waist. Then, I tucked my feet under his calves. He grunted slightly but didn't loosen his hold.

"No more fur at night. Deal?"

The blankets and his chest muffled my voice, but I knew he heard me. He kissed the top of my head, the only part exposed. I smiled, figuring it meant yes.

The next morning, my cell phone rang, waking me. Still wrapped in Clay's warmth, I didn't move right away. He reached over me, plucked it from the bedpost, and handed it to me. Only Sam and Rachel had my number.

I could hear movement in the house and looked at the display, expecting Sam's number. Instead, it was one I didn't recognize.

I answered with a questioning, "Hello?"

"Gabby, I found her, but..."

"Luke?" I hadn't heard from him since we'd left the Compound.

"Yes. I understand you think she's important, but she's not even eighteen. How am I supposed to get her to come with me?"

I sat up excitedly and knocked back the covers in the process, exposing both Clay and me to the cool air. Clay grunted a complaint.

"I can't believe you actually found her! I need to talk to her. If she's like me, which I think she is, you had better bring her to the Compound. I hate to admit it, but the Elders need to know."

"Fine. You better be there when we get there," he said with an edge. The line went dead.

I pulled the phone from my ear to look at it, puzzled. Luke never had an edge.

Slowly, I grinned. Had I been right? Was he now dealing with his potential Mate? Smiling hugely, I hoped she gave Mr. Confident a little hell.

Chapter Eighteen

With the freeze came the night Rachel thawed toward Clay-the-man.

A heavy snow started to fall just as Clay and I went to bed. His arm curled around my waist, and my head rested on his shoulder. Asking him to sleep beside me was the best decision I ever made, and it made me finally understand that *I* determined the pace of our relationship. He had waited patiently for me to invite him in and would wait patiently for the next step, whatever I decided that would be.

My phone rang and pulled me from my warm cocoon. I recognized the number and answered it.

"Hey. I'm coming home," Rachel said. "It's snowing too badly to go to Peter's." She'd caught on that Clay spent the night often.

"Thanks for the heads up," I said with a laugh. "We'll see you soon."

Clay got out of bed as I ended the call. Puzzled, I watched him dress in warm clothes. He left the room. The back door opened and closed. A minute later, I heard the rasp of a shovel on the driveway. I smiled, moved to his warm spot, and burrowed in.

The sound of the plow scraping past disrupted the silent world and kept me awake. Clay stayed outside, keeping the entrance to the driveway clear until Rachel came home. I heard her thanking Clay as they came in together. He didn't say anything in return, but I imagined he gave her one of his rare nods.

When he returned, I flipped the covers back for him and moved out of his place.

"I was just keeping it warm for you," I lied.

He laughed and pulled me close. Even after being outside so long, he still warmed me.

My lids grew heavy, and he kissed the top of my head.

WITH THE LONG holiday around the corner, I needed to cross a few things off my mental checklist. First, I needed to pin down my next victim for a power swap. After that, I needed to talk to Sam and hope for answers.

I'd planned to test my ability on Rachel before I went back to the Compound, but Clay watched me closely. Since he knew something happened when I touched other people, he subtly kept everyone out of reach. I pretended not to notice so he wouldn't become even more protective.

Luck turned in my favor when Rachel texted and asked me to meet her and Peter for lunch. Having just left my morning class, the timing couldn't have worked better. She suggested a small ma and pa diner close to the campus; the same one Clay and I had walked to so long ago for our sunrise breakfast. I quickly agreed, told her what to order for me, and rushed over the scraped sidewalks to my car.

I cautiously drove the few blocks to the diner. The salt on the roads made everything slushy, and my worn tires liked to slide when I least expected. I eased into the crowded parking lot and snagged a spot near the door.

Through the windows, I spied Rachel and Peter already snuggled in a booth. The waitress had just delivered our food, and they didn't notice me park or get out of the car. They stared at each other. I saw their lips moving in quiet conversation. Rachel kept stopping to grin at Peter.

I opened the door, briefly blasting the patrons with the frigid air. It caught Rachel and Peter's attention. They wore secret smiles as they watched me approach. I slid in across from them, the vinyl seat squeaking, and peeled off my hat and gloves. The warmth of the room heated my cheeks and turned them red in seconds.

"Hi, guys. This is a nice surprise. What's the occasion?" As soon as I said it, I noticed the glint on Rachel's ring finger. "Oh, wow..." It came out sounding as stunned as I felt. The rational side of me said it was too soon, but the part of me that saw them together and saw their synchronized pulses knew it was perfect.

"Peter proposed last night, and I said yes." Rachel's happiness bubbled from her.

I stood and reached across the table to hug her. She bounced up from her seat and excitedly hugged me back. I grabbed hold of the opportunity. Focusing, I repeated what I'd thought and felt the other times I'd shocked someone. Was she doing the right thing? Was Peter the right one for her? What if I was wrong? I dredged up all my concerns and hope for her, held it tight within me, and then let it flow through to her.

The shock jolted us apart immediately. The intensity of it burned my fingertips. Rachel settled next to Peter with a surprised laugh. I sat too, smiled, and opened my sight wide, forcing the full view of the world as I'd seen when I'd shocked Luke. It strained me a bit, but I didn't let go. This time, I really looked. The tiny sparks of all living beings covered the world. I focused the view so I could see the occupants of the diner in detail.

Peter and Rachel pulsed in time as usual. I expected Peter to be different, somehow, to signify his match with Rachel, but I couldn't see anything unusual. They did appear a bit dimmer like their lights had faded. I remembered that happening when I'd touched Luke, and I quickly pulled back from such a close-up view.

While I looked at Rachel's tiny spark, something caught my eye. Faint pulses rippled out from her. Much like the ripples made by a pebble thrown into a pond, they spread outward, passing through all other sparks. One approached Charlene's spark. Instead of passing through, it bounced off and came speeding back.

Startled, I scanned the sparks, zooming in and out as needed until I identified five uniquely colored sparks like me. The ripples didn't pass through them. Instead, they bounced off and came flying back. Right at me, not Rachel.

The return wave of the spark midway between Charlene and me hit. I absorbed it, and a wave of dizziness rushed through me. That was the first indication of the drain I'd felt previously. I watched Charlene's wave approach and knew that when it hit, I'd get worse. It made sense now, why I grew weak and sick shortly after transferring my ability. Each hit of return energy knocked me further on my butt. If I'd paid more attention to it before, I would have noticed it when I shocked Nicole and the other girls. But why had it acted differently when I'd touched Luke? Why had just one of the five become focused? I still had so much to figure out. For now, the clock ticked, counting down the time until I would turn into a shaking mess.

I'd noted all of this in the few short seconds it'd taken for Rachel's surprised expression to clear.

"I'm so happy for both of you," I said before she could say anything about my momentary pause.

I smiled while I braced myself for Charlene's energy wave, just minutes away.

"Gabby, after Peter proposed, we both decided we'd tortured you and Scott enough and should get our own place. So as soon as we find something, I plan on moving out. I wanted to give you as much time as possible to find a roommate before I actually left."

I nodded and smiled at her as if I understood. Would another roommate really put up with Clay-the-moody-dog, or Clay-the-mute-man? I couldn't blame them for wanting to find their own place. I knew she missed Peter when they were apart.

She picked up her fork and started eating her salad. Peter took another bite of his BLT sandwich. My burger and fries sat before me, still untouched.

Her announcement and the continued strain of staying focused on the vast scale of lights for so long took their toll. My head started to pound. I saw the second wave rush toward me and couldn't help the slight wince when the pounding in my head increased to full force. I clenched my teeth to keep them from chattering.

Thankfully, Rachel still wore her love-goggles and didn't notice.

"Don't worry about me. Clay will be there enough that I'll make him pay the other half of the rent. So, did you set a date?"

The conversation turned to wedding plans until Peter glanced at his watch and reminded Rachel of their next class. She pouted playfully. I smiled, barely holding back a shiver, and assured her we'd make time to talk wedding stuff soon. The third wave hit, stunning me. Two to go, and they weren't far off.

"You feeling all right?" Peter asked as they stood. "You look very pale."

"I'm fine. I skipped breakfast, and I think my blood sugar is getting revenge. It will pass." I picked up a fry and ate it. My stomach rebelled.

"You should have that tested," Peter warned, helping Rachel into her jacket.

I nodded and reached for the ketchup while they walked out the door. Squirting a big pile on my plate, I looked up in time to wave to Rachel as they backed out of their spot. I pretended to nibble on a fry as I watched their car. Once they left, I dug out my cell with shaking hands and dialed Dale's Auto Body. It looked like I would need to miss a few more classes.

Dale answered after the third ring.

"Hi, Dale, it's Gabby...Clay's girlfriend." It felt weird giving myself that title, but I pushed it aside. Bigger issues to deal with. "If he's there, can I talk to him?"

Dale chuckled. "Sure, but I don't imagine it'd be much of a conversation."

I heard him call out to Clay. A moment later, a husky voice said, "Hello?"

After not talking to me for so long, hearing his voice startled and annoyed me slightly. He would talk to a perfect stranger, but not me? I opened my mouth to say something about it, but the pain in my head insistently prodded me to get on with the important news.

"Clay, I did it again. I'm at the diner where we had breakfast. I need you to come get me before it gets worse."

He didn't say anything for so long that I looked at the phone to see if I still had a signal. The screen said disconnected. Would it have killed him to say, "Okay," or maybe even, "Bye," before hanging up? His hello had been too shocking to recall the sound of his voice.

I sighed and put my cell away. With Sam's frequent calls and Rachel's occasional texts, my remaining minutes dipped into the double digits. I needed to adjust my budget to buy more airtime. Did life really need to throw me this many curveballs? And all at once?

I forced myself to eat more of my mostly untouched meal so the waitress wouldn't bother me as I waited.

The last of the waves hit me. Only determination and a hand over my mouth kept me from whimpering. After about ten minutes, I settled the bill and watched out the window for Clay, barely checking the need to curl into a ball and lie down on the padded bench. The waitress kept a close eye on me, probably thinking she would need to clean up barf soon. She might.

Dale's huge tow truck pulled into the parking lot. Clay opened his door and leapt out while it still rolled to a stop. Through the window, he spotted me. His eyes never left me as he strode in and Dale pulled away.

Clay still wore his greasy coveralls, and with his hair pulled back, he looked like an angel—a grimy one—coming to save me. Again.

"Hi," I whispered, tilting my head to meet his gaze. ·

His eyes softened as he looked me over.

My legs trembled just sitting there, but with so many students from campus, I wouldn't leave by any means other than my own two feet. I handed him the keys to my car, slid out of the booth, and reached for him. Standing, I wrapped my arms around his waist. I hoped it looked like I wanted to snuggle instead of holding myself up. He maneuvered us out the door and to my car with no trouble.

Minutes later, he carried me through the back door. He knew the drill and gave me a drink before he tucked me into bed.

CLOSE TO DAWN, I woke feeling much better. The shivers had faded while I slept, and the lingering headache was manageable. The full bladder wasn't.

I snuck to the bathroom, hoping not to wake Clay. But when I got back, the light was on and he lay awake waiting for me. With his hair still back, I easily read his expression. I hated when he looked at me like that. All disappointed and hurt.

I stalled saying anything until I slid back under the covers. Warmer, I met his gaze.

"I'm sorry. I didn't plan it..." Technically. "...but I think I've figured out what I am, Clay. I'm like a GPS for werewolves. I can find people. Not just people but compatible Mates like me." My feet refused to warm so I tucked them under his legs. He didn't even flinch. Probably because I did it all the time.

"When I touched Rachel yesterday, I really paid attention. I saw the energy I release when I shock a person. It goes into them and pulses outward, passing through almost everyone else. And everyone this energy passes through fades in my mind, almost dimming to the point of non-existence. Five people didn't fade, Clay. In the whole world, there are only five. Six if you include me. And when the energy I release touches them, it bounces off to come crashing back on me. That's what's been knocking me on my butt."

Unsure if I should bring up the rest, I played with the quilt for a second. He nudged me, and I smiled at him. I should know better. Even when he didn't like what I had to say, he listened. He always listened.

"It was different when I touched Luke. With him, I zoomed in on one specific spark, a yellow-violet one on the east coast. The paper I gave Luke? That was directions to find her. I think she belongs with him. I think I found his Mate just by touching him." I grinned when I recalled the phone call from Luke. "I don't think he appreciates my help, though."

Through my entire monologue, Clay lay on his side, up on an elbow, and watched me intently. His serious expression conveyed his concentration.

When I finished, instead of shrugging as I expected, his head snapped toward my bedroom window. He snarled softly as he threw off the covers and crouched on the bed, head moving to track something I couldn't see.

I scrambled to my knees, staring at him. Fangs exploded from his mouth, and his ears changed. Now I knew why Luke had laughed at Clay's partial transformation, but I didn't find it a bit funny as I watched.

Clay remained frozen in a crouch, listening. I held my breath and strained to hear what he heard. The beating of my own heart filled my ears.

Both our heads turned toward a chuffing laugh near the window. A taunt to draw Clay out.

I opened my mouth to point it out but never made a sound. Clay's hand darted out and nudged me backward. I lost my balance. As I tumbled over the edge of the mattress, he leapt toward the bedroom door. He cleared it and switched off the light before I even landed on the floor.

The front door slammed against the wall. The explosive sound echoed through the house as did the chilly breeze that gusted along the floor. I shivered, hidden in the semi-darkness beside the bed. The door closed itself on the backswing, cutting off the cold.

I righted myself as I caught my breath. Luckily, I'd landed on a pillow, which I'd knocked off with me. Any recovery I'd experienced while I slept had vanished as soon as I hit the floor. My head pounded with renewed vigor, but I thought clearly enough to wonder if Rachel had spent the night here or with Peter. The sudden noise outside distracted me from my thoughts.

Loud snarls and low growls filled the air.

Despite Clay's obvious wish that I stay down, I risked a look over the mattress as my eyes adjusted to the gloom. The window gave a soft glow from the streetlights. The sound of my frightened breathing echoed in the room. I quieted it, pulled myself up, and crawled over the bed toward the window. Cautiously, I inched the curtain aside to peek out.

Clay and another man fought in the snow on the front yard. I cringed at the sight of Clay's bare feet and chest. The challenger at least wore shoes and a shirt.

Clay swiped at the man, ripping a good portion of his shirt away. Good. Clay wouldn't be the only cold one.

They skirted the direct glow of the streetlight but didn't stick to the shadows closest to the house. The neighbors would not only be able to hear them but see them as well. Hadn't the idiot challenging

Clay thought of that before he approached our house from the front? Pack law forbade public shifting.

The snow crunched under the challenger's feet as he rushed Clay. Clay spun and avoided the charge. He used the man's momentum to trip him and knock him into the snow. As the man fell, he shifted noticeably.

Clay shifted further as well. His mouth extended to enable the use of his fangs. I cringed at the thought of the neighbors spotting him. There would be no way to explain away the disconcerting appearance of his ears and fangs.

The other man rolled and rose to his feet. His head had almost completely contorted to wolf form. My eyes rounded. He snapped at Clay, narrowly missing Clay's chest. His attempt distracted Clay from blocking a well-placed punch to his gut. I cringed then silently cheered when Clay gave back as good as he got.

The sky began to lighten, and down the road, a few of the streetlights blinked off. They needed to end this soon, but the fight didn't seem to be winding down.

Their movements increased in speed until they mostly blurred. I heard each time one of them connected—the solid thunk of it reverberated through the house—but didn't see anything. I hoped Clay gave more than he received.

Twice, the other wolf feinted away from the house, but Clay refused to follow, forcing the challenger to come back to him. Clay would not distance himself any farther from the house and leave me unprotected. The other wolf's attempt had me wondering.

Knowing I'd regret it, I stretched my sight. I saw another blue-grey light nearby and began to doubt this fight was just another Mating challenge. As quickly as I opened my spark-filled view of the world, I closed it. It hurt, and I couldn't afford to distract Clay with my pain.

I studied the man fighting Clay. He didn't look like the same werewolf who'd attacked us on our way back from breakfast. The sprinkling of fur starting to cover his skin appeared lighter than the original challenger's dark grey fur.

Despite their noise, I heard the back door open. So did Clay.

In a fierce move, he hit the other werewolf in the head with a sickening crack. The man dropped to the ground. Clay didn't wait to see him land. He turned and ran for the house before I could even think to scramble under the bed and hide.

The front door slammed again. I thought of the damage and winced. The temperature in the room dropped further.

Clay and the new werewolf met in the living room with a thud. I didn't think, just sprang from my crouched position near the window to scramble over the bed. It might have been safer to stay hidden, but I worried more when I couldn't see what was happening.

I eased off the end of the mattress and edged closer to the door, trying to make them out in the dim light of the living room. I stared at the fight raging in front of me.

Two shapes struggled in the center of the brown rug. I identified Clay by his long hair. His back was to me. The other man had his arms wrapped around Clay, attempting to squeeze him. Clay fisted his hands together and hammered them down on his attacker's face. They broke apart, the attacker almost bumping into the TV.

Cold air wrapped around my legs. I glanced at the front door, which stood ajar, but didn't move to close it.

When I looked back at the men, I had a clear view of the attacker. I stopped breathing and stared at the man, stunned.

I'd grown accustomed to the stomach acrobatics I suffered every time I looked at Clay. Feeling them when I looked at this new wolf devastated me. I gasped in a ragged breath, hurt by fate's cruelty. The sound distracted the newcomer, who met my eyes with recognition then calculation. Clay took advantage and brought the man down like he had the one outside. The sickening thud made me cringe.

Without thought, I moved out into the living room and stared down at the unconscious man. His short, sandy blonde hair contrasted with the brown of the rug. It moved in the breeze that swept the floor. I didn't feel the cold as I studied his tall, lean frame. He had no facial hair. Except for the tall part, he looked like Clay's opposite.

How could I feel that pull for two men? Sam assured me that I would know when I met the right one because there would be a pull, a burning curiosity like no other. This didn't make any sense.

The man's hand lay on the carpet close to me. Some of his fingernails had shifted to glossy black claws before Clay had knocked him out. Looking closer, I saw his ears had shifted, too.

"What do we do, Clay?"

I looked up at him and found him watching me closely. I shivered and didn't look back at the man on the floor. Having all the doors open made the heat kick in, but it did little to warm me.

"He's part changed. With all the noise, I think the police will be here soon. Can we leave him here like this?"

Clay nodded and motioned me back into the bedroom. His knuckles bled, and he had the start of another black eye. I wanted to go to him and hug him but felt too confused. Instead, I turned away to hide my watering eyes.

In the distance, I heard sirens.

Clay put me back into bed then left, closing the door behind him. Moments later, I heard the back door close and then nothing as the sirens got closer.

Fate or not, I belonged with Clay. I wasn't sure anymore if I was his prize or punishment, though. Regardless, he'd earned my loyalty. Reacting to someone other than Clay felt like cheating, and it bothered me a lot. I didn't know what to do about it or how to stop it. It wasn't something I could talk to Clay about. I had hurt him enough already. If I could trust Sam, I could maybe ask him.

The sirens quieted with a chirp before they reached the house. Muted red and blue lights danced on my bedroom wall by my head. I wondered what Clay planned to tell the police. No matter what I'd just felt for the man passed out on the living room floor, I trusted Clay completely. He had a plan, and I just needed to wait.

But Clay didn't come back in. Instead, I heard a knock on the front door and the murmur of several voices. Exhaustion and pain, from pushing myself too soon, shivered through my body.

AN HOUR LATER, THE FULL LIGHT OF A NEW DAY—WEDNESDAY morning, the beginning of Thanksgiving break—lit my room.

Clay, still bloody from the fight, stood with the officers to show them out. They had his written statement and my phone number since I didn't plan to stay in the house for a few nights. I'd decided we'd go to the Compound a day early. I'd waited long enough. I had too many questions to answer on my own, and a certain Elder waited for me there. I needed to talk to him.

The police believed we'd experienced a simple break-in. Their deduction suited me fine. I could just imagine the line of questioning I would have endured if I'd mentioned the men had broken in to kidnap me. After seeing the second man, I had no doubt that had been their intent.

The front door closed, and I listened to Clay walk through the house and close himself in the bathroom. He needed to wash the dried blood from his face. It had served its purpose and hidden his noticeably advanced healing from the police.

Flipping back the covers, I got out of bed and started to dress. The dizziness and headache that had returned when I fell off the bed had faded while they questioned me.

I finished dressing, grabbed my messenger bag, and began to cram clothes into it. My mind wasn't on packing, so I didn't treat it any more gently than Clay or Luke had when they had packed it. How had I felt anything for that man on the floor? It shouldn't have been possible. Agitation burrowed deep. When I turned toward the door and saw Clay watching me, I dropped my gaze to the floor, unable to meet his calm regard. He sighed, stepped aside, and motioned for me to lead.

In the kitchen, Clay had my jacket and shoes waiting. I slipped them on, remembering at the last minute to call Rachel to let her know what had happened. Thankfully, she hadn't been home. She promised only to come back home with Peter, just to be safe.

Clay didn't say anything as we got into the car, which was normal, but I sensed his extreme tension. My stomach churned with guilt. However, I didn't know what to say, so I closed my eyes and tried to nap. Still needing to regain my strength, sleep wasn't too hard to come by.

Several times, I woke to the sound of him tapping his grey nails against the steering wheel. When I opened my eyes to look at him, I could see his elongated canines. At those times, I wanted to reach over and pat his leg, but I held myself back.

When I woke to see his ears pointed too, I quietly studied him for a few minutes. I knew I was the cause of his agitation. He'd sensed my withdrawal. I hadn't wanted him to see my confusion. I wanted to talk to Sam first—before saying anything to Clay. But my approach obviously wasn't the right one. Clay had stuck by me through everything. I needed to trust that he wouldn't turn away from me after I revealed what had happened.

"Clay..."

He paused his tapping.

"Could you pull over for a minute?"

He glanced at me, lifting a concerned brow, but did as I asked. The tires crunched on the snowy shoulder. He stopped the car then turned toward me.

A sad smile lifted my lips. I hated to see him like this. I tapped my lips. I needed affirmation that we still had our connection, and he needed assurance I was fine.

His tight grip on the steering wheel loosened, and he shook his head in amusement. I held my breath as he leaned toward me.

Clay cradled my face in his hands and kissed me tenderly. I clutched his shirt, dragging him closer. When he opened his mouth to nip my bottom lip, I groaned and willingly let him in. We steamed the windows. My lungs burned for air. Finally, I had to pull away to catch my breath. He wrapped his arms around me and placed small gentle kisses on the top of my head.

His neck hovered in my line of sight. I could give him what he wanted. A quick bite, and I wouldn't need to worry about other potential Mates. I could Claim him as my own. But I didn't want to hurt him anymore. Physically or emotionally. I pulled back from our make-out session.

Clay gave me one last kiss on the lips then put the car in drive. The smooth, tan skin of his very human ears called my attention as did his clean, pink nails. He looked content, no longer tapping his fingers while he stared ahead at the snow-covered roads.

I turned away and pretended to sleep, condemning myself for my lie. My hesitation to Claim Clay didn't stem from a concern that I would hurt him. No, just like Sam said, I selfishly didn't want to give up my plans.

Deep down, I was unwilling to bend and try to make it work.

WE ARRIVED at the Compound just as the sun's last rays sank below the tree-topped horizon. Vehicles crowded the parking area. I didn't worry though. Holidays always drew a crowd.

Clay grabbed my bag then walked around to open my door for me. Staying close, we walked inside the Compound. Jackets and shoes filled the entry. It meant cramped quarters for the holiday, but I'd done it before.

We went to the apartment I usually stayed in with Sam, but another family with small cubs had commandeered it. After several minutes of knocking on doors, we gave up trying to find an apartment in the main Compound. We turned down a hall I typically didn't travel—the unMated wing—and found the majority of the dorm quarters also occupied. Several men passed us as we searched. They gave us curious looks as they scented the air. I stayed close to Clay.

Clay and I grabbed the first open dorm room and put our stuff on the twin bed. We would figure out our sleeping arrangements later.

"I need to talk to Sam," I said once we were back in the hall. Clay nodded and led the way to the main hall.

Charlene and her crew had done a wonderful job decorating the large room. Cornucopias with harvest produce sat on each of the long tables. Several turkeys with feathers made of construction paper hands hung on the walls. The cubs had obviously partaken in crafts while visiting. It amused me that Charlene insisted on celebrating the US holiday while living in Canada. Her extended adopted family didn't seem to mind. I could hear women laughing in the attached kitchen. Fresh pumpkin pie perfumed the air.

In the midst of all of the decorations, I spotted Sam. He sat with his back to me, conversing with several other men at one of the many seating areas in the main hall. I noticed the weary slope of his shoulders. Part of me—the part that lived with him for so long and thought of him as "Grandpa"—wanted to run over and hug him. I ignored that part.

Before he noticed me, I strode over and interrupted their conversation.

"It's time we talked," I said, tersely.

He turned toward me with a hesitant smile then quickly nodded to the others, who got up to move to another group.

"Gabby, I didn't think you'd be up until tomorrow."

Clay and I shared a glance. The main hall didn't afford privacy since all the werewolves present would hear me. Then again, very few places in the Compound qualified as private to that degree. Normally, I wouldn't care who heard me, but I had the mystery of the blue-grey werewolves to solve. I did a quick scan of the room and managed to hold back a wince of pain.

Clay gave an annoyed grunt but gently rubbed my back. He'd become adept at knowing when I used my gift.

In the brief glimpse, I'd noted the sparks all appeared normal. Well, for a werewolf anyway. But it only assured me to a degree. Although I didn't think Sam responsible for what had happened, I still wondered if he might know something about it.

"We came early because two werewolves tried breaking into my house." I watched Sam closely as I said it.

"What?" Sam said, giving Clay a sharp look. Sam appeared genuinely upset and concerned.

"He's still not talking," I said. I slumped into the chair across from Sam. "I believe their intentions were to kidnap me."

Clay lowered himself into the chair next to me. He always stayed close, and I couldn't imagine it any other way. If it hadn't been for Clay, the men probably would have taken me. What would have happened then? I thought about the blonde man who'd been lying on the floor, and my stomach clenched with worry. My troubled gaze swung to Clay.

Clay met my look with calm, brown eyes. Staring into their depths, a tense breath eased out of me. Sure, I had questions, but I wouldn't let the answers to any of them affect the tie Clay and I had.

I gave Clay a small worried smile then turned my attention back to Sam. Different colored lights...a pull to another man when it should only happen once...I could come up with only one possible explanation.

"Is there more than one kind of werewolf?" I asked bluntly. Maybe I'd stir up trouble with my public questioning, but I was tired of waiting.

Sam frowned and leaned forward. "Not sure what you mean, exactly."

Sam watched me closely. I nibbled on my lip and thought back to the original challenger. Physically, he'd looked like any other werewolf. So if Sam didn't already know about another kind of werewolf, I didn't think there would be a way for him to differentiate. Then I thought of the last one I saw on the floor.

"When you go fur, what color variations are possible? Different shades of fur, eyes...what about nose or nails?"

The door to the commons opened, and a few more werewolves drifted in, slowly walking toward other groups. While they progressed across the room, they kept their heads tilted, listening as if already aware of the important conversation occurring in our small group.

"What does this have to do with—"

I held up a hand. "Bear with me, Sam. I need answers to give answers."

Sam turned his attention to Clay.

"I already told you, he still isn't talking. Look, is there another Elder I can talk to? One willing to answer my questions?"

I wanted to take my harsh words back when Sam's face fell.

The expression cleared after a moment, and he slowly answered. "Fur is like hair and varies just like a human's. Same with the eyes. We are more like dogs when it comes to our noses. Mostly dark, but we sometimes have unusual markings. Did you see an identifying mark, Gabby?"

I ignored his question. "What about the nails?"

He shrugged. "Shades of grey. Mostly a dark grey."

"Black?"

"Well, like I said, a dark grey is possible."

"No. I mean black. A very glossy black you could see your reflection in."

Sam remained introspectively quiet for a full minute. The intense silence claimed my attention. Looking around, I caught the eyes of a few others in the room before they quickly looked away.

"I don't think I've ever paid that much attention to our claws before. But, no, I don't believe so."

I slumped back in my chair, thinking. Everyone in the room watched me, waiting for what I'd say next.

Could there really be another species of werewolf? The sparks I saw indicated the possibility. But if I followed that line of reasoning, did that then mean I was another species of human? Maybe these werewolves just had different abilities. I chewed on my lip for a minute. What about the nail color? Could that small difference carry enough significance to classify two separate species? I was grasping. I needed to grasp. If there were two kinds, it could explain why I had two potential Mates.

Frustrated and still tired from my stunt with Rachel, I scowled and got to the heart of my angst. Sure, I wanted to know what the color differences meant, but I needed to know why I felt what I did when I saw that man.

Sam cleared his throat, and I ignored him. Someone spoke softly farther back in the room. Others moved restlessly.

So what if I felt the same pull for another guy? It just meant I had a choice. Wasn't that what I'd wanted all along? Yet, now that I had options, I couldn't see myself walking away from Clay...not for school, not for a career, and not for some creep who snuck into my house.

I peeked at Clay, unable to hide my turmoil. He reached out, offering his hand. His hair hid his eyes again, making it hard to read him. I looked down at his hand, calloused and so real.

Realization dawned. Clay and I held the answers. I kept my eyes trained on his hand to hide my thoughts. When I'd focused on Luke, I saw the yellow-violet spark. When I'd focused on Rachel, I'd expected to see Peter, but I hadn't. Human vs. werewolf testing. If I was right about different species and tried the same test with Clay, I foresaw two possibilities. I would see myself as Clay's Mate or I would see two potential Mates for myself, thus supporting my theory of another werewolf species.

Doubt crept in. What if I didn't see myself? What if it didn't work that way, and I saw the werewolf that Clay had knocked out?

I needed to know.

Lacing my fingers through his, I closed my eyes and focused. I held onto my need to find the perfect Mate for Clay and my hope I'd see myself.

The shock jumped from my hand to his, and my vision of the real world narrowed. I held my breath, terrified of the answer. My second sight exploded into existence. Not the great void filled with billions of sparks, but with the vibrant intensity and color of the sun. The white-yellow core pulsed, its energy radiating outward, cooling to a molten orange. Hope flooded me as I realized my own spark filled my vision.

The vision closed, and my eyes once again focused on the real world. My hand still rested within Clay's, but I caught the change in his expression. Clay glared at me. He knew what I'd done, but I couldn't feel bad about it. Joy filled me. I'd been right. It didn't answer my question about the variances in sparks, but I didn't care. It had given me the answer I needed.

I smiled sweetly and leaned over to kiss him lightly on the lips. When our lips touched, something tangible changed. The joy I felt remained, but something else crept in. I pulled back, eyes wide. My heart hammered, and my stomach clenched as I stared at him, unable to look away. Mesmerized.

In shock, I realized what I'd done. I'd transferred my pull to him. Only he wasn't pulling in men. He pulled me in, and the force of it consumed me. He represented a hot fudge sundae to a diet-starved girl. Even knowing that what I felt was a result of my power, I couldn't ignore it. He was so handsome, so perfect, and so clueless as he continued to scowl at me.

His fingers still twined through mine, but I needed more from him. I needed an affirmation of us as a pair. I wanted to touch his face and smell his skin. I wanted to hold him tight and never let go.

With speed I never imagined I possessed, I moved from my seat to his, straddled his lap, and leaned my forehead against his. He grunted in surprise but otherwise didn't move.

Breathing in deeply, I smelled the soap he'd used and closed my eyes. His hair tickled my nose. I pressed my lips to the tip of his nose. My heart twisted painfully. His hand came up, lightly resting on my side. It heated my ribs. The contact of each finger branded me. Better, but not enough. My mind kept chanting, "More." I opened my eyes and smiled.

Forgetting our audience, I ran my hands through his hair and pulled back to kiss his exposed forehead. His cautious brown eyes met mine. I lost myself in their depths for several moments as I recalled the first time I saw them. On his driver's license. I needed more from him. No more hiding from each other.

I tilted my head and kissed his cheek. The whiskers abraded my lips, but I didn't mind. I moved lower, finding his lips. He didn't resist me but didn't join in as he had in the car. I frowned slightly. A stab of doubt pierced my heart. This didn't feel right, yet. He still hid from me.

Nudging his jaw with my nose, I made room to nuzzle his neck. My lips skimmed his smooth skin. His pulse jumped under my mouth. Finally, he reacted. Both his hands came up, holding my sides, kneading me, encouraging. My breath quickened, and my heart hammered. Yes! This was right.

Something took possession of me. With one hand, I gripped his hair and tugged it. He tilted his head to the side and exposed his neck, giving in willingly. My eyes traced his neck where his pulse skipped erratically. The beat matched my own. I couldn't look away from that clean-shaven spot. I recalled when he had started shaving it. He'd known I would need to see it. For this. I kissed it lightly and felt him shudder. Before the shudder ended, I bit him hard on the same spot. Hard enough to draw blood.

The taste of his blood on my tongue broke the hold he had on me and created a new one somewhere deep inside. I pulled back slightly to look at the small marks I'd left. They had already begun to heal.

The pull he had on me and the euphoria of the moment faded as the horror of what I'd just done washed over me.

Clay stared at me in stunned silence...versus his everyday silence. Behind me, someone moved and called attention to the fact that we still had an audience. A Claiming typically occurred in private.

A deep blush seized my cheeks, and embarrassed tears began to gather. I wiped the blood from my mouth with a shaky hand. I didn't regret Claiming him but wished we could have talked first. I needed reassurance. Would this mean I'd have to quit school? Would he want me to live in the woods with him? If he did, I owed it to him to try after everything he'd done for me.

Then, a really ugly question floated to the surface. Had I just forced him?

Panic bloomed in my chest. Before I could scramble off his lap, he reached up and gently stroked my hair. I froze, hands braced on his chest for stability, ready to flee.

"I've been waiting for that since the moment I saw you," he said in a deep and husky voice. He sounded like a midnight radio DJ.

Hearing his perfect voice ignited my temper. *Now*, he could talk? I scowled at him. The man had the audacity to laugh then scooped me up into his arms.

The room around us erupted in cheers, and I hid my blazing face in his chest, my thoughts a confused jumble. I felt him walk but didn't have the courage to look up to meet the faces of the people who'd witnessed our Claiming. The sounds of cheering faded as he moved out of the commons. My tears of embarrassment dried before they spilled over.

Part of me couldn't wait to get him alone and yell at him for not talking to me for so long. Another part of me wanted to skip talking altogether and get back to the kissing part. And yet, another part of me wanted to ask his thoughts about my gifts and the lights I saw.

When he carried me into our little room and set me on my feet after closing the door, I did none of those things. I stood mere inches from him still too stunned, and very unsure, to do anything but stare. Where would we live? How would we support ourselves? What about my education? His job? Was he upset I bit him under the influence? Should I tell him about the other wolf? Did he have ideas about the weird colored lights?

I trembled. He no longer smiled, but his eyes still twinkled.

"Why?" My high, strained voice made me sound like a child. I cleared my throat and tried again. "Why wait until now to talk?" Apparently, my curiosity had won.

He quietly studied me for a moment then opened his arms. I didn't hesitate and stepped right into them. I needed his comfort. He tucked me against his chest and gave me his explanation in a simple, heart-melting way.

"If I'd spoken, even just one word, I would have never been able to hold back what I feel for you. You would have run."

I remembered the day he'd plopped down on the towel next to Rachel. Had he arrived any other way, I would have tried to kick him out. If that wouldn't have worked, I would have...run. Even then, he'd known me. I hadn't been ready for any monumental life changes then and wasn't sure if I was now.

I pulled back and met his gaze.

"Can I finally get answers from you now? You'll keep talking?"

He smiled at me and nodded. Well, he'd never be a chatterbox.

"Do you think I'm right about the—"

With sudden seriousness, he interrupted me. "Now's not the time. We'll talk later."

"No way, we're talking now. If not about that, then something else. I've waited over six months to hear your voice."

He didn't look too motivated to talk, yet.

"You owe me. I bit you." It sounded a little backward, but he smiled for a moment before the look turned puzzled.

"How are you feeling?"

His question gave me pause. Where were the waves of backlash? Shouldn't I feel sick or something by now?

"Good, actually." I'd felt great since I bit him.

Curious, I stretched my awareness. Two of the waves had already hit me, but I hadn't felt a thing.

"It's weird, but I don't feel sick." No backlash. Did that mean I would no longer have a pull on men? The idea excited me. I tried pushing my sight further, and it worked.

In Clay's arms, I focused easily, seeing things I'd missed before. The humans dominated the majority of the space while the werewolves claimed an insignificant portion. Far to the east, a large gathering of blue-grey werewolves hid among the humans. I stayed focused on their group, concerned. If they congregated together, they understood their difference.

"I think we need a safe place to talk." Although werewolves tried to respect each other's privacy, I didn't want to chance anyone overhearing what we needed to discuss.

Clay nodded but glanced at the door without moving. I followed his gaze, and my shoulders slumped as I looked at the wood panel. I had a good idea who hovered outside. He'd given me my answers and now wanted his own.

I slipped from Clay's arms and yanked the door open. As I had expected, Sam leaned against the wall opposite the door. Waiting. Probably listening, too.

"Sam, since we don't have any privacy, we'd like to use the conference room. There are a few things we need to discuss."

"I couldn't agree more," Sam said, motioning for me to lead.

"Clay and I, Sam," I clarified as I stepped from the room. "I don't have any answers for you."

"Gabby—"

"No. Now, it's your turn to be bossed around and told what to do. I did what you wanted and Claimed one of you. Lay off." My stomach churned, and a little fear crept in. Talking to Sam like that was like poking a bear with a stick. Though he'd never given me reason to fear him, he could rip my head off in a blink. I never forgot that.

Sam didn't say anything behind me but continued to follow me. I didn't turn around to look but knew Clay followed Sam. I needed to stop baiting Sam and smelling like fear. It didn't help any of us.

I opened the door to the soundproofed conference room and turned to face Sam. He'd schooled his features to appear perfectly calm and blank, but his spark glowed like a fanned ember.

"Sam, I'm trying to do what's best for me, Clay, and the pack. There's a lot I haven't told you, things I haven't told Clay. Give me some time to sort everything out. I need to make sure your goals mesh with mine before I can fully confide in you." He looked hurt by my words, but I didn't regret them. I was trying to be honest and give him what information I could to help explain my behavior.

He studied my face for a long moment then stood back and let Clay join me in the room. "I'll be here."

I nodded and gently closed the door. I'd figured he would wait.

When I turned to Clay, I found him watching me. He looked puzzled. Probably trying to figure out what I hadn't told him. He knew so much already. But what would he think about my reaction to the man who'd broken into our house?

I rubbed my hand through my hair. "I'm not sure where to start."

He pulled me into his arms. "Anywhere. I'll listen."

He always did. I smiled and started with the easiest thing. "I can see everything, Clay. Without pain." I pulled out of his arms and continued to look. "Even without touching you, there's no pain. I can see so much more than before. Why?"

"It's our link."

"Wait. I thought the link happened when..." I didn't really want to bring that up. We'd moved a little fast with the Claiming, and I didn't want to seem overly eager about the Mating. No mixed signals.

He read my hesitation and quirked a smile. "The full link happens after the Mating is completed. With the Claiming, we have a more limited version of that connection." His smile faded, and he looked at me sincerely. "It can still be broken. If there's another potential Mate out there...by biting him, you can break our bond and create one with him."

My jaw dropped. I couldn't believe he'd said all those words. I hoped he didn't say that potential Mate part because he thought I still doubted us.

"Don't use up your word quota for the day." He grinned, and I stuck out my tongue before getting serious again.

"Clay, I won't be biting anyone else. Ever. But I do have something to tell you. When those wolves attacked...the second one..." I trailed off, trying to find the right words. I didn't want to hurt him. This should qualify as the best day for us. Would telling him turn it into the worst? He nudged me as he often did when in his fur. It made me smile sadly as I admitted the truth.

"I felt the same pull with him as I do with you. I don't understand why that would happen. Sam said just one. Experiencing that with someone else confused me and made me feel horrible like I cheated on you."

He sighed and shook his head, smiling softly at me. "I saw what happened. It worried me, but the kiss in the car helped me understand how you feel. Don't worry about it."

He'd known all along? His impatient finger tapping made more sense now.

I met his eyes and smiled back. His easy acceptance of everything that'd happened finished melting my heart.

"I love you." My admission took me by surprise.

I didn't see him move. He embraced me again, crushing me in a spinning hug. The room twirled around us at a dizzying speed, and I didn't attempt to focus on it. Instead, I looked down at Clay's face. He wore a huge smile. I grinned back and noted his canines were normal for the first time ever.

"Oh!" I squirmed to get down, excited at the size of his teeth. He grudgingly released me. "Please, can we get rid of the beard?" Yes, I hopped from foot to foot like a kid begging for cotton candy. I wanted to see him just once without facial hair. If he wanted to grow it back, I wouldn't mind. I'd fallen in love with him as he was, after all.

He nodded, laughing at me.

"And I still want to get my degree. Can we stay where we are until then?"

Before he could say anything, his eyes shifted to the door. My joy-filled smile faded. I still needed to figure out what made Elder Joshua different from other werewolves. No doubt, it related to me in some way. Why else would I be able to see the colors? For a moment, I thought about my mom and all of the questions I would ask her if she still lived.

I stepped closer to Clay and laid my head against his chest, wrapping my arms around his waist. "Everyone I've ever loved this way I've lost," I said, recalling my earliest memories of my mom and grandma. I hugged him close. "Don't let me down."

"I won't. You're stuck with me forever," he whispered as he held me close.

I pulled back enough to meet his eyes and knew, without a doubt, I'd found the perfect man. He *would* stand by me. Always.

I kissed his lips, wishing we had time to be just Gabby and Clay, the newly engaged couple. Then, I smiled. We would have time.

Eventually. Like he said, he wasn't going anywhere, and neither was I.

Something chirped behind me. It took a second chirp for me to recognize the sound of my own phone. I groaned at the interruption but pulled back from Clay's warm embrace, not quite leaving it, to pluck the phone from my back pocket. Luke's number flashed on the screen.

As soon as I hit "talk," Luke spoke in a rush without waiting for my greeting.

"Gabby, I have a problem," he shouted over the roar of an engine. Something popped loudly in the background. Luke swore. The phone went dead.

The three-second conversation left me speechless. I pulled the phone away from my ear to look at it. What the hell was going on? Safe in Clay's arms, I stretched my senses and searched for Luke. I found a yellow-violet spark and a lone blue-green spark—Luke...and the other spark like me—swarmed by blue-grey sparks.

"Clay, I don't think I have a choice anymore. Something's happening to Luke. The other werewolves are all around him. We need to get Sam." I turned to look at the door. "I don't know who to trust."

Clay nodded and leaned his forehead against mine. "I'll stand with you, always."

Our gazes met, and I felt the pull, that tug on my insides that indicated she was my Mate. She felt it, too, because she stopped walking.

I started toward her, unable to keep my gaze from drifting to her neck. One bite and she would be mine.

Then her scent registered. Fear. Panic. Disgust lit her features. Shame flared in my gut.

The horror in her beautiful hazel gaze tore through the euphoria that had built in my chest. What was she seeing? The long hair, the scruffy beard? That was just the outside. There was more to me than that.

MELISSA HAAG

CLAY'S
HOPE

CLAY'S HOPE

CLAY, WE NEED YOUR HELP.

Winifred's voice interrupted my contemplation of the scene before me.

When? I sent back.

Tonight.

I didn't respond or ask why. The Elders knew I would come, just as I knew the reason they'd called me.

For a moment, I continued to watch the house from my place hidden within the trees. The woman in the window moved around the kitchen, cooking dinner. Passing the table where her son sat doing his homework, she stopped to kiss the top of his head. The boy started speaking. The distance and the closed house kept me from hearing everything, but I heard her response. She congratulated him for his high score on a math test. Love lit her gaze as she turned to study the boy's bent head.

Exhaling, I turned away from what I would never have. A family.

With an easy lope, I started the journey to the Compound, the meeting place for my kind. Werewolves. As I traveled, I thought of the human boy and his mom. We werewolves were similar to humans in some ways, yet different in so many others.

One of our differences was the Elders, like Winifred. A group dedicated to the wellbeing of all werewolves. Once a werewolf took the oath to serve our kind, they became an Elder. Through an oath, Elders gave up their right to put their wants before the wants of our race as a whole. It wasn't a subjective promise but a mental bond that ensured our safety. While the bond allowed an Elder to communicate with any of us directly, it also served as a death sentence if the Elder ever acted in a way that wasn't in the best interest of our survival...such as finding a Mate.

Like an Elder, I would never have a Mate. It wasn't that I'd taken some oath that prevented it. No, the possibility of a Mate for someone like me, an outcast without a pack was...well, I'd be more likely to wake up with the ability to turn into a bear instead of a wolf.

The Elders knew it, too. That was why they called on me to help at Introductions, gatherings to introduce an eligible female to the unMated of our kind. Yet another way we differed from humans.

I'd heard the call for this upcoming Introduction weeks ago. The Elders were giving all the unMated time to journey to the Compound. That meant there would be hundreds of males there. One lucky wolf would find himself a Mate. It wouldn't be me. A brief surge of jealousy clawed at me, but I shook out my fur and the feeling.

When the Elders called for my help, it was to keep the peace among the males. Then I'd leave again, returning to the woods and my isolated life.

The image of the humans remained in my mind as the miles slowly disappeared under my paws. While my father was alive, I would have never gone so close to their home. Since he'd died though, I found myself wandering closer and closer. I knew why. I missed him. And though I had no memory of my mother, I missed her, too. I missed belonging to something.

Maybe it was time for me to submit to Thomas and join his pack. The thought filled me with disgust. As much as I wanted to be a part of something, to be able to stay in one place for more than a night, I didn't think I'd be able to bow to another person's whims again. After all, my father had been a good leader, but I'd struggled against many of his rules.

The scent of a cougar tickled my nose, and I veered to the south to avoid its territory. Cougars worked differently than werewolves. A lone cat could hold its own territory. A werewolf, like me, couldn't hold a territory alone. It made having a home without a pack impossible. But the idea of a place of my own settled in my gut. I couldn't keep a place as a werewolf, but I could maybe find a place as a man.

I recalled the woman in the window. Could I live like that? Walking on two legs day after day just to be able to call someplace home? The idea made my skin feel tight and itchy, and I didn't have to think long on it. Not a chance. I was meant to run on four paws, not walk on two feet.

I stretched my stride until I ran.

THE COMPOUND TEEMED WITH UNMATED. They paced between the trees, a restless tension pervading their movements. A few already faced off, trying to determine the strongest and their order in the upcoming Introduction line. Poor fools.

I ignored the fight that broke out and loped in the direction of the back door. The unMated could fight all they wanted out there. As long as they kept it away from my post at the Introduction door, I had no problem with them. I briefly wondered what female had caused such a large gathering. Generally, paying attention to the females was a lost cause. Too bad the ones getting their pelts kicked in the trees hadn't figured that out yet.

Several piles of picked over clothes waited at the back door.

Charlene's doing most likely. She must have anticipated the arrival of so many. I grabbed what I needed at random. Loose pants and a shirt. A shiver rippled over my flesh at the odd furlessness. How long had I gone this time between shifting?

Dressed, but still cold, I went around to the front door and helped myself to one of the jackets on the hooks before ambling to the kitchen. One of the perks of coming to the Compound. Food.

Charlene was moving around in the kitchen, checking this and that. She reminded me of the woman in the window.

She looked up and nodded to me as she walked past.

"Buns are in the warming oven. Stew's on the stove. Help yourself, Clay."

She left the room, and I stared after her. I'd been to the Compound maybe five times in my life. Three of those times had been before I hit puberty. How she remembered my name was beyond me.

The scent of fresh bread pulled me toward the ovens. Heat poured out when I opened the door. The sight of a full tray of golden buns made my mouth water. Reaching in, I grabbed several. One went in my mouth, the rest in the large pockets of my jacket. With my pockets stuffed full, I padded back outside to take up my place near the Introduction door. The heat of the buns warmed my side as I leaned against the building and pulled the first one out of my pocket.

I ate slowly, watched the fighting, and waited.

Vehicles continued to roll into the yard over the next hour. Men crowded into the woods near the door I guarded. A few strolled by to size me up but weren't stupid enough to try anything. One on one, they wouldn't stand a chance. More than one on one would bring the Elders. Elder intervention meant banishment from the Introduction. None of them wanted to miss their chance at a Mate.

A louder vehicle pulled into the yard. A truck by the sound of it. Silence spread throughout the woods when the engine cut.

They're here. Winifred's voice penetrated my thoughts. *Are you in place?*

Yes, ma'am.

Good. Let us know if you have any trouble.

I eyed the men who started to line up before me and prepared myself for a long night. The sun would rise before the female met everyone.

Anticipation held the men closest to the building. Quiet, they listened for a hint of sound from the room behind me. Further into the woods, the men started fighting again, establishing a pecking order.

It wasn't long before I heard Winifred again.

Let the first ten in.

"Ten," I said with a nod to the men in front of me. Standing back, I opened the door, waited for them to file in, then closed it again.

The number surprised me. Ten usually meant an older female; I hadn't thought there were any older ones still hiding in the wild.

After a minute or two of silence, I heard a woman's voice.

"Thank you for coming."

She sounded young, not old. Why ten, then?

The scrape of many feet on the floor alerted me to the end of the Introduction. I opened the door to let the rejected men out, and a hint of something warm and sweet drifted out with them. I lifted my nose and sniffed, trying to identify it. Had one of them been to the kitchen?

Motioning for the next ten, I tried to place the scent. My stomach rumbled. I should have stuffed more food into my pockets.

I closed the door after the last man entered and listened to the girl say thank you again. At the shuffle of footsteps a few moments later, I opened the door once more. Again, that trace of something delicious trailed behind them.

Would it be against the rules to ask the Elders for a food break?

I waved the next ten in and closed the door.

The extended silence in the room pulled my attention from the puzzle of the smell.

After several minutes, I heard the girl speak.

"It's nice to meet you."

Feet shuffled on the floor, and I hurried to open the door.

"A moment, please," she said before anyone stepped out.

The sound of her determined steps told me she was crossing their little tape line. The Elders wouldn't like that. I almost smiled.

"Gabby, wait," Sam, one of the Elders, called.

Briefly, I wondered if I should close the door to keep her in, but decided the Elders could deal with her. I had more than enough to deal with outside.

A petite blonde stepped through the door. Her scent hit me hard, and I froze. Mate. The word bounced around in my head. My canines lengthened, and my vision wavered as I struggled to maintain my form. Mine.

She continued a few more steps, with the Elders right behind her, and then stopped. I inhaled slowly, breathing in the scent that had tempted and teased me until now. With my gaze locked on her, I almost stepped forward. Reason stopped me, and I glanced at the men who stood before her, silently watching, equally stunned that she'd left the Introduction room.

If I spoke up now, I'd face countless challenges. I would win...for a while. But every wolf tired eventually, and there were too many out there still waiting for a chance to scent her. Better to wait. She was safe with the Elders present. I glanced at them to see if any had noticed my reaction. They weren't paying attention to me, though. After all, I wasn't here for a Mate. They were watching the others. As was she.

Motionless, she stood before the waiting men. I couldn't see much of her face, just the back of her head and her stiff stance. Scenting the air, I detected a hint of her distress and a stronger whiff of anger. She was upset.

"Sam," she said, turning to face him.

Sam uncomfortably looked away.

She turned back to the men.

"No more fighting. There's no need to wait or fight for your place in tonight's Introduction. I will meet you all."

A growl almost escaped me. Though I knew it would be safer if she did meet them all, I didn't want any other male near her.

"Start a line here, and I'll walk it. If I am not right for you, there is no need for you to remain after I've passed you. You may leave and know that I am honored by your presence here tonight."

I curled my hands into fists and eyed the men who poured from the woods. They had no chance. Turning my gaze back to her once more, I tried to steady myself. She moved forward with grace.

Gabby. My Mate.

Several passes up and down the line thinned the number of waiting men, and I willfully unclenched my fists. The Elders noted a few names, but she showed no interest in any of them.

Finally, the last man nodded to the Elders and walked away, and there was no one left. The reality of having a Mate suddenly hit me hard. Adrenaline pumped into my blood. She really was mine, and soon she'd turn to face me.

What if she didn't show interest in me? My hands shook. I held my breath as she turned, waiting for our eyes to lock. But they didn't. She was watching her feet as she approached the door. It was the first time I'd fully seen her face. She was perfect. Her blonde hair was pulled back into a ponytail and freckles dusted her cute nose.

I shifted impatiently, and the movement seemed to draw her attention. She looked up at the last moment. Our gazes met, and I felt the pull. My father had told me about the phenomena. A tug on your insides the first time you see your Mate.

She felt it, too, because she stopped walking, and her mouth dropped open a little.

I stepped out of the shadows.

"You have got to be kidding," she said softly.

That she felt the same disbelief I had made my pulse leap. I started to walk toward her unable to keep my gaze from drifting to her neck. One bite and she would be mine.

I was halfway to her when the change in her scent registered. Fear. Panic. She was frozen in disbelief, but not as I'd been. Disgust lit her features. Shame flared in my gut. Had I mistaken the pull?

The closer I got, the stronger the smell of disgust poured from her. The horror in her beautiful hazel gaze tore through the euphoria that had built in my chest. What was she seeing? The long hair, the scruffy beard? That was just the outside. There was more to me than that.

My hope withered. I should have known better.

Unable to stay for more, I turned and walked to the front of the building.

Behind me, I heard her speak again.

"Sam, I've more than fulfilled any obligation I had to you or the pack. I'd like to leave tonight."

As much as it hurt to know she didn't want me as badly as I wanted her, I couldn't let her leave without trying again.

I went straight to the blue pickup. Her scent wrapped around the thing. I breathed it in and realized she wasn't just any female. She was the compatible human I'd heard about. There'd only been one other human like her. Charlene. And she'd changed the fate of the packs. Gabby was different, special, and her presence explained the huge crowd for the Introduction.

There was a mystery around these two women. The Elders didn't know why they were compatible with us, but Charlene and Gabby represented a chance for more potential Mates. The Elders were trying to find more like these two and had set laws to protect them. This changed everything.

I couldn't treat her like other females, and my heart sank as I realized what that meant. I couldn't Claim her; she needed to Claim me. Based on her reaction, she didn't want that. But giving up wasn't an option. I had the standard six months to court her and try to win her over. Six months. The enormity of the life-changing event that had just occurred threatened to bring me down. I needed patience. But first, I needed to stop her from leaving.

I needed a plan.

Eyeing the truck, I popped the hood and looked inside. Vehicles always had amazed me. I studied the engine for a moment, inspecting all of the connections, then I reached in and started unscrewing what I could.

"Want some tools?" someone asked behind me.

"Sure."

Humans couldn't run like wolves. Without the truck, she wasn't going anywhere.

TOOLS MADE quick work of removing most of the parts. I examined things as I took them apart. The way the oil flowed through the system was ingenious. There were a few other systems I needed to figure out: fuel and coolant. But the overall picture was simpler than I'd imagined.

Several of the rejected men watched from the porch but I didn't pay them much attention. I was waiting. Gabby had made her intention to leave clear. She'd show up eventually.

As soon as she walked out the door, my gut clenched again as her scent drifted to me.

Son, I acknowledge your interest. There was a brief pause before Elder Sam's voice continued in my head. *I do hope you know how to put my truck back together when you're done.*

I didn't acknowledge him. Instead, I continued to use the ratchet. My hand started to shake again. She had no idea how desperate I was for any sign of acceptance from her. Just one sign. Any sign.

"Gabby, honey," I heard him say. "I don't think he wants you to go just yet."

"There's more than one vehicle here," she said.

I swallowed hard. That wasn't what I'd hoped for. She was afraid, I reminded myself. She just needed time.

"If we go inside to ask anyone else, we'll come back to more vehicular murder," Sam said.

He was right. I wasn't about to give her up. She was mine.

"Fine," she said. Not looking was killing me. I glanced up as she stepped off the porch and marched toward the main gate.

"You won't get far," Sam said.

She hesitated at the edge of the yard light then plunged into the darkness that surrounded the driveway. It didn't take long for her to disappear from sight, and I ceased ratcheting to listen. She didn't stop walking as I'd hoped she would.

When she reached the point where I couldn't hear her anymore, I set the tools aside and started to follow. Her scent led me. I wouldn't lose her.

STUDYING the motel Gabby had checked into, I remained crouched near the tree line. There wasn't much to see. Two parked cars occupied the small parking lot, and through the office window, the man at the desk leaned back in his chair and stared at a small television. I glanced again at the window for Gabby's room. A light shined through. Did that mean she was still awake, though?

She'd walked so far, her feet dragging long scuffs in the dirt along the shoulder of the road. She'd been exhausted. I'd thought she would have turned back before she reached the motel. Yet, she'd kept going, her desperation to leave clear. And, my desperation to keep her had me crouched behind a bush.

Rubbing a hand over my face, I regretted not catching her while we walked. I wasn't sure what to do next. I couldn't risk knocking on her door and trying to talk to her. She'd been upset the first time she'd laid eyes on me. I doubted the second time would go much better as tired as she was.

The light in Gabby's room dimmed considerably, drawing my attention. A plan formed. Slowly, I grinned in the darkness and stood. She didn't need to cooperate...she just needed to sleep through it all.

Keeping to the shadows, I crept toward the motel. Outside, I pressed my ear to her door, listening. The sound of her deep breathing made me smile. She was already out. Time to move.

The round handle resisted when I tried it, and a frustrated growl escaped me. It would have been easier if she hadn't locked it. I twisted the knob sharply and heard the locking mechanism break. Holding my breath, I listened again. Inside, her breathing remained steady. I eased the door open, watching for a security chain. Nothing. I opened it wider and slipped into the room, quickly easing the door closed behind me.

Gabby lay on the bed, the bathroom light shining on her hair. She was curled on her side, a hand resting under her cheek. My heart clenched tight in my chest at the sight, and I reached up to rub the ache. Mine. I exhaled slowly and tore my gaze from her to look around for her things. There wasn't much. Her shoes were neatly by the door, telling me a lot about her personality, and her bag near the bed. I found her toothbrush next to the sink where the stench of rotten eggs, from the faucet, lingered.

With everything stowed away, I removed my jacket and lengthened the strap of her bag. Unable to look away, I watched her as I fit the bag across my back, out of the way. My palms began to sweat. I planned to carry her to the Compound. Touching her, holding her, for over an hour...my skin rippled, and I closed my eyes for a moment to steady my control.

Opening my eyes, I moved close to the side of the bed and pulled back the covers. She didn't move. I took my time to cover her with my jacket. My hands shook when I bent to slide my arms under her.

She weighed nothing to me as I lifted and settled her against my chest. She murmured and nestled her cheek against my neck, and I froze, unable to breathe. My heart hammered hard in my chest. Pure want boiled in my veins. Bite me, I thought. I held still, hoping, but she didn't move.

After a moment, I realized she wouldn't, and I calmed enough to walk to the door. Using my foot, I nudged the door open and walked out into the night, carrying the most precious thing in my world. I held her to me, enjoying the feel of her in my arms as I kept to the shadows. Avoiding the road and its noise, I went to the woods.

I took my time, walking carefully, not wanting to jar her. What would she do if she woke? If she woke while I held her, she'd most likely be angry. If I were lucky, she'd bite me in her irritation. I shuddered and tried to push that kind of thinking aside. It wasn't helping my control.

What would I do if she woke? I studied her features, the way her lashes fanned against her cheeks, the freckles that sprinkled the bridge of her nose, her soft lips. I struggled to keep moving as I stared at them. What would she do if I kissed her? Would she run again? Probably.

I tore my gaze from her and studied the woods around us. Leaves crunched under my bare feet. In the distance, frogs croaked. Nearby, the animals quieted until we quickly passed. At this pace, it would take less time to return than it had to leave.

What would she do when she woke up and found herself back in her room at the Compound? I frowned as I considered her reaction. She wouldn't be happy, that was for sure, and that wouldn't work well for me. Mad people didn't listen, and I needed her open to reason when we first talked. How could I keep her from being angry?

I remembered something my dad once told me about my mom.

She was good at confusing the hell out of me until I didn't know what to do or say. That was when she usually got her way.

Glancing down at Gabby, I wondered if I could confuse her enough to get my way. The ache in my chest returned. I couldn't rub it. So, I pressed her closer. It helped.

As I expected, it didn't take long before I entered Thomas' territory. Fortunately, she hadn't woken. She'd barely moved. I should have been thankful for that but was too busy dwelling on the fact that I'd need to let her go soon. My fingers twitched with the need to hold her tighter.

Instead, I paused and crouched near the ground. Balancing her in my lap, I studied her for a moment. Although a gentle breeze played with her hair, her peaceful expression never changed. I wished I could be there when she woke. Reaching down, I grabbed a handful of leaves and began to tuck them into her soft hair. Unable to help myself, I touched her face. My fingers left behind streaks of dirt. I cringed. Hadn't meant to do that.

She looked like she'd walked herself back to the Compound. With a grin, I lifted her again, my hands likely leaving dirt streaks on her clothes. She shifted in my arms, and I froze. She made a small noise and settled her hand against my chest. Again, I had to focus on breathing.

She was mine. She'd figure that out. I just needed to give her some time and find a way to give us a chance to talk. When she didn't move again, I started out, closing the distance to the Compound.

There were still a few males wandering about, but no one paused to speak with me when I entered. A few cast worried glances at Gabby. Probably the leaves. I stopped to drop her shoes near the entry. I planned to put some mud on them too. Then, I padded my way to her apartment. It was easy to find. Now that I had her scent, I could trace it anywhere.

I shifted her to one side so I could tap on the door. Sam opened it right away, a surprise lift to his expression at the sight of Gabby in my arms.

"Is she all right?" he asked. His gruff voice gave away his concern.

I nodded and stepped forward. I didn't want to have a conversation while I held her. If she woke up now, in my arms, looking like a mess...well, it wouldn't be good.

Sam quickly moved out of my way. I strode into their apartment and followed her scent to the bedroom. As gently as possible, I shifted her in my arms and pulled down the covers then tucked her in.

She didn't know it yet, but I'd take care of her, always.

I STOOD OUTSIDE, WORKING ON THE TRUCK, AND EVERY TIME THE MAIN door opened, I tensed. The sun had risen a long while ago. Each passing hour made me more nervous. What would I say to Gabby when she did appear? Should I apologize right away? No, it was better to gauge her mood first. The leaves might do the trick.

It wasn't until well after the sun rose that the door opened, and her scent drifted into the yard. My palms started to sweat as I listened to her step onto the porch. When she stopped, I swallowed hard, and glanced her way. She had lifted her face to the sun and closed her eyes. Leaves still clung to her hair and dirt streaked her face, making her look wild. My chest grew tight. Mine. She was mine.

I wanted to hold her again. Touch her face. The need made my skin ripple. Shifting my focus to the truck, I located another bolt and quickly set the ratchet. It took two tries. The rippling faded but my nerves didn't.

The sound of her movement had me inhaling deeply as I waited for her to cross the yard. Her annoyance and confusion salted the air. But no anger. That was good.

She didn't say anything until she stood next to the hood.

"We weren't officially introduced last night. My name's Gabby. Gabrielle May Winters."

I straightened and turned toward her. The sun glinted off her hair as she stood there with her hands in her pockets. She was such a tiny thing, looking up at me, studying me with her wide brown eyes. My response died before I opened my mouth; being so close to her robbed me of what I'd been thinking. Instead, I wondered if she liked what she saw. Last night's reaction made me doubt it.

"Sam said that your name is Clay."

She'd talked to Sam about me? My pulse leapt. That was good, right?

"Listen, Clay, I know you think I'm the one for you..."

The direction of her thinking made it hurt to breathe. I knew what she was getting at. She didn't believe she was my Mate. She continued as if she hadn't just verbally kicked me between the legs.

"I don't have a sense of smell to depend on, like you do. Although the Elders say to trust the instinct of werewolves, I don't trust blindly. I really want to go home. If I asked to borrow someone else's car, would it live?"

I turned back to the truck to hide my pain. According to what I'd heard, she'd been living with Sam for years, learning our ways. Why couldn't she understand that I wouldn't give her up? Without seeing what I was doing, I lifted the ratchet.

"Ok. I'll take that as a no," she mumbled.

Her understanding made me hopeful, and I turned back to her.

"Clay, I'm not trying to be rude here, but I'm struggling to figure us out. What's the plan?"

She knew I had a plan? Panic had me scrambling for the words to defend my actions. She didn't give me time, though.

"Am I just supposed to stay here until you decide I'm not really your Mate?" she asked softly.

Ouch. Any relief I would have felt over her not knowing about the leaves left with her continued, brutal denial of our connection.

She wrinkled her nose and sighed slightly. Scenting the air, I found a thread of frustration.

"Would it help speed things along if we spent a little time together?"

The abrupt change in her thinking left me stunned. Hell, yes, I wanted to spend time together. A ripple of excitement coursed over the skin of my arms, and I hoped she didn't notice as she stared at me expectantly, waiting for an answer. I didn't trust myself not to say just that, so I shrugged. I didn't want to seem too overeager.

"Do you talk?"

My heart stopped. Hadn't I been? I thought back. Nope. Not a word. She'd think me stupid, now. What could I say? Cringing, I turned away toward the truck and struggled to come up with something that didn't end with "don't leave."

"Ok. No talking. Got it."

Shit.

Maybe silence was better, anyway. Desperation had me about three seconds from begging. For what, I didn't know. Probably for any scrap of affection she'd willingly surrender to me. Yeah, it'd be better if I just kept my mouth shut.

She sighed, pulled her hands from her back pockets, and leaned against the truck. Chin in hands, she watched me as I pretended to know what I was doing to the truck.

"You seemed to like the idea of spending time to get to know each other," she said.

I turned toward her again. How could I not? Her voice, her face, everything about her called to me.

"But what's the point in spending time together if you don't want to talk to me? Isn't the point to get to know one another?"

Oh, I wanted to talk, but I doubted she wanted to know how lonely I'd been or how I felt now that I'd found her. Or that I understood having trust issues. Disgusted with myself, I turned back to the truck. Yeah, I really needed to keep quiet or my insecurities would have her running.

Then, she sighed and straightened away from the truck. I almost broke when she walked back to the main entrance. What would she do if I called her back? Probably beg me to let her leave. I couldn't have that. Not yet. She hadn't given us, or the idea of us, a chance.

I stayed by the truck, trying to figure out what to do next. Puking seemed like an option. It still felt like she'd kicked me between the legs.

Patience, I reminded myself. I needed to give her time to adjust to the idea. She was right. She wasn't like werewolves. She had no sense of smell to help her. She felt the pull, though. I was sure of it. That meant she'd be back. It had to.

The sun slowly trekked across the sky as I doggedly worked on the truck. There wasn't anything else to do while I waited. When the door opened again and her scent reached me, I exhaled in relief. She stepped out, and I studied her from the corner of my eye. Her damp hair was free of leaves, and she wore a pair of cotton shorts and a tank top.

She started walking across the gravel in her bare feet. I turned and watched her approach. Just seeing her coming toward me eased some of the doubt that had crept into my head.

I frowned as Gabby winced with each hurried step. Then, I looked at the gravel surrounding the truck. I wanted her to stay and talk but she wouldn't be able to do that without shoes. I studied her, wondering if she would let me pick her up to sit her on the truck. I doubted it. I used my foot to clear a spot, pulled the rag from my pocket, shook it out, and set it on the ground. It was dirty, but it was better than standing on the gravel.

She took the last few steps and stood on the rag with a sigh. The dash across the gravel had set her pulse racing loudly.

"Thanks," she said, looking up at me and sounding breathless. Her light brown eyes sparkled in the light. My gut clenched with the pull, and I itched to touch her but noticed her anxious scent.

"Sam just told me that you're to be confined to a room for the remainder of the day. With me."

I frowned, trying to think of a reason why the Elders were interfering. I'd done everything they'd asked of me. Sam had acknowledged my Claim. They had no right to upset her by forcing her to spend time with me.

"They want to see how we react to each other so they can determine if you really do have a Claim to me." She spoke quickly as if hurrying to share a secret.

If I had a Claim to her? Sam had acknowledged me. I growled, frustrated.

"What? You don't want to spend time with me?" she said, sounding surprised.

Not spend time with her? I looked down so she wouldn't see just how badly I wanted that. Though I wanted it, I wanted her to spend time with me willingly. Not through force.

"You do want to spend time with me, don't you?" Her soft, uncertain words had me opening my mouth. At the last second, I closed it and shrugged, unable to give her the real, desperate answer.

"So, it's not me. Don't you like being indoors?"

I would go anywhere she was, but I couldn't say that either. I kept silent and met her gaze hoping she'd understand it wasn't her.

"Ok. If it's not me and not being indoors, then what?"

She didn't let me guess where she was going for long.

"You don't want to be told when or how to spend time with me. You don't want someone telling you what to do. Is that right?"

Wrong. But I could see this wasn't about me. It was about her. I studied her, waiting for her to say what she needed to say.

"Yeah, me either."

She didn't want to be told what to do. Was she afraid being my Mate would mean we would start telling her what to do? No one would. Not even me. But that didn't mean I had to let her go. It just meant I needed to give her space and time.

She stepped off the rag, bent down to pick it up, shook it out, and handed it to me.

"I lied to you, Clay. I thought maybe if you knew how it felt to have your choices taken from you, you'd understand why I want to leave. It's nothing personal."

This was about last night and about the truck. Her honesty didn't make her plea to leave less painful. How could I give her what she wanted yet give us a chance?

I took the rag and turned back to the truck, thinking quickly as I picked up a ratchet and started to loosen yet another bolt.

"Your instincts say I'm the one. I don't have those instincts. Instead, I just keep thinking how I don't even know you. And the little bit Sam's told me...that you spend most of your time in your fur...well, it doesn't help me understand how there can be anything between us. I have no fur. I can't just run off into the woods with you.

"I've enrolled in college—one I chose—despite Sam's opposition. Do you know why I picked it? Because it was far enough away that I knew it'd be harder for people to tell me what to do. Major decisions, up until this point, have been made by others based on what they thought would be best for me. Sure, they ask me what I think and try to consider it, but not always. How do you think Sam got me to Introductions for the past two years? It wasn't by asking me each time if I felt like going."

Sam forced her? This wasn't good.

"I don't mean to sound heartless. I've been through enough Introductions to know what they mean to your kind. I'm not trying to throw your traditions back in your face. I'm just asking for some compromise. Don't ask me to forget the one thing I've chosen on my own.

"If you're serious about me, then come to the city with me and learn while I learn. We can get to know each other."

Hell, yes!

"I need that in order to even consider the possibility of us. I know I'm asking a lot. You'd need to start talking, stop growling, and bathe. No offense meant, but you look like a crazy man the way you are."

Damn. That hurt. But she'd struck on an idea. A better plan started to take shape, and I hid my smile.

"I know it wouldn't be easy on you. You'll be surrounded by people. It'll probably be uncomfortable after you've been on your own for so long. But we'd be able to spend time together, to get to know each other—the normal, human way—and see how things go. We'd both be giving a little, then. Well, you'd be giving a little more, but...will you think about it?"

There was nothing to consider.

As she walked away, I eyed the truck, thinking of everything I would need to do to be human.

IT WAS late by the time I thought I had all the pieces back where they belonged. I made my way into the main building, heading toward the kitchen first. The place was deserted, but as usual, Charlene had something for a quick meal in the refrigerator. I wolfed down the meatloaf sandwich in four bites then pushed through the double-doors and walked the halls to Gabby's apartment.

Before I knocked, I listened for any sign someone was awake. After several moments of hearing nothing, I knocked lightly, not wanting to wake her. Inside, I heard movement. Sam didn't make me wait long before he opened the door.

"Need the keys," I said.

Sam looked me over with bleary eyes, then shuffled over to the counter to pick up his keys.

"You've decided to let her go?" he asked, handing them over.

Not likely. I debated what to tell Sam. I was still mad at him for the role he'd played in getting Gabby here.

"We came to an agreement," I said.

"Really?"

"She said I should live with her, get to know her."

Sam's tired air disappeared.

"Did she now?"

"She did. But she thought she was scaring me away by saying it." I lifted the keys. "I'll bring these back in a bit."

He nodded, and I left, taking the keys outside. The truck started fine, and the rumble of the engine brought a smile to my face. It had less of a rattle now. I turned it off and went back inside.

Sam must have stayed up because he answered the door before I knocked. He looked just as beat and could barely keep his eyes open.

I handed him the keys.

"Don't tell her I spoke."

I waited until he nodded then I left again.

Outside, I swiped my hair back from my face and considered my next move. I needed to keep her guessing. If she didn't know what I had planned, she couldn't say no. I stripped from the clothes, tossed them on the porch, then took off in my fur, heading south to Sam's place.

Everyone knew where the Elders lived. They belonged to all of us, not just the packs. They were there to help. I'd never asked for help, and I wouldn't start now; but I wasn't going there for help, anyway.

Now that Sam had acknowledged my Claim and knew Gabby had invited me to college with her, he'd take her back home. That played right into my plan. To show her I had no interest in telling her what to do or stopping her from attending a school she'd chosen, I wouldn't approach her again until after she moved. But, that didn't mean I planned to ignore her for the summer. I meant to study my Mate in a setting familiar to her.

So I made my way to Sam's place, taking my time as I traveled. The trees and fields gave way to roads and houses then city blocks.

People in town weren't friendly to my kind. They tended to yell "get" at me as if I were a dog. I ignored them, kept moving, and slowly closed the distance between Gabby's home and me. As towns grew closer together, I traveled at night, keeping to the shadows.

Seven days after leaving the Compound, I found Sam's yellow house. I sat in the shadow of a tree across the street in a neighbor's back yard. The spot afforded me a view of Sam's picture window.

Gabby walked into the room, carrying a bag on her shoulder. I only got a fleeting glimpse as she passed, but it was enough to resurrect the feelings of hope. I'd have a family again. She just needed time.

Chapter Four

For the next several weeks, I did what I'd always done. From a distance, I watched what I wanted most.

Gabby woke, left for work early each morning, and returned late each night to eat a rushed dinner then go to bed. The more I studied her, the more she became a puzzle to me. She didn't interact with people. In fact, she tended to avoid everyone except the elderly.

Why was she so desperate to go to college? Her speech about me being uncomfortable surrounded by people didn't make sense. I'd thought she meant I would be uncomfortable around all the people she knew since I planned to stay near her. But, she maintained a very withdrawn lifestyle. I didn't see a problem...unless she planned to change that. Did she want to become more social? Meet people her own age? Men? The thought made me clench my fists.

When does she leave? I sent the thought to Sam as I watched her speak with an elderly man at her first job.

Second to last week of August. I'll drive her.

I nodded though I knew Sam couldn't see it. I was tempted to ask if she'd questioned him about me, but whether she did or didn't wouldn't change what I planned.

Keep her safe.

I will.

Turning away, I made the trip back north. There were things I'd left behind, papers my father saved for me after my mom's death. He'd shown me the hidey-hole three times as I grew up, making sure I knew how to find it. In the human world, those papers proved I existed. I'd need them, now.

It took three days to reach the spot and another half-day to get to the Compound and grab some clothes. After I dressed, one of the primary Mated pair's pups gave me a ride into town and dropped me off at a shopping center.

"Want me to wait?" he asked.

"Nah. I'm wearing fur from here. Thanks for the ride, Paul."

The boy nodded and left.

I went into the store and found one of those tag machines humans used to label their pets. Grinning, I bought myself a dog tag.

What's the address of her new place? I sent the thought to Sam.

After his reply, I went to look at the map pinned to the wall near the checkouts. I'd never traveled that far south but figured I'd be there in plenty of time. I had weeks yet.

I left the grocery and walked a ways out of town before I stripped out of my clothes. Using the shirt, I tied everything into a pouch I could carry with my mouth. Then, I shifted. My skin barely tingled as fur covered me. It was getting easier, which was good. Hopefully, I'd be doing a lot of shifting in the next few months.

Picking up my bundle, I set out. Instead of heading toward Gabby's new address, I detoured and made the long journey to Sam's once more. I needed to see her again. Now that I knew she existed, I could think of little else.

I arrived well after dark on the third day. No light shone from Sam's house, and I knew Gabby was most likely sleeping. I settled in behind the neighbor's house across the street, sleeping between their hedges and a fence. Before dawn, I shook out my fur and left my spot to watch Sam's place. A light turned on. Through the windows, I watched Gabby move around the house. Seeing her again, feeling the pull she had on me, only made me more sure I was doing the right thing.

I waited for her to leave for work, breathing in her scent one last time before I continued south.

It didn't take long to reach the address Sam had given me. The house looked small in comparison to Sam's but nice enough as houses go. I scouted the neighborhood before I settled in to watch the woman who lived there. She wasn't around much, and the neighbors seemed to mind their own business. It was a generally quiet neighborhood, especially during the day.

Taking advantage of the quiet, I broke into the house to have a look around while the woman was away. I wanted to know more about Gabby's new roommate. The first room, the kitchen, was clean and uncluttered. The roommate's bed was made, and the top of her dresser was clogged with every piece of jewelry imaginable. Scarves hung over the posts on each side of her mirror, and several pictures were tucked into the mirror frame. One of a dog caught my attention, and I smiled.

The rest of the house checked out fine. Only her scent perfumed the air. No males. Good.

I studied some of the mail stuck to her fridge, then carefully let myself out to settle in for the wait.

FROM THE HOLE I'd dug under the neighbor's shrub, I watched a light turn on early the day Gabby was due. The woman, Rachel— I'd read her name on the mail—started to open the windows. It was still pleasant out, summer not yet ready to leave. After a while, the smell of cleaning products drifted out. The neighborhood slowly woke as she cleaned and sang to some music. I stayed where I was, watching through the fence.

For such a small house, it took some time before she finished and the music turned off. It wasn't long after that the front door opened.

The neighbors had already left their house so I crawled out from under the shrub and stretched. In the distance, I heard the familiar rumble of Sam's truck. A tightness grew in my chest. She was almost here. As much as I wanted to see her, I didn't want her to see me. Not yet.

Quietly, crossing through the yards, I made my way to the end of the block where Sam's exhaust already clogged the air. I crossed the street then cut between yards, putting another block between Gabby and me. I didn't want to chance her spotting me. Sitting in the front yard of an empty house, I waited, listening for Sam's truck again.

I imagined it would take some time to move her things in and for Sam to talk to Rachel to ensure Gabby would be safe there. But it wasn't long before the truck rumbled to life once again. The distant noise made my pulse jump, and I took a steadying breath. It was almost time. I was nervous as hell about approaching her.

After a moment, Sam's truck passed. He nodded to me, and I nodded back.

Take care of her. It wasn't a command from an Elder, just a request from someone who cared.

I will.

I sat in the shade, impatiently waiting for the right amount of time to pass. I wanted her to settle in, to feel comfortable.

A car zipped past me, and I did a double take at the passenger. Gabby.

Damn it.

I caught a glimpse of Rachel's animated face before they sped out of view. Where were they going? Sam had barely left. What was Gabby doing? Rachel had seemed excited about something. What?

A sick feeling settled into my gut. What if Rachel had taken Gabby somewhere she could meet other men? Human women seemed to do that a lot.

I pulled my lips back in a silent snarl. I could try to follow them but knew I'd lose their trail with all the traffic in town. So I turned and made my way back to the house.

For three hours, I paced their backyard before I heard a car slow near the house. I darted behind the shed and waited.

The sound of Gabby's voice as she laughed at something Rachel said made my insides twist. Then I heard Rachel say something about sunbathing. Gabby agreed and followed Rachel inside. I frowned. They weren't leaving again, were they? Nothing was going as planned.

The building frustration fled as I realized what I'd just heard. Gabby didn't talk to women her own age. In the weeks I'd watched her, she'd avoided them. Why was she talking to Rachel? Something about Rachel was different. But what?

A few minutes after they'd disappeared inside, Rachel reappeared with towels in her arms. The breeze blew her scent toward me, and I lifted my nose. Excitement added a hint of sweetness to it. I watched her shake out the towels and lay them on the deck.

My idea had been to approach Gabby once she'd settled in so she'd know I was there to join her. I had on the tags I'd made to help drive home that point. But maybe approaching Gabby wasn't the best course.

I silently stepped out from behind the shed, trotted across the yard, and up the steps before Rachel noticed me. With her back to me, she settled onto the far towel. If I'd been in human form, I would have wiped my sweaty palms on my pants. Instead, I took a fortifying breath, then lay down next to her.

She squeaked and jolted away from me as she turned to look at what had brushed against her.

Her face was inches from mine. She didn't scream as I'd half-expected. With a grin, she offered her hand. Mentally sighing, I dutifully sniffed her. She grinned wider when I finished, then she reached out and scratched behind my ear. It actually felt pretty good. Better than scratching it myself.

"Where did you come from, handsome?" she said softly. Her hand brushed down my neck—it made me slightly uncomfortable—and ran over the rope holding my tags.

"What's this?" Her fingers hooked under the line, and my tags jingled. I wanted to grin as she brought the piece of metal around to read it.

"A good home, huh? I wonder if Gabby likes dogs."

Probably not. I sighed, laid my head on my paws, and gave Rachel my best woeful look.

"Aw, I'm sure she does. Look at you. What's not to like?"

My thoughts exactly.

Just then, Gabby stepped out in a pink bathing suit that left more skin exposed than covered. The sight of her soft pale stomach had me raising my head and swallowing hard.

"Gabby, look," Rachel said in a pitch that made my ears ache. "A dog!"

Had my future not been riding on this moment, Gabby's reaction might have been comical. Her eyes rounded as she froze and stared at me.

Small, pink triangles of material covered her chest and small, tight shorts covered her bottom. I stared, letting the image burn into my memory. Gabby in a swimsuit. I swallowed again and tried to breathe. I decided pink was my new favorite color.

Rachel's fingers continued to ruffle the fur around my neck. I met Gabby's gaze, wondering if she minded. I doubted it. Still, it made me uncomfortable to have Rachel touch me in front of Gabby. I didn't want Gabby to doubt I was hers.

Turning my head, I moved out of Rachel's reach. Rachel shifted to a sitting position and tried to reach me again.

"It just walked up the porch steps and lay right down. I nearly peed myself. Have you ever seen a dog this big before? What kind do you think it is?"

I gave up and let her pet me again while I held Gabby's gaze. The breeze carried the sour tang of doubt and suspicion.

"And you're not going to believe what its tag says," Rachel said. "'If found, please provide a good home.' Isn't that funny?"

She ruffled my neck fur, which made my tags jingle, but I ignored her as I waited for Gabby's reaction.

"Yeah. Funny."

She didn't sound amused. She turned away as if to go back inside.

"His tag also says his name is Clay. What do you think? Should we keep him?"

Gabby spun and stared at Rachel. I didn't need to smell her shock and disbelief. Who had she thought I was?

"What?" she said, disbelief clear on her features.

She glanced back down at me.

Did she seriously think I'd let some other pup come here?

"Aw, you aren't allergic are you?" Rachel asked. "The lease says a single pet is allowed as long as it's licensed."

Gabby hesitated as she continued to stare at me with distrust. Unwilling to consider what that meant, I sighed and laid my head back on my paws. The move had softened Rachel; maybe it would work on Gabby.

"No, I'm not allergic," she finally said.

"Good. He's so cute!" Rachel scratched behind my ears, and I closed my eyes pretending it was Gabby.

"I'm going back in," Gabby said, bursting my dream. I leapt to my feet before she reached the door and moved closer. She looked down at me, then at Rachel.

"Looks like another guy who can't take his eyes off you," Rachel said.

What did she mean by that? Who else had been looking at Gabby? I glanced at her suit again and clamped my jaw shut.

"Living with you is going to be a riot." Rachel laughed and picked up the towels. "Let's all go in. The neighbor's tree is going to shade the deck soon, anyway."

Gabby opened the door, and I quickly darted in past her. I sat just inside the door, waiting for her. She held the door for Rachel, and I worried that Gabby might try to run again. But she didn't. She took a deep breath and followed Rachel in.

"We can keep him. But he's going to shed everywhere," Gabby said as she walked away.

Her irritation kept me glued to my spot. I wouldn't press her. I was in the house, and she hadn't run. For now, that was enough.

RACHEL MOVED TOWARD THE REFRIGERATOR. ALTHOUGH SHE continued speaking to me—some nonsense about me being a good dog—I barely paid attention. Instead, I strained to hear the faint murmur of Gabby's voice. She was talking to someone. Probably Sam.

"Do you eat people food?" Rachel said, straightening from the fridge.

I forced my gaze from the arch, through which Gabby had disappeared, and gave Rachel my attention. She quirked a smile at me.

"Well, I'm sure you'd be willing, but should you eat people food?"

She put her hands on her hips and studied me for a moment.

"Dog food is essentially ground up meat and stuff, right?" She turned again and opened the fridge. "Hey, Gabby?" she called as she stared into the brightly lit interior.

I turned to stare at the arch.

From Gabby's room, I heard quick movements, then the door

opened. I waited and was rewarded with the sight of her marching into the kitchen. She wore pants and a top that covered her stomach but not her arms or shoulders. I stifled the urge to sigh. I sure did like her swimsuit better.

"What's up?" she asked, looking at Rachel, who was still bent over looking in the fridge.

"Do you think I can feed him leftover steak?"

"I'm pretty sure people food is bad for dogs. We can pick up some dog food for him in the morning. He'll be fine overnight."

Yep, she was mad at me. That was okay. I could wait her out.

She sat at the kitchen table, pulled her legs up, and wrapped her arms around her knees. The position made her look lost, alone, and scared. I wanted to shift and hold her, but I knew I was the cause of her concern. Only time would reassure her that I had no intention to mess with her big plans. I just wanted to be with her, and hopefully, one day, take care of her as a Mate would.

Her stomach growled, and I felt a moment of frustration. I couldn't take care of her like this, though.

"But dinner does sound good," Gabby said. "I should have thought of groceries while we were shopping."

Groceries meant food. I should be able to provide that for her. Yet, I'd watched the humans enough to know my skills wouldn't help much. I needed a way to earn money. I knew human's had jobs. Charlene, Thomas' Mate, was big on the werewolves going out and getting jobs to help support the werewolf community. That was one of the many reasons my father had chosen to live away from the pack.

Gabby and Rachel's conversation faded as I considered my options. I had the paperwork I needed in order to get a job. But I didn't think that would be enough. Though I'd studied humans from a distance, I wasn't sure I knew how to be human.

Gabby stood, drawing my attention as she went to a cupboard. I lay down, rested my head on my paws, and watched. I was here for her. I wanted to show her that a Mate was an asset, but she was right. We didn't know each other. How could I prove I was what she needed when I didn't have any idea what she needed?

"What kind of movies do you like?" Rachel asked.

The question caught my interest. I knew so little about Gabby. And so did Rachel. I wanted to grin. That would only help me.

"Action-comedy, I guess," Gabby said. "I don't watch movies often."

Rachel gave Gabby a plate, and I finally noticed that hot pepperoni scented the air. My mouth started to water. It'd been a while since I'd eaten.

"Let's eat this in the living room and watch a movie," Rachel said.

I stood and moved toward the living room before either of the girls took a step. If I was sneaky, maybe I could steal a slice from Rachel's plate without being noticed.

Rachel laughed behind me. "I think he's going to fit right in."

I stretched out in front of the couch, trying to take up as much room as possible so they would both need to sit close to me. I wanted Gabby close because I'd missed her. And, Rachel...well, I wanted her pizza. I wouldn't take Gabby's food. She needed it.

Rachel picked out a movie, and I watched closely as she fed it into the machine. Interesting. She picked up a long piece of plastic and pushed one of the buttons on it. Then, they stepped over me, one sitting at each end of the couch.

The screen came alive with color. Sure, I'd seen a few TVs through windows. But after hearing the high pitch squeal that the humans didn't seem to hear, I'd decided it wasn't interesting. This was different. Being in the same room, being able to hear the real life sounds along with the images, made it interesting, and for a while, I forgot about the pizza. However, when Gabby shifted positions and set her plate aside, my hunger returned. I stared at the piece on her plate. I didn't want to take her food; but if she was full and offered it, I wouldn't say no.

"Just one bite?" Rachel asked, seeing the direction of my

attention.

"If he's never eaten it before, he might throw up. Are you willing to clean it up? I'm not."

Yep, Gabby was still mad at me.

Rachel stuck out her bottom lip in a pout but returned her attention to the movie. Gabby went back to watching the movie as well. She sure had a cold heart. How long would it take to thaw? What if it never did? No, it had to.

Hoping to distract myself from my negative thoughts and my hunger, I tried to watch the movie as well. However, movement from the corner of my eye caught my attention.

I watched as Rachel tore bits of pizza from the main slice, then nudged them to the edge of her plate. Going for innocent, I nonchalantly turned my head and grabbed them with my tongue. Rachel and I worked through a whole slice that way.

By the end of the movie, I was really starting to like her.

"Fine," Gabby said when the first credit rolled. "Give him the steak."

Steak? My mouth watered in earnest. Rachel cheered and hopped off the couch, but I didn't follow her when she called to me. I turned and looked back at Gabby.

"Your choice, bud. Not mine," she whispered.

What was my choice? To follow Rachel, a person willing to feed me, or stay by Gabby so she could glare at me while I starved? Starving almost seemed like a valid option when I thought of it like that. But, I stood and walked to the kitchen. Let her think she was pushing me away. I was just biding my time and gathering my energy. She had to sleep eventually.

Rachel already had the steak out when I walked into the kitchen.

"I'll warm it up for you," she said with a pat to my head. I didn't like all the touching and patting but if it meant steak, I'd put up with it.

A moment later, I heard Gabby stand and walk our way.

"Thanks for the shopping and movie, Rachel. And the leftovers. You've made this feel like home in less than a day."

Her words and sad smile twisted my heart. Did she want a real home as much as I did?

"But I'm beat and going to bed. See you in the morning."

She walked away but looked back at me. It gave me hope. I held her gaze for a heartbeat before she blushed and hurried to her room.

Rachel pulled the plate from the microwave, distracting me from my thoughts.

"Here you go, Clay," she said, setting the plate down. She'd cut it up into tiny pieces for me. Why couldn't Gabby be that nice? I sighed and bent my head to eat.

"What's wrong? I bet you need something to drink, too." She moved to another cupboard while I wolfed down the meat.

A bowl appeared next to my plate, and I lifted my head to stare at it. When in my fur, I drank from streams and puddles. It never bothered me before. But the idea of eating out of dog bowls in Gabby's home soured the meat in my belly. At least she wasn't awake to witness it. I dipped my head and drank.

Rachel puttered around the kitchen behind me, adding water to a machine on the counter and setting some kind of clock on it. Thirst quenched, I watched as she opened a tin of coffee grounds. The scent brought me back to the Compound and a simpler life.

My father had raised me in the woods, telling me it was far safer than the human world. After hunters shot my mother, I'd known he'd only wanted to protect me. Yet, he'd made my life harder because he'd hidden us away.

Anything I knew about humans I'd gleaned from watching them or by interacting and learning from my kind at the Compound. What I knew wasn't enough to build a life with Gabby.

I sat back on my haunches to watch Rachel. She noticed my attention.

"Do you need to go out?" She moved to the back door and opened it. "Here you go. Come on. Get going."

She expected me to defecate on command? Humiliating.

I stood and stiffly walked outside, reminding myself that to her I was a dog. My pride could handle the bruising. I went outside, checked on my hole under the bush, then ran a block away to relieve myself. The human ways were already getting to my head. I couldn't do anything in the yard Gabby walked in. It just wasn't right.

Rachel stood on the back deck, watching for me when I returned.

"I thought you took off on me," she said.

I harrumphed. She kicked me out then worried I wouldn't come back? She didn't make sense.

She stood aside and let me in, then locked the door behind us. I trotted ahead to the living room and eyed Gabby's closed door. I could wait until Rachel went to bed, then shift and let myself in, but it would be better if an accomplice took the blame for my unwanted invasion.

"Night, Clay," Rachel said, moving to her room.

I whined.

She stopped, backed up a step, and looked at me. I sat near the end of the couch, staring at Gabby's door.

"I don't know, bud. She doesn't seem to like you much."

I whined louder and inched closer to Gabby's door.

Rachel sighed. "If she gets mad, you're going to be the one out of a home."

I stood and moved another foot toward Gabby.

"All right, all right." Rachel crossed the room and opened the door for me. I slid by her and gently hopped up on the end of the bed. Rachel eyed me for a minute, but I just settled my head on my paws and closed my eyes.

She shook her head and closed the door. I lifted my head and turned to look at Gabby. She slept peacefully already, her steady breathing shallow and slow.

Breathing deeply of her scent, I set my head on my paws again. I belonged beside her, but I knew not to push my luck.

GABBY WOKE WITH A STRETCH, HER FEET BUMPING AGAINST MY RIBS. She'd done that often during the night, and I'd welcomed each nudge. Any contact was good contact. Apparently not this morning, though.

She sat up abruptly and glared at me.

"No," she whispered. "No dogs allowed on my bed."

I sighed, laid my head down, and closed my eyes. I'd hoped for a nicer morning.

"Seriously, Clay. Don't you think this is just a little inappropriate?"

Not in the least.

"Fine." She braced her hands on the headboard and tried to use her feet to push me off the bed. I opened one eye to watch her strain. I wanted to laugh at her efforts but didn't think she'd appreciate my humor.

She stopped and glared back at me. "If you shed all over my comforter, I'm locking my door at night." She got out of bed. "With an eyehook."

I lifted my head in surprise as she stomped from the room. Her threat didn't worry me. I could get past an eyehook. No, my surprise was that she'd just openly accepted me sleeping in the same bed. Granted, she'd been angry about it. Still, it was a sign she was already coming around. I wanted to grin and shout. Instead, I listened to Rachel ask if Gabby wanted coffee.

I perked up, ready to catch Gabby's answer.

"No. I'm more of a milk or orange juice person."

I listened to Gabby join Rachel in the kitchen. Should I join them? Had I given her enough time to cool down?

"Going to work?" Gabby asked.

"Yep. Sorry to leave you on your own so soon. I'll be back around five. If you need anything, just call my cell. If I don't answer, leave a message, and I'll get back to you," Rachel said. "Oh, when I went to bed, Clay whined at your door, so I let him in. Hope that was okay..."

There was a notable pause. See, I thought to Gabby. Rachel let me in. I hoped Gabby would let go of just a little of her anger.

"Yeah, that's fine," Gabby said.

I could hear the lie in her words.

"Have you thought of taking him to a vet?" Gabby asked.

I groaned and let my head drop to the bed, missing Rachel's answer. Going to the vet didn't bother me; Gabby's stab at revenge did. I felt our connection and knew she did too. How could she so completely ignore it?

"Talk to you tonight," Rachel said.

The back door closed, and I listened to Gabby walk toward me. I didn't move, just watched the doorway for her.

"First," she said as soon as she appeared, "I'd like to clarify that this does not qualify as getting to know each other. Second, you smell like wet dog. If you want to continue to sleep in my room, on my bed, you'll let Rachel give you a bath when she gets home."

I snorted. As if I'd let another woman touch me...more than she already had.

"Third, once I'm awake, you get out. I know what you are, and I am not changing in front of you."

I couldn't hold back my grin on that one. I hadn't even given changing a thought.

Not willing to give her a reason to bar me from her room, I hopped off the bed and gave her the privacy she wanted. Sitting just outside her door, I listened to her move around. Because of a rustling of material, I knew she made the bed. The sound of drawers opening and a zipper told me she was dressing. What would she want to do today now that we were alone? She obviously had getting to know each other on her mind.

The door opened, and she froze when she saw me.

"What are you doing?"

I thought it pretty obvious. Waiting.

She walked around me and went to the kitchen. I followed her and watched her grab a key. She moved to the door, and I trailed her. She stopped and looked at me.

"I'm going for a walk, and you're staying here," she said.

We'd never get to know one another that way. I growled my disagreement. There was no menace in it, but her scent turned sour with fear, anyway.

"Please don't do that. Unless you really *are* trying to scare me."

Frustrated, I stopped making the sound.

"And don't crab at me. I'm not the unlicensed dog without a leash. Do you want me to talk Rachel into buying a pink collar for you?"

Pink? Hell, yes. I chuckled, her threat only reminding me of her swimsuit. Rather than have a standoff that would only upset her more, I turned and walked into the living room. I'd let her have a head start and then follow her.

"See you later," she said from the door.

I watched her walk past the picture window. She never even looked back. I went to the back door, shifted my paw just enough to open it, then closed the door behind me and followed her at a distance.

The walk wasn't bad, but I didn't like the attention she received from the men she passed. I kept quiet about it and continued to watch from a healthy distance. Once she reached a cluster of brick buildings, she turned around. I darted behind a parked car and watched as she retraced her steps.

She stopped at a store and reemerged carrying several bags. They looked heavy, and I wished I could help her. Based on all our previous interactions, I knew how she would respond. Negatively. So, I watched her struggle until we were a block from home, then I darted through the backyards to arrive before her.

I lay on the porch and listened to her steps as she shuffled up the drive.

"Nice to know you can let yourself out," she said as she passed me. She nudged open the door and kicked it closed behind her before I even stood.

I barked loudly and watched her through the door as her shoulders fell in a sigh. But she turned and let me in.

"What? Can't let yourself back in?"

She went to the table and reached into one of the bags.

"Look what I got you." She pulled out a small bag of dog food.

I gave a playful growl, hoping it wouldn't scare her again.

"You want to look like a normal dog don't you? Well...as normal as a dog your size can look, anyway." She set the bag of food on the floor next to my bowl of water, which I refused to look at, and went back to unpacking.

"These are for you," she said, holding up soap and a toothbrush. "You have two choices. You can use them when Rachel's gone, or you can wait until she's back, and I'm sure she'd be happy to help you."

She really thought I smelled? I'd thought she'd said it just because I'd annoyed her. Embarrassed, I stood and left the kitchen. As soon as I cleared the arch, I shifted into a man and walked into the bathroom. I knew how to shower. I'd used a bathroom at the Compound.

A startled yelp told me Gabby had followed me. My lips twitched. Serves her right. A bar of soap and toothbrush clattered to the floor a second before the door slammed shut.

"You could have waited until I put the stuff in there," her muffled voice came through the door.

I bent, picked up the soap, and set the toothbrush on the counter. Then I turned on the shower. I knew better than to step right in, so I waited a minute for it to heat up. It only took one cold spray for a guy to learn his lesson.

Standing under the water, I went to work with the soap. I bathed regularly but always as a wolf. Perhaps that made a difference? It hurt a little to know she didn't like my natural scent, and I reminded myself I wasn't dealing with one of my kind. The rules changed with a human. I knew that. All of us knew the rules.

A knock at the door pulled me from my thoughts.

"I have a towel for you," she said, her words muffled by the door. "If you're still in the shower, I can open the door and toss it on the toilet seat. Okay?"

The water was still running, where else would I be?

"Okay, I'm coming in."

The door slowly opened. I listened to her throw the towel on the toilet and waited for the door to close again.

"My toothpaste is the one marked with the pink nail polish on the cap. I'll let you use it as long as you promise not to squeeze the tube from the middle."

I was already taking a shower, and she was setting rules about squeezing from the middle of the tube? Cupping my hands together, I gathered a good amount of water and tossed it over the curtain. The woman was cold, cruel, and picky. And I still wanted her.

She squeaked.

"You're cleaning that up."

Finally, the door closed.

I sighed and went back to scrubbing. I washed my hair twice and sniffed myself. I reeked like the soap she'd given me. Hopefully she liked the smell. I turned off the water, pulled back the curtain, and reached for the towel.

After drying, I picked up her tube of paste and correctly squeezed it from the end. Then, I scrubbed my teeth until I foamed like a rabid dog. Rinsing, I wondered what she'd have me doing next.

I set the toothbrush back on the counter, tossed the towel to the floor, opened the door, and shifted to my fur.

She sat on the couch with a book raised high enough to block her view. I couldn't help but laugh. What was she so afraid of?

Padding across the room, I waited for her to look at me. She didn't. I hopped up on the couch.

"Don't get too comfortable," she said, relaxing her hold on the book. "I don't know Rachel's rules about pets on the furniture."

She shifted her position, curling her legs under her, then leaned over to sniff me.

My heart stopped, and I held myself still. She'd moved toward me. She'd wanted to sniff me. The embarrassment over her request that I bathe left, and I waited for her reaction.

"Much better," she said, straightening.

Approval. I wanted to laugh and hug her. Instead, I watched her. Did she realize what she'd just done?

She turned back to her book, oblivious, and I wanted to growl in frustration. After a while, I calmed down and started reading over her shoulder. That was one human thing my father had insisted I learn. Their words. I needed to know them, speak them, and read them to keep myself safe.

So I sat beside her for hours, reading until her stomach rumbled.

She stood, and I hoped like hell she wouldn't pour me a bowl of dog food. If she did, I'd change in front of her again and raid the fridge for myself. As she walked past the bathroom, she paused and stared down at my towel.

"Next time, fold it over the edge of the tub," she said.

If I had hands, I would have run them through my hair. The only thing I'd done right since arriving was using soap. It was depressing.

She went to the kitchen and started putting together two sandwiches. I stayed out of her way but watched her closely. Each deliberate move held a subtle grace that highlighted her calm beauty. Though I told myself I watched her to learn more about it, the truth was that I just liked to watch her. Seeing her soothed me.

"I'm guessing your bowl of dog food will always be full," she said as she set a plate with a sandwich on the floor.

I glanced at the sandwich she'd made for me. The simple meal meant she was continuing to acknowledge the man within me. She sat at the table, completely unaware that she'd given me hope again. I ate my sandwich in two bites.

"So, we have a week before my classes start up. What's your plan?"

Plan? I tilted my head to study her.

"Did you want to try to enroll in any classes? Study anything?"

The only thing I wanted to study was her. I lay down and stared at my plate. So far, the information I'd gathered didn't amount to much.

"Okay...well, if you change your mind, let me know."

She washed our dishes then went back to reading. I waited for her to get comfortable then joined her on the couch. She didn't seem to mind when I leaned against her and read over her shoulder. In fact, when she read, she didn't seem to notice me at all.

Was that a good thing or a bad thing? For now, I figured it was good. If she didn't notice me, she couldn't object to me. Later, well, I hoped with enough time she wouldn't want to ignore me.

SEVERAL HOURS and another dry ham sandwich later, I stood by my bowl. It was in line of sight of the couch, and I was thirsty. But thirsty enough to drink from the bowl where Gabby would see? I wasn't sure.

Outside, I heard a car pull into the driveway. A door opened. Steps thumped on the deck. Then the door swung open, and Rachel swept in. She threw her keys on the counter, and her eyes zeroed in on me. This couldn't be good.

In her left hand, she held a collar and a leash.

Hell, no.

Rachel knelt in front of me with a smile. I narrowed my eyes at her, and when she tried to wrap her arms around my neck, I dodged.

"Come on," she said softly, trying to wrangle me.

I kept moving.

"Just hold still."

Not likely, woman.

She heaved a sigh and sat back on her heels to stare at me.

I'd been kicked out, ignored, poorly fed—two sandwiches were a snack in my mind—told I stunk, and now Rachel wanted to collar me. Not happening.

"This is a joke," she said.

Gabby laughed from the doorway, surprising me. I glanced at her and saw her amusement. When Rachel tried again, I ducked under her arms. Gabby grinned wider and met my gaze.

"Here." She held out her hand to Rachel. "I'll try."

"Good luck," Rachel said with a chuckle as she got off her knees and handed over the collar.

I watched Gabby closely as she approached.

"It was the biggest collar they had," Rachel said. "I don't even know if it fits. He wouldn't let me get close enough."

Gabby knelt in front of me, still clearly amused.

"Clay, if you want to be able to go anywhere with us, you need a collar we can clip a leash on. Not just the twine you have holding your tag around your neck."

Did that mean she wouldn't try to leave me behind again? I was still debating if I could put up with a collar when she leaned forward and wrapped her arms around my neck. I held still and closed my eyes. She could do whatever she wanted as long as she kept touching me. Her light movement brushed over my fur, and I barely held back a shiver.

"At least it's not pink," she said with a pat, and I realized she'd already removed my tags and collared me.

She stood quickly and turned away.

"Hey, I wouldn't do that to him," Rachel said with a laugh. "No pink for our man. I don't know why he sat still for you and not me."

Rachel came toward me and bent to kiss the top of my head. I sighed.

"He's moody," Gabby said, meeting my gaze.

Me? Moody? I gazed after her as she left the kitchen. Would I ever understand her?

RACHEL STOOD, AND I HUFFED A RELIEVED SIGH. SHE WAS TOO FOND OF rubbing my fur. I hoped Gabby would eventually come around and stand up for me.

"Hey, Gabby," Rachel called as she walked to her room. "Want to go out with me tonight? Girl's night out? Hit a few clubs?"

My head snapped up, and I strained to hear Gabby's answer from the bedroom. She had better say no or she'd have a wolf trailing her, causing mass hysteria.

"Um, thanks for the offer, but I think I'll stay here. I want to be sure I'm settled before school starts."

I heaved a relieved sigh.

"All right," Rachel said. "I just didn't want you to feel like I'm abandoning you. I hate staying home, and when I'm not working, I like to go out. If you ever want to come with, just say."

Not happening.

"Sure."

Gabby's half-hearted answer reassured me. I sighed and went back to contemplating my bowl. Now that I had a collar, I really didn't want to drink like a dog.

Rachel reemerged dressed in a short skirt that barely peeked out from under her jacket. Where was she going dressed like that? And she'd wanted Gabby to go with her? I'd drink out of the bowl and start eating dog food before I let Gabby go out like that.

Rachel patted me on the head on her way out the back door. I lingered in the kitchen, listening to her get into her car and drive off. Then, silence held the house. Had Gabby gone to bed? Taking a chance, I shifted, went to the sink, and got myself a glass of water.

Would Gabby remember she'd said I could join her? I finished my drink, set the cup aside, then hesitated. If she didn't remember, she'd kick me out. Better to wait until she slept and not push her.

I shifted back into my fur and waited fifteen minutes then quietly padded to Gabby's door. It wasn't shut all the way, a sign she'd remembered. I smiled. Maybe she wasn't as opposed to me as she seemed.

I pushed the door open with my nose and jumped up on the end of the bed. Inhaling her scent, I settled into my designated spot. With some luck, I wouldn't be at the end of the bed much longer.

"Get out," Gabby said as soon as she woke.

Her less than charitable tone let me know she wasn't as close to coming around as I'd hoped. With a quiet sigh, I hopped off the bed and exited the room. The house was quiet since Rachel had already left. That woman barely slept.

I settled on the couch to wait for Gabby and whatever she had planned for the day.

When Gabby emerged, she passed me without acknowledgment then wandered around the house for a bit. She'd seemed bored, a state of existence I understood well, so I stayed out of her way. After only a few minutes, she shut herself in her room again, which I found odd.

Inside her room, I heard the faint sound of a zipper and the rustle of clothes. I hopped off the couch and moved closer to the door, trying to listen. She was changing? She'd just gotten dressed.

I'd barely sat down to wait when the door swung open. Gabby, wearing her swimsuit, stood within the doorway. My gut clenched at the sight of her pale limbs and smooth stomach, and I thanked whatever thought had inspired her to change. My mouth went dry as I studied every inch of her. I itched to touch her again, to hold her in my arms.

With effort, I lifted my gaze. Did she know how much I loved that suit? Had she changed just for me? Her wide eyes and the livid blush that stained her cheeks gave me my answer. She hadn't.

She stepped back and slammed the door. Too late, I realized I'd screwed up by openly showing my interest in her. I wanted to yowl my frustration, but I kept quiet. We were learning each other. We were bound to make mistakes. Patience. I just needed patience.

When she reemerged wearing shorts and a bitty top, she ignored me and marched out the back door. I followed cautiously and watched her disappear into the garage. A minute later, she pushed the lawn mower out.

She bent to check a few things and push a button. I only gave what she did half my attention. The rest of my focus remained on the curve of her backside.

She yanked back on a cord, and the mower started with an annoying roar. Too soon, the air filled with its stink. But the view of Gabby's legs as she pushed the machine back and forth made the smell endurable.

When she finished, she cast an annoyed glance my direction. She didn't like me eyeing her in her suit; now, she didn't like me watching her mow the lawn. What did she expect me to do? Frustrated, I ducked into the house and took another shower to cool off and to wash the exhaust from my skin.

I dried myself, correctly draped the towel over the edge of the tub, then opened the door a crack. Shifting to my fur, I nudged the door open further and wandered out to look for her.

She sat on the couch reading again. I padded across the room and jumped up next to her. This time, I didn't earn a sniff. Disappointed, I settled in for another long, hungry morning and afternoon.

She barely moved or acknowledged me the entire time. The only highlight to the day was the end of it...and the memory of her in her swimsuit. Yeah, that image wasn't ever going to leave me.

Gabby went to bed, and I waited again, unsure of my welcome. But I found her door unlatched and sighed in relief. How could I feel so hopeful and dejected at the same time?

I hopped up on the bed and stared down at her.

The need to touch her clawed at me. Quietly, I shifted into my human skin and shivered slightly as I moved from the end of the bed to lie beside her. Carefully, I eased myself onto my side. I didn't dare slide under the covers. Face to face, I watched her sleep; ever so carefully, I brushed a fingertip along her cheek. Her soft skin begged for more, but I withdrew my hand.

She confused me and seemed cold at times, but she was mine. Eventually, she'd come to terms with that.

I inhaled deeply, breathing in her scent, and closed my eyes.

A CHANGE in her breathing woke me. I quickly shifted to my fur before she caught me in her bed without clothes on. That wouldn't end well for me.

Her eyes snapped open and locked onto me.

"Now, just hold on," she said. "You're a dog. Act like one. Fur stays at the foot of the bed."

I pretended to mind as I moved to the end of the bed, staring at her the whole time, but I didn't. I was too grateful she hadn't caught me sleeping naked next to her.

"Don't give me your doleful eyes. This is your choice, not mine."

Wait. Did that mean—

"Not that you'd get to sleep next to me in your skin, either. So, don't even think about it."

We were starting to think alike, I thought with a grin.

"If you don't like the end of the bed, you can always sleep on the floor."

The floor? No. My spot was beside her. I just needed to help her figure that out.

After she kicked me out so she could dress, she joined me in the kitchen and spent a lot of time staring at the newspaper. While she did that, I considered what I could do to help her see me as her Mate. An unlocked door at night was a good start. I wanted more than that. I wanted to be the one she talked to when she was upset, the one she came to for comfort, the one to hold her for the rest of her life—

She stood suddenly, jarring me from my thoughts. When she moved to get her house key and her bag, I quickly got to my feet and waited by the door.

She scowled down at me but I didn't flinch away from her gaze. I wore the degrading collar. She wouldn't be leaving without me. For good measure, I shook my neck to jingle my tags.

Sighing, she reached for the leash and clipped it on. I gloated. On the inside.

As soon as we were outside, she pulled a phone from her pocket and dialed a number. I listened to her conversation and found out she wanted to go see a car.

I agreed she needed one. That forty-minute walk to those brick buildings, where she planned to take classes, was too long for her to make each day. There were too many men along the way. Plus, it would get colder. A car would help keep her away from men and out of the cold.

Side by side, we made our way to the address the man had given her. The place wasn't hard to find. An old car sat parked on the front lawn. Gabby paused on the sidewalk, studying the vehicle. It wasn't any worse than what I often saw at the Compound.

"Hello," a man called from the garage.

I swung my gaze to the man as he stepped out and walked toward us. He seemed average height for a human. Middle aged and carrying a bit of extra weight, as they tended to do. He barely glanced at me as he approached. His fixated stare at Gabby made my fur bristle.

"I'm Howard. You called about the car?"

"I did," she said, and without giving her name, she turned toward the car before he could offer his hand. Smart girl.

I lingered, watching her back as she moved away.

"It's a decent car for the price," he said, moving past her and popping the hood. She peeked inside, and he moved close to her. Too close.

I nudged him aside and jumped up, bracing my paws on the front end. The man yipped like a startled pup but backed away as I wanted. Ignoring him, I stared at the engine, comparing what I saw to Sam's truck. I nodded to myself. It looked similar.

"I'll take it," Gabby said.

Just like that? She had too much trust in people. He hadn't even told her much about the car. It didn't seem to matter to her, though.

"Do you have the title ready to sign over?"

"Sure. Let me run inside."

A few minutes later, I contorted myself to sit in the very cramped passenger seat as we drove away.

The car needed a good cleaning. It reeked of stale smoke.

THE REST of the week followed a very similar pattern. She read a lot, made a trip to purchase more books—I rode along and dutifully waited in the car—then she started to read those, too.

Some of the subjects were interesting. Woman's literature

fascinated me. It wasn't the context but the concept. A whole class just about women's books and the impact they had on the world. Did they have a men's literature?

Monday, when she grabbed her keys, I jumped to follow her to the door.

"Your license only wins you so much freedom. Dogs aren't allowed on campus and definitely not in the classroom."

I growled. There was no way she was going to that place full of men without me.

"Clay, I'm putting up with you in my house and on my bed. Don't push this."

Her tone and scent had me backing off. I wouldn't push. A ride in the car would have been convenient, but I could just as easily follow her on foot.

I JUMPED onto the couch with a sigh and flopped down. I now understood why humans hated Mondays. The campus had been chaos, and following Gabby had been impossible. Security had chased me off the grounds, then chased me again when I returned.

I needed clothes, I needed to blend, and I needed to shower before Gabby came home, which could be any time. Her schedule remained a mystery to me. Lifting my head, I glanced out the window. I hadn't wanted to leave the campus yet, but wasn't given a choice. The last security guard had fired a pellet gun at me.

A familiar car pulled into the driveway, and I huffed a sigh. I'd forgotten about Rachel. So much for a shower.

"Clay," she called as soon as she opened the door.

I stood and jogged to her just so she wouldn't keep yelling.

"Hey, bud! Look what I brought you."

She opened her foam container and showed me a half-eaten burger. It almost made up for her attempt to get Gabby to go out with her. She set it on the floor, and I wolfed it down. The bacon on the burger made me want to groan. I hadn't eaten anything since leaving the house.

"You sure are hungry." She glanced at the dish. "Don't you like your food?"

Nope, but I'd have to remember to get rid of it every now and again so Rachel wouldn't worry about it.

"I wonder when Gabby's coming home..." She stepped to the fridge and lifted the top few layers of paper held to the side by a magnetic clip.

"Today's a late one."

As I swallowed the last bite, I realized she was looking at Gabby's schedule. Rachel glanced at me.

"Stay home and hang out with you or go out?"

Go out. Go out.

"What do you think?"

I turned my back to her, trotted to Gabby's room, and hopped up on the end of the bed, hopefully making it clear I didn't want to hang out with Rachel.

She peeked into the room and grinned at me. "I don't get why you like her so much. She doesn't feed you good stuff like I do. Better remember that."

She didn't seem mad or offended by my preference. Only amused. She went to her room, and I listened to her change. The woman rarely closed her door.

A few minutes later, I heard her leave her room and walk to the kitchen.

"Clay. Come on, Clay. Time to go out."

The indignities I suffered. I hopped off the bed and dutifully went outside. She watched me through the door this time. Who watched like that? I strode behind the shed, stood there for a suitable amount of time, then returned to the yard. She opened the door as soon as she saw me.

"You're such a good boy," she said, scratching my head. "I'll bring you a treat when I come home."

I wouldn't lie to myself. The food treats tempted me.

As soon as her car pulled out of the driveway, I shifted to my skin and looked at Gabby's schedule. She wouldn't be home for a while yet.

With a sigh, I went to take a quick shower, then waited for her on the couch.

JUST BEFORE I grew bored enough to start chewing on the table legs, I heard her car in the driveway. I hopped off the couch and hurried to the back door. Seeing her again made my chest ache. How could I miss someone I didn't understand or know?

She didn't acknowledge me when she stepped inside. She let her bag drop to the floor with a thump and moved to the fridge.

"I'm starving." She wasn't talking to me, but herself.

I stayed out of her way as she moved about, grabbing what she needed to make two sandwiches. She absently handed me one when she finished and stuck hers in her mouth, freeing her hands so she could carry her bag to her room. I quickly chomped my food down before she made it to the arch and followed her. Did she even realize I was here?

I wasn't expecting her to feel the way I did, but her complete indifference hurt.

In her room, she tiredly kicked off her shoes and set her bag on the mattress. She took a bite of her sandwich with one hand and started to read one of her books. Her gaze didn't leave the pages as she eased onto the bed and curled her legs under her, getting comfortable.

Hopping up on the bed, I joined her. She didn't flinch at all as I curled up beside her. In fact, she didn't do anything but read for a long time.

Eventually, she started to yawn.

"Come on, Clay. Out. I need to change." A yawn punctuated her request.

Suppressing a sigh, I hopped off the bed and left the room. When she opened the door again, I waited until I heard her get into bed before joining her. The soft rhythm of her breathing changed within minutes, letting me know she slept.

The next day followed the same routine. She woke, kicked me out, and left for class. I followed her to campus to make sure the piece of junk car didn't break down on the way, then went home to wait for her.

I was beginning to see why other people had made decisions for her. Her choice to go to college didn't seem like a smart one. It was boring as hell. But, I was near her, and if reading all the time made her happy...I sighed. I would just need to accept it.

Though I would have rather held her attention, I didn't mind watching her read. Observing her, I began to learn her body language. When she read something that confused her, she chewed her lip. When she read something interesting, she wrote it down. When she doubted what she read, she pulled out another book to see what that said. She often became so engrossed she forgot to drink anything at night; and she always studied until she yawned for the third time.

My time alone in the house was much harder to endure. I chafed at the situation, wishing I knew what to do to integrate myself into her life. Desperation drove me to pick up one of her textbooks. Maybe understanding what she read would give me insight into why she read it and her life. Instead, I quickly discovered why she went to bed after the third yawn.

Once I grew tired, the words tended to swim around in my head and made very little sense. I managed two chapters of biology before I closed that book and moved on to a different one. I picked at random from her dresser.

When she came home that night, she tossed me a sandwich, like she had the night before, and went to her room. She seemed to notice I'd moved her books around. I watched her study them, wondering if I'd upset her. She didn't say anything, though, just picked one up and started reading.

The next day she didn't come home with her usual distracted air.

"Hey, Clay," she called as she pushed through the door.

I stood abruptly from my normal waiting spot near the stove, wondering why she needed me. The movement drew her attention, and she looked at me with a slight smile on her face. My heart leapt at the sight. Was she actually happy to see me?

"Brought you something," she said.

The fact that she'd thought of me while she was out made me want to grin. My patience was paying off. I was sure of it.

Then, she pulled three books from her bag and set them on the table. Books? She'd brought me books? Of course she did. She read constantly, and had given me something that meant a great deal to her.

I eyed the titles. Books about plants and wildlife. Though I doubted they contained anything I didn't already know, I turned to Gabby, trying to figure out how to thank her for thinking of me. But she was already digging in the fridge, my moment of attention already gone. With a sigh, I waited, ready to accept my sandwich and follow her to her room.

That night, after she and Rachel went to sleep, I went to the kitchen, grabbed one of my books, and stayed up late reading. As I thought, the book didn't offer anything new; but it was better than her textbooks.

The following morning, after I returned from campus, I tried to continue reading but grew frustrated. The books were fine. The waiting at home wasn't. I wanted to walk with her to each class and face the men there as a man. Though she seemed to tolerate me, I didn't think she was ready to accept me openly. I needed to find a way to make myself useful, a way for her to need me.

Giving up on reading, I stared out the window. What could I

offer her that she would need? She didn't seem to need or want a man's attention or affection. I recalled her sigh last night when we'd run out of ham. She needed someone to bring her food. Unless she liked fresh rabbit—which I doubted was the case—I needed money and a job to provide for her.

A car drove past, and I smiled.

If Gabby was willing to bring me books, maybe I could teach myself enough about cars to be useful to her. The rusted thing she drove would need attention eventually.

That night, after she went to sleep, I eased off the bed and shifted to my skin. I tore a page from one of her notebooks and picked up a pen. With the pen against the paper, I hesitated. How should I start? How would I end? Love, Clay? I sighed, looked at her curled under the covers, and knew I needed to keep it simple for both our sakes. She wasn't ready for even a hint of what I felt for her. The brief encounter with her in her swimsuit proved that.

I wrote the word *mechanics*, then leaned the paper against the stack of books she'd brought me. Hopefully, she'd understand.

As soon as she moved, I was awake. I held myself still as she sat up and brushed her hair out of her face. She looked over at the dresser, as if sensing something was out of place, and got out of bed. She picked up the note, stared at it for a moment, then turned to glare at me.

"So you can write words to me, just not speak them?"

I wanted to cringe. I hadn't considered that.

"Whatever. You're going to get caught creeping around the house at night."

However, when she returned home, she had several books on mechanics and one on do-it-yourself home repairs.

Chapter Eight

GABBY WAS DEEP IN THOUGHT AS SHE READ NEXT TO ME ON OUR BED. Since bringing me the books on mechanics, time with Gabby had become more special. She had seen right away that I couldn't turn the pages on my own and told me to nudge her when I needed a flip. She'd unknowingly given me permission to touch her. And over the past week, I'd read fast and brushed my nose against her bare leg as often as I could.

Tonight, her scent clouded my senses, and I swam in my own paradise as she sat beside me. I didn't mind that she didn't seem to notice me because I knew what was happening. She was accepting not only my presence but me, too.

Though I'd already decided to learn more about mechanics to help her, her acceptance pushed me harder to learn faster. I needed a way to show her what she meant to me. What her acceptance meant to me.

So I absorbed the information on the pages. The basics of an engine were easy to grasp, but the practical application was a bit harder. I couldn't work on her car during the day, mostly because she was gone at school, and partially because I knew she wasn't yet ready to see me as a man. So at night, I carefully used her car as a test subject with the tools I'd procured here and there from the neighbors.

Soon, I moved from the engine basics to a deeper understanding of the subsystems and the hi-tech tools needed to troubleshoot them.

I was reading about those tools when I heard a car pull into the drive and another pull in front of the house. Lifting my head, I listened to Rachel's familiar step as she walked down the drive. Then, she was speaking to someone.

I nudged Gabby, and she automatically turned my page for me. I smiled and was tempted to kiss her for her consideration but decided to nudge her again. The second nudge broke through her concentration. She finally looked up and met my gaze. I looked pointedly at the closed bedroom door. We both heard the front door open and Rachel speaking.

"...and this is where I live. Please have a seat, and I'll change quickly. My roommate and our dog should be around here somewhere."

"No rush," a man answered. "Our reservation isn't until six."

Gabby looked at me, her eyes wide and her scent clouding with worry. Why would it worry her that Rachel brought a man home? I didn't care for it either; but after seeing the way Rachel dressed when she went out, I'd known it would be inevitable.

Rachel knocked on Gabby's door, and Gabby jumped slightly. Her behavior puzzled me. Gabby rushed to close the book in front of me and called, "Come in."

The words were barely out of Gabby's mouth when Rachel walked in still wearing her clothes from her job at the hospital. She reeked of chemicals and sickness. Though she smiled, her flushed cheeks had me worrying. Gabby wasn't like me; she could get sick. I hoped Rachel stayed back until she washed.

"There you are," Rachel said, closing the door. "Come meet Peter." She walked closer to Gabby and dropped her voice to a whisper. "Don't kill me, but he has a friend without a date tonight, and I said I had a friend without a date tonight...please come with."

A what? I turned to stare at Gabby, who groaned. Anxiety drifted from her. I didn't know what a date meant, but Gabby didn't seem to like it. The fact that Rachel had brought a man home and now wanted Gabby to leave with her, worried me.

"Don't do this to me, Rachel. This won't end well, and you'll probably never forgive me."

"Come on...please?" Rachel said as she sat on the bed next to Gabby. "I really like this one."

Frustratingly ignorant, my confused gaze bounced between the two women.

"That's the problem. Remember what I said? It's always a guy who ruins a friendship."

I didn't remember that conversation, but Rachel seemed to. Not that it appeared to stop her from begging.

"I don't want to go out tonight," Gabby said softly, desperation changing her tone.

Go out. I knew that term. That meant leaving dressed in short skirts. I glared at Rachel. No amount of leftovers would atone for this.

Gabby glanced at me, then gave me a nudge. Was the nudge because I was glaring or because she wanted me to bite Rachel? I was willing to bite.

"I like having a friend," Gabby said.

Something in her tone stopped my glare, and I turned to study her. Gabby held herself back from people. I'd witnessed that over the summer and when I'd followed her to school. Yet, she wasn't that way with Rachel. She relaxed around her. I'd noticed that right away. Could it be that Gabby was as lonely as me?

"If he hits on you, then it wasn't meant to be. Don't worry so much," Rachel said with a smile.

Rachel pulled Gabby off the bed, and I hopped down, sticking close to Gabby. I wasn't sure what they'd decided. Were they going out or was Rachel just introducing Gabby to the man in the living room?

In the living room, a man with light hair and light brown eyes sat on the couch. He stood as soon as he saw the women. Or, rather, Rachel. His gaze didn't waver from her, the scent of his attraction flooding the air.

Good. He could have Rachel. Not her leftovers, though. Those were still mine for putting up with the damn collar.

Rachel stepped aside and introduced Gabby, whose anxiety spiked a moment before it disappeared. The man met Gabby's gaze, politely nodded, and went back to staring adoringly at Rachel.

I studied Gabby as she exhaled in relief. What had she expected from the man?

Rachel was saying something as she inched her way to the arch, but I didn't really hear her words until she said, "Tell her about Scott." I whipped my gaze to Rachel, who had already disappeared around the corner to her bedroom.

Beside me, Gabby's fading anxiety flared with an edge toward panic. I glanced at the man, but he was still where he'd been, staring at the empty arch where Rachel had been, obviously infatuated with her. Who was Scott, and why the panic from Gabby?

Gabby made a small noise that drew Peter out of his daze.

He cleared his throat and looked at Gabby. She took a soft, deep breath. Nothing he could hear, but I did. She was trying to calm herself. I wished I understood what was upsetting her.

"Nice to meet you, Gabby."

"You too," she said, sounding normal. "Want to sit?"

She motioned him to the couch and took the chair for herself.

Continuing to observe her, I lay on the floor between them. As if sensing my attention, she glanced at me and then back up at the man.

"This is Clay," she said.

I turned and found Peter staring at me.

"He's huge," he said.

"Yeah. So, who's Scott?" Gabby said, asking what I wanted to know, too.

Peter looked back up at Gabby. "Oh, a friend of mine. He's also in med school. We had plans to go to O'Donell's tonight for dinner and a drink or two. Then, I ran into Rachel and invited her to join us. We thought it'd be more fun if you could come, too."

A date meant meeting another man? Not happening. I looked to Gabby, waiting for her to say no, but Rachel came back into the room just then, dressed in a skirt so short I could see her underwear if I wanted to look.

"Of course you will, won't you, Gabby?"

There was a silent exchange between the two that had both wearing a pleading look.

"Okay," Gabby said slowly, giving in. "But I need to be home early enough to let Clay out."

What? I was too stunned to react.

"I'm sure he'll be fine for that little while." Rachel waved her hand dismissively at me, and I made a choked noise. What had just happened?

"Go get dressed," Rachel said, waving Gabby toward her room.

Gabby stood, ready to listen to Rachel, the short skirt queen. Gabby's willingness finally broke my control. There was no way she was leaving with Rachel and love-boy to meet up with some other guy.

I stood and rushed to block Gabby from entering her room. She eyed me and tried to step around me, but I cut her off.

Rachel laughed. "Come here, Clay. Come here and let Gabby get ready." She squatted down and patted her leg. She was lucky I didn't have fingers at the moment.

Ignoring Rachel, I continued to block Gabby. She had to understand. I wasn't okay with this.

"I've never seen him act like this," Rachel said.

Because I'd never been this angry with her and Gabby. I almost bared my teeth. Only Gabby's considering gaze kept me sane.

"I'm surprised you have such a wild looking dog," the man said. "It seems too big compared to the house...and the two of you."

Gabby shook her head ever so slightly and dropped to her knees in front of me. She wrapped her arms around my neck, hugging me. My pulse stuttered with her mouth so close to my neck. I forgot to breathe, but lack of air wasn't what made my chest ache and my gut clench.

Bite me, I pleaded silently. Show them I'm yours and you're mine.

Instead, she spoke softly near my ear.

"I'm not crazy about the idea either, but you have to let me go and stop acting weird."

Have to? No. I didn't have to.

She pulled back.

"Ready to be good, Clay?" She stood and scratched me behind the ear...just as a pet owner would do.

The pain in my chest grew worse, and I turned, went to her room, and jumped up on the end of her bed. She followed me in, closed the door, and folded her arms. An edge of anxiety lingered in her scent, warring with her growing anger.

"I am not changing in front of you."

Exactly. I grinned at her and lay on the blanket. Her eyes narrowed on me for a moment, then she shrugged.

"Fine. I'll change in the bathroom."

She turned and pretended to study the clothes hanging in the closet. She was bluffing. She had to be. But why? Did she want me to be jealous? I already was. The idea of the hours she spent around men while on campus each day nearly drove me insane. She didn't need to add a date. What did she have to prove? She already owned me. I was here, in the human world, trying to figure out how to blend into her life, trying to make us work. What more did she want from me?

Gabby reached for a skirt just as short as the one Rachel wore. Not in this lifetime. I growled.

"Zip it." She grabbed some kind of silky top. It had more material than the skirt.

She really meant to go. I sat up and started to vent.

If you're trying to make me jealous, it worked. Put it down. You're not going anywhere, especially wearing any of that.

Of course, all she heard was barking. Still, it felt good to actually say something to her.

She spun toward me, her eyes wide with shock.

"What the hell, Clay? Cut it out."

Like hell. You know you belong to me. I'm trying to be patient but this is asking too much. You can't go to dinner with another man while feeding me dog food and making me drink out of a bowl.

Rachel burst in without knocking, and the man right behind her. I stood and yelled at both of them.

Get out and take your man-boy with you.

"What's wrong?" Rachel asked, her gaze bouncing between me and Gabby.

As if she didn't know. I growled and barked nonsense just because I was so pissed at the way things were turning out.

"Nothing," Gabby said, yelling over me. "Just give me a few minutes to calm him down, okay?"

Calm me down? I stopped barking and glared at the three of them. Gabby walked toward me with the clothes still under one arm. I growled at them, and she faltered. A hint of fear drifted to me, and I immediately felt guilty.

"Uh, I'm not so sure you should do that right now," Peter said.

I will jump off this bed and mark you if you don't leave now.

"Enough," Gabby said forcefully, her voice echoing in the small room.

I snapped my mouth closed but bared my teeth at the man.

Gabby gave me a hard look, then turned toward the pair.

"I'm fine. Thank you. Just give me a few minutes to change."

Once they left, shutting the door behind them, Gabby closed her eyes and took a slow breath as if she were the angry one. I couldn't believe it.

When she turned to look at me, I glared at her. Sure, I'd known she hadn't wanted me here, but I thought she understood our connection. I hadn't been searching for a Mate. I hadn't wanted her any more than she'd wanted me. No, that wasn't quite true. I'd never hoped for a Mate because I thought it impossible for someone like me. I had no pack, no family, no way to offer protection and safety other than with my teeth and claws. Just because I hadn't hoped for a Mate didn't mean I didn't want one. I wanted her. Badly. Why couldn't she see that?

"Will you bite me if I sit next to you, Clay?"

I snorted and the rest of my anger left me. She was just as lost as I was. I needed to remember that. I sat back down and waited.

"You know I don't understand dog, right?"

Which was a good thing.

"It'd be so much easier if you just told me what was wrong."

She finally turned to face me. When her gaze met mine, I saw the turmoil there. I'd done that. Regret pounded at me, and I wanted to shift so I could use my hand to cup her face and try to erase the mess of emotions sparking in her gaze. I wanted to kiss away any thought of meeting another man. How could she not know what was wrong? I sighed and nudged the clothes she still held.

"You don't like the clothes or that I'm going out?"

All of it, I thought with a nod.

"You don't like both?"

I lay down on the mattress, glad we finally understood each other.

"You're really frustrating me, Clay."

What?

She moved to get up, and I growled, nowhere near ready to stop trying to communicate.

"Now, hold on..." She stood, turned, and put her hands on her hips as she eyed me with annoyance.

"I'm trying here, Clay, and you're not. So stop growling at me. Got it? And so what if I go out? Do you trust me so little? Have you not been paying attention? I'm not comfortable around guys. It's not as if I'm going to go out tonight and come back with a boyfriend or something. So, just chill out about your Claim, all right?"

So she did understand and meant to go anyway? I growled in frustration.

"We're not talking unMated males," she said softly. "They're just men."

I laughed in disbelief. Just men? All men, whether werewolf or human, were a threat to the tenuous hold I had on her.

I hopped off the bed and moved toward her. She stepped back, worry in her gaze, and I felt ashamed again. I'd done that. With my anger and impatience, I'd scared her.

"Sorry."

I could hear she meant it. I should be the one apologizing to her.

"Let me think, Clay."

She sat on the bed, and I watched her think for a moment.

"Can we compromise? I don't want to spend the entire year sitting at home with a possessive dog who won't talk to me."

I resented that she'd called me a dog, but I understood her point. If only she were ready to deal with me as a man and potential Mate.

"What if we went somewhere dog friendly? There's a bar with cute little bistro tables on the sidewalk. If you're on your leash, you could come."

Again with the dog reference. I turned around and faced the door so she could change. If she was set on going, I wasn't going to let her out of my sight for a second.

"Is that a yes? I'm taking that as a yes. If you turn around while I'm changing, I'm going to have you neutered."

I laughed at her threat. She was thinking of my—the soft rustle of material distracted me. I swallowed hard. She was changing. Right there behind me. A tremble raced down my spine. I ached to shift.

A slight movement caught my attention. I glanced up, and my world stopped. In the mirror, I watched her pull her shirt over her head. The thing she wore underneath was like her bathing suit but with slightly wider straps and in all white. Pure, like her. I wanted to touch her so badly I shook with need. She pulled a new top over her head, and suddenly, her gaze met mine in the mirror.

Give me a sign, I thought, and I'll change into a man to touch you. Just one sign.

"Hope it was worth it," she said. "You're on the couch tonight."

That wasn't what I'd hoped for.

She walked past me to open the door, and I saw she already wore the short skirt. She looked amazing. Sexy. I wanted to pull her back into the room and bar the door.

"All set, but can we change our plans?" she asked as she stepped out. "I think Clay was freaking out because he knows we're leaving. He's been left alone so much this week..."

Following closely behind Gabby, I didn't miss Peter's doubtful look. Rachel made pity noises and came at me. I narrowed my eyes at her, but she didn't seem to notice.

"What if we went to that bar with the bistro tables that you were telling me about?" Gabby asked.

"That'd be perfect. It's still nice enough out. Besides, I think this is the last week they do the outdoor dining. We should go before it's closed for the season."

Peter spoke up. "Are you sure he will be okay? He looked pretty aggressive in there."

Aggressive? That was nothing. I was ready to show him my teeth when Rachel's hand stilled on my head. She looked at Peter.

"He's never done that before. I think Gabby might be right. We've been leaving him alone a lot."

See, even your woman wants me along.

"I even forgot to let him out this morning before I left," she said.

Why did she have to go there?

"Let me grab my shoes," Gabby said. "I'll follow you guys in my car just in case I need to leave early."

"I'll let Scott know about the change in plans," Peter said.

It would be better if he didn't tell Scott about the change in plans. I hated Scott, and I didn't even know him. Somehow, I didn't think biting him at first sight would win me any points with Gabby.

"I'll let Clay out." Rachel got up and started calling to me. I glanced at Gabby, giving her my best is-she-serious look. Gabby's gaze held no pity.

"You know the drill. Go do dog business."

Patience, I reminded myself as I stood and left the room.

As soon as Rachel closed the door behind me, I went to the passenger side of the car and opened the door. I wished I had some clothes. If I did, I would've thrown them on and went with Gabby like I was supposed to. What would she do? Probably throw a fit. She was too willing to see me as a dog and not at all willing to see me as a man.

I sighed and waited for her. She stepped out a minute later, shaking her head at me. It seemed I was constantly disappointing her. She opened the door and got in.

"You're going to be seen doing stuff a dog shouldn't do."

A dog. Yep, that's how she saw me, and that knowledge ate at me.

"That or someone's going to call the cops because a naked man keeps popping up in my backyard."

And if I wasn't a dog, I was still a crazy man in her mind. I suppressed a defeated sigh. Couldn't she give me some hope?

"You okay?"

I looked at her, wondering if she could see my pain.

"Fine," she sighed when I didn't speak. "No growling, no

biting, no barking. Pretty much no anything but acting like a passive, well-behaved dog." As she spoke, she backed out of the driveway and turned onto the street to follow Peter's car.

"I'm really nervous about this and don't want to worry about you, too."

So she'd guessed my plan to bite Scott? I heaved a sigh and looked out the window.

For the next few minutes, she just drove.

"Clay, you should know...men make me uncomfortable because of the way they act around me."

I turned to watch her.

"They usually start flirting or ask me on a date. Most girls would be flattered, but if you really pay attention, there's something unnatural about it. It's like they can't help themselves. And sometimes, after I tell them no enough, they walk away with...I don't know...a look. Like they've been caught doing something they're ashamed of. I just want to try for normal tonight, okay? It'll be hard enough being in a public place. You'll see. I just need to know you're not going to make it any harder on me."

She'd just told me men wouldn't leave her alone, then wanted a promise that I wouldn't react? Yeah, right. I went back to looking out the window, already knowing I'd do as she asked...because she'd asked.

She reached out and ran a hand lightly over my shoulder. My tension and anger left me with that single touch. She was my world. There wasn't anything I wouldn't do for her. Except give her up.

"Does it bother you when I pet you?"

Fear that she'd stop kept me from laughing. Instead, I curled up as tight as possible and shifted my position to lay my head in her lap. She laughed, a quiet husky sound that made me want to wrap my arms around her.

Too soon she pulled into a parking spot, and I had to sit up again. The calm I'd gained quickly fled. We were here so Rachel and her new friend could introduce Gabby to another man. I wanted to bare my teeth, but Gabby's increasing worry stopped me. She didn't want to be here, either. She'd said as much.

She snapped the leash on me and opened her door. I followed her out and stayed close to her side as we walked.

While Gabby talked to Rachel and the man-boy, I scanned ahead, looking for the man they meant Gabby to meet. He was hard to miss. As over groomed as a poodle, he stood near a table. I glanced at Gabby. She wouldn't be interested in that. Would she? She had remarked on my smell and seemed to like me better right after I groomed.

Gabby's step hitched the slightest bit as she noticed the man. Was that a sign of interest? Jealousy balled in my stomach. The man's smile changed as he caught sight of Gabby.

I could feel my hackles rising and tried to calm down. A light touch, Gabby's hand on my back, soothed me, and I managed to walk to the table without growling.

"Scott, this is Gabby," Peter said.

"A pretty name you don't hear often," Scott said, pulling out a chair for her.

His smooth words annoyed me. Gabby hesitated to sit in the chair he offered. Good girl.

"Would you mind if we switched spots, Scott?" she asked. "That way our dog won't be so close to people walking by. He's very friendly, but big. I don't want anyone to be intimidated by him."

"No problem," he said, pulling out his own chair for her.

I moved with her; and as she sat, I lay between her chair and Scott's, making sure to push his chair further away. And, there I stayed through all Scott's annoying attempts to hit on Gabby. He wasn't obvious about it, just small little remarks like the comment about her name. I did my best to ignore it. After all, I was between them, and his words couldn't actually touch her.

Yet, the longer I stayed at her feet, the more I resented the man at the table. It should have been me.

"Why not have a drink with us, Gabby?" Scott asked.

Gabby shifted slightly in her chair. "I'm a bit younger than the rest of you."

"Really? How old are you?"

"Eighteen. I'm not much of a soda drinker either, so water works. How much longer until you graduate?"

I almost picked my head up. Why had she asked that? Was she actually interested?

"It depends on how far I want to go. Peter told me he declared his major freshman year and has never changed. I, on the other hand, have changed twice. I like what I'm learning now, so I hope I won't change it again, but you never know. What about you?"

"I'm going for massage therapy. So, I won't be here as long as the rest of you."

"Massage therapy? I hear they ask for volunteers to come in for those classes. If you ever need someone to practice on, let me know. I'd be happy to come in."

The man reached across the table, and I tensed, ready to jump up, but the arrival of their food saved him. I nudged Gabby's bare leg with my nose. When she glanced down at me, I showed her my teeth. That was all the warning I was going to give her. If Scott touched her, he'd feel my bite.

"I think you'll both be in some of the anatomy classes next semester, Gabby," Peter said, drawing her attention. "If you want a study group, you should let Rachel and I know. I've already been through them. And since you're graduating in spring, I know you have, too."

"Thank you, Peter, but I really do study best on my—"

"That's a great idea," Scott said. "We should start now so the class won't be so hard later. What do you think about Tuesday nights?"

I bumped her leg again. She was not studying with him.

"It's a good idea to get a head start—"

Woman, I thought in warning and bumped her harder.

"But I'm so swamped with classes and homework now that I don't even have time to take poor Clay for walks."

She reached out and patted my shoulder. I turned my head to gloat, but saw the man's gaze dip to Gabby's shirt and froze. She must have noticed his attention too because she immediately straightened and took a quick bite. That was the only thing that saved him from a beating.

Exhaling slowly, I worked to calm down but the man tried to shove his chair closer. I braced myself, unwilling to give a hairsbreadth. He noticed and glanced down at me. I kept my head down, trying to control my temper.

"What's your dog's name?" he asked.

"Clay," Rachel said.

"Nice name," Scott said.

Liar.

"Let's take him home after this and go out to a new club that opened downtown."

I wanted to give Gabby what she desired, my good behavior, but he was pushing it. There was no way I'd let her walk away with him without a challenge.

"Rachel?" Gabby said.

My heart froze. What was she asking Rachel? Was Gabby seeking her permission to bring me home?

"I see it," Rachel said.

"See what?" Peter asked, echoing my thoughts.

"Exhaustion. She's been studying like crazy." I lifted my head enough to witness Rachel wave over the waitress and ask for boxes and the check for the two of them. Finally, some sense from that woman.

"And she needs rest, not a night out. Although, I am really glad we came."

Gabby reached for her purse on the back of the chair, knocking my leash loose. Scott moved to grab her hand. Oh, hell no. I stood, unable to take any more, and everything on the table rattled when my shoulder bumped it. But, I'd successfully blocked Scott from touching her.

Gabby turned away, not looking at either me or Scott. Good. Scott was eyeing me again; I was eyeing his leg.

The waitress returned with the bill and the wrapped up leftovers, breaking the tension. Gabby paid, and Rachel gave up digging in her purse.

"I better drive her home," Rachel said, looking at Peter as she stood. "You have my number. Give me a call if you want to do something next weekend."

Gabby stood too, turning her back on Scott to step toward Rachel.

"Rachel, you can stay with Peter. I don't mind taking Gabby home," he said.

I bet he wouldn't mind.

With her back to him, Gabby didn't catch Scott reaching to stop her. I sprang forward and propelled her out of the way with my head. She looked down at me, but before I could nod toward the car, Rachel spoke up.

"No, Scott. I think we're done for tonight." She waved to Peter then grabbed Gabby's hand.

As the two started to walk away, seeming to completely forget about me, Scott shoved his money at the waitress and stood, his intent clear. I darted in front of him and crouched low. The man's singular focus on Gabby cost him. He tripped over me and fell to the ground. I stood and ran after Gabby, who was looking over her shoulder at us. I nudged her back to keep her moving. The man wouldn't stay down long. Both women moved at a pre-jog walk.

"I'm sorry," Rachel said, once we were almost to the car. "You told me, but I didn't really get it. Even the men sitting around us were eyeing you."

They were? I glanced back, but everything looked normal. I'd been so focused on Scott, I hadn't noticed anything else.

"No big deal," Gabby said. "You should see me in some of my

classes. 'No' is the most common word in my vocabulary. Scott's reaction was worse than most because he already considered me his date. If you say 'no' consistently and to everyone, it doesn't get so bad."

I looked up at her and studied her sad face. She dealt with men like that all the time? Suddenly her standoff attitude toward just about everyone made a lot more sense.

She handed Rachel the keys. "You really can drive."

Rachel took them and opened the door for me as Gabby walked around to the passenger side. I hopped over the seats to get to the back, then lay down so I could watch out the front—and be closer to Gabby.

Halfway home, Rachel stopped at a gas station.

"Tonight's an ice cream night. Be right back." She jumped out and hurried inside.

Gabby dropped her head back against the seat and sighed. I lifted my nose, trying to scent her mood. Melancholy. What part of tonight had made her sad? I doubted it was my interference; and although I'd bared my teeth in warning, I'd behaved as she'd asked. For the most part.

She reached out and started to stroke my head and ears. I sighed and relaxed, enjoying her touch. At least she didn't seem to be upset with me.

She looked out the window, and her misery grew stronger. I lifted my head, worried about her.

"I'm fine," she said, meeting my gaze. "How are you doing?"

She was worried about me? With an ache growing in my chest, I pushed myself forward a bit so I could lay my head on her lap.

The door opened, and the unexpected sound made me flinch. I hadn't even heard Rachel approaching. I hadn't been listening because when I was around Gabby, all my senses belonged to her.

If Gabby noticed my reaction, she didn't comment. Instead, she gave my ear one last caress and then released it so I could make room for Rachel.

As Rachel drove and they talked about ice cream, I struggled to think of what I could do next. Though I wanted Gabby to see me as a man, and more specifically her Mate, she was starting to see me as a companion. She was talking to me more.

We pulled into the driveway, and I jumped out just behind Gabby, not ready to give up the closeness we'd experienced in the car. When she went to her room, I reluctantly stayed with Rachel, half-listening to the woman's babble about how I was such a good boy.

It didn't take long for Gabby to reappear, dressed for bed.

"Where's my chocolate?" she asked.

I could scent something off. She was still upset, and I moved to her side. She patted me gently.

Rachel handed over a small container of ice cream.

"I'm going to go change. Want to watch a movie or something?" Rachel stripped out of her shirt on her way to her bedroom, but I didn't look. I wasn't interested. I was too busy studying Gabby's face as she took a small bite of ice cream.

She covered her ice cream with the lid and put it in the freezer.

"What do you think?" she asked, looking at me. "Stay up and watch a movie, or go to bed early? Lead the way."

I turned and went to her room, hopping up on the bed.

"Rach, we're just going to go to bed early. 'K?" Gabby said from behind me.

"It's okay. Go ahead. I won't keep you up with a movie, will I?" I listened to Rachel flop on the couch and watched Gabby move to stand in our doorway.

"I'm so tired I doubt anything will keep me from sleeping."

"'K. Night, Hun. Thanks for going with me even if it did suck."

"Don't worry about it. Night."

Gabby turned and closed the door. In the living room, a high-pitched, electronic squeal, a sound I'd grown used to, filled the air as Rachel turned on the TV.

Something in Gabby's expression softened as she looked at me, and it suddenly hurt to breathe.

"Thanks, Clay," she said, walking around the bed. She paused and bent over me. I held myself completely still and closed my eyes as I felt her lips on the top of my head. A noise escaped me, part pain, part need. She moved away too quickly and crawled under the covers. Her feet slid under my chest, seeking my warmth.

She didn't realize how these simple gestures reassured me. Her small touches meant acceptance. I sighed. I had patience to see this courtship through until the end. But, the torture of it might kill me.

I waited until Rachel went to her room and the house quieted before I eased off the bed. I needed to go for a long run.

Outside, I left the yard, sticking to the shadows and avoiding houses with dogs. This wasn't the first night I'd snuck out for a run. Sleeping in the same room with Gabby was as calming as it was stimulating. Her scent seeped into my senses while I slept, and I often woke physically uncomfortable. A run usually helped.

Toward the campus, a few of the houses thrummed with music and muted voices. I stopped to watch the males and females interact and hoped Gabby would never want to go to a party.

Chapter Nine

It took longer than I'd intended to run off the steam from the evening's events, and it was close to dawn when I let myself back in. Standing there naked in the kitchen, I heard Gabby softly call my name and smiled.

I shifted, went to her room, and jumped onto the mattress. She exhaled when I lay on her cold, roaming feet.

"Thanks."

Yep. She needed me. I closed my eyes, content with that thought. Just as I started to drift off, she spoke.

"Hey, Clay. Wanna go get breakfast with me?"

Of course she wanted to go to breakfast after I'd stayed up all night. Not thinking clearly, I sighed and left the bed again.

"You could have said no," she said with a soft laugh.

I watched her get out of bed, grab clothes, and walk to the bathroom.

As I stared after her, a thought occurred to me. She wanted to go to breakfast with me. That meant a restaurant. Restaurants didn't allow dogs, which is how humans saw me. Did that mean she wanted me to be a man? I cursed to myself. I still didn't have any damn clothes.

Refusing to lose an opportunity, I trotted to the back door and sat to wait.

She didn't seem surprised to see me when she emerged.

"You up for a walk?" she quietly asked.

I still had fuzz between my ears because it took a minute to figure out what she was asking. Walk to breakfast or drive to breakfast. Before I could think of how to respond, she grabbed the leash, clipped it on, and then loosely wrapped it around my collar.

Curious as to why she wasn't holding her end, I looked over at her.

"What? I'm following the law...you're on a leash. Let's go."

She didn't fool me. She knew she didn't need to hold the leash because I wasn't a dog. She was starting to see me as more. The thought chased away my need for sleep, and I stepped outside with her and stood near as she locked up.

We walked in the direction of the campus, close to the same route I'd taken, only this time on the main road. Everything seemed a little quieter now. I listened to her breathing and steady heartbeat as I scanned the shadows. I wasn't worried about my kind as much as I was her kind.

We'd made it halfway to campus when I heard the faint scuff of shoes ahead.

"So what do you like for breakfast?" Gabby asked. "Oatmeal?"

I laughed as I scented the air. What was oatmeal? She smiled at me.

"Yeah, I was thinking you're more a steak and eggs kinda guy."

The faint musk of a man tickled my nose. Older. Not a threat.

"Who you talking to dar'lin?" he called as he stepped out from the shadows across the narrow street. His sudden appearance made Gabby's heart race.

"My dog," she called.

"Clay," she whispered. "Can you bark mean?"

She was afraid, and she was coming to me for safety. I grinned and barked as she asked.

"Damn," the man said, keeping pace with us on the opposite sidewalk. "That thing on a leash?"

"Yep, but there's no holding him back. I'm safer letting him go, or he'd just drag me along."

The man laughed. "I bet. Have a good morning." The man turned at the next corner to walk around the block.

"You trust that?" Gabby said as she stared in the direction the man had disappeared.

I grunted in annoyance. He was a human. Did she really think so little of my ability to protect her?

"Me neither," she said as if my grunt had been an agreement. "And thanks for warning me there was someone close by."

Her sarcasm wasn't lost on me, and I snorted.

I smelled the diner before I saw it. The scent of cooking meat set my mouth to salivating, and my stomach growled.

"Since they don't allow dogs, I'll go in and get our food for carryout," Gabby said when we reached the diner.

Sitting near the door as she went inside, I watched her. The place was empty except for a woman walking around the tables so I wasn't too worried.

The two spoke, and the woman wrote something down on a piece of paper that she then passed through a little window. Gabby remained inside for several minutes, until two white boxes appeared in the little window. The woman handed them to Gabby. Gabby turned, smiled at me through the door, and joined me outside.

I followed her to a long piece of cement in the parking lot. She sat down and set the boxes on the ground before her. Then, she opened one. The aroma teased me, but the small hunk of meat inside, which she proceeded to cut into tiny pieces, was a letdown. I could have eaten that thing in three bites.

She nudged the container in my direction as soon as she

finished, and I just about inhaled the meat. I was starving. Rachel hadn't given me her leftovers last night, and I wasn't about to eat the dog food.

"I hope you're a slower eater when you're in your skin," Gabby said.

There was censure in her voice. I stopped and looked up at her. She immediately blushed and looked away.

"It's just that you eat faster than me. That's all."

No, there was something more. Did I shame her? Did she still think of me as an unkempt wild man? I bathed every day now.

Pushing aside my hunger, I ate slowly, savoring each bite as if it were my last. It could be if she didn't start seeing me as a man soon. When I finished, she offered me her leftovers, guilt souring her scent. I almost refused, but my commonsense outweighed my pride. I took care to eat slowly, though.

After she threw away the containers, we started back home. She remained quiet as we walked. The light scent of her continued guilt wasn't enough to hide another scent that suddenly gusted on a breeze.

I lifted my nose and inhaled. A male. Not human. A challenger? The Elders had acknowledged the tie I had to Gabby; there shouldn't be any challengers, yet. I knew the rules and understood I only had six months to win my Mate over before others of my kind started to challenge me. How much time had already passed? Three months since I first saw her? Maybe four? I still had a few months to try to win her over.

I growled low, a warning to the one who approached, and stopped walking. Gabby froze beside me.

"What is it, Clay?" she whispered. "What should I do?"

I couldn't let her fear distract me. I listened to the thump of the male's feet as it ran toward us.

I growled louder, angry at this pup's audacity, and tensed, ready for a fight. Gabby retreated a few more steps behind me. Good. She knew not to run.

The steady pounding of paws on the ground stopped as the challenger leapt toward us. This was no pup. I braced myself as my opponent flew from the darkness. He collided with me, and I snarled as I twisted away from his snapping teeth and dug in my feet. My claws grated against the pavement as we slid closer to Gabby.

When the other wolf pulled back to regain his footing, I saw an opening and took it. Lunging forward, I aimed for his face. His lip and nose ripped under my teeth, and his blood coated my tongue. My opponent cried out in pain, and I grunted in satisfaction and let go, giving him a chance to concede.

Instead of giving in, the mutt tensed, ready for more. I growled a low warning to let him know I wouldn't be so lenient again. He snarled in return and tried to circle me. Gabby moved with me, so I remained her shield.

She was worried and afraid. I was neither. I watched him closely, waiting.

"Hey!" Gabby yelled.

The other wolf's blue gaze shifted to Gabby as a light turned on in a nearby house.

"Whose dog is this? Someone help me get him off my dog!"

She didn't really think this was a normal dog, did she?

Another light went on in the house, and I lunged forward, taking advantage of the distraction. The other wolf dodged just in time, avoiding a second bite. The first bled freely, coloring his muzzle.

He swore at me, then lunged again. I turned so he caught me in the shoulder. The impact was harder than I'd expected, and it knocked me off balance for a moment. I went for his foreleg, exposing my neck. The other wolf grunted in pain as my teeth sank in.

As I'd anticipated, the mutt still went for the opening. His teeth clicked against the metal that studded my collar. The wolf growled, pulled back, and made to try again. I released him and backed away. Gabby shuffled back a step behind me.

As I moved, the damn leash uncoiled from its place under my collar. The other werewolf noticed, moved forward, and tried to step on the trailing end. I twisted sharply, flicking the end of it out of the way.

Someone whistled shrilly. "Duke! Come here, Duke."

"The noise has everyone waking up, whoever you are," Gabby said, proving that she understood this was a challenge. "You don't have enough time to finish this. It'd be better to leave now since Clay won't be able to chase you."

She knew I wouldn't leave her.

"Someone's going to call the police, and when they get here, they'll see a dog that's neither licensed nor leashed. You'll either have to change and expose yourself, or let them take you away thinking you're a dog."

He and I continued our slow circle.

The front door of the house closest to us opened, and a man shined a flashlight at us.

"Can you help me?" Gabby called to him.

I understood what she was doing but didn't like it. I could take care of this challenger on my own.

"Do you know whose dog this is? It came running at my dog from the direction of your backyard."

"It's not ours. Want me to call the police?" he yelled over the snarls and growls.

My opponent swore under his breath, turned, and sprinted for the darkness from where he'd come.

I watched the other wolf retreat. With his withdrawal, the challenger conceded. For now.

"Did you see what kind of dog it was?" the man called as he left the safety of his house to look at his side yard where the wolf had disappeared. He cautiously shined his flashlight to search for it, and I moved closer to Gabby.

Gabby didn't answer the man. Instead, she fell to her knees beside me and buried her face against my neck. My skin tingled. Did she have any idea what she did to me?

Then I felt her shaking as her hands roamed over my neck and head. She was worried and was checking for injuries, yet another sign of affection. She let out a shaky breath and leaned against me.

"Ma'am? You okay?"

The man pointed his flashlight at us but stayed near his house. Across the street, a door opened, distracting the man.

"They okay, Mike?"

Gabby lifted her head and met my gaze. "You okay?" she whispered.

I kissed her cheek, a long lick.

"Next time I'll just carry the leash," she said.

I noticed a sheen of tears before she turned away. She cared about me. I knew then that it was only a matter of time before she realized it, too.

"We're okay," she said as she stood. She kept a hand on my head. "The dog was as big as Clay here but had dark grey fur."

"Doesn't sound like any dog from this neighborhood, but I know there are some big dogs a few blocks away. Do you want me to call the cops?" The man started toward us.

She picked up my loose leash and nudged me. Her worry was getting stronger, which I thought odd. To quote her, it was just a human man.

"Nah. I think we're fine," she said, taking a step back.

I was studying the man and noticed a sudden change. His interest in Gabby had gone from concerned citizen to potential Mate. My temper flared, but I quickly smothered it. In the car yesterday, she'd said men acted weird around her. Rachel had claimed to notice it at the restaurant. Was this what they meant?

I continued to study both the man and Gabby. Gabby was beautiful. I couldn't argue against that. Yet, the man's reactions to every word and every move she made seemed too much, and it concerned me. If what she said was true, that men typically always acted like this around her, what really happened to her each day when she went to campus?

She assured the man we were fine and reluctantly gave him her phone number in case the police did come. When she turned away, I felt her unease and stuck close to her.

My poor Gabby. I wanted to reassure her that I wouldn't let the human bother her, but I didn't think she'd appreciate me shifting to my skin to tell her. She wasn't ready yet. Plus, the stress of the encounter with the challenger seemed to have left her shaken.

She looked around constantly. I did the same so she'd know I was still guarding her.

It wasn't until we were halfway home that I noticed there was something odd about her gaze. It was almost unfocused. I'd seen her deep in thought before, but this was different. It was as if she was looking at something I couldn't see, and that made me edgy.

Gradually, I noticed her steps began to lag. Her already pale face grew more so, and she wore a slight grimace as if the rising sun pained her.

It didn't take scenting her to know she was exhausted. I wanted to get her home, wrap her in my arms, and lay in bed with her. But it wasn't meant to be. As soon as we rounded the back of the house, I saw Rachel.

"There you are!"

Gabby's hand flew to my neck, and her heart skipped a beat.

"Nice morning for a walk," Rachel said, moving toward us, oblivious to the scare she'd just given Gabby.

As Rachel reached out to pet me, Gabby uncurled her fingers from my fur. She had quite a grip.

Rachel played with one of my ears, and I shook my head to get her to stop. The woman had no boundaries. She laughed and bent to kiss the top of my head. I caught Gabby's gaze and rolled my eyes at her.

She smiled slightly and seemed to relax. I'd hoped she would save me but ridding her of worry worked, too.

"I made a call this morning and can get Clay into the vet for his shots," Rachel said as she tugged the leash from Gabby's hand. "I figured after the way he acted last night, we should have him current...just in case."

Gabby stared at Rachel for a long moment, then her shocked gaze locked on me. Was she going to save me or did she still want revenge?

Panic flavored Gabby's scent as she looked back at Rachel.

"You okay, Gabby?" Rachel eyed Gabby with concern.

"Uh, I didn't budget for it," Gabby said.

"Don't worry. I can cover it for now, and you can pay me back."

"Let's all go."

I tilted my head, trying to figure out what Gabby might be thinking. She wasn't telling Rachel no, but she wasn't happy about sending me to the vet, either.

"No offense, Gabby, but you look like hell. I think you'd be better off with some quiet time. Don't worry; we'll be fine."

Rachel was right. Gabby looked like she hadn't slept at all. Worried about her, I nudged her toward the door just as Rachel tried to tug me toward the car. Rachel scolded me, but I ignored her. I nudged Gabby again.

"Would you mind giving him your standard pep talk? I don't know why he only listens to you. I'm the one that feeds him treats."

Except for last night, I thought. You let me starve.

Rachel handed Gabby the leash. Gabby rubbed her forehead and then bent to give me a hug.

"Is it safe for you?"

To go somewhere with Rachel? I snorted. The woman was a bit free with her hands, but I could handle her.

"I'm so sorry about this," Gabby said softly, her breath tickling my ear in the most pleasant way. "I'll need to call Sam and let him know what happened."

She was right. The Elders needed to know that there was a challenge before the six-month mark. I didn't want someone approaching Gabby when I wasn't around. Living with her like this was hard enough.

She straightened, looked me in the eye, and smoothed a hand over the fur on the top of my head.

"It's your choice," she said as she dropped the leash and stepped back.

I eyed Gabby and knew Rachel was right. She needed some rest. Maybe leaving with Rachel would give her that time. It would also get Rachel out of the house so Gabby could call Sam to tell him about the challenge. I sighed then followed Rachel to the car door.

"The control you have over him is weird but cool," Rachel said as she waited for me to get all the way in.

"Yeah. Just don't be gone too long. He'll get upset."

"The vet's just a few minutes from here. We should be back soon." She climbed behind the wheel, closed the door, and rolled down her window.

Because of the open window, I smelled Gabby's wave of panic a second before it showed on her face.

"Just don't have him neutered! Or anything that involves blood or blood work. It's expensive, and I promised him he'd keep his jewels."

My jewels? I knew what that meant and couldn't stop from laughing. I definitely needed to leave now that I knew the direction of her thoughts.

"Maybe we should have the vet check his lungs," Rachel said. Her comment and worry did nothing to dampen my amusement.

"He's fine. Think cost," Gabby said from the deck as Rachel backed out of the driveway.

Rachel pulled in front of a small brown building. As soon as she opened the back door, I smelled dog feces. Where had she brought me? I'd figured vet meant doctor but this had to be wrong.

"Come, boy. I bet you get treats inside."

Unless it was a medium rare burger, they could keep their treats. I heaved a sigh and hopped out of the back.

We walked to the door, which she opened to let me in. Inside, a man sat with his pit-bull. The thing took one look at me and started to whine. Good. The woman with the Chihuahua was another story. That little chew toy started yapping at me fiercely. The woman looked at me with disdain.

Go ahead...set the yapper down.

She held it close as she spoke to the woman behind the counter.

"Come on, Clay," Rachel said, tugging the leash to the bench opposite the pit-bull.

I followed and sat beside her once she positioned herself on the bench. Then, I watched. Once the yapper left, the woman came from behind the counter. She offered the pit-bull a treat to coax it onto the scale. It got another treat so it held still. And yet another treat to go into an exam room. I stared at the plaque on the door. Exam Room 1. I looked at the other door. Exam Room 2. I looked at the scale, the woman approaching with the treat, then Rachel as I realized what she'd done. She'd brought me to an animal doctor. How degrading.

I stood before the woman reached us and went to the scale. There, I stood still hoping she wouldn't try to feed me one of those dried cakes. It didn't smell bad. But I wasn't a dog and wasn't about to eat something humans fed to a dog.

"Wow. This is Clay, right? He's very well trained," the woman said, watching me.

She read the scale and made a note on a piece of paper.

"Yeah, we haven't had him for long. We don't know much about him, actually. Shots, age...it's all a mystery."

Shots? What the hell was she talking about?

"Well, we'll take a look and see what we can tell you. Let's go in here."

She opened the door to Exam Room 2. I ignored her treat and walked in.

"Hmm..." she said, watching me. "What does he eat at home?"

"Well, we bought him dog food, but he doesn't seem to like it. I've given him some cooked steak and other meat," Rachel said, her voice laced with guilt.

"Perhaps we can recommend a different dog food. Though dog foods do contain meat, they also contain other essential vitamins and minerals dogs need that they won't get from just eating steak."

This new woman needed to stop talking. I moved closer to Rachel, defending my sole food source.

The door, opposite the one we'd entered, opened. Another woman walked in.

"Good morning," she said, looking down at me. "My, you're a big one." She looked up at Rachel. "Shelly mentioned there are no records. Can you get him to jump up on the table?"

"Yeah, no records," Rachel said, standing. "I'm not sure he'll listen." Rachel looked at me and patted the low metal table.

"Come on, Clay. Up here."

The sooner I did what they wanted, the sooner we went back to Gabby, I reminded myself. I hopped up on the table and fought not to roll my eyes at the new woman's praise. She held out her hand. Did she really expect me to sniff her? I looked at Rachel. She smiled at me and nodded.

"It's okay, Clay. She's just going to look you over to make sure you're healthy."

I'm healthy.

Still, I turned back to the woman and pretended to sniff her. She praised me and offered me a biscuit. I turned away, but she kept trying until I took it in my mouth. Then I set it on the table between my feet.

"Has he been eating well?"

I'm eating fine, I thought as I listened to Rachel repeat her explanation. As she spoke, the woman ran a hand along my side, down my legs, then cupped my unmentionables. The move shocked me so much I froze in panic as she groped me.

"He's not neutered. Let's see if he'll let me look at his teeth."

Yes. Anything. Just please let go.

I endured a thorough exam of my mouth and ears. They talked shots, and I put up with a few pokes. Human medicine I might have to worry about, but I doubted animal medicine would cause any issues.

When the woman put on a rubber glove and asked Rachel to hold my head, I grew suspicious. The words "anal glands" sent a shock of panic through me. I jumped off the table and backed toward the door. What did they do to dogs here? That yappy Chihuahua made more sense. It had probably been screaming for help.

"Um, I think he's done cooperating for today," Rachel said slowly as she watched me.

The woman tried coaxing me with a variety of treats, even the lunchmeat from her sandwich, for the next several minutes before agreeing that I'd had enough. There was no bribe on the planet that would get me back up on that table.

"If you notice him scooting on the carpet, you should bring him back."

Not in her lifetime.

GABBY WAITED on the porch when Rachel pulled past the corner of the house. I stayed as I was, lying on the backseat. After the indignities I'd suffered, I wasn't speaking to Rachel—not that I spoke to her before—and I wasn't yet sure how I felt about Gabby. Had she sent me to that place knowing what they wanted to do to me? She'd told Rachel not to let them unman me; she'd tried to protect me. Yet, she'd said nothing about the last procedure.

Rachel opened her door.

"How'd it go?" Gabby asked. I could hear her anxiety.

"He took it like a champ."

I shuddered at what more I might have taken if that woman would have had her way.

Rachel opened the back car door. Nauseous, I lifted my head and stood on shaky legs. When the pack spread information about the human world, no one had specifically mentioned vets as animal doctors. I considered contacting one of the Elders with a warning but didn't want to admit how I'd come by the knowledge.

Deep in thought, I slowly climbed the deck steps and moved to Gabby's side.

"What'd they do to him?" she asked.

Her worry broke my reverie.

"He wasn't acting like this when we left. I swear. I think he's hamming it up for you." Rachel patted my head with a laugh, and I realized, unless I wanted Gabby probing—I cringed at the use of the word—into what had happened, I needed to act normally.

I straightened and walked with purpose to the door. Gabby sighed, her relief obvious. I glanced at her and winked. She quickly looked at Rachel, but that woman was already in the house.

Gabby followed her in.

"So what shots did he get?" Gabby asked as she poured some orange juice. She took a small sip a little too casually, then glanced at me. I wished I knew what was going through her head. Moments like this made me yearn for her to stake her Claim. The connection it would give us...well, there'd be no doubt what she was thinking or feeling then.

"Just rabies. The vet had a hard time determining his age by his teeth, but thought him to be in his prime," Rachel said.

Gabby choked on her juice.

"That's great," she said in a raspy voice as she glanced at me.

I couldn't help the small smile that curled my lips because I knew she was thinking of me as a man in that moment, not the dog that I'd been treated like for the past hour.

"Hey, while I was waiting for him, Peter called."

Rachel had been waiting for me to come out of the corner—where I'd stayed until the woman with the plastic glove left—when her phone had chirped. I'd been too preoccupied to pay attention to her conversation.

"He said he had a good time last night and hoped Scott hadn't ruined his chance by coming on too strong. He's never seen Scott act in any way but smooth. He naturally thinks Scott's falling hard for you."

I stared at Rachel and considered biting her. She'd put me through enough today.

"I'm just repeating." She held up her hands with a laugh at Gabby. "Anyway, Peter said Scott's already been bugging him about getting your number to set up another date. Given what you told me, I said no, that last night was just a friendly get together and that you were seeing someone else."

Gabby and I both let out relieved sighs. Rachel noticed mine, though.

"You know, sometimes that dog creeps me out with how human he acts," Rachel said, shaking her head. "Anyway, I'm going to meet up with Peter for another try at a date. We're going to see a movie; and this time, I'm not asking you to come with." She had a huge smile on her face as she walked past us toward her room.

"Thank you!" Gabby called to her.

For the rest of the weekend, Gabby studied, and I stayed glued to her side. She didn't talk about her call with Sam, and I kept quiet about the vet visit.

Monday, as soon as the house was empty, I left to roam the neighborhood. It was time to start acting like a human and gather some clothes for myself. A pair of socks pulled from a back porch, some worn and ratty boots pulled from a garage, a t-shirt pulled from a line. I picked things I knew weren't likely to be missed. The pants were harder, but I finally found a pair dangling from the branches of a barren tree. The tree belonged to one of the houses closer to campus, one that tended to blare music late into the night. I looked around and, hoping no one was watching, shifted my hands and limbs just enough to climb the tree. Pants in my mouth, I jogged home.

By Tuesday evening, I had a set of clothes. With clothes, I could shift into my skin and get a job. I had some mechanical knowledge, thanks to the books Gabby brought me. Now, I needed to figure out who would hire me. Since Gabby found a car by reading the paper,

I decided I would spend the next day looking at the paper to see if it had any information about jobs.

Wednesday morning, during the rush before she left for class, I watched Gabby race downstairs to throw in a load of laundry. I'd watched her do this countless times and already knew what dial to turn, what button to push, and what detergent to use.

As I sat on the steps watching her, I realized I couldn't wear what I had. At least, not as they were. All of it smelled like someone else, and I knew how meticulous Gabby was about my scent. I'd need to wash everything.

Gabby raced back up the stairs and almost ran me over on her way out the door. As soon as her car left the driveway, I went out to the neighbor's bush and brought my cache of clothes into the house. Then, I waited for the washer to finish.

In the privacy of the basement, I shifted into my skin and removed Gabby's clothes from the washer. Then, I hesitated. I wanted to put them in the dryer for her. Would she thank me or would she want to know what I was doing down here in the first place? Uncertain, I set her wet things in the basket then loaded the washer with my items.

Once the machine started to fill with water, I shifted and went back upstairs. I'd started making myself a single sandwich every day from Gabby's supplies while she was away at school. She hadn't mentioned anything, so I figured it was okay to keep doing it. While I had my paws on the counter to get the bread, I heard an odd noise.

I tilted my head and listened. Something clunked. I pushed away from the counter and took off down the stairs. The machine was shaking and thunking.

In a panic, I shifted and opened the lid. The machine quieted, and I looked down into the grey water. I couldn't see a thing. What had made that noise? The boots, maybe? I closed the lid gently and waited for it to start again. It squealed when it tried.

I stopped the machine again, canceled the program, and

listened to the water drain. Then, I attempted to start it again. It made worse noises the second time; and I knew, without a doubt, I'd managed to break it.

"But how?" I tugged at my beard in frustration.

If Gabby came back and found out that I broke—

I looked down at her wet clothes then back at the grey water. I couldn't afford for her to be mad at me when we were just starting to make progress. Teetering with indecision, I looked at her clothes once more. I'd make this little lie up to her. Decided, I plunged my hand into the water and started pulling out my items.

One of the bootlaces gave me trouble. Wound around the base of the center pole that twisted back and forth, the thing didn't want to come loose. The boot had also wedged itself between the center post and the drum. No doubt, my boot was the "how" behind the machine's behavior.

Once I had my things draining in the utility sink, I put Gabby's wet things back into the washer. With the boot and string removed, I tried to start the machine once more. It filled as it should, but as soon as the post started to twist back and forth, it made awful noises.

A car pulled into the driveway, and I froze. A door opened and a moment later, I listened to Rachel's familiar tread on the porch. She wasn't supposed to be back yet.

I grabbed my wet things, shoved them behind an empty cardboard box, and shifted back into my fur just as the back door opened.

I barked just as an annoying dog would do when there are strange noises in the house.

"Clay?" Rachel called.

No...it's your other dog barking, I thought. I still hadn't forgiven her for the vet.

She came down the steps, and I pointedly looked at the washer as if the noise it made wasn't enough of a clue.

"Oh, no!" She flew to the machine and quickly opened the lid like I'd done. After studying things for a few moments, she turned to me.

"We're going to have to call someone, I think. I don't know anything about this stuff." She pulled her cell phone from her pocket as she walked back upstairs.

I followed her closely, thankful she hadn't noticed the wet trail that led to my hidden clothes.

SEVERAL HOURS LATER, I sat at the top of the steps, watching the man downstairs. I could just barely see him from my position.

Rachel was waiting in the kitchen for Gabby, which was the same reason I was at the top of the stairs instead of downstairs learning. Rachel and I had been down there with the man when he'd pulled the machine out to look at the back. While I'd been learning, she'd been eyeing the man in a potential Mate way. I wondered if that meant she was no longer with Peter. I doubted it because she still smelled of him.

The sound of a car coming down the road pricked my ears. Gabby's engine and exhaust system were distinct and easy to identify. As soon as Gabby pulled into the driveway, Rachel dashed out the back door.

"You are brilliant!" Rachel said, still outside.

"What'd I do?" Gabby's words were faint.

"There's a hot repairman working on the washer in the basement."

Hot? I looked at the man again as he bent over to pick up a tool.

"Thank you for breaking it," Rachel said.

She and Gabby walked into the house.

"I didn't do anything but throw in a load of laundry before I left," Gabby said quietly.

I turned to look at her. Did she suspect something?

"Hey," Rachel said. "I'm not blaming...I'm just thanking."

"But, I thought you were into Peter," Gabby said, echoing my thoughts.

"I am. It doesn't mean I don't window-shop. Go down there and flirt with him and see if we can get twenty percent off our bill."

Flirt? Before I could get even more upset with Rachel, Gabby snorted.

"I will not. It'd be safer to send Clay down there to learn how to fix it than me trying to get us a price break."

Done.

"If our dog starts fixing things, we're hitting the road and making some money," said Rachel.

The man started up the basement stairs, and Rachel's face lit with anticipation while Gabby eyed the basement door with dread. I backed up a few steps, positioning myself between her and the door, trying to reassure her with my presence.

Her look of dread changed to one of appreciation when the man reached the top of the stairs. The man didn't miss her appreciative look, either. He flexed for her. I briefly considered nudging the man to send him falling down the steps.

Gabby flushed and turned to Rachel.

"I have to go pick up my ring before Clay gets here. He'd be heartbroken if he found out I bent a prong on the setting already. Plus, my hand feels naked without it."

She held out her left hand and gave it a wistful look.

What ring was she talking about?

"The dog?" the man asked with a puzzled look at Rachel.

Gabby laughed nervously. "We named the dog after my fiancé. He has a good sense of humor and likes the dog, too."

She said it so fast I could barely understand her. By the time the words sank in, she was already out the door. I wanted to run after her. Was I the fiancé, the dog, or both?

Stuck with two human witnesses, I couldn't shift to let myself out the door and chase her down. Instead, I listened to her car peel out of the driveway.

It took another hour before the man left and longer still for Gabby to reappear. When she cautiously walked in, bags looped over her arms, I was waiting for her.

She set down the bags and peeked around the corner before she spoke to me in a whisper.

"You better keep reading the books I bring home. You can be our repair guy. It gives me the willies that he knows where I live."

I nodded just as Rachel turned the corner from her bedroom. She paused mid-stride, her eyes wide.

"Did he just nod?"

Gabby smiled. "Yep. I've been working on it with him. He caught on really fast. The nodding isn't bad, but his smile can be a little scary."

Her pulse tripped, giving away her lie. Rachel stared at us for a moment then shook her head.

"You're weird, Gabby, but in a good way. Anyway, it was one hundred and twenty-five dollars to fix the washer. I covered your half. With the vet bill, you're up to one hundred, minus the burger and drink from disaster night."

I saw Gabby's cringe.

"Okay. I'll run to the bank after class tomorrow." She chewed her lip for a moment, and I scented her concern.

My mistake had cost her.

It took the rest of the week for the boots to dry; and when they did, the leather cracked. I could have dealt with that, but the toes of both boots also curled up, making them difficult to wear. Frustrated that the effort hadn't resulted in something I could wear to go job hunting, I hid everything back under the neighbor's shrub and knew I'd need to find some other footwear.

Friday afternoon, I lay beside Gabby, resolutely reading yet another book. I heard Rachel's car pull into the driveway much too quickly, then her rapid steps on the porch. I lifted my head.

"Gabby!" she called in a panicked tone.

Even with Gabby's cute little human ears, she picked up on the wrongness of Rachel's pitch.

"In here!" she said as she flew from the bed toward the door.

The two almost collided when Rachel burst into the room.

"What's going on?" Gabby asked, pulling back.

Gabby liked keeping a physical distance from people. Even Rachel. She didn't seem to like touching. It made each pat on the head even more special.

"Peter broke and told Scott he had plans to go to dinner with me tonight," Rachel said, out of breath.

"So...?"

I liked that Gabby tended to echo my thoughts when it came to Rachel.

"Peter's coming here to pick me up, and Scott's coming with."

My ears twitched involuntarily.

"Gabby, I don't think he's going to take no for an answer tonight. Peter can't shake him."

Scott was going to end up in the hospital. After the week I had, I wasn't in the mood to deal with him nicely.

Gabby groaned, flopped back on her bed, and landed on me. Full body contact with her back. I didn't care. I loved it. She even reached back to pat me and apologize.

"Sorry, Clay." She froze then bolted up right. "I've got an idea! Rachel, if you have any clothes that would say I've been dating a guy for a while, can I borrow them?"

Wait, what?

"Sure, but who are you dating?"

Yeah. Who?

Rachel moved out of Gabby's way as Gabby rushed from the room. I jumped off the bed and followed. She crammed some shoes onto her feet as she walked to the door, almost falling twice along the way. I stared at her wondering what she was doing.

"I'll let you know when I bring him home. Come on, Clay," she said, holding open the door.

She wanted me along? I hurried through the door.

She rushed to the car, opened the door, and waved for me to get in. I was barely out of the way when she pushed in behind me and slammed the car door. I studied her as she careened out the driveway.

"You're here to keep me safe, right?"

I grunted in surprise. It wasn't a rhetorical question. She really wasn't sure.

I'm here to keep you safe and more, Gabby, I thought. But I remained quiet, waiting for her to state her point.

"Then, I need you to be more than my dog."

I tilted my head at her, unsure how to take that comment.

She glanced at me nervously.

"I need you to put on your skin. Be my date tonight. Please?"

She wanted me. My pulse leapt, and the ache that had slowly eased over the days spent lying beside her came back with such force that I struggled to inhale. She wanted me as a man, as her date. I almost shifted right then.

"You took a shower today, right?"

Like a well-aimed porcupine quill, her little dart dug deep. I snorted.

"Do you know what size you wear? Shirt, pants, shoes?"

I blinked at her. I had no idea. I put on things that looked like they would fit. Everything I'd found, I'd tried on.

She didn't seem bothered by my lack of answer. With a slight squeal of tires, she pulled into an open space in a huge parking lot and slammed on the brakes. I almost hit the dash.

"I'll be back in a few minutes," she said. She was out the door before I could nod.

I stared after her and watched her disappear into a store. What was she up to? Scott was coming; and instead of just leaving the house, she was asking me to be her date?

A slow smile spread on my lips as I began to see her plan. She wanted to show the man that I had a Claim on her. She didn't want to avoid him; she wanted to stop any future interest. I stood and stared at the store with pride. She wanted me.

She ran out of the store a few minutes later with a bag hanging from her arm. She opened the car door, tossed the bag at my feet, slid behind the wheel, and backed out, all in a matter of seconds.

Her driving made my stomach turn as she raced home.

Gabby pulled into the driveway, came to another jarring stop, then killed the engine as she opened her door. Rachel stood by the back door, waiting. The clingy dress she wore didn't bode well for Gabby because I doubted the stack of clothes in Rachel's arms was much different.

"Where's your date?" Rachel asked as she scanned the car. "The guys are going to be here in fifteen minutes."

Gabby waved her back into the house. "He'll be here in a few minutes. I hope."

I followed just behind Gabby and saw her toss the bag into the bathroom.

"Let's go in my room, and you can help me pick what to wear."

"Really?" Rachel's excited squeal made me wince. It wasn't the pitch; it was how she would dress Gabby.

They disappeared around the corner into the living room while I stayed by the bathroom.

"I need something a little tropical or hippie-ish," Gabby said as she closed her bedroom door.

I looked at the bag. What had she purchased? I walked into the bathroom, then shifted and closed the door. In the bag, I found some weird cloth pants, a matching shirt, and sandals. Even without growing up human, I knew I'd look like an idiot. I knew what men wore. It wasn't that.

But she'd asked me to be a man for her. I sighed and started the shower. Though I'd already bathed, I knew how she was about my scent.

I listened to the murmur of their voices through the walls. Then suddenly Gabby's voice rose, and I could clearly hear her.

"...because I'm cheap, I got him some clean clothes from the summer closeout racks..."

So it was money behind the selection and not annoyance. That relieved me but also concerned me. I was eating her food, breaking her washing machine—the cost of the vet was all on her—and now she had to buy me clothes, too? I'd wanted her to become dependent on me. Instead, I was dependent on her.

I stepped into the shower and quickly washed. When I finished, I refrained from shaking off. Gabby didn't like the mess that made. I used my designated towel, dried, and hung it over the edge of the tub. Then I stared at the clothes. There was a package of shorts and a pair of pants. I looked the package over. Underwear. Hmm. They didn't have that at the Compound. Shrugging, I opened the package and shook a pair out. I eyed it. It looked...small. I stretched the sides out, in doubt. Maybe it would work, but was it necessary?

She wouldn't have included it if it wasn't. At least from her point of view. I stepped into the underwear and carefully pulled them up. They held everything as firmly as the vet. I tugged the legs down and won an inch of breathing room. Resigned, I stepped into the pants. They fit all right and were comfortable enough. The shirt was snug across my shoulders. If I needed to grab Scott, I'd rip a seam. No grabbing Scott, then. Unless he really deserved it.

Someone tapped on the door.

"Do you need help?" Gabby's whispered words reached me through the door.

I nervously looked at myself in the mirror, ran my fingers through my long hair and beard, then eyed the sandals. I wasn't wearing them or going to another dinner with Scott, Peter, and Rachel. The first one had been worse than a run in with a skunk.

"Please hurry, Clay," Gabby said.

Taking a deep breath, I opened the door. Gabby waited for me in a pretty knee-length, cream skirt and a light yellow top that showed her neck and collarbones. She had her hair back and something about her eyes looked different. She stole my breath most days, but in this moment, she made me want to drop to my knees.

As I stared at her, her gaze swept over me, lingering on the shirt and my shoulders. I was worried that she was thinking it didn't look right. Then a slight change in her scent hit me. Interest. I wanted to shout and laugh. Instead, I calmly put my hands in my pockets and let her look her fill.

With a pink tint to her cheeks, she looked away.

"Brat," she said under her breath, and I wasn't sure if she was talking to me or herself. Then she cleared her throat and said, "You'll do."

Behind her, Rachel smirked at us. Gabby turned and caught her amusement.

"Quiet from the peanut gallery."

The doorbell rang. Rachel ran to the front door, and Gabby slowly followed. I trailed behind her, watching the gentle sway of her skirt.

"Come on in," Rachel said to Peter.

Peter stepped in, and Scott followed just inches behind. Peter's nervousness clouded the room. Scott's lust quickly overpowered it, though, and I fisted my hands in my pockets and stepped closer to Gabby. The man's gaze flicked to me, and I knew he saw the possession in my stance.

"Hi, Peter," Gabby said. "Nice to see you again, Scott. We were going to join you guys, but Clay just got off of work a little while ago and suggested he and I take advantage of the empty house tonight."

A lie I would happily die to see come true.

I watched anger color Scott's face.

"Isn't Clay your dog?"

I didn't care for his tone and narrowed my eyes at him.

"We named the dog after my boyfriend. It's a bit of a joke. Clay, meet Peter and Scott, Rachel's friends."

Scott's shoulders slumped at Gabby's words. I wanted to gloat, but Gabby's sudden remorse and anxiety worried me. Taking a risk, I lightly set my hand on the small of her back to comfort her. She didn't flinch or move away. My mouth went dry and my throat closed at her acceptance of my touch. My breathing grew shallow, and I struggled to control my emotions...my need to turn her around and touch her face and hair.

"Peter, Rachel, I'm sorry to back out on you, too, but I think I'm going to head home," Scott said, distracting me. "I've been fighting a cold all week." He turned and left.

Rachel softly asked Peter to get her jacket and eyed Gabby.

"Are you sure you want to stay in?" she asked Gabby, as Peter helped her with her jacket.

I studied Peter. He was crazy about Rachel. I could see it in the way he looked at her and touched her, and I could smell it. If they were my kind, I would have surely scented a Claimed pair. How could he stand being apart from her each night?

"We're sure," Gabby said, waving them toward the door. "Don't come home early."

When the door closed behind them, she exhaled slowly and turned toward me. I reluctantly let my hand drop. She smiled at me nervously.

"Home free. Thank you, Clay."

I put my hand back in my pocket and waited. Would she ask me to change back? Tell me to leave?

"Um..." She seemed just as uncertain as I was. She took a breath. "Did you want to do something since we're both dressed up?"

She wasn't going to send me away? I shrugged, trying not to show how happy she'd just made me. I didn't want to ruin my chance to spend time with her in my skin.

"You can talk to me, Clay," she said.

Oh, I wanted to. I wanted to tell her how beautiful she looked right now. And ask if I could touch her hair. But, I kept my mouth shut. She wasn't ready. She'd run.

"Okay, do you want to go out or stay in?"

Stay in. I figured, deep down, she wanted that too. I moved to the couch and sat in the middle.

She hesitated then looked at the space available on each side of me. I loved watching the warm light in her soft brown eyes as she considered her options.

"I'm going to go change." Her voice shook. "I'll be right back."

My heart stalled, and as she turned, I sprang from the couch. She couldn't leave. If she did, she might not come back out of the room. I caught the back of her shirt between my thumb and finger. She froze and ever so slowly looked over her shoulder at me. I tilted my head at the couch.

Please don't go, I thought.

Desperate, but trying hard not to show it, I gave her shirt another gentle tug.

She took a slow, deep breath and hesitantly moved back to the couch. I wanted to go sit by her, but I knew she'd probably bolt. I could smell her near panic. Walking to the TV, I tried to figure out what I could do to ease her uncertainty of me. I picked the comedy I'd borrowed from one of the neighbor's homes. It was one Gabby had mentioned wanting to see.

I pressed play, stood, and walked toward the couch. She watched me closely, and I wanted to stand taller because of it.

Sitting next to her, I tried to focus on the previews. It was no good. I'd sat too close. Her scent wrapped around me, as usual, but her leg pressed lightly against mine. Despite two layers of material, it felt too much like skin on skin. My gut clenched with want.

It took half the movie for her to start to relax beside me. Then, she laughed at something. Though I stared at the TV, I had no idea what had just happened. I remained completely focused on her. But the sound of her amusement made me chuckle. I wanted to hear that sound every day of my life.

When the movie ended, she leaned forward to stand. The motion hitched up her skirt an innocent inch. Innocent or not, I knew I needed to calm down. As she moved to the TV, I shifted and slipped out of my clothes at the same time. Moving with the blurred speed that came natural to my kind, I folded the clothes neatly so she would know I appreciated her gift and set them on the couch. Then I left via the front door.

I ran fast and hard for ten minutes, covering miles before returning to the back porch. A hint of buttery saltiness drifted in the air, and I heard Gabby moving around within the kitchen. Changing directions, I went to the front. I opened the door and smelled popcorn. Quietly, I closed the door and settled onto the couch in my fur to wait for her.

She stepped into the room a moment later with a big bowl in her arms, spotted me, and smiled. She was happy to see me.

"There you are. Want some popcorn?"

She turned around and went back into the kitchen, got another bowl for me, and set it on the floor by the couch. I wasn't sure if it was because she was seeing me as a dog or because there wasn't much room left on the couch. Then she settled in next to me and curled her legs up to tuck her feet under me.

Why hadn't she done this when I was a man? I sighed, moved closer, and laid my head on her legs. She'd asked me to change into my skin for her, I reminded myself. Our relationship was growing. She'd come to accept me in my fur. She'd do the same with my skin. But would it be in time? At the rate we were moving, her acceptance would come long after the six-month mark.

I only half watched the movie that played. Mostly I focused on her. What would it take to move things along?

She absently ate a piece of popcorn, and my heart skipped a beat. How could I react to her like this all the time, but she barely reacted to me at all? I couldn't think like that. It wasn't a fair comparison. Like she'd said in the beginning, she was human. She didn't have the instincts I did. I needed to help her see I was meant to be the one for her.

She glanced at me as if sensing my regard and then smiled. She offered me a piece of her popcorn. I nipped it from her fingers. I wasn't hungry. I just wanted a taste of her. My tongue barely swept against her finger, but she didn't seem to mind. She ate another piece, then offered me one. The fourth time, I licked the back of her hand. It was a kiss, but would she know that?

The movie fully captured her attention, and she stopped eating and feeding me. I shifted my position, lying closer to her.

When the movie ended and she got up, I wanted to groan and pull her back. Sure, we slept in the same room every night and read side by side, but this had been actual snuggling; and I wanted more.

Instead of going to the kitchen with the bowl, she set it on the floor and moved to the TV to start another movie. I grinned. She'd liked it too, hadn't she? The smile was well suppressed when she turned around and rejoined me.

The second movie was more action-suspense than comedy. Halfway through the movie, she'd dug one of her hands into the fur at my neck, and the other lightly worried one of my ears. She was nervous because of the movie, and I was turned on as hell.

The front door opened just then, and Gabby jumped—nearly yanking my ear off—and screamed. Yeah, that helped cool me down, as did Rachel's stunned face.

"And that's why I don't watch suspense movies," Gabby said, putting a hand to her heart. Rachel and I both started laughing.

Gabby was just so damn cute. I kissed her exposed stomach and settled down.

She gently tugged on my ear. "Cut it out," she said softly.

So she did know when I kissed her. The insight made me want to try again. Too bad Rachel was watching.

"When did Clay leave? I thought he'd still be here after you said

I shouldn't hurry home." Rachel kicked off her shoes and flopped sideways on the chair.

Gabby turned off the movie. "Nah, I turned my back, and he took off on me."

She patted me on the head, and I snorted. If I would have stayed, she would have been the one running out the door.

"It's okay, though, I have my favorite guy here."

Inside, I soared.

"He was a little scary looking if you ask me," Rachel said.

Scary? That was the clothes, not me.

When Rachel reached over to pet me, I moved slightly and arched a brow at Gabby. She better say I wasn't scary.

Gabby looked like she wanted to laugh.

"When I first met him, I told him he looked like a crazy man. I still think he's crazy, but he's also nice and dependable."

I sighed. I was scary, crazy, nice, and dependable; but the idiot repairman had been hot?

"So does he ever act like Scott?" Rachel asked.

"No way," Gabby said quickly. "Most guys talk about themselves to try to impress me, or they just act scary obsessive. Clay's different. I don't think I affect him like I do other guys." She paused for a long moment. "I think he just likes being with me."

Finally! She got it.

"And I'm grateful that I get to be normal around him."

Rachel laughed. "You sound like you're really serious about him. Why didn't you talk about him before this? And why didn't you say the dog had the same name? We could have changed it."

I watched Gabby, wondering how she'd explain around that.

"I wasn't sure if or when he'd make an appearance. And I like the name Clay. Besides, he doesn't mind."

Rachel made a small noise neither agreeing nor disagreeing.

"We should probably talk about overnight visitors," Rachel said. "What rules do we want to set?"

"Um...no loud noises?"

"Come on!" Rachel laughed louder. "I meant, weekends only? Maybe guests till midnight on weekdays? Notice needed? You know, that kind of stuff."

Rachel's grin said she was up to something. It probably had to do with Peter, who'd been standing outside the front door the whole time.

"I don't know. I trust you and your judgment, and you can trust my lack of a social life. I really don't think I'll see Clay very often, so you don't need to worry."

"Oh, he'll be back. I saw the way he watched you. Are you sure the only rule you can come up with is no loud noises?"

"Yeah, I think we're fine."

"Great!" she said with a huge grin. Then she cupped her hands and yelled, "Peter!"

The front door immediately opened, and a sheepish looking Peter entered.

"You were supposed to text me," he muttered uncomfortably.

Gabby laughed. "Come on in, Peter. Clay and I were just going to bed."

Definitely. I jumped off the couch, and Gabby moved to follow me.

"Night, guys," she said as we walked into her room.

"Another early Friday night for us," she whispered after she closed the door.

She got into bed, and I jumped up on the end. I didn't mind an early night if it meant lying with her.

Gabby stayed awake a long time, and I wondered if she could hear the giggling and other noises coming from Rachel's room, too.

GABBY SHUFFLED OUT OF HER ROOM. SHE HADN'T FALLEN ASLEEP UNTIL early morning. I hadn't slept well either, thanks to the love noises coming from Rachel and Peter.

I followed Gabby closely, unhappy that Peter was not only still in the house but also taking a shower. Gabby didn't seem to notice. She went straight to the fridge, stood in front of the open door for several long minutes, then looked around the room. Her gaze locked onto the orange juice container in the recycling bin.

She glanced at me, and I wanted to shake my head in denial. I had nothing to do with emptying that drink. I had tried a sip of it once, just to see why she liked it so much. I'd left it alone after that. She shared enough with me already.

A noise in the bathroom diverted Gabby's attention. She tilted her head and narrowed her eyes in that direction, and I heaved a sigh of relief.

"Great. Another non-coffee person," she said.

She shuffled to the faucet, grabbed a glass, then tipped the handle. She started to mumble as she jiggled the handle in earnest.

It wobbled loosely, and the water didn't come out like it usually did.

"Looks like I'll have to call the hottie plumber back," Rachel said as she walked into the kitchen.

"No, thanks," Gabby said quickly. "And no big guy showing two inches of crack, either." She turned off the tap with only a third of her glass full. "I was going to go pick up Clay later, anyway. I'll have him look at it."

Excitement coursed through me. She wanted me to wear my skin again.

Rachel looked up in surprise from the coffee tin. "Really? No-talk, leave-early Clay?"

Quiet woman, I thought, not liking the skepticism in her tone.

"Yeah, that one. Not the dog."

"I believe you said you didn't think he'd be around much," Rachel said with an odd grin.

She really needed to stop talking. I didn't want Gabby to remember that.

"Don't remind me. I'm probably going to need to beg."

Not likely. I doubted Gabby would need to beg me for anything ever.

"Does he know much about plumbing?" Rachel asked as she moved to the sink to fill the coffee pot.

"Don't know...we don't talk much."

Although she said it with humor, I knew that really bothered her. I watched her set her glass aside.

Soon, Gabby. We'll talk soon.

AFTER PETER AND RACHEL LEFT, Gabby emerged from her room dressed for the day.

"Wanna come shopping with me or stay here?"

Silly question. I walked to the door, and she drove us to the grocery store. As usual, I waited in the car as she strode across the parking lot.

It took almost an hour for her to reappear; and when she did, she moved fast as if she expected someone to come tearing after her. I watched behind her closely. No one was following her.

She caught my gaze and smiled at me. Then her gaze drifted to the truck pulling into the spot next to us. I turned and saw a man getting out. His determined, possessive expression had me tensing. What was it with human men around Gabby?

"Hi, there. Need a hand?" the man said as Gabby stopped her cart near the trunk of our car.

"No, thanks. I got it."

The man didn't move away.

"My name's Dale. I own Dale's Auto Body on South Mitchell. You should bring your car by. It looks like it might be due for an oil change."

What? I'd just changed it. Don't believe him, Gabby, I thought to her.

"That's a nice offer, but my boyfriend does the oil changes," she said as she opened the trunk, momentarily blocking my view. My heart seized for a minute. Did she know?

I ducked down and watched them in the narrow strip at the bottom of the window. Gabby didn't look upset, just in a hurry. Probably because Dale still hadn't left.

"He's a handy guy, then?" Dale asked as he grabbed the potatoes and set them in the trunk, a move that brought him closer to Gabby.

I shifted my paw into a hand, ready to open the door if need be.

"Yes, very," Gabby said. Her pulse remained steady, indicating she believed what she said. I wanted to shift fully but not because of the man outside.

"I'm sorry, I didn't catch your name," he said.

Gabby met my gaze and rolled her eyes. Although she found the man's attempts at courting her humorous, I did not.

"Gabby," she said, closing the trunk. "Thanks for helping me with the groceries, but I need to get going. My dog's been in the car for a while already."

Gabby swiftly shoved the cart into the empty space beside us and turned toward her door. She hadn't been fast enough. Dale now stood between her and the car door. I hopped from the back seat to the driver's seat, ready to let myself out and remove the man.

"We have an opening at the shop," I heard him say. "If your boyfriend's looking for work, send him by. We'll see how good he is."

I wanted to laugh. Whether or not he was serious, I'd be seeing Dale again soon.

Oblivious that I was now in the driver's seat, he opened the door for her. I growled a low warning. He looked down at me in surprise and backed up a step.

Gabby was quick to get in and pull the door from his loose hold. She had the engine started and was pulling away before the man thought to move again.

"Well, that was a challenge if I ever heard one," she said as she reached over to pet my head.

Human men weren't a challenge; they were an annoyance. But, that one might just be helpful.

"However, no challenges until you fix the sink," she said with a smile.

When we got back to the house, Gabby grabbed the things from the trunk and carried them into the house.

"You go shower while I unpack. Then you can look at the sink and see if we can avoid calling that big-headed plumber back."

I went to the bathroom, shifting just after I rounded the corner. Gabby hadn't followed me after that first time. I turned on the water and let it warm before stepping in.

A few minutes later, Gabby tapped on the door.

"I'm coming in, so please stay behind the curtain."

I grinned and rinsed the shampoo from my hair as I waited for her to gather the courage to open the door. It took several heartbeats.

"I have some clothes for you. Better stuff for looking at a sink than what I bought yesterday." She paused a moment. "Clay, I'm so sorry. I'm being rude and making assumptions." She took a deep breath. "Will you look at the sink? Please?" She was teasing me. I could hear the laughter in her voice. I cupped my hands under the water then squeezed them together, aiming the squirt of water over the curtain.

"Ok, ok. I'll just leave the stuff here on the floor. If something doesn't fit," she said, her voice taking on a nervous pitch, "or you don't like it, leave the tags on it, and we'll take it back. I guessed on the shoes. Some of the stuff isn't for now, but I figured you could try it on."

Why was she so nervous? Beyond the curtain, I heard a rustle of clothes. Was she taking back what she'd gotten me? My curiosity had me turning off the water.

She squeaked and fled the bathroom. I chuckled and pushed aside the curtain. On the toilet, she'd laid out socks, those tight underwear, a pair of jeans, and a t-shirt. A pair of grey and blue running shoes waited on the floor beside the toilet. All of it new.

First the car guy, now clothes. Finally, things were falling into place for me.

I eagerly dressed but left off the shoes and socks. I wasn't planning on going anywhere and didn't want to dirty anything more than I needed to. Everything fit well. She'd done a good job guessing at my size. Maybe she'd been paying more attention to me in my skin than she'd let on.

Grinning, I stepped out of the bathroom. But Gabby wasn't there. Curious, I checked the kitchen. Not there either.

I peeked in her room and saw her sewing a flannel shirt. It was large. Too big for her. The ache in my chest surged. She was sewing my shirt. I quickly left before I did something stupid, like tackle her with a hug.

From the basement, I grabbed a few of the tools I'd collected, then went back upstairs to work on the faucet. It wasn't too complex. The handle seemed as if it was simply loose.

I leaned closer, studying how the handle was connected. Behind me, I heard Gabby walk into the kitchen and pause. She didn't say anything or move, and it took all my effort to remain focused on the sink. Did she like the clothes? Did she like seeing me in my skin again?

Finally, she moved. I listened to her walk to the fridge, open it, then walk to the table and set a few things down. Her movement stirred the air enough that I caught the subtle change in her scent. Interest. In me.

My canines grew larger. With care, I set down the wrench I'd been using. It took all my willpower to walk past her and go down into the basement where I stood for a full minute, shaking. I listened to her steps on the floor above me. If she had any idea what she'd just done...I closed my eyes, took a deep breath, and ran my tongue over my teeth, willing them smaller.

It helped calm the shaking, but the teeth didn't budge. I went to the small pile of tools and grabbed the Allen wrenches I'd acquired. Unable to stay away from her any longer, I headed back up the stairs.

Gabby glanced at me when I reappeared.

"The shoes didn't fit?" she asked as she moved to the potatoes on the table.

I shrugged, having no idea if they fit. Shoes were the last thing on my mind. As I walked past her, I inhaled her scent again, needing to know if the interest had been a fleeting thing. It was still there, a light and fragile sweetness added to her already enticing scent.

"So they fit, but you didn't want to wear them?"

How did she know me so well? Because we were meant for each other.

I bent to the sink again and started checking which size Allen wrench I needed. Behind me, she shifted in her chair, and I listened to the rasp of the peeler as she removed the potato's skin.

"Did you like them, or should we take them back?"

Return them? I almost straightened from the sink, but she kept talking in a rush.

"I wasn't sure what style you liked. There were several different colors. They're cheap shoes, but I figured it was better than walking around barefoot in the snow. That's got to be cold, even for you."

She was worried I didn't like the shoes. I turned and looked at her. Interest and now concern.

"I just don't want you to think you have to keep them if you don't like them. It won't hurt my feelings if we take them back. Just wear the flip flops for now, and you can come in with me next time and pick out what you like."

She quickly stood and went to the stove.

While her back was turned, I used my speed to get the shoes and socks from the bathroom. I couldn't tell her I hadn't wanted to put them on and risk wrecking them before I had a chance to use them to get a job. But if I didn't do something to show that I liked them, she'd take them back. There was no way I'd surrender a single item she picked out for me. Not even the underwear.

I sat in the kitchen chair, put on the socks, and was in the middle of tying the shoes when she turned again.

"No, no, no, Clay," she said in a rush as she moved toward me. "I wasn't saying you *had* to wear them."

I knew that. But I also knew they were a gift from her, and by not wearing them right away, I'd hurt her feelings.

"It's okay to bring them back if you don't like them."

I finished tying, stood, and looked down at my feet. The shoes hugged the sides of my feet, but I had room to move my toes. They were much more comfortable than the ruined boots. Gabby remained where she was, and I was certain her gaze never left me. I wanted to look up, but I didn't trust myself. Instead, I moved to finish working on the sink.

"You like shoes, but you don't wear them much. Right?"

I shrugged again, wanting her to keep talking to me, but she turned back to the stove and fell silent. She didn't seem upset by anything so the quiet wasn't uncomfortable. In fact, it seemed pretty typical of our time together. Sometimes, she didn't feel like talking. I didn't mind those quiet moments with her.

The aroma of bacon, eggs, and potatoes had my mouth watering, and I couldn't wait to eat. I finished the faucet and tested the work, happy to see a full stream of water.

"Good to have a handyman," she said.

She'd called me a man. I wanted to pick her up and spin with her in my arms. Instead, I took the tools back downstairs and spent another minute trying to calm down.

When I returned, she had two plates on the table. She already sat at one side. My gut clenched. Our first real meal together.

I sat across from her, kept my eyes on my plate, and dug in. I nearly groaned. The bacon was loose just as I liked it, the eggs runny, and the potatoes crisp with bacon grease. I used my napkin often, worried I would have a yolk trail in my beard; Gabby liked me clean.

"What are the chances of trimming that beard?" Gabby asked.

I slowly wiped my mouth as I tried to figure out why she was asking. If she didn't like it, she would have asked about shaving it off. She'd said trim. Did she still think I looked like a crazy man? No, she'd told Rachel that was her first impression of me, not the current one. I decided to be honest about the reason behind the beard. It hid things, like my smiles when she was around...and my teeth.

Pulling my lips back, I flashed my smile at her. She froze for a second, her fork suspended in midair, and I detected a hint of fear. I closed my lips to hide my elongated canines and focused on my food again.

"Do they stay like that all the time?" she asked.

I debated if I should answer. She'd been afraid just seeing them. But she was asking questions. About me. Getting to know me. I wanted that. We needed it. But how could I explain why my teeth were big without scaring her more?

Taking my last bite, I stood and moved to the sink while I tried to decide if I should answer her question.

Abandoning her food, she followed me and leaned against the counter. Though I didn't look at her, I knew she was still studying me.

"Is this something you don't want to talk about?"

I shrugged.

"Is it something I need to guess, or can you explain it to me?"

She really wanted to know.

I glanced at her, wondering how I could explain it. My teeth were always out around her. It was worse when she gave me signs that she was starting to like me. Care for me. Her interest in me really hit hard. How could I show her that her nearness was the influence? The answer was crazy simple—show her that she could make it even more pronounced.

Slowly washing my plate and fork, I considered how she would react if I scented her, nose to skin. She moved away from the sink to grab her dishes. I went to the stove and washed that while I debated her possible reactions. There was only one way to know for sure.

I returned to the sink where she rinsed her plate. Her calm posture reassured me. Setting the washrag aside, I leaned against the counter and crossed my arms as I waited for her to finish.

We stood just a few inches apart, and when she turned to me, I could see the gold flecks in her light brown eyes. We watched each other for several moments. Her eyes dipped to my chest, and I saw her interest again. If she kept this up, I'd need to leave and lose a perfect opportunity to get closer. Yeah, not going to happen.

I uncrossed my arms and leaned toward her. Panic filled the air, and she froze. I inhaled, reminding myself I needed to be careful. I shook my head, trying to tell her not to worry, and pulled back.

Her throat moved with a hard swallow.

"You're trying to explain the teeth, right?" Fear still laced her words.

I nodded.

She studied me again, and slowly, the panic faded and interest returned. She took a deep breath.

"It's okay then. Go ahead, explain. I'll behave," she said.

I grinned and knew she'd caught me when her gaze dropped to my mouth. Maybe I needed a bigger beard.

Carefully, I leaned forward again. She didn't flinch away, and her scent remained clear of fear. As I neared, my teeth grew in anticipation. If she were my kind, I would bite her neck, Claim her, and end the waiting. But she wasn't my kind. She needed to bite me.

I didn't stop my approach until my nose almost touched her skin. Then, I inhaled deeply. Ah, what she did to me. I gripped the counter to steady myself and hoped she didn't notice.

She stiffened as I exhaled, and her pulse spiked. Even with fear flooding her, her scent called to me. I inhaled once more and lifted my head, exhaling as I went.

I was inches from her lips and so tempted. Would she still run? Had I given her enough time?

No. Her eyes were wide with fear and uncertainty. She still didn't trust that we were meant to be together.

I pulled back my lips, finishing what I'd started...an explanation for the beard.

She studied me, and slowly her pulse calmed.

"So, when you're around me, they're worse? I guess that means they're like that all the time."

I shrugged and took a step back.

A car pulled into the driveway, distracting Gabby. She left the kitchen in a rush. I sighed and quickly stripped out of the clothes, knowing our time was over. For now.

When Rachel walked through the door, I was in my fur and the clothes were in a neat pile on the chair.

Rachel smiled at me, petted my head, then caught sight of the clothes as Gabby walked into the room.

"Is there someone here?"

"Clay stopped by and fixed the sink. He figured he would leave a change of clothes because of last night," Gabby said.

Her smooth lies amazed me. I was glad I could hear the skip in her pulse to detect them because without it, there was nothing to give her away.

"Really? The sink's working? And for free?" Rachel moved to the sink to test it.

Gabby shrugged and grabbed the clothes, leaving me to deal with Rachel's good mood. When Rachel was happy, I endured hugs, kisses on the top of the head, and excessive petting. Done with her affectionate praise, she finally released me; and I shook off the feeling of her.

One of these days, Rachel's fondling would bother Gabby.

Monday, after Gabby and Rachel left, I went to Gabby's room to look for my clothes. Most of them were in her bottom dresser drawer. She even had the flannel shirt in there for me. I brought it to my nose and inhaled. Her scent was all over it.

Dressed like a man, I went to the basement and grabbed my wallet from where I'd hidden it after the washing machine incident. My fake ID wouldn't do much for an official job, but I had the feeling Dale's offer hadn't been official anyway.

With my wallet in my pocket, I left the house and settled in for the long walk to South Mitchell.

The garage was easy to find and looked better than most I'd seen back home. The square block building was painted white, but age and weather had dulled its pristine effect. Still, the place looked neat. A stack of four tires just outside the door held a sale sign. Four diagonally parked cars took up the space against the right side of the building, and a small fenced area hugged the left side. Two large bay doors stood open; in one bay, the floor lift had a car jacked into the air.

Dale was standing under the car and looked at me as I walked into the bay.

"Can I help you?" he said.

I nodded. "Gabby sent me. Said you had an opening for her boyfriend."

For a moment, Dale looked at me blankly, then a grin split his face. I'd expected guilt or denial, not amusement.

"I didn't think she'd actually send someone."

She hadn't, but I kept that to myself.

"I'm Dale," he said, coming over to me. He offered his hand, and I shook it.

"Clay."

"I'll be honest; I'm not looking for full-time help. This time of year, everyone starts remembering oil changes and winter tires. Once that's over, I'll be fine on my own."

I couldn't believe my luck. At best, I'd hoped he'd be able to point me to a shop that was hiring so I could use his name as a chance to get in somewhere.

"I'll work for cash whenever you need me," I said. I already knew that working for cash meant no need for my ID.

Dale considered me for a minute. "Cash?"

I nodded.

"This could work out," he said with a smile. "What experience do you have?"

I thought of Sam's truck. "Messing around, mostly."

"All right. Let's do a trial run. Ten dollars an hour. You can start with this oil change," he said, pointing to the car.

I nodded, and stepped further into my new life. An oil change was easy, something basic I'd read in the many books Gabby brought home and something I'd done already on Gabby's car. I found the drain pan he used off to the side, set it under the car, and started the oil draining. I went to the oil shelf he had in back and grabbed five quarts of the winter grade. Dale watched everything I did. It was a test I passed within twenty minutes.

"Good," he said with a nod. "I've got a few more for you to do."

The oil changes were fine. While I did those in the right bay, he pulled another car into the left. This one he didn't hoist up with the lift. Instead, he wheeled over a cherry picker. I continued with my task and watched him struggle for a few minutes. He made the engine look heavy, but I knew from Sam's truck it wasn't too much for me to lift on my own.

"Come give me a hand," he said after a few minutes.

He explained that the engine was slightly wedged and how we'd need to finesse it free so, once we had everything clear, the cherry picker could hoist it.

"Let me get an extra strap," he said, moving around me.

With his back turned, I quickly lifted the engine, tilting it and pulling it forward. Cleared, I started hoisting it with the cherry picker before Dale turned back to me.

"Nice," he said when he saw I already had it free. He glanced at me again, assessing me.

I shrugged and moved back to my current oil change.

Three hours later, he sent me home with an extra forty dollars in my pocket because of my initiative, and he also asked me to return around noon the next day.

As I made my way back to the house, I started planning what I'd do with the money. Gabby had some cash hidden in a box in her drawer. I'd seen her take from it a few times. I planned on putting a few bills there; hopefully, nothing noticeable. Since she'd just gone shopping, I figured I'd keep the rest in my wallet until she wanted something, like more of her favorite orange juice.

Once home, I showered and washed my clothes—except for the shoes. Rachel's car pulled into the driveway just after I put everything in the dryer. I quickly shifted, fear making my heart race as I sprinted up the stairs.

She stepped into the house, petted my head, and held the door for me to go outside. She didn't seem to notice the noise in the basement, so I went. She didn't watch me from the door, but instead went to her room. A few minutes later, she was back and let me in. She'd changed.

I watched as she scribbled a note and dropped it on the table. She seemed in a hurry as she patted me on the head and left. I waited until she pulled out of the driveway to read the note. She was going to dinner with Peter and would be home late. She'd been doing that a lot lately, staying out until long after Gabby went to bed.

An idea formed, and I grinned. I had clothes, a job, and money. Gabby was interested in me as a man. It was time to start showing her what I could be for her.

THE BAKED POTATOES WERE DONE, so I turned the oven down to keep them warm. The chicken breasts were still sizzling in the pan, and the corn steamed in the pot beside it. I looked at everything, trying to figure out if I'd missed anything.

Outside, a car pulled into the driveway. My pulse leapt. I looked down at my shirt to make sure it was still clean. Yep. White and tight. Just like it'd been from the dryer.

As Gabby walked through door, I slid the two chicken breasts onto their plates.

"Wow," she said. "I didn't know you cooked. It smells great." She closed the door, set her bag on the nearest chair, and moved to stand just behind me. Her scent wrapped around me. Then she inhaled deeply, robbing me of thought for a minute. Had she just scented me?

No, idiot. The food. I'm making dinner. For her. Stay focused.

I bent, pulled the baked potatoes from the oven, and added those to the plates along with a healthy portion of corn. Gabby moved away from me and grabbed us both a fork and knife from the silverware drawer before sitting at the table.

"So, other than cooking, how did you keep yourself busy today?"

Not ready to tell her about the job, I set the plates down and nodded at the last batch of books she'd brought me, which happened to be on the table. I'd finished the last one last night and had them there, ready for her to return.

"You read them all, already?"

I nodded.

"That's a lot to read in just five days. Are you skipping chapters?"

Her amusement confused me, and I looked up to see why that would be funny. She blushed slightly and cleared her throat.

"So, about the beard...are your teeth ready to play nice?"

I laughed. My teeth were ready to play. Nice or not didn't matter.

"Does that mean we can trim your beard?" Excitement filled her gaze.

I shook my head, wondering why she wanted the beard trimmed. This was the second time she'd mentioned it.

Her face fell, and she quickly looked down at her plate. I lifted my nose and tested the air. I'd disappointed her. I leaned back in my chair and studied her. Her interest made me happy; if a trimmed beard meant that much to her, I'd do it. But, I needed to understand why. My gut told me there was something more behind the request than her obsession with my grooming habits.

She glanced up, gave me a weak smile, and lifted another bite.

"This tastes great. Thank you for cooking. Do you have a favorite food? I can put it on the next shopping list."

Why was she changing the subject now? She pushed a few bites around on her plate, her discomfort growing. I picked my fork back up, still trying to figure out what had just happened.

"Actually, let's keep a shopping list on my dresser. When you think of something, you can add to it so I know what to get without guessing."

We ate the rest of the meal in silence. When she was done, she brought her plate to the sink, then returned to the table and started reading from one of her textbooks.

"If you want, when you're done, we can watch a movie," she said as I took my last bite.

I wanted nothing more. I hurried to clean up. When she moved to help, I waved her back to her seat. If she did her work while I cleaned, I'd have more of her undivided attention later.

While I finished washing the stove, Gabby packed up and then hovered in the doorway, waiting for me. Behind my beard, I grinned triumphantly. She wanted me. Sure, it was just my presence she wanted, but I knew there would soon be more.

We moved to the living room, and I picked out a suspense movie. It worked well for snuggling the last time.

"If I scream again when Rachel comes home, no laughing," she said as she curled up on the couch.

I started the movie and sat next to her. As she watched it, I concentrated on her. She immediately relaxed, just slightly leaning against me. Her pulse jumped several times within the first few minutes of the movie. And although I knew it had nothing to do with me, my pulse always leapt in response.

I frowned and actually focused on the movie when I felt her shiver beside me. It wasn't that scary. A few minutes later, just as the girl was about to enter the house, Gabby popped up from the couch and went to her room. Tilting my head, I listened to her pull something from her closet.

Gabby returned, wearing a hoodie. She'd been cold. Damn it. I could have put my arm around her.

I spent the rest of the movie mentally beating myself.

When the movie ended, Gabby sprang from the couch, surprising me.

"Hey, Clay. Do you like cookies?" she asked as she left the room.

I stood and followed behind her, wondering what had brought on that unusual question. She opened a cupboard and started moving stuff around, looking for something. I stepped closer, barely an inch behind her, wondering what she was after. There wasn't much in the cupboard.

"Shoot," she said, closing the doors.

She turned and let out a strangled "gah" when she saw me so close. I grinned. How had she not heard me?

"Har-har," she said with a grin. Her pulse raced wildly. "I told you no suspense movies. Life is scary enough without them. Oh, and false alarm on the cookies. We're missing some main ingredients."

If she really wanted to make cookies, why not get what she needed? I held up her car keys and jingled them.

"It's tempting, but unless I want to get a part-time job, I can't afford to keep spending the money I've saved. I've got to stick to the budget so it lasts till spring. If we can manage to keep the heat off until November, I should have cookie money for Christmas. That's when cookies are best anyhow. I'll just need to start wearing more clothes inside."

More clothes? I wanted to groan.

She took the keys from me and put them back in the dish on the counter. I barely noticed. I was the reason she was spending more than she'd planned. The money in my pocket was a good start but only if I used it to help her. I couldn't just give it to her. She'd ask questions I wasn't ready to answer.

Tomorrow, before I went to Dale's, I'd figure out what groceries we needed in order to make cookies. I'd find a way to get everything Gabby wanted.

WHEN GABBY LEFT FOR CLASS THE NEXT DAY, I DID WHAT I COULD TO help at home. I switched over the laundry she'd put in that morning—I was less afraid of breaking the machine now—folded everything once it dried, and washed the sheets she'd pulled from the bed.

While I waited for the laundry to finish, I looked at our supplies and made note of anything running low. I also found a cookbook with over a dozen cookie recipes. Each recipe had a slight variation, but all had the same basic ingredients: flour, sugar, butter, baking powder (or soda), and vanilla. I added those ingredients to the list as well.

Once I had the bed remade, the laundry put away, and the list in my back pocket, I headed out the door.

Dale was ready with a car on the lift in the right bay when I arrived. I checked the paperwork on his desk for what it needed, then started on the oil change. It felt good to have something to do while Gabby was at school. Reading had helped me from going crazy, but physically doing something was better.

It was close to dinner when Dale told me I could go. I knew I wouldn't make it home before Gabby did, but I still stopped to pick up some more laundry detergent, dryer sheets, toilet paper, and toothpaste. Those items would be easy enough to sneak into the house. The rest of the list, I'd save for another day.

If Rachel wasn't home and Gabby hadn't yet eaten, maybe I could cook her dinner again. The likelihood of Rachel's absence was pretty high. Rachel's social life had altered when she started seeing Peter, and I'd noticed a pattern. She typically spent Tuesday nights at his house, which meant Gabby and I would have tonight together.

Two blocks from home, I noticed the car. It was parked in front of our house and was hard to miss. As I watched, the brake lights turned on; and it pulled away from the curb. I frowned. I knew both Rachel's and Peter's cars, and the one that had just driven away wasn't either.

Something about the car worried me.

With a burst of speed, I made it to the garage to ditch the supplies, then let myself in through the back door. I found Gabby in the living room, standing with her forehead against the front door.

The scent of her fear and confusion laced the air. Worried, I stepped closer as she pushed away from the door.

When she turned and saw me, she started screaming, a blood curdling sound that nearly stopped my heart. With wide eyes, she clapped a hand over her mouth to stop the sound. In the silence, I heard her pounding pulse. Something had scared her before she saw me. What? Or who?

I inhaled deeply. There was a lingering scent in the air, barely there. I breathed in again, tracing the scent. She had something in her front pocket. Something not hers. I glanced down, caught a glimpse of white, and reached forward to pluck the business card out of her pocket. There was nothing but a name and phone number on it.

I looked at her and shook my head, wondering what had upset her so much.

She exhaled shakily and dropped her hand.

"Did you see who was here?" she asked with a slight tremor in her voice.

I shook my head, wishing I hadn't worked late.

"How did you know that was in my pocket?"

I lifted it to my nose.

"Have you ever met Elder Joshua before?"

I shook my head again.

"Have you ever smelled him before?"

Where was she going with these questions? Again, I let her know I hadn't.

She closed her eyes and let out a sigh. She was relieved I hadn't met him? Why?

Her unfocused gaze told me she was lost in thought. I gently tapped her forehead, wanting to know what she was thinking. She startled slightly and gave me a weak smile.

"You want to know what's going on in my head?"

I nodded. I wanted that more than anything.

"I'd like to know what's going on in my head sometimes, too," she said, looking a bit lost. "Let's make dinner while I talk. Let me know if you hear Rachel or anyone else."

I nodded, kicked off my shoes, and put them in Gabby's room before joining her in the kitchen. She was sitting at the table, her hands fidgeting. I went to the cupboard and grabbed some potatoes. She needed to keep her hands busy.

She didn't hesitate once I set the spuds in front of her. She started to peel, and I turned to get a pot out.

"That was Elder Joshua at the door. He stopped by because I haven't talked to Sam lately, and Sam asked him to check up on me. I guess he was worried after that challenge."

I took some chicken from the freezer and went to thaw the meat in the microwave, listening not just to her words but also her tone. She sounded pensive.

"Something was odd about him, Clay."

And then, she just stopped talking. Behind me, the peeler rasped against the potato and the microwave beeped. I took the chicken to the stove then went to her side. She didn't look up at me. I grabbed the peeled potato, purposely nudging her chair. It seemed to startle her from her thoughts, and I went to the sink to rinse the potato.

"I'm different," she said abruptly.

I turned from the sink and looked at her. Of course she was different. She was human...yet somehow connected to our world. I didn't see anything wrong with that. I shrugged.

"No. Really different. It's kind of hard to explain. Sam told me I was different when he met me, but he doesn't know all of it. He said that I was rare because I was one of only a few humans compatible with werewolves, just me and Charlene."

She sighed and dropped the peeler, obviously agitated. I quickly grabbed two more potatoes and handed them to her along with the rinsed, nude potatoes. She started peeling again, and I went to the stove and started slicing the chicken.

"Since as long as I can remember, I've seen lights. Not with my eyes, but in my mind.

"When I was younger, I had to close my eyes and concentrate to see a relatively small area around me. As I got older, I didn't need to concentrate as hard and could see a much larger area. Now, I can see these lights at will, briefly, with little effort, and over a longer distance. And I don't need to close my eyes."

I put a large portion of butter into the pot, started it, and added the chicken. Moving quietly, I took some broccoli from the freezer, still listening and trying to understand what she was saying.

"These lights are people, Clay. I can see the neighbors moving around in their houses right now."

I paused, stunned by what she was saying. No lie laced her words. How could I, someone who had no skill of any merit, be with someone so completely special? When she started speaking again, she sounded a bit hoarse, so I poured her a glass of water.

"It's not an aura I'm seeing. To put it in perspective, I can see a square mile around us, but in my mind, the area looks like an inch. The lights within that area are small pinpricks, but I can see them so clearly that they might as well be the size of quarters three inches from my face. And all those dots are the same color. Every human around us has the same yellow light with a green halo."

I handed her the drink and rescued the potatoes she'd cubed into tiny pieces. It would make cooking them quicker.

"Thanks," she said, taking a sip.

While she continued talking, I resumed cooking dinner.

"You and I, in the middle of those dots, stand out. I have the same yellow light as everyone else, but my halo is orange. I'm different from the people around us. Even from you. Werewolves have a blue core with a green halo. At least, that's all I ever saw in the past two years, until the night you were challenged. That werewolf had a blue-grey light."

Was she saying there was another kind of werewolf? I'd never heard of any, but that didn't mean it wasn't true. We'd kept to ourselves until Charlene's arrival and acceptance into Thomas' pack. Who really knew what was out there? And another species would explain why that werewolf had challenged me before my time was up.

She continued her explanation, speaking slowly as if trying to figure out the right words to use.

"Now, imagine my shock when I opened the door and saw a man, who introduced himself as Elder Joshua, with the same color light. Only the difference in the color of his eyes kept me breathing."

Her panic made sense, and I started to wonder. If there was another kind of werewolf, how could we have one as an Elder? Did the other Elders know about this? No, I doubted it. They were still trying to puzzle out why Charlene and Gabby were potential Mates for our kind. I wondered if the answer to that lay within what

Gabby was telling me, that there might be more species out there than we were aware.

"I've been like this my entire life, and I have more questions than answers about this second sight. Why are all humans green and yellow except Charlene and me? We're human. Why does Charlene have a red halo? Or me an orange halo? The only similarities are the yellow cores. I've been thinking the yellow cores mean human, but I don't know what the halos mean.

"And I'm sure that you've caught on to the whole guy situation. I call to them, somehow, as if I'm a beacon or something. Do I really send out some kind of signal?"

She looked up at me questioningly as I turned from the stove with a loaded plate in each hand. I handed one to her and studied her for a long moment.

I had noticed the attention she received. Some of it seemed a little intense, but she was beautiful and amazing. I felt intense around her, too, but I knew that was just the animal side of me. Humans were different. Gabby more so because of her compatibility with me. However, beyond the Mate pull, I didn't sense anything different about her.

I shrugged and shook my head.

"So nothing as far as you can tell? There's got to be a reason, a connection to it all." She sighed and played with the food on her plate.

I ate slowly, unsure how to react to everything she'd shared. Her revelation surprised me, but it didn't change how I felt about her. I didn't care that she saw lights in her head or that men found her attractive. It just meant we'd have an interesting life.

I quietly ate my food and waited for her to say more. Eventually, she did.

"I've never told anyone all of this. People figure out there's something different about me if they're around me long enough. But no one knows about the lights."

That she'd chosen to share her secrets elated me. It showed trust and progress in our relationship.

"I'm torn. Do I call Sam and tell him everything? Do I tell him the light of the guy who challenged you is the same light as Joshua? There's nothing concrete I can offer about the coloring or why I'm so worried about it.

"Why would a werewolf I've never met challenge you? And why does he share the same coloring as Joshua? So far, the lights have had a category: humans, werewolves, and compatible Mates. I don't think the challenger and Joshua can be compatible Mates because Charlene and I are uniquely colored from each other."

She shook her head then took her first bite. Her food had to be cold by now.

"Bet you're wishing you hadn't asked."

I shook my head slowly, still watching her. She was everything I wanted and more. I only wished she would have trusted me sooner.

She quickly finished her meal, and I took both our plates and cleaned up the kitchen while she sat at the table and did her homework. Her anxiety remained high, and I didn't know what to do to comfort her. I doubted she'd welcome a hug yet. At least, not from me while I wore my skin.

When I finished rinsing the sink, I left the room, stripped out of my clothes, and shifted. I returned to the kitchen, nudged her arm with my head, and looked toward the living room. She reached out and ran her fingers through the fur at my neck, then packed up her homework.

We watched some sitcoms before calling it a night.

OUR LIVES SETTLED INTO A PATTERN. I followed her to school, without her knowing, then went to work. On Tuesdays, Fridays, and Saturdays, Rachel spent her time at Peter's place. On those nights, I made sure I was home before Gabby so I could have dinner ready. On the nights Rachel was home, I let Dale know I could work late if he needed me.

The money helped. I started getting the things Gabby needed or showed interest in. Simple things like movies she mentioned to Rachel, basic food items, and some spare clothes for me. I always wore what she'd given me on the nights we were together, though, and hoped she understood how much I treasured them, especially the shirt she'd sewn.

Each night together she peppered me with questions, making a game of getting to know me; and as the weeks passed, I thought we'd progressed nicely. She was comfortable with me and seemed to really trust me. I wasn't ready to test our relationship yet, though. Fear that she would pull back stopped me.

When the questioning turned to what I did all day, I left my wallet on her dresser as a clue. Rachel was home when Gabby found it so she didn't say anything, but her expression spoke volumes. Curiosity and excitement played across her features. I sat behind her as she quietly opened it and started poking through the contents.

Her hesitant glances at me before she looked at each new thing were adorable but not as much as when she stared at my license. They'd made me pull my hair back for the photo. It was her first glimpse of my face. She stared so long that I started to laugh, not at her fascination but because she was fascinated. Just another sign of how much she'd accepted me.

But acceptance wouldn't be enough to keep the other unMated at bay, and our time to complete a Claim was running out.

Chapter Fourteen

I sat on the bed and watched Gabby get ready. A female from one of Gabby's classes had invited Gabby to a Halloween party. And Gabby had said yes.

She wore my favorite flannel shirt and a pair of my jeans. The jeans sagged on her and mostly covered the boots she wore. Thankfully, she'd belted the waist to keep the pants from falling off completely. I liked that she wore my clothes. It gave me a certain sense of possession...if only she weren't planning to leave and go mingle with other men at one of those party houses.

Most of Gabby's blonde hair was hidden under a ball cap. I tilted my head, studying her as she sculpted some thick sideburns with the hair gel. She was too cute to pull off being a man, but it was better than the cocktail waitress costume Rachel had given her.

When she started coloring manly looking eyebrows on her face, her cuteness dropped a level, and I started to worry. She was dressing tough. Human men weren't rational when they drank. Someone might take her attempt at toughness as a challenge.

"What do you think?" she said, turning around.

Unhappy with the situation, I jumped off the bed and turned

toward the door, pretending to ignore Gabby as I tried to decide if I would be able to follow her from a distance. That wouldn't help when she went into the house. I needed to go with her as a man, but would she let me?

Lost in thought, I didn't hear Rachel until the door was already opening. I jumped out of the way just before it hit me.

Rachel stopped and stared at Gabby in shock. For once, I agreed with Rachel's reaction.

"What the hell did you do?" she said.

"I'm going for dude. It's safe, right? What guy is going to want to hit on a guy even if he knows that underneath, it's a girl? Guys get weird about that stuff."

"You know what's going to happen?" Rachel said, sitting on the bed. "All the guys are still going to be attracted to you. Only they're going to freak out because you're going to make them think they're gay. You're going to get your ass kicked tonight."

I swore and rushed from the room. There was no way I'd let Gabby go without me now. Gabby and her classmate would just need to adjust to the change in plans.

With Rachel in Gabby's room, I shifted my hand, let myself out the back door, and went to the garage. Dale had given me some coveralls a few weeks ago, which I'd hidden in the back. I grabbed them, dressed with speed, and pulled back my hair. I wanted every man I encountered tonight to see my eyes and know the threat they faced if they got near her.

Less than a minute later, I was at the door again. I almost let myself back in, but remembered Rachel was inside, and knocked. It didn't take long for Rachel to answer. When she saw me, she grinned.

"I'm glad you're here. That girl's going to need someone to keep her safe tonight."

I nodded. Finally, we were on the same page.

"It's for you, Gabby," Rachel said loudly.

Rachel didn't move to invite me in, so I waited outside for

Gabby. As soon as she reached the kitchen arch, she stopped and stared. Slowly, some of the anger and annoyance left me, and I found myself grinning at her stunned expression.

Her scent changed the longer she looked, and it made my gut clench.

Someone knocked at the front door.

"I got it," Rachel said, grinning at us before she rushed from the room.

Gabby glanced down at my coveralls, read the name sewn on my chest, then met my gaze. "You have some explaining to do, I think."

My job had never really been a secret, no more than everything else I didn't say.

She turned away from me, but she didn't seem mad. I followed her to the front door where Rachel and another woman were talking. The woman wore a form-fitting dress to attract men. A mermaid or a siren; it didn't make much difference. It was good I meant to tag along.

"You're gorgeous, Nicole," Gabby said. "Are you going to be warm enough?"

Probably not. And, a sweater would help draw less attention.

Both of the women and Rachel laughed.

"Hey," Gabby said, "it's a valid question. It's the end of October for Pete's sake."

"I'll be fine," the woman said as her gaze locked on me. "Hi, I'm Nicole."

I nodded and stuck out a hand. She clasped it.

"Uh, this is Clay," Gabby said for me. "He doesn't talk much. And this is Rachel, my roommate. Are we ready?"

While they focused on each other, I turned, planning to beat Gabby to the car. In the beginning, she'd managed to leave the house a few times without me. I was smarter now. Silently, I left the room.

"Sure," Nicole said. "I parked on the street."

"Great. Let me grab my keys," Gabby said.

Already in the kitchen, I grinned at the keys in my hand and stepped out the back door. I was down the porch steps before she reached the kitchen. The missing keys would let her know what I had in mind if the overalls hadn't.

Sliding behind the wheel, I started the engine and waited.

A few minutes later, both Gabby and Nicole stepped onto the back porch and hurried to the car. Gabby sat up front with me, and Nicole slid into the back seat.

Gabby turned to look at Nicole.

"I don't know where we're going. Just tell Clay where to turn and be sure to give plenty of warning. This is the only car I have for the winter."

I knew her warning was for me. No doubt, she questioned my ability to drive. Although we'd grown closer, there was still so much she didn't know about me. I smiled as I backed out of the driveway and followed Nicole's directions to the party.

The car-crowded curbs worried me as we parked a few blocks away. Just how many men would I need to deal with tonight? I glanced at Gabby, her costume still a source of concern. She seemed unbothered by both her costume and the cold. Nicole shivered as we walked, but Gabby seemed fine. Dressing as a guy was still better than what Rachel had offered.

The blaring music began to hurt my ears as we neared the party house. Stuffed sheets, their version of ghostly decorations, hung from every tree in the yard. People crowded the front lawn in groups that overflowed into the neighbor's yard.

We caught the attention of a few men who turned to stare. Their gazes drifted to Gabby, confusion clouded their expressions, then they looked at Nicole.

"I knew you would make this fun," Nicole said with a laugh. "Oh, I see him on the porch. Do you think I should say hi?"

I had no idea who she was talking about, but I knew this wasn't going to be fun with Gabby's next words.

"Let's push our way through the crowd and get inside. We can warm up for a minute. It'll be more attractive if you're not stuttering with cold."

She wanted to go in? The windows rattled in time with the beat of the music. It wouldn't be pleasant inside, and getting there would be less so because we needed to navigate through the sea of men on the lawn.

Frustrated, I took Gabby's hand and started to lead her through an overly interested crowd. They willingly parted for us, turning as we neared though I knew they couldn't hear us. Gabby was right. It was as if they sensed her, as if she sent out some kind of signal. She'd told me. I'd just never seen it get this bad.

When we reached the door, a man tried to sell me an empty cup for three dollars while offering Gabby one for free. Gabby politely said no. What was he thinking? Who wanted an empty cup? Even for free?

I glared at him and pulled her inside as he continued to look at her with interest. Immediately, my eardrums wanted to bleed. The bass echoed in my ribcage and made my teeth ache.

I pulled Gabby through the crowded entry, into a packed living room, then shouldered my way to the small couch. I glared at the two males sitting there. They uneasily stood and left, making room for the women to sit. Alcohol fumes permeated the air. Uneasy with the mood of the room, I stayed near Gabby, sitting on the arm of the couch. The men around us were drunk and unpredictable. I didn't like it.

One of the males across the room caught sight of Gabby and made his way over.

When the man stopped in front of her, he swayed slightly on his feet. Gabby wouldn't look at him. Good girl.

The music decreased in volume as a softer song came on. I would have sighed with relief, but the man used the opportunity to try to speak to Gabby. The alcohol he'd consumed had impaired his tongue, making him hard to understand.

"Hey...wash shore name?" he asked.

"Go away." Gabby's quick response almost made me smile.

"Wanna go up shtairs? They have a pool table."

Nicole coughed, an attempt to hide her amusement. I was not amused. I narrowed my eyes at him and curled my hands into fists to hide my nails, which were slowly changing color.

"No. Go away." Gabby turned to glare at the man.

From where I was sitting, just slightly behind her, I caught the man's attention and bared my teeth. The flare of white snagged his attention, and his eyes widened before he started to nod and smile.

"Oh, god it man. Sheesh yours."

I nodded in return, and he moved away from us. Both women looked up at me.

"What did you do?" Gabby said.

After a moment's hesitation, I bared my teeth, showing my elongated canines. As I anticipated, she didn't like it. Worry tinged her usual scent, which was hard to pick up with all the odors in the room.

"If you keep those in all night, you're going to have sore gums tomorrow," she said.

I had no idea what she was talking about.

"Those are so real looking. You have to tell me where you got them," Nicole said.

Ah. She wanted Nicole to believe my teeth were fake. Just so long as the other men eyeing Gabby thought they were real, I didn't care.

"He won't say," Gabby said to Nicole. "Warm enough? Are you going solo or do you want backup?"

Nicole's obvious nervousness hadn't left her. She wasn't ready to talk to whoever drew her here; yet, I didn't think staying much longer wise. The men across the room were starting to frown at Gabby. Was it the challenge I'd feared she'd face or her pull?

While I kept my narrowed gaze on them, Gabby reached out to

pat Nicole's bare shoulder. They both yelped, drawing my attention.

"I'm so sorry, Nicole," Gabby said. "I was just going to tell you that we should say hi now, and I go and shock you, instead."

How had she shocked Nicole?

"No, I know what that was. It was a jump start." Nicole smiled at Gabby. "I'm going to go out there now. If I can't get his attention, we can go." Nicole stood and made her way to the door.

I turned my attention back to the men and found their stares no longer on Gabby. The men who had seconds ago frowned at Gabby now moved to follow Nicole. The sudden change, though welcome, had me puzzled. I glanced at Gabby and saw her studying the men as well.

She cast a worried glance in Nicole's direction and stood quickly. She almost fell, and I wrapped my hands around her waist to steady her, truly concerned. She didn't acknowledge me at all. Instead, she kept her focus on Nicole.

After a moment, Gabby slipped from my hold and started to follow. She seemed steady, but I stuck close and remained ready.

Where people had turned and moved for us on the way in, they completely ignored us now. I had to push people out of our way. Someone almost stepped on Gabby. I grabbed him by the back of the neck and turned him like a puppet.

Meanwhile, Nicole had no problem weaving through the crowd, and the distance she gained seemed to upset Gabby.

We made it to the porch as Nicole approached a man. I heard her say hello, and the man turned to Nicole with an eager smile. The attention he gave her reminded me of Scott.

Gabby didn't move to approach the pair. Instead, she worked her way to the railing to watch.

The men around Nicole all turned to stare at her. As I watched, I realized this was similar to how men paid attention to Gabby. A tad more intense, but I'd never seen Gabby in a dress like that around men. Just the thought made my hackles rise.

Gabby shifted from foot to foot, drawing my attention. A shiver shook her, but it didn't remove her focus from her friend. I watched the shivers increase and the group of men around Nicole grow. How long did we need to stay? The men were no longer a problem, it seemed, but the cold still was.

Apparently having the same thoughts, Gabby reached back, wrapped her petite hand around my wrist, and tugged my arm up. I didn't need any more of an invitation. I widened my stance and pulled her close, wrapping my arms around her. She leaned back into my chest, and I set my chin on her head, trying to touch her as much as possible. I told myself it was only to share my warmth.

"I don't feel good," she said. Her teeth clacked together as she spoke.

I lifted my hand to her forehead. She didn't feel feverish.

"Do I feel warm?" She twisted her neck to look at me, and I shook my head.

She didn't turn back around. Instead, she continued to gaze at me. A small smile lifted the corners of her lips, and her gaze softened. My heart stuttered at the change in her expression. Everyone around us ceased to matter. I knew what Gabby was thinking when her gaze dropped to my lips. I'd never wanted anything so badly than for her to follow through with her thoughts.

She seemed to shake herself from the moment.

"I think I'm ready to go, but I don't want to leave Nicole here. What are my chances of getting her away from him, you think?"

With a heavy heart, I turned my gaze from Gabby to glance at Nicole. The woman didn't appear to like all of the attention anymore. She seemed nervous again.

"I think now's a good time to s-see," Gabby said.

I loosened my hold but kept a hand on the small of Gabby's back as she moved forward. She shook with cold, and her plodding steps made slow progress. The people around us didn't seem to notice and would have easily pushed her aside in their pursuit of a good time...if not for me. I pushed back. People who didn't move were moved. A few grumbled, but I bared my teeth and dared them to take offense. Each one stumbled away.

When we finally reached the group, the men turned to glare at me as if I were interested in stealing Nicole from them. I was. But only so I could take Gabby home. She was worrying me. In all the time since we'd met, she'd never once been sick. Why now? And why were the men, who normally fawned over her, suddenly treating her like she didn't matter?

"Hi, guys," Gabby said to the group. "Sorry to interrupt, but we need to pull Nicole away for just a minute."

Nicole's smile widened as she glanced at Gabby then back at the men.

"I'll be back in just a bit," Nicole said to them. "Can someone get me a soda?"

She took Gabby by the arm and turned her around so fast I barely had time to move out of the way. I scowled at her. Couldn't she see Gabby was sick? You can't tug around a sick person like that.

Sticking with the pair, I followed them from the porch and across the yard, in the direction of Gabby's car.

"Thank you for that," Nicole said. "It was really weird the way they were acting tonight. I guess mermaid sends off the wrong vibe. I hope he remembers talking to me, though. I liked it until his friends showed up."

Impatience ate at me as I watched their slow progress. I wanted to pick Gabby up and carry her to the car. My concern hadn't yet outweighed my fear of her reaction though.

"Yeah," Gabby said. "He s-seemed okay. D-don't trust his friends."

"Are you okay?" Nicole asked, looking closely at Gabby.

Finally, she notices, I thought.

"I think I'm getting sick or s-s-something. Clay felt my head, but s-said I didn't feel warm."

"Is Rachel going to be home tonight? You said she's going to school for nursing, right? She'll probably know if there's something going around on campus. The nursing students doing clinicals always seem to know."

"Good idea."

Halfway to the car, Gabby noticeably flinched and started shaking more. She needed to warm up. I ran ahead and started the car. Then, I got back out and waited for them by the door. As soon as they were close, I opened the door for Gabby. She was too pale with dark circles under her eyes.

Nicole kept an arm around Gabby as she helped her into the front seat.

"Do I look as b-bad as I f-feel?" Gabby asked with a weak smile as Nicole buckled her in.

Nicole glanced at me, but I couldn't tear my gaze from Gabby as I circled the hood to get in. What had happened? She'd been fine all day. There hadn't been any signs of illness. Not a single sneeze or sniffle like humans tended to display.

"Well, you do look like you're coming down with something. I'm so sorry I begged you to come out tonight."

"Don't w-worry about it. It w-was r-really interesting."

Nicole closed Gabby's door and got in back.

I sped home because, despite the heat pouring from the vents, Gabby's shivering had gotten worse. Her teeth chattered nonstop.

The dark house was a welcome sight when I pulled into the driveway.

"I hope you feel better," Nicole said. "I'll see you on Tuesday."

Gabby only nodded as I parked by the porch. I immediately got out and walked around the front of the car as Nicole left. Gabby blinked slowly, miserably, as she watched me.

I opened the door and wrapped an arm around her shoulders. Keeping a firm hold on her, I helped her from the car and across the porch. As soon as I had the door open, she slipped from my hold, stepped inside, and started to tug off the flannel. I followed closely, ready to help in whatever way I could.

"Clay, c-can you get my towel?" she asked, pausing outside the bathroom to drop the shirt on the carpet.

A shower? I nodded. It would help warm her faster. I quickly went to her room and grabbed the towel. The closing of the bathroom door made me pause. She'd barely been able to stand. Would she be able to shower on her own?

I brought the towel to the bathroom door then waited. Inside, I listened to the small, mewling noises she made. Each one broke my heart and tested the respect I had for her privacy and my need to care for her.

Unable to stand another second, I tapped on the door. Just let me in. Please.

"J-just a s-sec," she said, her panic clear. "I'm not ready, y-yet."

A second later, I heard her bump into something. Taking a breath, I cautiously opened the door.

She stood by the toilet. She'd managed to get her shirt, socks, and shoes off, but her pants were obviously giving her trouble.

"Hey!" An unnatural flush crept across her pale cheeks as she crossed her arms over her chest.

If I wasn't so scared for her, I would have taken a moment to enjoy all the skin she'd bared. Instead, I tossed the towel on the toilet lid and moved past her without a glance. I turned on the shower so the water could heat up. Then with a burst of speed, I did what needed to be done. I moved back to her side, bent, and had her pants around her ankles before she could screech.

With my eyes averted, I remained by her legs to wait for her reaction and for her to step out of her jeans.

"Clay, g-get out!"

Her outraged demand just firmed my resolve to stay.

"Really, I c-can do the rest."

I tapped her leg and motioned for her to step out of the pants. After a moment, she placed a hand on my shoulder and did as I asked.

"N-now out, Clay."

I picked up the pants and stood, careful to keep my gaze glued to the wall tile, then shook my head.

"The h-hell you s-say!"

She almost made me smile. I set her pants on top of the towel then pulled back the curtain and held out a hand. While I waited, steam began to drift in the air, letting me know the water had warmed. When she took too long, I nodded toward the shower and tapped the tub with my boot. Couldn't she see she'd be warmer in there?

"You're s-staying until I'm in? So I don't fall?"

I was staying because I couldn't leave her. But I shrugged, willing to let her think what she wanted.

She sighed and, a second later, placed her cold hand in mine. Sure, she still wore her bra and underwear, but I highly doubted she'd appreciate my help with those.

As soon as she was in, I closed the curtain then hesitated. She wasn't steady on her feet. Would she fall when she tried to remove the rest of her clothes? I waited, but she didn't move an inch behind the curtain. And, I realized she wouldn't until I was gone. With a worried sigh, I turned and left.

As soon as the door closed, I heard material hit the bathroom floor.

After listening to the water run for five minutes with very little additional sound, I let myself back in.

"Clay?"

She sounded worse. Weak. I grunted so she'd know it was me. Who else would it be if not me?

I grabbed the towel, held it out, and averted my eyes again. The curtain rustled, then a moment later the water turned off. She plucked the towel from my fingers but remained hidden behind the curtain. I stayed as I was, facing the door with my hand extended, ready to help.

After some more rustling, she grabbed my hand and stepped from the shower. I knew how badly she felt when she scooted past me, wrapped in only a towel, and shut herself in her room. I picked up the bathroom to give her time to dress, then waited outside her door.

A long pause and short breaths followed each rustle of movement. Her pain tormented me. Yet, I knew she wouldn't welcome any further interference. The waiting became agony.

As soon as I heard her climb into bed and pull the covers up, I let myself in and turned off the lights.

In the dark, her teeth chattered loudly. I tossed her clothing on the floor, stripped out of my clothes, and tugged on a pair of shorts from the bottom drawer. She didn't make any other sound, just the clacking of her teeth, as I pulled back the covers and slid in next to her.

"I really hope you're wearing shorts or something," she said with a slight slur.

Her concern over what I wore didn't stop her from pressing her cold feet against my legs. She made a small noise, one of relief, and moved closer to me.

Seconds later, her breathing slowed. She slept. I wrapped my arms around her and pulled her to my chest, holding her as I'd wanted to do for months. My heart broke that it was because she was sick.

Please let her be all right, I thought.

I didn't sleep, just held her. Night faded to dawn, and dawn gave way to day. Still she slept without stirring. Each hour brought more helpless fear.

By mid-morning, Gabby finally stirred. My throat tightened at the feel of her feet moving under the covers. She groaned slightly and tilted her head back, shifting away from my chest. Her eyes were open but her gaze was bleary.

"I'm thirsty." The dry rasp of her words supported her claim.

I eased her from my arms and hurried to the kitchen, glad Rachel wasn't home yet. With a glass of water in hand, I returned to Gabby's side and helped her drink. She drained the glass in long swallows then curled up once more. She was sleeping before I set the glass aside.

Sitting on the bed, I studied her. Her skin seemed to have more of its normal color back. And the circles under her eyes were less pronounced. I hoped that meant she was better. The worry and fear that I'd held all night eased up, but only a little. Her need for more sleep when she'd already slept more than twelve hours didn't seem normal.

Taking her glass, I went to the kitchen to refill it just in case she woke again. I set it on her dresser and grabbed one of my books before settling on the bed beside her. She shifted in her sleep, moving close to me. I smoothed back her hair then forced myself to open the book and began to read. Though my eyes touched on the words, I read very little. How long should it take for her to get better? Should I reach out to Sam? I glanced at Gabby, knowing she wouldn't like that.

I stayed close, trying to read, until she started moving in her sleep.

Hoping she'd wake hungry this time, I went to the kitchen to make a very late breakfast. Rachel still wasn't home so I could move around freely. If she were home, though, maybe she'd know what was wrong with Gabby.

I'd just turned the bacon in the pan when I heard Gabby get out of bed. She didn't leave her room, though. She just moved around a bit. Probably grabbing her books.

I hurried to finish cooking then made a plate for her.

Carrying her food and a glass of juice, I nudged the bedroom door open and found her sitting up in bed, studying. When she looked up, I lifted the plate and glass unsure if she wanted it.

"Thank you," she said with a smile. "I'm starving."

Starving was good. That meant she was better. Right?

I stepped into the room as she tossed her book aside. She was ready when I handed her the plate with a fork and set the orange juice on the dresser. The enthusiasm with which she dug in surprised me. Eggs, bacon, potatoes, and toast vanished in minutes.

When she looked around for more, I handed her the glass of juice. She sipped it with a contented sigh and patted the bed next to her.

"Want to read by me?"

Yes and always. I grinned at her, collected the dishes, and left the room. As I finished up the breakfast dishes, she used the bathroom. Instead of hovering like I wanted to, I grabbed a book and settled on my side of the bed. I finally had a side, not just the foot of the bed.

She joined me a few minutes later, and we remained like that for the rest of the day.

Near dinner, I heard Rachel's car and closed my book. With Gabby sticking to the bed, I left the room to shift in the living room.

Rachel would just have to deal with a man's set of clothes on the couch.

Chapter Fifteen

Clay, time's up.

Sam's unexpected words sent a bolt of panic through me as I stared down at Gabby. She slept peacefully beside me, still recovering from whatever affected her last night.

Several males have approached Elder Joshua and requested permission to Introduce themselves to Gabby. Permission's been granted. Sorry, son.

Had it been that long? I thought back to the Introduction in spring and wanted to growl. It had. I'd been so focused on the progress Gabby and I were making, I hadn't noticed the passing time.

There wasn't much I could do about unMated males asking to meet her. I'd been given six months to win her over; and in their eyes, I'd failed. I knew better, though. Gabby was human. She was taking her sweet time to realize that she didn't just care about me but loved me.

Elder supervised only, I sent back.

I wasn't giving up, just ensuring her safety.

Though werewolf laws forbade us from Claiming a human—only the human could initiate the Claim—I'd already dealt with one unMated who'd challenged me when Gabby was around. She could have been hurt. If they wanted to start Introductions again, she needed to be in a controlled environment. Plus, the Elders would be there to note her disinterest in others and preference to me.

I reached out and gently touched Gabby's cheek. She was so fragile.

I'll see what I can do.

I growled. Not good enough.

Let them all know I'm challenging for the right to keep her.

Gabby shifted in her sleep. I calmed, wrapped my arms around her, and waited for her to wake up. When she did, she seemed better but still not herself. She stayed in her room, studying or napping. As the day wore on, no one bothered us, and I hoped that meant the Elders had agreed to chaperoned Introductions.

While she read, I tried to think of ways to broach the subject of Claiming. Deep down, I knew she wasn't ready yet. She'd let me sleep next to her only because she was sick. I had no doubt, when she felt better, I'd be back to the end of the bed.

Yet, I also knew I was making progress. She talked to me when she wanted to share news that excited her. She chose to have dinner with me instead of going out with Rachel. Whether she realized it or not, we were slowly working up to making things official. Just not fast enough.

WHEN GABBY WOKE Monday morning and started to dress for school, I tried to stop her. She was still weak. However, since Rachel had returned home late Sunday, I'd reverted to my fur. So my efforts were limited to what a dog would do and were easy for Gabby to ignore.

On her way out the door, she patted me on my head and softly said, "Don't worry so much."

How could I not? The rules had changed, and she still didn't know. Frustrated, I sat beside the door and listened to her car pull away. She had no idea just how much I did worry. Not only would she need to contend with human men but, possibly, werewolves, too.

Thankfully, Rachel left soon after. I let myself out and ran my route to campus, scenting as I went.

Though there were no signs of werewolves in the area, it didn't mean it would stay that way. I knew, as wolves, they wouldn't get too close, thanks to the security guards. But, what about as men?

I watched the students walking around campus for several minutes then turned away. Gabby was right. I was worrying too much. The men who wanted to meet her didn't want to hurt her. They wanted to talk to her, convince her that they were a better match for her. It was the Mating challenges that were the danger to her. As long as the challengers approached me when she wasn't near, she would be fine.

Back at the house, I dressed for work as usual and set out on the long walk. I expected someone to approach me then, but I arrived at the shop without incident.

Dale had the orders laid out on his desk so I could choose what to work on. He no longer regulated me to general maintenance orders. Anything he had on his desk was up for grabs. I'd noticed he usually left the heavy jobs on the top. I didn't mind. He paid me more when I did those.

I took the top order, found the keys for the car on the rack, then went to the lot to pull it into the right bay. Outside, a hint of something in the air made me pause. I inhaled deeply. Werewolf. It was faint which meant the challenger was watching me from a distance, sizing me up.

The tension I'd held since Sam contacted me, eased. It was a bit of a relief to know someone was out there. If he was watching me, he wasn't watching Gabby. It also meant that Sam had spread the news that I wasn't giving up my Claim. Anyone wanting to meet

Gabby would challenge me first. It wasn't required, but we had our pride. Though Gabby had technically rejected me by not completing the Claim within the six months, she was still allowing me to live in her house. Any man hoping to approach her wouldn't tolerate that remaining sign of her acceptance for me. Thus, the challenges. They wanted to prove to her that they were better in every way that mattered to a wolf.

I drove the car into the right bay and set to work as I normally would. No one approached the shop and the scent never grew stronger throughout the day. But I hadn't expected it would. Challenges weren't something we did out in the open. There was too much risk that humans would see what they shouldn't. When werewolves fought, we didn't always shift completely. Instead, we used the best of both our forms.

Near four, I cleaned up and went to the current order to make notes. It was early enough that I could settle up with Dale, face whoever challenged me, and still arrive home before Gabby so I could start dinner.

Dale stopped his work and came over when he saw me.

"Thanks for another day," he said, handing me money as he read my notes. "You see everything," he said, pointing to my comment about a few pinholes in the exhaust.

I shrugged. Some of the stuff was hard to miss when I had the car jacked in the air.

"See you tomorrow?"

With a nod, I tucked the cash in my wallet and left for the day. I didn't get very far.

The challenger's scent grew heavy near a vacant building at the edge of the business district. After a quick glance around, I veered off the sidewalk to track the scent around the building.

The cement block structure had a flat roof, and all of its windows were painted black from the inside. The faint scent of oil and exhaust still clung to it. Some kind of manufacturing plant, perhaps. Most likely insulated to help prevent sound from carrying to the homes not far away. Whomever I faced was smart to pick this location. No witnesses.

Around the back, I found the rear metal door ripped open and hanging at an angle. A blatant invitation. I stepped into the shadowed interior and pulled the door shut behind me. The large empty space made it easy to see my challenger. He waited in his fur in the center of the room.

I unzipped my coveralls and pulled off my shirt. He remained where he was as I stripped and shifted.

Moving toward him, I already knew the outcome of the fight. I saw in his eyes that he did, too. One on one, very few of my kind would be able to overcome me.

WHEN I WALKED out of the building, the sky was already dark. The challenge took longer than I'd anticipated, and I knew the only dinner I'd have ready in time was canned soup. It was something I'd picked up last week.

I jogged home, trying to keep a human pace; and before going inside, I hid my coveralls in the garage. Though Gabby knew about them, I wasn't sure Rachel was ready for more man clothes around the house.

Glancing at the clock, I wondered how Gabby's day had gone. No doubt I'd find out in a few minutes. It took me seconds to open the soup and dump it into a pot. As it heated on the stove, I quickly washed up. Though I'd won, the challenger had scored a few solid blows but nothing that wouldn't be healed by morning.

Gabby pulled into the driveway just as I poured the soup into bowls. Her slow steps thumped on the porch while I carried the bowls to the table. I glanced up as she opened the door. Looking exhausted, she dropped her bag on the floor, closed the door, and then shuffled to the table. With a weary sigh, she practically collapsed into the chair.

I sat across from her, watching as she took her first few bites of soup before I started eating too. We ate in silence for a few minutes.

"Are you going to tell me about the coveralls or where you got the money for groceries?"

Though she'd asked, she didn't look up to any serious conversation. She looked like she needed sleep. So I shrugged.

She sighed and pushed her bowl back. "I know I'm supposed to start asking you a bunch of questions, but I'm still too tired. Just don't be doing anything illegal, 'K? It would be hard to visit you in jail."

She got up and put the rest of her soup in a container. Despite my silent objections, she washed her own dishes then left me in the kitchen with my half bowl of soup. I quickly ate, cleaned up, and went to her bedroom. She was already curled under the covers and asleep.

The sound of Rachel's engine stopped me from lying next to her. I stripped, put my clothes away, and settled on the end of the bed, careful of my bruised ribs.

TUESDAY WAS A REPEAT OF MONDAY. Gabby went to school, and I went to work. The scent of werewolf drifted to me throughout the day, and I left early again. Like the day before, the scent grew stronger as I neared the vacant building. Only this time, it wasn't a single scent, but three. I knew I wouldn't make it home before Gabby.

Walking around the building, I retraced my steps. As I'd anticipated, the shallow bruises from the day before had already healed. I doubted I'd heal as quickly from three fights in a row. The bruising would go much deeper.

I stepped inside and found the three challengers. Though I could see they planned to fight as men, I stripped down to nothing anyway.

"Just give up now," one of the men said. "Sure you might win the first fight or two, but do you really think you can win three in a row?"

I waved the first one forward in answer.

The guy shook his head. "Whether you win this fight or not, Gabby's no longer yours. You had your chance. Elder Joshua has granted any interested male permission to approach her without supervision."

Shit.

I struggled to control my temper. I'd asked for controlled Introductions. Sam had said he would see what he could do. When I hadn't heard more, I'd thought...what had I thought? No answer didn't mean a yes.

With a growl, I launched myself at the first challenger. I needed to get home.

IT WAS past midnight when I left the building. I stopped at a gas station to clean up. I had a split lip and blood on my knuckles and in my beard. Most of the blood in my beard wasn't my own.

Letting myself in the back door, I listened for Gabby's soft breathing. She was safely asleep in bed. No other sounds drifted through the house, which meant Rachel wasn't home yet. Some of the remaining tension melted from my chest.

As I stripped and then changed into a clean shirt and shorts, I considered the challenges. I'd taken my time and paced myself, careful not to expend all my energy up front. But in the end, the third challenger had almost beaten me. What would Gabby have done if she'd woken, and I still hadn't returned? Her comment from Monday's dinner led me to believe she would have tried to find me, that we weren't done. Yet, what were we? Friends? I needed her to start seeing us as more than that.

I carefully lay next to her, wincing at the soreness along my back. She seemed to sense me in her sleep because she shifted closer. I put my hands behind my head and let her use me as a pillow. With her cheek on my chest, I wished I'd left off the shirt.

Once she settled, I sighed deeply and fell asleep.

SHE MOVED, a slight nod that rubbed her cheek against my chest. It was a pleasant way to wake up. She lifted her head, and I opened my eyes.

"It's annoying not being able to see you," she said softly as she propped herself up on her elbows to study me.

"If you don't talk, and I can't see your face, how am I ever supposed to figure out what you're thinking?"

She reached out to push my hair back, but I caught her wrist. She wouldn't like what she saw. I doubted the bruises had faded from last night.

"Seriously, Clay, what kind of bribe is it going to take for you to get rid of some of that hair?"

I bared my teeth, hoping my excuse would work this time, too.

"Can't we at least trim it back some?"

Her desire to look at me had me tugging her hand to my chest and laying it flat. I wanted her to see me, not just the outside but inside, too. My heart was hers. All that I was belonged to her.

She watched me with a slightly amused expression. Her tousled hair haloed her head in appealing disarray. Her lips parted, and my gaze drifted there. I could handle a thousand more challenges if only for one kiss.

Barely breathing, I lifted my free hand and tapped my mouth.

"What, you want me to be mute like you?"

She was killing me. I shook my head and reached out, cupping her jaw and lightly running my thumb over her bottom lip. My pulse thundered in my ears.

She froze, then her eyes widened. All trace of amusement fled her expression.

"Whoa!" she said as she flew from the bed, almost falling off it in her haste to put distance between us.

My hand slowly fell to the mattress. She didn't stop backing up until she hit the dresser, and then she clutched it as if she needed the support.

I saw her tremble and frowned. Had I misread our relationship? Did she truly not see me as a potential Mate? I waited. We watched each other. After a minute, she loosened her hold and nervously wiped her hand on her leg. I wished I knew what she was thinking.

As she continued to study me, her expression of fear melted away to one of slow amazement followed by a deep blush, which I found curious. Her amazement vanished and a sudden panicked look took its place. She was shifting through emotions too fast for me to understand. I'd thought the amazement and blush a good thing, but why had it caused her to panic?

Then her gaze drifted to my throat. I wanted to groan and close my eyes. Her reactions were confusing torment. Want me or don't, just decide soon.

She took several slow, deep breaths, wiped her hands on her pajamas again, then, finally she moved. She didn't flee the room, as I'd half-expected, but edged toward the bed. Her teeth caught her lower lip, making it hard for me to breathe.

"I have some questions before we talk about my bribe and your price."

What bribe? What price? I thought back to our conversation—her conversation—and realized she thought I wanted a kiss in exchange for trimming my hair.

She crawled back upon the bed and sat on her heels beside me. "Will you try to answer my questions?"

I waited, unsure of her questions.

"Are you able to physically speak?"

I nodded.

"Are you ever planning on talking to me?"

That question hinted at a long-term future. I smiled wide and nodded again.

"Clay," she said hesitantly, "were you asking for a kiss?"

I'd never wanted anything more. I nodded and reached out to twine my fingers with hers. She let me, and I ran my thumb over the skin of her hand.

"Clay, I can't even see your mouth to know where to kiss. I hope this bargain includes a shave."

My heart stopped. Was that a yes? I didn't move, afraid I was dreaming it.

She pulled her hand from mine so she could set both hands on my shoulders. I felt the slight tremble in her fingertips as she slowly leaned over me. Her nervousness almost blocked the scent of her anticipation. She closed her eyes a moment before her lips settled on me. She hovered there, lightly pressing her mouth against mine. I held still, wanting so much more and afraid to do something to scare her away.

She moved slighting, angling the chaste kiss as she reached up to gently brush her fingers along my face, exploring my forehead, ear, and jaw. I couldn't hold back. I tilted my head and started to nibble at her lips.

Her desire changed to panic, and I cursed myself as she pulled away and opened her eyes. Her shock and gasp made my heart sink.

Was she so afraid of a kiss?

"What happened?"

Her concern confused me.

"I thought werewolves weren't supposed to get hurt like this."

Crap. She'd moved my hair and was staring at my blackened face. Wait. Did that mean she hadn't minded the kiss, then? Before the thought could firmly settle in my mind, she bounded off the bed again.

"A deal's a deal. Go shower and shave. After you're done, we can play charades until I have the story behind the black eye."

Screw the black eye, I wanted her back on the bed.

"That or I call Sam."

I ran my hand through my hair in frustration, then sighed and sat up. The mood was obviously broken.

Swinging my feet over the bed, I turned away from her, ready to go take a cold shower when she came rushing over to me again. I didn't stand. She'd be able to reach my lips easier this way. Only she didn't rush to my front. She reached around me and tugged up my shirt. Somehow, I doubted her actions related to continuing our kiss.

"What happened?" she asked again, sounding really upset this time. She nudged my arm away from my side and leaned closer to inspect the bruises there. I held still, liking it when she ran gentle fingers over the marks.

"This is really scaring me, Clay. I thought werewolves were supposed to be this tough, nearly indestructible, race."

I fought three wolves, one right after the other. How tough did she need me?

"Is this why you were gone last night when I came home?"

She sounded sad and mad at the same time. I didn't think there was any correct answer so I remained silent. As usual.

"Fine."

She turned to leave, obviously angry, but I caught her wrist and gently tugged her to my side. I brought her hand to my mouth and kissed the back of it and then her knuckles, unwilling to let her leave angry. I knew I'd won when she brushed her fingers through my hair.

"I've lost everyone that's ever really mattered to me. I thought caring about a werewolf would be safer," she said softly.

I looked up, my heart breaking for the lonely woman reflected in her gaze. Then I pulled her into my arms. She'd never be lonely again. I wouldn't leave her, no matter what.

Eventually, she pulled away and mumbled something about making breakfast. She fled the room, leaving me to my thoughts as she cooked. I would have joined her, but I knew Rachel was still home.

Gabby cared for me. Her own words. But caring wasn't love. Though I'd happily take any form of affection she'd willingly give, I knew caring wouldn't be enough of a bond to stop the challengers.

Would it be enough to ask her to complete the Claim?

Chapter Sixteen

I STILL DIDN'T HAVE THE ANSWER WHEN GABBY RETURNED WITH TWO steaming plates. With a shy smile, she offered me one then sat on the bed beside me. We ate in silence. It wasn't easy to stay focused on the food. The lingering feel of her lips on mine, her hands on my shoulders, consumed me.

Her comment about finding my lips rang in my head, too. Could that be her obsession with trimming my beard? Did she want to see my skin so she knew where to bite? A tremor shot through me, and I hurried to eat. I needed to shave.

Before I finished, I heard Rachel leave. Good.

Gabby took our plates and left the room. While she washed dishes, I slipped into the bathroom with scissors and a razor.

I trimmed back the whiskers from around my mouth and shaved everything from my neck. A shudder of anticipation rippled over me as I stared at the exposed skin in the mirror. Now, I was ready for her to bite me and Claim me as her own.

After a quick shower, during which I heard her pause often outside the door, I dressed and tried to calm myself. Would she Claim me right away? My gut clenched at the thought, then reason kicked in. Probably not. She wouldn't rush into it. But, she might kiss me some more.

With that thought in my head, I reached for the doorknob but a knock on the front door stopped me from stepping out. I turned back toward the mirror and scowled at myself. Why now? I ran my fingers through my hair in frustration. Unsure if Gabby wanted me to make my presence known, I waited and listened as she went to answer the door.

At Gabby's faint words, I curled my hands into fists.

"Morning, Sam. This is a surprise."

I wanted to curse and hit something. Sam showing up was not a good sign.

"Um, don't get me wrong, I like seeing you, but is there a reason you're here?"

The impatience in Gabby's voice helped calm me. She wanted to see me because she knew I'd shaved. For her.

"We'll wait for Clay," Sam said.

With a deep breath, I reached for the door.

Gabby turned to look at me as I padded into the living room. Excitement made her eyes shine. I wanted to go straight to her, wrap my arms around her, and let her inspect me for as long as she'd like. Too bad Sam stood by the door watching us.

Still, I focused on Gabby as she focused on me. Her gaze took in my clothes then zeroed in on my face, and, lastly, my exposed neck. There, she lingered. My pulse jumped. Could she see what she did to me with just a glance?

Finally, she met my gaze again and smiled. Behind her, Sam shifted, drawing my attention.

"You know why I'm here, Clay."

Gabby glanced at Sam, a trace of annoyance coloring her expression.

No doubt, he was here because of the challenges. Did he honestly think I would step aside so easily?

"I'm told you didn't take the news well."

I shrugged and crossed my arms. I thought I took the news that other men would be coming after my woman with a fair amount of grace.

Gabby caught my shrug and frowned.

"What's going on? What news?" she said, glancing between Sam and me.

"You didn't tell her?" Sam said.

Crap.

"He's not talking to me, yet," Gabby said.

Sam shook his head at me. "You've dug your own hole then, son." He looked at Gabby. "A group of Forlorn have asked Elder Joshua to approach you for an unofficial kind of Introduction. Joshua approved, but he made it clear they were to keep it brief and then leave, unless any of them had a further request of him."

Anger spiked through me. I still resented how the Elders were handling this.

A bitter tang reached me, and I realized I wasn't the only one struggling to control myself. Gabby's fists were clenched at her sides as she glared at Sam.

"I thought I was done with that. We had a deal." She crossed her arms, looking too much like me. "I know I said I was done."

Sam's expression shifted slightly to one of pity. "Honey, there are rules we must follow to keep peace in the pack. Clay had six months to convince you of his suit. That time has passed. That means unMated can once again approach you, with permission."

Gabby's face flushed.

"That's complete crap," she said. "First of all, I didn't reject anyone. Second, no one ever told me about this stupid rule." Her voice rose, and she started jabbing the air with her finger as she made each point. She seemed to realize it suddenly and dropped her hands to her sides again. "You know what? I don't care what the pack rules are. I gave you my word and my time. Now, I expect you to keep yours. I worked hard to get here, Sam. I won't let anyone take this away from me."

"By not completing the Claim, you've become eligible again. Charlene was granted a special consideration because, at that time, we weren't even sure a Claiming would be possible between a human and a werewolf. Now that we know it is, you fall under the same rules," Sam said.

"No, I don't. Is this why Clay was beat up?"

I snorted. Beat up? Sure I was a bit bruised, but she should see the other three. Apparently, making any sort of noise during her current volatile mood was a wrong move because she whirled on me.

"Feel free to jump in at any time," she said, arching a brow at me. She was beautiful all the time, more so when angry and flushed.

"Gabby," Sam said from behind her, "it's the reason he's been fighting. He's not relinquishing his tie to you. Every time an unMated shows up here, he will challenge that man for his right for Introduction. Did Clay get beat up? Only as a byproduct of handing out beatings."

She remained focused on me while he spoke, and as she began to understand, her angry mask fell away, replaced with one of concern. She swallowed hard then turned back to Sam.

"Why is two years of school too much to ask for?"

"And after that?" Sam said. "Then you'll want time to establish your career. Let's face it. There will never be a perfect time for this in your life. You just need to make the best with what you have."

She flushed again and stalked toward him. I moved closer, concerned. In theory, Sam would never hurt her. She was a female and the future of the pack. But he was a werewolf with a temper like any other.

She poked him in the shoulder.

"No, Sam, you do. I'm not your pawn in this game you play with women's lives. I went to your Introductions and fulfilled any obligation I felt I owed you for the roof over my head. You have no say in who I see...or what I do, unless you intend to drag me back to the Compound and physically force me to bite someone."

I'd been silently cheering her on until the last part. The idea of the Elders forcing her to bite someone else ripped a growl from me.

As if it were a signal, she stepped back and moved closer to me.

"It's time for you to leave, Sam. Don't come back."

I could see her words hurt Sam, but I didn't feel any pity for him. He'd brought this on himself by not standing up for her rights, too. His decisions had hurt her.

"You were never an obligation to me, Gabby." She looked away from him. He looked to me then. "You know it'd be safer for both of you if the Introductions continued at the Compound. If you keep going like this, there might be someone you won't beat. Are you willing to risk leaving her alone, then?"

Think of her safety.

I clenched my jaw.

I am. Sending males to Gabby unsupervised was your choice.

Gabby glanced at me, her gaze drifting over my bruises before she turned and went to open the door, a pointed demand for Sam to leave.

"All right, then," Sam said quietly. He walked to the door and turned toward Gabby. "Gabby, call me anytime. I'm here to help you, no matter what you might think right now."

She nodded, but her eyes glittered with anger. After he walked out and she closed the door behind him, she remained facing the door for a few seconds. I watched her take several long breaths and knew she was trying to calm down. Was she angry at me? I could care less if she remained mad at Sam.

I moved closer, wanting to touch her, but waited.

She turned to look at me and reached up to run her fingers through the whiskers along my jaw.

"Much better, but I'm going to keep at you until it's all shaved off, and maybe a haircut, too."

At her first touch, my teeth lengthened so I showed them to her again.

She didn't seem to care. She spent time studying my face and tracking her fingers along the skin of my forehead and eye. I knew she was tracing the discolored areas and wished I knew what she was thinking.

With a sigh, she stepped away. She didn't seem mad. Pensive, maybe.

"I need to get ready for class. Before I go, would you show me where you got the coveralls from?"

I smiled slightly and nodded.

Less than five minutes later, we were pulling up to Dale's shop.

She was looking around with interest until Dale moved to the partially opened bay door.

"Dale from the parking lot?" she whispered, looking at me in surprise. I nodded and wondered why she remembered Dale so well. Dale waved when he saw it was me.

I got out and moved around to open Gabby's door. I knew she was curious, but maybe having her meet Dale a second time wasn't such a good idea.

Gabby stepped out as Dale walked toward us.

"Hi there, Gabby. Glad Clay finally brought you around." He held out his hand, and she clasped it briefly.

Why was I so jealous over a handshake?

"I have to tell you that I was surprised when Clay showed up and was as good as you boasted. Although, it doesn't look like he's been taking care of your car."

Bull crap. What was Dale playing at?

"I'm always running back and forth to my classes. It's hard to give it up for any amount of time." She shrugged. "Speaking of which..." She glanced at me. "I really need to get going, or I'll be late. It was nice seeing you again, Dale. I hope stopping in was okay. I really wanted to see where Clay was working."

"Stop by anytime." Dale waved as we walked back to the car.

"I'm sure there was some type of logic to picking that place," she said as I drove home. "Someday you'll have to tell me about it."

After she dropped me off, I dressed for work. No doubt Dale would have some questions for me.

When I got there, Dale joked about my black eye and teased about keeping men away from Gabby but otherwise let me work. He wasn't too bad for a human.

By the time I finished the last work order, I was ready to go home and spend time with Gabby. I couldn't stop thinking about our kiss.

My distraction didn't keep me from noticing the scent of several wolves in the abandoned building. I rolled my shoulders and cut around back, hoping it wouldn't take me too long to send the new challengers on their way. I didn't like the idea of Gabby spending any time alone in the house. Hopefully, Rachel would be there tonight.

T HE HOUSE WAS QUIET WHEN I SNUCK IN JUST AFTER NINE IN THE morning. On a Saturday, that wasn't unusual. Still, I inhaled deeply as I entered, checking to see if trouble waited for me. Gabby and Rachel's scents drifted in the air along with a faint trace of Peter's but no hint of any werewolf's. I let out a relieved sigh and slowly made my way to Gabby's room.

I was exhausted and couldn't name a spot that didn't ache. Quietly, I disrobed and dropped my clothes on the floor. Gabby would flip if she saw the number of bruises I had now. I shifted quickly and hopped up on the bed, already half asleep.

She moved slightly as if I'd disturbed her, but her feet didn't search for my warmth like they normally did. She must really be out. I curled up and closed my eyes.

She moved again, her breathing oddly shallow.

I lifted my head and looked at her as she attempted to sit up. Her eyes were open but she still looked like she was sleeping, her moves uncoordinated.

"C-clay, we need to get to the Compound. Can you drive?"

Her stutter worried me as did the wince on her face when she tried to sit up again.

She managed to lift herself and slide from the mattress, but she only stood on her shaky legs for a second before she sat once more. Her head hung down as if it hurt too much to lift it. I shook off my exhaustion and inhaled. Her scent was off. What was wrong? Was she sick? I knew she'd pushed herself too hard after whatever had happened to her at that party.

Confused and worried, I hopped off the bed, quickly shifted back to my skin, and slipped on my jeans. Before I could button them, she moved to stand again.

This time, I was there to steady her with an arm around her back. She willingly leaned into it. Beneath my arm, she trembled.

She lifted her head, and her reflection in the mirror seemed to catch her attention. I could understand why. She was pale with dark circles under her eyes.

Her glazed eyes drifted from her reflection to mine, and my eyes narrowed. I knew that glazed look. She'd been the same after the Halloween party. I inhaled deeply, near her hair, pulling in the lingering scents of alcohol, perfume, and my kind. Had she seriously gone to another party while I was fighting?

"A lot happened last night while you were gone. Rachel talked me into going clubbing. I'll tell you about it on the way."

Guilt filled her eyes; and she looked away, but not far. Her gaze swept over me appreciatively, lingering on my stomach. I almost sighed. One look and she wiped away my anger and made me want to grin. I was hopeless around her. She shivered, and I reached for her forehead just to be sure she wasn't actually sick. No fever, just like last time.

I continued to watch her in the mirror as her gaze finally gained some focus and ever so slowly drifted upwards. She was eyeing every piece of exposed skin my chest offered. Suddenly, she squinted and scowled. It wasn't hard to figure out why. She was glaring at the bite someone had given me.

Then the scowl cleared, and she sighed.

"I need to use the bathroom then start packing."

After what happened with Sam, I knew something serious had to have happened for Gabby to want to return to the Compound. Maybe she thought the Elders could help with whatever was happening to her.

Not liking the idea of going back, but needing to do anything I could to get her well again, I nodded and helped her through the door. She leaned heavily on me as each slow step brought us closer to the bathroom.

I heard movement from Rachel's room and wanted to groan. A second later, Rachel stepped into the hall. She glanced at Gabby whose head hung low, then at me.

"Hi, Clay. How'd you get here?"

Gabby and I paused, and Gabby forced her head up as she answered Rachel.

"I called him. Sorry, Rachel, I didn't want to bug you."

Rachel's gaze drifted to me. She eyed my chest and the jeans I still hadn't managed to button. Her perusal made me nervous even though a hint of her concern for Gabby remained in her eyes. I didn't trust her. The last time she'd looked at me with concern, the vet had nearly unmanned me.

"It's okay; I get it," she said, still eyeing me.

Gabby shivered again, drawing Rachel's attention. I wanted to hug Gabby.

"Are you sure you should be going?" Rachel asked.

"Yeah," Gabby said as I helped her take a step toward the bathroom. "Clay's going to pack for me, and then we'll go. Oh, and he came by last night, saw the dog out, and took him home. We'll take him with, so don't worry."

As soon as Gabby reached the tiled floor, she grabbed the door and shut it, leaving me in the hall...alone...with Rachel.

Slowly, I turned to face her. She grinned at me, her eyes again sweeping my bare chest. I fought the strong urge to cover myself with my hands. She grinned wider. I sidestepped her and backed toward the bedroom. By the time I reached Gabby's door, Rachel was laughing softly. That woman had issues.

I closed the door, pulled on a shirt, and buttoned my pants. Then, I grabbed Gabby's bag and started stuffing it. I didn't pay much attention to what I threw in. I was busy listening for Gabby and for Rachel. I didn't want Gabby to fall. She'd barely had the strength to walk. And, I didn't want Rachel to...well, corner me.

After I had the clothes, I grabbed our toiletry stuff from the top of Gabby's dresser then shut the bag. Since Gabby was still in the bathroom, I put on my shoes and brought the bag to the car.

My breath fogged as I tossed the bag into the backseat. It was too cold outside for Gabby. I quickly started the car, then headed inside to grab a blanket and Gabby's shoes. I took everything out to the car and made a little nest in the front seat for her. The heat was finally blowing warm.

When I came back in, Gabby was out of the bathroom and shuffling her way to the closet. Probably on her way to find shoes, which were already in the car. In two steps, I was behind her and scooped her up in my arms.

She squeaked in surprise but smiled up at me.

Rachel stepped out of her room as I made it to the kitchen. I didn't slow down.

"When you're feeling better, let's talk about rental rates," she called after us with a snicker. "And I'm not talking about the house!"

Not in her dreams. Ever.

Outside, I held Gabby close, trying to keep her warm as I opened the passenger door. Carefully, I set her on the blanket. She twisted in her seat and pulled her phone from the bag in back before she sat facing forward again. Her breathing was shallow and strained. Exhaustion painted her face paler with each passing minute. I was worried.

I closed the door, and as I jogged around the hood, I watched her buckle. She drew her legs under her and huddled under the blanket.

Sliding in behind the wheel, I closed the door quickly to keep the heat in. She continued to shake beside me. I reached over and tucked the blanket around her. She clutched her phone in one hand and the edge of the blanket in the other. Her knuckles were white on both.

I gently soothed my fingers over her skin then focused on backing out of the driveway. Beside me, she struggled to stay awake.

I almost told her to go to sleep but knew talking would have had the opposite effect on her.

"I don't want to keep going on like this," she said once we cleared town.

What did she mean by that? I glanced at her, feeling the cold weight of worry in my chest. She caught my look.

"I don't mean being with you. I like that. But I don't like seeing you bruised."

I smiled at her concern, and she scowled.

"There's nothing amusing about it. I don't like worrying."

She lifted the phone and dialed. Her arm trembled as she brought the little device to her ear.

I heard Sam answer.

"I'm on my way," she said. "Put out a call for tonight only."

I stopped breathing as she disconnected. The road blurred before me. Put out a call? Elders did that for Introductions. They put out a call to all unMated males. What was she doing? Had she really given up on us?

She tossed the phone on the back seat. It immediately started to vibrate.

"It's not what you think, Clay. I don't want to do another Introduction, but something happened last night. Like I said before, I went out with Rachel to a club downtown. Not one of my best decisions, but I think I've figured out what's going on with me."

I'd been right, then, and she did need the Elders' help. She had my attention.

"Remember the party with Nicole? When I touched her, I gave her a huge shock. That happened again last night. I think I can transfer my gift, that thing with guys, to other people. I didn't know how it happened the first time. But I think I've figured it out.

"Last night, these two women at the club had been on their own until Rachel and I—and the groupies I'd collected—joined them. When we made to leave, the women had been so disappointed. They knew the guys would walk away when we did. I felt so bad for them that I went to...I don't know...pat them, I guess. I'd just meant it as an 'I'm sorry' gesture, but then it happened again just like before. A huge shock."

Her words were slurring. She was exhausted. I wanted her to sleep, but I also wanted to know what the hell a shock had to do with setting up formal Introductions at the Compound.

"Both times I was thinking about how I wished I could help find the person they were meant to be with. And, I think that's the key. I don't understand why I can see the lights, but I know it must be all tied together because when I try to use my sight, it hurts. Really bad."

I could feel Gabby's gaze on me. She was obviously waiting for a reaction. However, I was still waiting for the reason we were heading north to push her in front of the very men I'd been fighting the last few weeks.

"Oh, yeah. Before I shocked those two, a Forlorn came up behind me and started a conversation. My fish finder still worked then."

I knew she meant the lights she could see in her head.

"There were more werewolves in the crowd, Clay. The one talking to me said he just wanted a chance to say hi. He was very persistent so I told him I would see them at the Compound for an official Introduction. They left right after that but gave me the impression that if I didn't show up, they'd come looking for me. I got the feeling they'd been pushed too far."

They'd been pushed too far? I'd known something like this would happen. One of them had scared her. I wanted to hit something. Damn the Elders. They should have never allowed unsupervised Introductions. What were they thinking?

"Has it been the same werewolves trying to see me or is it always different?"

What did it matter if I was fighting the same werewolves or different ones each time?

She sighed, almost as if I'd spoken aloud, and snaked a hand out from under the blanket to touch my leg.

"It hurts to see you like this, Clay. If I have to put up with an Introduction to keep you safe, then that's what I'll do."

And, again, she melted my anger. This time with just a touch.

"I'm sorry, Clay," she mumbled sleepily. "I wish I could just get over my need for freedom and Claim you. We both know you're the one. I just don't want to lose myself."

She immediately fell asleep.

I ignored the tear trailing down to my beard.

THE COMPOUND WAS TEEMING with unMated when we pulled to a stop before the porch. Gabby slept in her seat. She hadn't stirred once during the long drive.

Men watched as I got out and circled to her side of the car. One made a move to stop me.

"She's not yours any longer."

I stopped walking and stared at the man. He had no hope to challenge me but there were many others behind him, still and watching.

"She's sick," I said, glancing at them all.

Sam, get out here, now.

A moment later, the door swung open; and Sam strode out. Counting on his presence to keep things peaceful, I ignored everyone and turned back to the car to open Gabby's door. She didn't move when I unbuckled her or when I lifted her, blanket and all, from the seat. When I straightened, Sam was right there to close the door.

He studied the dark circles under Gabby's eyes then looked at me. "What's wrong?"

"Sick."

His gaze drifted to the men watching us before settling back on her.

"How long has she been like this?"

"Last night. Took her three days to recover last time." Now that I knew we weren't here to help her, I didn't want her to try to go through an Introduction.

"Why did she call this morning?"

I shrugged, unwilling to answer something that should be so obvious given the number of men listening to us.

Sam's silence spiked my impatience.

"She needs a bed."

Sam nodded. "Yes. Right. You know the room."

He remained beside the car, looking at the unMated he'd called to the Compound, as I carried Gabby inside. I could give a damn about the men he'd called.

Those who passed me in the hall glanced at Gabby but let me continue without protest. I reached the room and shifted her weight to open the door. Once inside, I took her straight to the bed, lay her down, then went for a glass of water. She'd be thirsty again when she finally came out of whatever spell she was under.

Returning with the drink, I set it aside and sat beside her, gently smoothing back her hair.

I hated this helplessness. Though she'd explained what she thought had happened, I didn't know how she wanted me to handle the situation here. Sam would have more questions. What did she want me to tell him, if anything?

Sam came in a few minutes later.

"Thanks for bringing her. I'll care for her from here."

Dismissed? Not likely. Angry, I looked up at him.

Sam sighed.

"Having you here will cause problems she's in no condition to deal with. She's sleeping. I'll keep an eye on her. Go get something to eat."

I didn't like it, but he was right.

Several hours later, Sam found me in the room I'd taken for myself.

"She's asking for you."

I was up and out the door before he had time to say more. Based on the last time this happened, she shouldn't be awake yet. Was she really better?

Letting myself into the apartment without knocking, I quietly approached her room. I could hear her moving around. I stopped at the door and leaned against the jamb to study her. She was leaning against the bed and digging through her bag. She moved slowly; and, from the faces she made, her head still ached.

She caught sight of me, reached into her bag, and pulled out her pink bikini.

"Really, Clay? You're killing me. Where are my jeans?"

Her playfulness, despite her pain, made me smile slightly. She studied my face for a while. She tended to do that whenever I pulled my hair back so she could see me. I loved the attention.

She blinked slowly, and I knew she was still too tired to be up.

Sparing her from further searching, I stepped close and, without looking away from her, pulled the jeans she wanted from her bag.

I held them out and tapped my lips, needing confirmation that she really did want to be with me like she'd said in the car.

She smiled widely. "A kiss for the jeans?"

I nodded; but, instead of kissing me, she pulled the jeans from my hand and tossed them on the bed.

Then she further surprised me by stepping closer and placing her hands on my chest. Her fingers branded me through my shirt.

"I don't need bribes to kiss you, Clay. Come here."

My heart burst, and I claimed her lips. She opened for me, sweetly and willingly, as she curled her fingers in my shirt. If she thought I'd tried to move away from her, she was mistaken. I wrapped my arms around her and held her close. Her lips parted and nibbled at my top lip. She was killing me again. I reached up to cup the back of her head, wanting more. And she gave more. Standing on her toes, she slid her arms around my neck and opened to me further. The feel of her tongue running over my bottom lip almost undid me.

I growled and struggled not to crush her to me. When she used her tongue again, I opened my mouth and captured hers, kissing her like I'd wanted to when she'd first walked out the Introduction room's door.

Her pulse jumped wildly, and I knew I needed to ease off. It was too much for her right now. But, her lips begged me to stay. With effort, I pulled away. She whimpered, and pride filled me. She wanted me. She'd told the truth. I just needed to be patient a little longer and let her get over her fears. That knowledge eased some of my frustration.

I kissed her cheek, then her forehead, trying to calm her.

With a shaky exhale, she wrapped her arms around my waist and rested her head on my chest. I held her close, waiting for whatever she might do or say next.

Unfortunately, Sam walked into the apartment before she did anything. She sighed and pulled back. Reluctantly, I let her go.

She looked up at me.

"Can you come with me for this, or will that cause more problems?"

"It would be best if he stayed away, Gabby," Sam answered from behind me.

She leaned to the side to look around me.

"I didn't ask what was best. Best went out the window years ago, Sam, when 'making do' moved in. Is he allowed?"

Sam sighed. I didn't turn to look at him. I kept my focus on Gabby and the emotions playing across her face.

"It's allowed. He's unMated, but he's considered rejected. He'll be challenged by everyone for his place in the Introduction order."

She glanced at me. "Do you want to be there?"

I nodded.

"All right then. Sam, please head over and get things ready. Clay will walk me there. Clay, I just need to change, then I'm ready."

Sam didn't move, and she arched a brow at him until he left grumbling about Mating fights and sick women who didn't know when to stay in bed.

Gabby turned her arched brow on me. I wisely retreated so she could change.

From the living room, I listened to her move. At one point, she sat still on the bed for several minutes. Sam was right. She should still be in bed. I wasn't about to tell her that, though. Instead, I poured her a glass of orange juice and waited for the door to open.

When she walked out, she didn't look much better. Beautiful, as always, but tired and pale.

I offered her the glass of juice. She smiled and gulped it down.

"I need just a minute in the bathroom. Can you find my shoes for me?"

Shoes? I watched her use the wall for support as she shuffled her way to the bathroom. She didn't need shoes because she wasn't going to walk anywhere.

She closed herself into the bathroom, and I went to her bedroom for her slippers. I listened to the water run and the soft sounds of her brushing her teeth. Slippers in hand, I returned to the hall. She wouldn't like it, but tough. I set the slippers on the floor so she could step right into them.

By the time the door opened again, she looked paler. She glanced down at the slippers.

"Where are my shoes?"

I shrugged and pointed to the slippers. I wasn't going to negotiate.

She stepped into them without another word, and before she lifted her head, I picked her up and settled her against my chest.

"I can walk, Clay."

I shook my head and moved toward the door. What she'd done to get to the bathroom hadn't been walking.

Shifting her slight weight to one arm, I opened the door and stepped into the hall. She sighed, wrapped her arms around my neck, and leaned her head against my shoulder. I loved it. When her fingers started playing with the back of my hair, I decided I needed to start carrying her everywhere.

The few males we passed in the hall stopped and stared, their irritation plain. I wouldn't be welcome at the Introduction. Carrying her would be an insult to every unMated who had shown up. I didn't care. She was mine. They needed to know that.

At the intersection of halls which led to the Introduction room, she stopped me.

"No, go outside and around back. I won't go in that room ever again."

Her voice wavered a little at the end, and my hold tightened. If she didn't want to go in there, then she wouldn't. No Elder would force my Mate.

I turned around and went to the main entrance. I carefully set her on her feet, grabbed a spare jacket from one of the hooks, and helped her put it on. She studied me as I took the time to button it up. Hopefully, she was thinking of kissing me like I was her. I didn't try, though. She needed rest, not a racing pulse.

When I finished, I picked her back up and carried her outside. She shivered lightly in my arms as I walked across the dark yard toward the back of the building. Just before we reached the corner, she patted me lightly on the chest.

"Put me down, Clay. I'll walk now."

I stopped but didn't let go. Why was she doing this? She was still trembling and weak. She should just tell Sam to piss off. My fingers twitched as I suppressed the urge to growl. I could smell the men around the corner. Too many for her to walk among them.

"It'll be okay, Clay. There are a lot of fast people here. I won't fall on my face."

I studied her in the moonlight. She gazed up at me, her expression open. She didn't want to do this. She was doing it for me. To keep me safe. I wanted to hug her and hold her to me. Instead, I did as she asked and set her on her feet.

She walked steadily around the corner with her shoulders back and head high. I kept close, a secondary shadow.

Three Elders stood by the back door. They ignored me and watched Gabby. Gabby ignored them and looked at the gathered men.

"I'm Gabby. There will be no Introduction order. I won't have anyone left out, or leaving without a fair chance. So, instead of the stuffy cabin, let's just do this out here."

As she continued forward, the males lined up. She shivered again. It was small, but I noticed. Some of the men did, too.

"I believe the Elders mentioned I was ill; so if I start to stammer, bear with me."

She moved forward, and I stayed close to her. Most of the men ignored me. A few bared their teeth at me after she passed. I paid little attention to them or the Elders trailing behind us. My focus remained on Gabby and the shivers that occurred with increasing frequency.

Her proud stance melted away with each step, bowing her back and curving her shoulders. About halfway down the line, Gabby slowed. I thought she might be ready to call for a rest, but she didn't.

The men beyond her watched her with worry as she stopped completely. Then she gasped, the sound ringing in the silence, flinched, and touched her head as if in pain.

With a burst of speed, I stood behind her, ready to catch her. The werewolf she faced looked at me in confusion, then at her, and finally the Elders who'd quietly followed us until now.

"Gabby," Sam said, his voice heavy with worry and warning. It was too late for that.

She held up her hand.

"A moment, please," she said, sounding strained.

I kept my hands out, ready to grab her as she slowly straightened. She breathed deeply, as if orienting herself, then glanced at me. Worry filled her eyes. She held my gaze as if trying to tell me something. What, though? She was weak from sharing her ability with those women. She wouldn't have her pull on men here. Besides, it only seemed to affect human men. No, it couldn't be that. Why else would she worry? The answer hit me, and I looked at the men around us. She'd tried to use her sight. But why? The males watched us. Nothing seemed out of place.

While I studied the woods, she turned to the men in front of her.

"I'm sorry. Like I said, I'm not feeling well. The pain in my head just took me by surprise."

We all heard the lie in her words, but no one commented. She took another steadying breath and started moving again. Only, this time, her progress was slower and her steps more labored. Tremors shook her, confirming that she'd used her gift and exhausted herself.

I wasn't the only one watching her with concern. Each man she passed glanced at the Elders trailing us, as if wondering why they hadn't put a stop to this. I wondered the same thing.

After a few more steps, Gabby halted.

"A f-face I know. I'm here as p-promised."

I eyed the man she stared at. Who the hell was he and how did she know him?

"I see that, Little One," he said. "Although, it looks like you should be in bed, instead."

Curling my hands into fists, I tried to control my anger at his use of a pet name.

"I would b-be if people would j-just leave me alone. B-but it's not meant t-to be. So, you know my name, but I d-don't know yours."

"Luke Taylor, love."

Love? I wondered if I could knock his British accent out along with a few teeth.

Luke-the-Brit held out his hand. Gabby glanced at it and hesitated. I ground my teeth together, jealousy ripping through me when she reached forward and wrapped her hand in his. She paled, exhaled heavily, and swayed on her feet. Luke's slight smirk disappeared.

I held myself ready. To catch her. To fight for her. To do whatever she needed of me.

Gabby's heart started to beat loudly as if overtaxed. She made a small sound between a gasp and a moan. I inhaled deeply and noted her scent had changed, too. Mellowed. I started to pace just behind her, my focus on both of them.

Luke frowned at Gabby.

"I need to talk to you," she said, her words slurred. "Don't leave until I do."

Luke looked as surprised as I felt.

"Clay," she whispered. Her head lolled to the side as she tried to find me. "Catch me."

She let go of Luke's hand and fell against me.

"Is she okay?" Sam asked. He stood beside me, his hand extended to touch her forehead.

I couldn't stop the growl as I lifted her into my arms and settled her against my chest.

"You pushed this." A tremor ran over my arm. Fur appeared and disappeared. "These women aren't like us. They're fragile. You know that. You say you're protecting them. Who's protecting them from you?"

The males around us shifted in agitation. They were thinking the same thing. The Elders should have put a stop to this Introduction. They'd all sensed her exhaustion and witnessed her frailty.

Sam looked down at Gabby, her pale cheek resting against me, and I had the satisfaction of seeing guilt pass over his features.

I stepped around him and carried her inside, hurrying to get to her room. Anyone I passed moved out of our way. Word of what had happened had already spread.

Charlene stood by the apartment door and opened it for me. She followed me in as I strode across the small space to Gabby's bedroom.

"Do you need anything, Clay?"

I paused and looked back at Charlene. In the door, a man stood behind her. He looked like her and Thomas. His gaze was locked on Gabby, reflecting a sad worry. I clenched my jaw against a new wave of anger. Damn the Elders.

"Just tell them to stay away."

She nodded slightly, looking concerned. "I'll do my best."

She turned, shooed the man away, and closed the door. I could still hear them, though.

"Will she be all right?"

"I don't know, Jim."

"She's like you and Michelle, right?"

"Let's talk about this later."

Their voices faded as I set Gabby on her bed. I removed the

jacket, tucked her under the covers, and turned off the light. Her pale skin seemed to glow in the soft light from the main room. No discernable rise and fall of her chest moved beneath the covers. She was too still, and it scared me.

Frustrated and angry at my helplessness, I went to the kitchenette to get a glass of water. Please let this be like last time, I thought, carrying the glass back to her. I closed the door, set the glass beside the bed, then lay on the covers next to her.

I laid my hand on her chest to measure her shallow breathing. She'd obviously used her power again. And this was the worst she'd ever been. What if—? I wouldn't let the thought finish.

"Please wake up from this," I whispered in the dark. "I can't live without you."

Hours passed. Worry ate at me. Twice I heard Sam moving in the living room, but he didn't disturb us. I lingered in the dark, listening for any sign that Gabby was improving.

When she finally moved slightly, my throat tightened with emotion. She tried to speak, but she could only make a dry, raspy noise. I gently slid an arm under her and lifted her enough to give her a drink. She sipped slowly, each swallow sounding loud and painful, until she tilted her head to show she'd had enough.

She'd barely drunk anything. Before I could encourage more, I saw she'd left again. Was it sleep or had she fainted?

The worry returned. Why had she touched Luke? I'd kill the Brit next time I saw him.

It was several hours again before she woke to sip more water. Again, she barely managed anything. The wait until the next time she moved wasn't as long, and I began to hope. Was it a sign of improvement?

For two days, we existed in darkness. I only left the bedroom once to get more water. Charlene came once more to ask if I thought Gabby needed to go to the hospital. I wasn't sure. Could

Gabby survive on so little water? Charlene had left before I'd decided on an answer.

I was about to leave and call Charlene back when Gabby shifted again.

"Water," she whispered.

Sliding an arm under her, I lifted the glass to her lips. She didn't sip. She gulped. My eyes watered. I lowered her back to the bed, set the cup aside, and waited, listening to her breathing. It sounded stronger. Would she stay awake this time?

"How long have I been sleeping?" she asked.

I wrapped my arms around her and hugged her close. Relief coursed through me.

"I really hope you're Clay," she said.

A laugh escaped me. As if I'd let anyone else near her.

"Can we turn on a light?"

As soon as I left the bed, she tried sitting up. I watched her struggle in the dark. Every move looked strained. Turning on the light probably wasn't a good idea. She needed more rest. But I wanted to see her. Really see her. I waited to click the lamp on until she leaned against the headboard. She squinted, and her eyes watered. She reached up to rub her eyes and brush a tangle of hair from her sallow face.

After blinking for a minute, her gaze met mine.

"Clay, I think I know what's going on. Can you help me up? I need a shower."

She wanted me to help her move around again? Not happening. I shook my head.

"Clay, now's not the time to put your foot down. This is really important."

It was exactly the time to put my foot down. She'd been out for two damn days. I felt aged from how much I'd worried over her.

She tried to sit up further but couldn't. She winced as if her head hurt.

"Okay. Maybe you're right." She rubbed her forehead. "Can you get me something for my head, please? It feels like it's going to explode all over the walls."

A request I could easily fulfill. I leaned over, smoothed back her hair, and kissed her forehead. She smiled tiredly at me. It was hard to leave the room, even for medicine for her. But, I did.

The living room was empty. I let myself out of the apartment and closed the door softly behind me. I'd need to be quick. I didn't want anyone to see I'd left Gabby's side. They'd know she was awake, and I wasn't about to let anyone near her just yet. She needed rest. A lot of it.

When I returned, the shower was running in the bathroom. I growled. Stubborn woman.

Moving toward the door, I listened. The water splashed slightly so I knew she was already safely in the tub. I sighed and set my hand on the door. She'd better be careful in there.

I returned to the kitchenette, set the pills down, then went to the bedroom. If she was set on cleaning herself, I might as well clean up her room, too. I stripped the bed. It smelled like Gabby, which I liked; but it smelled of sickness, too. I wanted no memory of the last two days.

The water turned off as I remade the bed with clean sheets. I hurried to find what else I thought she might need. Socks, slippers, and her hairbrush waited on the quilt when I finished.

I listened to the sounds of her moving in the bathroom. Every slight noise was spaced apart as if she moved very slowly. She had to be exhausted again.

I grabbed a fresh glass of water and the pills and waited for her outside the door.

She didn't leave me waiting for long. She pulled open the door and yelped when she saw me. Guilt and pain stole over her features. She knew she shouldn't be up yet just as she knew I didn't want her up. She held the door for support, her knuckles white.

I offered the pills in one hand and the glass in the other. She took them both. I waited until the pills were down and the glass empty before I picked her up.

She sighed and rested her head against my chest as I moved toward the bedroom.

In the doorway, I hesitated. Would she want to brush her hair first or just go back to bed? She studied the room then turned toward me. She leaned in and kissed my cheek, surprising me. I really hoped she wanted to go back to bed.

"You are so sweet, and I truly appreciate this, but I'm not going back to bed, Clay."

Damn.

"I need to see Luke."

I clamped my jaw shut and swallowed the growl that wanted to surface along with some cussing. With care, I stepped into the room and placed her on the bed. Then I stalked out of her room, seething.

After watching over her and worrying for two days, she wanted to see Luke? What happened to knowing I was the one?

The apartment door suffered my anger. My ears burned, and I knew they'd shifted. I glanced at my arms as I walked the halls and saw fur. I tried to pull the change back but couldn't. I was too pissed to concentrate. I needed to find the Brit. I didn't care why Gabby wanted to talk to him or what kind of connection or—I swallowed—affection they had. I owed him for his part in the last two days of hell I'd lived through.

I narrowed my eyes and scented the air. There were too many trails here. If he'd stayed, though, he would probably be in the common room.

Since it was close to lunch, the room was full when I pushed my way through the double doors. Hesitating just inside, I looked around. People stopped eating and stared. Conversation faded to silence.

Luke's copper head was hard to miss. He lounged in a stuffed chair near one of the unlit fireplaces. When he saw me, a wide, mocking grin split his lips. I stalked toward him. When I neared, he stood.

I hit him hard and fast. His smug, cocky expression changed to one of surprise just before he fell over. I grabbed the cuff of his pants and started dragging him, caveman style.

The base of my spine itched, and I knew I now sported a tail.

Despite the punch to his face, Luke was still conscious. And my new tail caught his attention as I pulled him out of the room. His mad laughter reminded me of a braying ass.

I wanted to hit him again and struggled to maintain any remaining thread of control as we passed through the halls.

Just before we reached the apartment door, I inhaled and pulled myself together. The tail receded as did my ears and fur. I opened the door and pulled my quarry in behind me.

Gabby stood in the living room, staring at us in shock. Probably because the Brit was still laughing.

As I kept tugging my burden forward, she came to herself and rushed to close the door behind us. When I reached the middle of the room, I dropped Luke's leg and turned back to the door, which she still blocked. I didn't care. I didn't want to hear what she would say to him. I didn't think I'd be able to hold it together much longer.

I crossed the room, and she leaned back against the panel. When I made to reach for the knob, she held up her hand.

"Clay, I need you to stay and listen. Please."

She was killing me.

"Please," she said again. "Give me a chance."

Then she touched my face. Her warm fingers coaxed me until I met her gaze. She looked worried and sad, and I knew I'd stay.

"I've asked so much of you already and know it's not fair to ask again, but I am."

I sighed, reached up to cup her face, and gently smoothed my thumb over her cheek. Behind me, I heard Luke move. Dropping my hands, I turned. Luke lay where I'd left him. The smirk was back as he watched us. He needed to lose the smirk.

I walked toward him on my way to the couch and kicked him in the ribs as I stepped over him.

Luke grunted and started to sit up, his laughter finally starting to quiet.

"Most people wouldn't laugh while being dragged through the Compound like that," Gabby said, watching us. She stayed by the door.

Luke stood and turned toward me with a grin.

"I've never seen anyone hold a transformation like that. He was man, but the fangs, ears, fur...it was amazing, and hilarious, mate," he said as he settled himself on the couch.

"Um, isn't that a sign that he's in an extreme emotional state?" Gabby said.

Luke continued to smirk at me. I could feel his hilarity over the unmentioned tail.

Gabby walked behind Luke and smacked him hard on the back of the head.

"Meaning, you should stop trying to annoy him."

I grinned. Maybe this conversation wouldn't be so bad.

She walked around Luke and came toward my chair. She then gingerly perched on one of my knees. She'd picked me. In front of him. He didn't look so smug anymore.

I wrapped my hands around her waist and pulled her back into my lap, turning her until I could see Luke, too. She settled against me.

"Luke, what happened when I touched you? What did you feel?"

"One hell of a shock. Listen, did you bring me here for a reason, or was it just to rub your relationship with him in my face?"

"It's for a reason."

She tried to lean forward, but I kept her on my lap with an arm around her waist. She didn't fight it.

"How long have I been sleeping?"

"Two days, love. Everyone's been pretty worried, and the Elders are waiting to talk to you."

"I bet."

I felt her attention drift and watched her study the apartment door. When she winced and held her head, I knew what she'd done. She'd tried to look at the lights in her head.

"Crap."

I made an annoyed sound at the same time I rubbed her back. She needed to stop trying to use her abilities.

"Listen," Luke said, sounding hesitant, "I think you should still be in bed, Little One. No disrespect intended, but you don't look well."

He was right. I mean, she was beautiful; but she did look sick and like she needed more sleep.

"I know you're right, but I can't go back to sleep yet. I need you to tell me what happened."

"I don't know what happened, love. You shocked me, told me not to leave, then fainted. After that, Clay picked you up and ran inside with you. He hasn't let anyone near you for two days. We only knew you were still alive because he didn't take off into the woods."

"And after Clay left, what about you? What did you do?"

Luke began to look uncomfortable.

"Uh, I went out for a bit then came back here."

"The constant attention probably went to your head," she said under her breath.

I understood then that she'd done to Luke what she'd done to Nicole. Yet, his cocky attitude in the common room probably meant it'd been women he'd pulled in.

Luke looked up at Gabby, seemingly surprised that she knew what had happened. He had no idea just how special Gabby was.

"Did you meet anyone special while I was out?" she asked, glancing at the door again.

I wondered if she knew who waited in the hall. The soft movements told me more than one person waited, but not who. My guess was Sam and perhaps another Elder.

Luke shook his head, answering her question.

"Luke, there is so much I don't understand, and I really need your help." She nodded toward the door. "I need some time to myself to understand what I'm feeling."

Luke and I both stared at Gabby. Her nod toward the door was the only thing that stopped me from being upset by the words. She wasn't talking about her feelings for Luke. But I wasn't sure what she was trying to tell him, either.

Luke looked from her to me then back again. He opened his mouth to ask a question, hesitated, and then glanced at the door once more. Finally, he stood.

"I'll be around," he said.

The door had barely closed behind him when a knock sounded.

She turned in my lap, met my gaze, and shook her head. I slid an arm under her legs, and standing with her in my arms, I glanced at the door. I knew she didn't want to talk to whoever waited, but I doubted the Elders would be put off for long. She'd fainted during the Introduction and had been out for two days. And when she woke, the first thing she'd done was talk to Luke. They would want to know why.

I turned and carried her to the bedroom. There I set her on the bed, covered her, and closed her in her room.

With no choice, I went to answer the apartment door. Sam stood on the other side as I'd expected. There were several other wolves with him. Most likely spectators drawn by my removal of Luke from the common room. No other Elders, though.

I stepped aside to let him in.

"Where's Gabby?" Sam asked, eyeing the closed bedroom door.

"Bed," I said softly. "She's still sick."

Sam took a step toward her room, and I stepped in front of him. It was dangerous to challenge an Elder. If he really wanted to, he could physically force me aside or simply command me to move. Instead, he sighed and looked at me.

"Is she getting better?"

"She woke up. That's something."

"Clay, I know you're upset with how we handled the Introduction, but this is better for her."

"Did it look better?"

He sighed again and ran his hand through his hair. "Let me know when she wakes up again. I want to talk to her." Then he turned and left.

I went back to the bedroom and found Gabby already asleep. Lying on my side, I pulled her close and closed my eyes, ready to sleep for the first time in days.

Instead, her conversation with Luke replayed in my head. Her comment, "I need some time to myself," took on new meaning. The key was her look at the door. She'd known the Elders were out there listening. The way she'd held Luke's gaze afterward...she'd been trying to get him to understand something.

We needed help leaving the Compound without the Elders catching us.

A NOISE WOKE ME. Gabby's stomach. It growled again, and she shifted in her sleep. I smiled and waited for her to open her eyes. The lamp was on, illuminating her features. She looked better. Less pale.

Her breathing changed, a sign she was awake, but she didn't open her eyes. She was thinking. I'd seen her do that many times. Gabby wasn't the type to just shoot out of bed. She liked to take a minute. I figured she used that time to make a plan for her day. She seemed to like making plans and sticking to them.

I gently brushed her hair from her face. She opened her eyes and turned her head to look at me, and my heart swelled at the emotion I saw there.

"Do I say good morning or is it close to good night again?"

Smiling, I reached for her hand and brought it to my mouth. A noise from the apartment stopped me from pulling her into my arms. Frowning, I turned my head and focused. The sound of the apartment door closing barely reached me.

Sam hadn't returned since our last talk. Could it be him? I tensed as the bedroom door opened.

Luke poked his head in.

"Better hurry. You carry her, and I'll grab her things," he said, looking at me.

I didn't hesitate. I leapt off the bed and scooped Gabby into my arms, covers and all. I couldn't believe Luke had understood Gabby. I'd barely understood her.

She squeaked as I lifted her. Blankets covered her face, and she shook her head to dislodge them since her arms were pinned. Her scowl made me grin.

Luke already had Gabby's bag and was cramming her things into it. I turned and left the room, Luke trailing behind me. Moving quickly, we quietly raced through the halls and made it out the main entrance without being seen. I was sure we'd been heard, though.

In the dark yard, the car faced the gate. Luke must have moved it. With a burst of speed, I reached the car and shifted Gabby's weight to pull the handle. The door's loud groan made me cringe and move faster.

I settled Gabby inside and buckled her in. As I moved away, Luke took my place to hand her bag in. She took it as I jogged around the hood, but she motioned for him to wait. She grabbed a scrap of paper from her bag and quickly wrote something. She handed it to Luke with a wave, keeping silent.

Luke quickly closed the door. As he scanned the note, I started the car and slammed it into gear. When I looked back at him, Luke was already on a motorcycle. I took off in a spray of gravel. As I'd expected, the noise brought someone to the door.

The motorcycle roared to life and quickly zipped past us. Luke saluted Gabby with a grin then disappeared from sight.

Sam stood on the porch, his gaze locked on us.

We need to talk to her, son.

She doesn't want to talk.

I waited for a reply, but none came. A relieved sigh escaped me. Gabby didn't notice.

She laid her head back, closed her eyes, and fell asleep. She didn't stir the whole way home or when I pulled into the driveway and turned off the engine. I sat for a moment, watching her.

She still had dark circles under her eyes, she hadn't eaten, and she hadn't told me what exactly had happened when she'd touched Luke. Hopefully, the next time she woke, she'd eat then start talking.

Chapter Twenty

I DIDN'T GET MY WISH. GABBY WOKE JUST A FEW HOURS AFTER I PUT her to bed.

Since Rachel was home, I was back in my fur, lying in my usual spot, when I felt Gabby move. She reached for her phone and checked the screen. I knew what she'd see. Sam had called it twice since we'd left.

"Crap," she mumbled when she squinted at the display.

I thought she was referring to Sam until she left the bed saying, "I'm going to be late."

Did she seriously think she was going to school? I hopped off the bed and planted myself in front of the door.

She didn't notice as she grabbed clothes. When she turned and saw me, she paused.

"Clay, I have to pee so bad it hurts. Can you move, please?"

I narrowed my eyes at her. Did she really think she had me with that? Although I couldn't hear a lie, I knew her well enough to guess what she was doing. I stepped away from the door, letting her believe she'd fooled me, and watched her grin and leave.

As soon as she'd closed herself in the bathroom, I hid her keys in the towel drawer. She needed more rest to recover, not a day on campus.

When the bathroom door opened, she didn't walk into the kitchen as I'd expected. Instead, she went to her bedroom and brushed out her hair. It took her awhile, and I regretted not brushing it for her after her shower. I watched from the doorway. Each stroke moved slower than the last. She was so tired. Why was she so determined to leave?

She set the brush aside and left her room. In the kitchen, I heard her pause. I took my time joining her. She turned to glare at me as soon as she saw me.

"Clay," she whispered. "Give 'em to me." She couldn't yell because Rachel was still asleep.

I sat down in the archway.

Gabby sighed and looked around once more. I wanted to shake her. Gently. Instead of looking for her keys, she should eat something. Then, go back to bed.

"Please, Clay. I think I'm figuring out what's going on with me but won't know for sure until I talk to Nicole. At school. I need the keys."

I remained mute and unmoved. She could ask Nicole tomorrow. Meanwhile, I could hear Rachel stirring as Gabby continued to stare at me. I knew it wouldn't be long before Rachel would be coming into the kitchen.

"If I can't find my keys," Gabby said, "I'm going to walk."

Rachel passed behind me just as Gabby finished speaking.

Gabby's expression was hilarious, and I almost laughed.

"Gabby, you need to get out more and stop talking to the dog," Rachel said, closing herself in the bathroom.

Gabby glared at me; and I sighed, knowing I'd lost. I didn't want her walking. Standing, I went over to the drawer, shifted my hand, and grabbed out the keys.

"Thank you," she said.

Then she left.

I considered following her but Rachel was still in the bathroom and would notice if I was missing. So, I heaved a sigh and lay on the floor by the door.

It didn't take Rachel long to finish her morning routine, which still included touching me way too much, before she then headed out the door. Once she left, I shifted and dressed for work. Gabby would be at school already, and Dale was probably wondering if I'd show up today.

A chill wind whipped around me on the walk to the shop, and I hoped Gabby had dressed warm enough. The right bay door was half open. Ducking under, I found Dale working on a single car. He didn't hear me, so I went to the desk to look at the orders. There were more than usual. It meant that my absence had put him behind.

I picked the hardest one left over from the day before and grabbed the keys.

"Didn't know if I'd see you today," Dale said from across the shop.

"Gabby was sick."

"Ah. Yeah, well, I'd want to take care of her too...if she were mine."

He turned back and started working on his car before I could decide how to take his comment. Brushing it off, I went to get the first car. I had other wolves to worry about. I couldn't start worrying about human men, too. But I did. All morning, and all afternoon. Gabby was run down. Would she be able to fend off men like she usually did? Wait...would she need to? She'd said she lost her pull the last time this happened.

After finishing the jobs left over from the day before, along with half of the current day's jobs, I decided I'd done enough. I looked around and noticed Dale was sitting in his chair, filling out his last order. Perfect timing.

"Need to head out," I said, returning the keys to the rack behind the desk.

He glanced at the clock, then opened his cash drawer.

"Don't worry about it," I said. "We'll settle tomorrow." I just didn't want to wait for him to figure out how much to pay me.

He stopped and glanced at me.

"She that sick?"

I shrugged.

"Go. Take care of her, man. You two call me if you need anything."

I nodded then hurried home. The house was empty. Gabby would be home in an hour, and Rachel might not be home at all. It'd give me enough time to clean up and make something for dinner.

I grabbed some fresh clothes and went to shower. While the shower still ran, I heard the back door open. A grin spread on my face. Good thing I came home early. I quickly shut off the water, dried, and dressed. When I stepped out of the bathroom, the house was quiet. She was probably putting away her books. I went to the kitchen and opened a cupboard to see what I could make for dinner. We had some onions and potatoes on the bottom shelf. I grabbed an onion just as I heard her walk into the kitchen. I turned with a smile on my face. Then froze.

Rachel and I stared at each other.

Shee't. Busted.

My smile fell, and I started to panic. I hadn't been in my skin around her since...I struggled to think back. She glanced at my hand; and slowly, she started grinning at me. That worried me more.

"Making dinner?" she asked, looking at the onion I held.

Was that bad? I gave a single, hesitant nod.

Her smile broadened. "I'll help."

Help?

"What are we making?"

My panic skyrocketed. If I spoke, she'd say something to Gabby.

I went to the freezer, pulled out our bag of frozen chicken, and held it out to Rachel. She took it.

"Chicken, then?"

I nodded again.

"What do you want me to do with it?"

I pointed to the microwave. Every time I pointed or nodded, she grinned; and I realized my muteness amused her. She started to defrost the chicken while I quickly diced the onion. With the onion browning, I got out four potatoes.

"What's next?" she asked, turning with the thawed meat.

Trading the potatoes for the chicken, I pointed at the table. She sat and started dicing. I seasoned and sliced the chicken.

"So is Gabby feeling better?"

I shrugged.

"It's sweet of you to come here and make her dinner. Are you here often when I'm not home?"

I glanced at her unsure if she was upset by the idea. Her expression was closed but her scent sweet. She was amused.

Instead of answering, I washed my hands then took the diced potatoes from her.

"I'm glad you're keeping her company. She doesn't get out much."

Moving to the stove, I added the potatoes and a bit of oil. Everything sizzled as Rachel kept talking.

"It's not good for a person to close themselves off from other people. Without social contact and communication, a person's mental health could deteriorate."

Rachel stood and came to lean against the wall near the stove. She studied me for a long moment. I kept my eyes on the browning potatoes.

"How's your mental health, Clay?"

I glanced at her. If she was thinking of taking me to another doctor...

A car rumbled into the drive. Gabby was home. I'd never been so relieved in my life.

Rachel pushed away from the wall with a smirk and moved to the cupboards. I added the chicken as she set the table.

"Do you work around here, Clay? Live nearby? I know nothing about you. Tell me a little about yourself."

I kept cooking. Where was Gabby? I strained to hear her footsteps as Rachel kept up her one-sided conversation.

"Shy? Don't worry. How about I tell you a little about myself? Let's see...I'm a nursing student, which I'm sure Gabby's mentioned. I'll be graduating next spring. I love summer and can do without winter."

Gabby finally opened the door and stepped inside. She looked pale again. Definitely exhausted. She glanced at Rachel then me before moving into the room and closing the door. I remained focused on the food in the pan while Rachel walked past Gabby to get silverware.

"You didn't tell me he could *cook*," Rachel said.

"He cooks, he cleans, he warms up my feet at night, and he keeps the toilet seat down...so hands off. He's mine."

My heart flipped. Rachel laughed good naturedly, but I barely heard. He's mine. The words warmed my insides. Did she realize what she'd said? I turned to look at her. She met my gaze for a moment before Rachel distracted her again.

"How you feeling?" Rachel said, touching Gabby's forehead. "I asked Clay, but he didn't say."

Rachel gave me a pointed look, and I shrugged and went back to cooking. Everything was almost done.

"Not the best, but it's getting better. I think it's mental exhaustion, nothing contagious."

"Mm," Rachel said. "I still think you should go to the doctor. Could it be something you didn't think of yet? Pregnant?"

What the...?

My heart seized, and I dropped the spoon. It hit the stove,

spattered me with potato shrapnel, and bounced back at me. Swallowing hard, I tried to catch it and fumbled a bit before my brain started working again and I was able to close my fist around the wooden handle.

Gabby. Pregnant. The thought consumed me in the best way. A family. I wanted that. I swallowed again and caught the silence behind me. Without looking, I went back to stirring the food.

"No," Gabby said with a hint of humor. "Now, behave."

I turned off the stove and brought the pan to the table. Rachel thanked me as I scooped a portion onto her plate. Gabby smiled when I did the same for her. The remaining food, I dumped onto my own plate.

It wasn't bad eating with Rachel there. She kept up the conversation, asking Gabby questions about her weekend and her day. Her scent told me she really did worry about Gabby. So did I.

After Gabby finished, Rachel shooed her out of the kitchen with orders to rest while we cleaned up. Rachel turned on me with a grin and started talking about a cute pair of shoes she'd found. As I washed off the stove, I wondered how Peter put up with such a talker.

By the time we had everything clean, Gabby was lying asleep across the bed on top the covers.

"Good night, Clay," Rachel called from her room just before she closed her door. It was way too early to go to bed. At least I didn't have to hide the fact I was spending the night.

Gently picking Gabby up, I pulled back the covers. Then I removed her socks. She'd be more comfortable without her pants, but I wouldn't be. I pulled the covers up, tucked her in, and kissed her forehead. Her nose wrinkled in her sleep when my whiskers brushed her skin. I chuckled and reclined next to her. Not yet ready to sleep, I read for a while. She didn't move much, but I glanced at her often. I had to. With two words, she'd made it impossible to look away. He's mine.

I read for a while, slept a bit, then woke and read some more.

The sun rose and still she slept. That was what she should have done yesterday.

Finally, she yawned, stretched, and opened her eyes.

"Good morning," she said, pulling the covers up to her chin.

I closed my book and studied her. She had more color back.

"I want to talk to you but keep falling asleep. If I do it again, wake me up."

Not a chance. I slid an arm around her and pulled her against my side. She smiled and relaxed.

"During the Introduction, when I said my head hurt, I saw a man step away from the line. I know how your kind views Introductions. It didn't seem right, so I peeked at his spark. It hurt like hell, but I saw he had the same color light as Elder Joshua and the wolf that'd attacked us. I thought maybe it could be the same guy–that he needed to leave because you'd recognize his scent. Then, I saw three more, further away. Something's going on, but I can't figure out what.

"I know you didn't stay with the pack full-time, but did you ever notice any of them acting differently?"

I shook my head, and she sighed. Smoothing her hair back, I wished I had the answers she wanted.

Her phone vibrated, but she didn't reach for it. Usually, only one person called her. Sam.

"If only I could trust Sam. If I could ask him questions about Elder Joshua without him repeating them, I might be able to figure this thing out."

After the way Sam had handled the Introduction, I wasn't willing to trust him, either. He'd jeopardized Gabby's wellbeing with his need to adhere to our customs. I wondered how long it would take for the challenges to resume.

Would he keep them away long enough for her to fully recover?

AFTER ALMOST A FULL week of silence, Gabby finally answered one of Sam's calls.

We were in her room sitting on the bed reading, as usual, when her phone rang. She stared at it for a moment, sighed, and picked it up. I stayed where I was and listened to the stilted conversation. I wanted to know if he'd push the Introductions again.

After he asked if she was feeling better, he asked if she'd come back to the Compound over the long Thanksgiving weekend. She avoided a direct answer, and he tried apologizing for his actions. She made non-committal noises, obviously still mad and not yet ready to forgive. Then, he asked what had happened to her during the last visit.

Our gazes met briefly, and she answered vaguely that she had been sick. A long moment of silence passed. When he spoke, he didn't comment on her answer but asked again that she consider coming "home" over holiday break. She said she'd think about it then hung up.

I thought that call was a signal that life as we'd known it would resume. However, for the next few weeks, no challengers approached me, and Sam continued to call Gabby daily. Most of their brief conversations touched on weather, school, or investments. Anything pack related stayed off limits. He was genuinely concerned about her, but Gabby had lost whatever trust she'd once had in him.

She talked to me often, trying to reason out her ability. She felt certain that the answer lay in the transfer. So I kept a close eye on her to ensure she didn't pull that stunt again. I didn't leave for work until she left for school, and I made sure I returned home before she did. I was tempted to follow her, too, but resisted. It seemed less likely she'd use her abilities on someone at school. She wanted to study the effect. That made Rachel the most likely candidate. So, when Rachel was around, I stayed in my fur. Mostly because I could get away with more as a dog. But partly because I thought she'd eventually notice the missing "dog" when I was around. Plus, that woman talked too much when I was a man.

On one of the rare nights Rachel stayed in, she started talking to Gabby about me. I lay curled on the floor next to Gabby, listening and amused.

"You are so weird about him. What is it about the guy that keeps you coming back?" Rachel sat on the couch, folding her clothes.

Gabby smiled slightly and turned the page of the book in her lap before answering.

"You don't know him like I do."

"How can you know him at all when you two don't talk?"

"You don't need to talk to get to know someone. You just need to listen," Gabby said.

I watched as her eyes stopped moving over the words in her book. Her gaze met mine, and a smile twitched her lips. I wondered what thought put it there.

"But that's what I'm saying. He doesn't talk. What are you listening to?"

Gabby laughed. "Actions speak louder than words. He's there when I need him, he's kind and caring, he keeps me safe; and as you've seen, he cooks and cleans. What's not to like, Rachel?"

Yeah, Rachel, what's not to like? I wanted to hug Gabby. Rachel's grumbling told me she disagreed with my suitability for Gabby. So I stood, walked over to her, and lay down on one of the blouses she was trying to fold. Take that.

She laughed and tried to move me, but I just laid my head on my paws. I caught Gabby's wide grin and winked at her.

Shaking her head, she went to the kitchen and opened the fridge. I was glad she was looking for more food. She didn't eat enough. I'd been stopping at the store after work trying to tempt her with different things. Mostly, what I bought went unnoticed. Tonight, though, I was pretty proud of what I'd found, a big double-chocolate cake. Sure enough, Gabby honed in on it.

"Can I have a piece of your cake?" she asked.

"I thought it was yours. It was here when I got home," Rachel called back.

I moved off Rachel's clothes to watch Gabby. As she continued to stare at the cake, her expression softened.

I smiled. I just needed to be patient a little longer...

My patience paid off when the snow started to fall the week before Thanksgiving. The wind howled, and despite having the heat on, it was still chilly inside.

I lay at the end of the bed in my usual spot. Gabby had just crawled under the covers. Even with her feet under me, she shivered. I didn't see how. She wore two or three layers.

"Screw this," she said, sitting up. Then, she pulled off her sweatshirt and tossed it toward the closet.

I lifted my head, watching her and wondering what she was up to. She lay back down but started wriggling under the covers. A minute later, her sleep pants sailed across the room.

"Clay, will you keep me warm tonight?"

What? Hell, yes!

I shifted as I jumped off the bed and grabbed a pair of shorts to yank on. A second later, I pulled back the covers and slid in next to her where I belonged. Hopefully she couldn't see my toothy grin in the dark. I just couldn't help it. She wasn't sick and she wanted me in bed with her. I wrapped my arms around her and pulled her close. She snuggled in. I grunted when the ice cube she called a nose pressed against my bare chest, but I didn't let go.

"No more fur at night. Deal?"

My heart felt like it had exploded in my chest. She was telling me I should sleep with her every night. As a man. Sure, I knew she only wanted me for my body heat. But I didn't care. She could have me in whatever way she wanted me.

She fell asleep quickly while I stayed up most the night enjoying the feel of her wrapped around me. It was different from when I'd slept next to her when she was sick. Her hands moved often, finding a new spot on my chest or waist to warm themselves. I didn't want to miss a moment of it.

When her cell rang early, I wanted to groan. It was Sunday, the day Gabby usually slept in. Bonus snuggle time. Hiding my disappointment, I quickly reached over her, grabbed the phone, and handed it to her.

She glanced at the display and frowned.

"Hello?" she said.

"Gabby, I found her, but..."

"Luke?"

I scowled. Why was he calling her?

"Yes. I understand you think she's important, but she's not even eighteen. How am I supposed to get her to come with me?"

Gabby pulled away from me and sat up. I grunted, annoyed with Luke.

"I can't believe you actually found her. I need to talk to her. If she's like me, which I think she is, you had better bring her to the Compound. I hate to admit it, but the Elders need to know."

"Fine. You better be there when we get there," he said, sounding annoyed.

Good. At least I wasn't the only annoyed one. He'd ruined what could have been the best morning of my life. I refrained from sighing as Gabby got out of bed. At least there was tonight.

It wasn't just the next night, but every night, that Gabby folded back the covers to invite me in next to her. And, each day I went to work, with no signs of challengers waiting. I lived in a state of bliss.

Daydreaming of sleeping next to Gabby, yet again, I barely heard the shop phone ring or Dale's answering, "Hello, Dale's Auto Body." Last night, she'd been so cold she'd practically slept on top me the entire time. If I concentrated, I could still smell her on me.

"Clay! It's for you."

I straightened away from the hood of the car I was working on and frowned. No one knew to call me here. Still, I went to the phone.

"Hello?"

There was an indrawn breath, then a moment of silence. The wait wasn't long.

"Clay, I did it again," Gabby said, her voice sounding strained. "I'm at the diner where we had breakfast. I need you to come get me before it gets worse."

Damn it. I hung up the phone.

"Dale, I need a ride. It's Gabby."

"Okay. Let's go."

I jogged out the door, and he hurried to catch up. Who had she managed to find at the diner? I'd been so sure she would go after Rachel.

"Where to? Should we call an ambulance?"

"The diner on Main. No. She's just sick, again," I said as he pulled out of the lot.

He just shook his head and kept driving. When we pulled into the parking lot, I had the door open before he even stopped.

"Come back when you can. Take care of her."

I nodded and leapt out.

Through the window, I spotted her. She looked pale. Her bottom lip trembled when she caught sight of me. I pulled open the door and strode to the booth where she sat.

"Hi," she whispered, tilting her head to look at me. The pain in her gaze worried me.

She handed over her keys then started to slide out of the booth. I helped her to her feet and wrapped an arm around her shoulders, holding her close. Fine tremors wracked her body as she shuffled alongside of me. I wanted to be frustrated with her—why did she need to keep hurting herself like this—but concern outweighed frustration as I maneuvered us out the door and to her car.

Once I had her in the car and buckled up, she shut her eyes. Her breathing hitched several times as I drove home, and she didn't move when I picked her up and carried her inside. I knew she was awake, though; so after I tucked her into bed, I got her a glass of water. She drained it, then lay back with a tooth-chattering sigh.

I stripped to my shorts and slid in with her. This wasn't the kind of snuggling I'd had in mind. I hated this. Hated the worrying. She didn't understand her abilities and neither did I. What if she had a finite number of zaps in her? What would happen if she used them up? Would she burn herself out? Would she not wake up?

I held her, and I worried. At some point during the night, I pulled her close so that her head rested on my chest. Then, I just listened to her breathe.

Close to dawn, she moved. She lifted her head, and I felt her look at me. Keeping my eyes closed and my breathing steady, I silently waited. She was thinking about something.

She carefully pulled away from me, and I felt the mattress move as she got out of bed. I opened my eyes to watch her leave the room. That she was up and walking meant she was through the worst of it. I heaved a relieved sigh and got up to turn on the light for her so she wouldn't trip getting back into bed. Sitting against the headboard, I listened to her wash her hands and then leave the bathroom.

When she reached the bedroom door, she paused and eyed me. I studied her in return. She did appear to have more color. Although I was relieved, I was also annoyed. What possessed her to keep transferring her power? I hoped she'd explain. I needed to understand; but more, I needed to hear her say she'd never do it again.

Biting her lower lip, she closed the door and slowly turned back toward me. She wouldn't meet my gaze as she walked back to bed and burrowed under the covers once more.

"I'm sorry," she said softly. Then, she finally looked up at me. "I didn't plan it...but I think I've figured out what I am, Clay. I'm like a GPS for werewolves. I can find people. Not just people, but compatible Mates like me."

I wanted to sigh. I didn't care that she could find others like her, not when I'd just spent over sixteen hours waiting for her to wake up.

She tucked her cold feet under my legs and kept talking.

"When I touched Rachel yesterday, I really paid attention."

When had she seen Rachel? I almost swore. I'd known it would be her.

"I saw the energy I release when I shock a person. It goes into them and pulses outward, passing through almost everyone else.

And everyone this energy passes through fades in my mind, almost dimming to the point of non-existence. Five people didn't fade, Clay. In the whole world, there are only five. Six if you include me. And when the energy I release touches them, it bounces off to come crashing back on me. That's what's been knocking me on my butt."

She played with the quilt for a second, and I nudged her to keep her going. I still hadn't heard, "I'll never worry you like that again, Clay."

She smiled at me then resumed talking.

"It was different when I touched Luke. With him, I zoomed in on one specific spark, a yellow-violet one on the east coast. The paper I gave Luke? That was directions to find her. I think she belongs with him. I think I found his Mate just by touching him." She grinned and said, "I don't think he appreciated my help, though."

I remembered the phone call and agreed. However, I was glad he was off chasing some other female.

A faint laugh outside the house caught my attention. I turned my head toward the window, staring out into the dark. The soft sound continued. Someone was in the driveway, slowly circling to the front of the house. Other than the laugh, there was silence.

I felt Gabby move on the bed behind me. The laughing grew louder. Whoever was outside had heard her move. Only one of my kind could hear that well. I growled and threw off the covers.

Fangs exploded in my mouth, and my ears changed as I struggled to control my rage. For weeks, the challengers had met me in the abandoned shop, respecting the need to keep Gabby safe after that first challenge. Why would someone come here now?

I saw a slight movement through the blinds. He was standing on the front lawn in the shadows. I narrowed my eyes, and he grinned wide and laughed loudly. He could see us because of the light.

With a burst of speed, I knocked the pillows off the bed then bumped Gabby off, too. As she tumbled over the edge of the mattress, I leapt toward the bedroom door, cleared it, and switched off the light before she landed.

I flew out the front door and found the man crouched low, ready for me. Snow crunched under my bare feet as I moved toward him. His lips parted with a growl, and he moved to the side, studying me. I snarled back as I sized him up. His shoulders were narrower than mine, his fingers, thinner, but I outweighed him. I'd use that. But first, I needed to know his skill.

Moving in a blur, I rushed him and swiped at his torso with my changed nails. Material ripped, but he managed to move out of the way, just skirting the direct glow of the streetlight before he rushed at me. I twisted, turning with his attack to avoid being hit. As he passed me, I used my foot to tangle his. He growled as he fell, and I retreated a few steps toward the house, ready for his next attack.

The man snarled, and when he lifted his head, his eyes had dilated. He was losing control, on the verge of change.

"We need to take this elsewhere," I said quietly, aware of the houses around us. How long until someone heard us?

His skull moved under his skin, reshaping, and he crouched low again as his mouth reshaped, too. He wasn't ready to listen. I focused on allowing my mouth to change, making it easier to bite him. A good hold on his throat would send him off and end this before it got out of control.

He lunged forward, his mouth opening. I leaned back, avoiding his bite, and drove my fist into his gut.

Down the road, a few of the streetlights blinked off.

He backed away from me and sidestepped, as if trying to circle around me. Instead of following, I moved closer to the house and shadowed his step to the side. He snarled and charged me. This time, I didn't back away.

I met him with a fist to the face and enjoyed the sound of the low thud, until he drove his fist into my ribs. Grunting, I came back with a right fist to his jaw and a left to his ribs. We moved fast, striking and dodging. I did more dodging than he did. His breathing became harsh.

Twice more he tried to feint away from the house, but I refused to follow.

He growled softly and tensed to attack again. A faint noise behind the house caught my attention. Someone was on the back porch.

I growled and grabbed the man by the back of his head. As the back door opened, I put everything I had into the next hit. My fist met his temple with a crack. I opened my hand, and he dropped. I didn't wait to see him fall.

The front door still stood open. Rushing through it, I barreled into the next challenger who was crossing the living room.

The man ducked low and wrapped his arms around my waist, ready to drive me to the floor. I fisted my hands together, lifted them, and slammed down onto his back as we started to move. He straightened, trying to clip my jaw with the back of his head, but I jerked out of the way. Not far enough. His arms whipped around me and started to squeeze. He had more to him than the last guy, I felt it in his arms. Hands still locked, I brought them down on his face, again and again, hammering at him as he tried to crack my ribs.

From Gabby's room, I heard movement.

He released me, and we broke apart.

Gabby gasped. He looked over my shoulder, and I knew he saw her. His expression changed to one of adoration then swiftly to calculation. I knew that look. I had the same one months ago when I first saw her and felt the pull. Angry, I fisted my hand and hit him in the temple, bringing him down as I had the one outside. He landed hard.

Behind me, Gabby moved. I turned to watch her. She remained focused on the man on the floor. She looked horrified. Yet she studied him for a long while.

"What do we do, Clay?" she said finally.

She turned toward me and shivered. The front and back doors were both open. She needed to get back in bed.

"He's part changed. With all the noise, I think the police will be here soon. Can we leave him here like this?"

Her worry wasn't just for keeping our race hidden. She'd felt something for the man on the floor, and it was tearing me up to think any of her worry might be for him. So, I nodded and motioned her back to the bedroom.

Sirens screamed in the distance as I tucked her into bed and closed the door.

When I returned, there was no limp form in the living room. The back door closed as I eyed the blood-free carpet. I glanced out the front window. The lawn was clear. They'd both run.

I waited in the front door as the police pulled up.

My face hurt. I had no doubt I looked like a victim as the officers in the first car opened their doors. Good thing they couldn't see the other guys and their busted faces.

"Sir, I received a complaint that animals were fighting in your back yard...what happened to you?" the first officer asked as the second watched me.

"I need to report an attempted break in."

Then the questions started. Did I know who had attacked me? Had I ever seen my attacker before? Could I describe him?

I knew they wouldn't accept short answers.

"My girlfriend and I were inside when we heard a noise out here. I came out to investigate after telling her to stay inside. As soon as I was out, someone hit me from behind. We scuffled a bit. He was about my height but smaller in the shoulders. Dark hair. Hazel eyes. Nose had a bump in the bridge. His teeth were yellow. He had a friend in back. I heard his dog growling. I managed to knock the guy out on the front lawn," I stepped further out the door to the spot in the snow, "here. Then I went running back inside." One of the officers glanced at my bare feet.

Damn.

"I think the adrenaline rush is fading," I said calmly. "My feet and hands are freezing. Mind if we go inside?"

The one who'd spoken waved me in. As soon as I was inside and had the door closed, I started up again, speaking softly.

"Once I knocked the one out in front, I ran back in here. Gabby's been sick," I waved to the door, "and I was worried when I heard something from the back. It was a good thing I came in. He was standing right here," I moved to the center of the room. "He landed a few good punches, but I managed to knock him out, too. Gabby had gotten out of bed. We heard the sirens. I helped her back into bed, made sure she was okay, then came out to wait for you. When I came out, they were both gone."

"We'd like to talk to your girlfriend."

"Okay. Just knock on her door. I doubt she's sleeping."

Chapter Twenty-Two

AFTER THE POLICE SPOKE TO GABBY, WHOSE PALE, FRIGHTENED expression gave more credibility to my story, they took pictures of my hands, face, and the entry points.

Once they left to go bother the neighbors with questions, I closed myself in the bathroom to wash. Most of the cuts were starting to knit together. Beyond the sound of running water, I listened to Gabby move around in her bedroom.

During Gabby's conversation with the policemen, she had told them she didn't want to stay the night and had said we'd be staying with family during the holiday. She'd given them her cell number for the follow-up they said they would need to do.

I knew her desire to leave had little to do with her safety. She had questions. She was afraid of what had happened when she'd looked at the man on the floor. So was I. How could she feel the pull for another werewolf? Sure I knew Gabby's scent appealed to all werewolves, but the pull was supposed to be unique, something only one werewolf could experience when he saw his Mate for the first time. And I wasn't mistaken. She'd felt the pull for me and for the man I'd knocked to the floor. What did it mean?

I sighed, dried my face and hands, and quietly left the bathroom. Gabby had dressed and still moved about her room, her actions tense and jerky. She shoved clothes into her bag with an aggression I seldom saw in her. I leaned against the frame and watched her for a while.

When her bag was full, she turned toward the door, then froze. Her gaze immediately dropped to the floor, avoiding mine. It hurt. I was as confused as she was over what had happened, but it didn't change how I felt about her. Did it change how she felt about me, though?

I sighed, stepped aside, and motioned her through the door.

She grabbed her phone and called Rachel to let her know what had happened and to warn her not to come back without Peter. After she hung up, I quietly followed her out to the car. She moved around to the passenger side, still not looking at me.

Clenching my jaw, I got in behind the wheel. Was I losing her? I couldn't stay quiet. I had to say something. But what?

I backed out of the driveway and started out toward the Compound.

Anything I had to say right now would lead to begging. Females didn't like begging.

Tapping my fingers against the wheel in frustration, I tried to think of something, anything, to start a conversation about what had happened.

It took a moment to realize her breathing had slowed. I looked over and saw her head tilted loosely to the side. She was asleep. Great.

For the next hour, I kept going over the fight. I'd knocked the guy out. He lay on the floor, eyes closed. Gabby stepped out of her room as if in a trance, her eyes focused on *him*. I'd scented fear, confusion...but also interest.

I gritted my teeth. My canines poked into my lips. Nice. I was losing control and Gabby. The steering wheel crackled beneath my grip.

I went back to tapping. It didn't help. My ears itched. Beside me, Gabby shifted in her sleep. Her scent wasn't helping.

"Clay..."

I paused my tapping.

"Could you pull over for a minute?"

I glanced at her. Was she sick? She didn't look pale, just worried. I braked and slowly pulled over, careful of the snowy shoulder. Once the car was in park, I turned toward her.

A sad smile lifted her lips, and then she tapped them.

My tight grip on the wheel went slack. Was she saying she wanted a kiss? My heart leapt. I swallowed hard and tried to pull back the change. I didn't want to hurt her. It wasn't working. I needed to know everything was good between us before I'd calm down. A kiss would help with that.

She studied me just as I inhaled deeply. Her scent lacked the confusion it had held earlier. A sweet hint of interest gave me hope, and I lifted my hands to cup her face. Her expression softened. This woman...I couldn't live without her. I smoothed my fingers over her soft skin as I leaned in. She reached out and grabbed my shirt, pulling me closer until my lips met hers. I swallowed a groan. She was still mine.

Her lips parted, and she bit my bottom lip. It was like a kick to the heart. I opened my mouth for her, and she made a small noise as our tongues touched. My teeth shrank as I claimed her mouth, taking what she surrendered.

We steamed the windows before she pulled back. I wrapped my arms around her, unwilling to let her go yet. I kissed the top of her head and just held her.

Her fisted hands opened and flattened against my stomach. It wasn't a push away. It was a touch, an acceptance. I kissed her one last time, then straightened in my seat.

She fell asleep after a few minutes of driving, but it didn't matter. Whatever was going on in her head, she was still with me. That was all that mattered.

WE ARRIVED at the Compound at dusk. Cars crowded in front of the building, making it impossible to park close. And that was fine with me. I turned around and parked near the drive. Just in case.

Gabby woke as I turned off the car. She gave me a sleepy smile and started to untangle herself from her blanket as I got out. I walked around to her side, opened the door for her, then grabbed her bag.

The buildings were lit up, and few people milled around outside as we walked to the main door. Jackets and shoes filled the entry, and I could hear conversations from the rooms around us. Both signs of a full house.

Gabby led the way to her usual apartment, but we found there was another family with cubs already occupying it. She tried other apartments, but they were full, too. It wasn't a surprise. The families always came in around the holidays.

Giving up on the apartments, she turned toward the hall that was usually reserved for the unMated males. When she went to knock on the first door, I caught her wrist and shook my head. I knocked. I didn't want any of them to think she was looking for an offer. The majority of the dorm quarters were also occupied. Several men passed us as we searched and gave us curious looks as they scented the air. Gabby stayed close.

We took the first room we found open and put her bag on the twin bed. It would be enough to hold the room.

"I need to talk to Sam," she said, looking at me.

I'd figured as much and wondered if Sam would be in a talking mood. Keeping my doubts to myself, I nodded and led the way to the common room. Decorations were everywhere. Cornucopias with harvest produce sat on each of the long tables. Several turkeys with feathers made of construction paper hands hung on the walls. The air still smelled like glue, laughter, and pumpkin pie.

Sam sat with his back to us, speaking with several other men at one of the many sitting arrangements. Gabby picked up her pace and stepped ahead of me, her gaze focused on Sam.

She strode up to him and interrupted the conversation.

"It's time we talked," she said.

He turned toward her. There was no surprise in his expression. Someone must have let him know we were there. He smiled at her and nodded. The others in his group got up and moved away.

"Gabby, I didn't think you'd be up until tomorrow."

She glanced at me. The room didn't afford privacy with our keen hearing. I wondered what she was going to say. She glanced around the room, then her gaze became unfocused. She winced, and I knew what she'd done.

I grunted in annoyance but rubbed her back. If there were an off switch for her ability, I'd figure out how to keep it off permanently.

"We came early because two werewolves tried breaking into my house." She watched Sam closely as she spoke.

"What?" Sam said, giving me a sharp look.

Why didn't you contact me?

I don't like how you help.

"He's still not talking," Gabby said, unaware of our exchange. She moved to sit in the chair across from Sam. "I believe their intentions were to kidnap me."

I sat in the chair next to her. Her scent changed. Confusion again. Her troubled gaze swung to me, and I knew what she was thinking. The man on the floor. He didn't matter if she didn't let him matter.

She gave me a small smile as if reading my mind then turned back to Sam.

"Is there more than one kind of werewolf?" she asked.

The question surprised Sam, and even though I'd briefly considered the possibility, it surprised me, too.

Sam frowned and leaned forward. "Not sure what you mean, exactly."

Sam watched her closely as she nibbled her lip.

"When you go fur, what color variations are possible? Different shades of fur, eyes...what about nose or nails?"

The double doors opened and a few more werewolves drifted in, slowly walking toward other groups. Gabby had everyone's attention and word was spreading fast.

"What does this have to do with—"

She held up a hand. "Bear with me, Sam. I need answers to give answers."

Sam turned to me.

"I already told you," she said, "he still isn't talking. Look, is there another Elder I can talk to? One willing to answer my questions?"

Sam's face fell but his expression cleared after a moment. "Fur is like hair and varies just like a human's. Same with the eyes. We are more like dogs when it comes to our noses. Mostly dark, but we sometimes have unusual markings. Did you see an identifying mark, Gabby?"

"What about the nails?" she asked, ignoring his question.

He shrugged. "Shades of grey. Mostly a dark grey."

"Black?"

What was she getting at? What had she noticed that I hadn't?

"Well, like I said, a dark grey is possible."

"No. I mean black. A very glossy black you could see your reflection in."

I struggled to recall the color of the nails of the men I'd fought as Sam remained introspectively quiet. Nothing came to mind. I'd been busy fighting and worrying about Gabby.

During the silence, Gabby became aware of the room and looked around. Everyone was suddenly looking elsewhere.

"I don't think I've ever paid that much attention to our claws before. But, no, I don't believe so."

Gabby leaned back in her chair, obviously lost in thought. Everyone in the room watched her, waiting for what she'd say next.

Her scent changed with the array of emotions she experienced.

Worry, anger, interest. I caught Sam inhaling slowly and knew he'd noticed, too. After several moments of silence, Sam cleared his throat. She continued to ignore him, and he glanced at me. I shrugged. Gabby wasn't the type to rush into things. Someone spoke softly further back in the room. Others moved restlessly.

When she glanced at me with her scent bleeding confusion, I offered my hand. I couldn't guess what she was thinking, but I could offer my support. She had it unconditionally since the moment I saw her. She looked down at my hand, hesitated, then reached for me.

As soon as we touched, I felt it. A zing of energy. Her fingers laced through mine, and her scent faded.

I scowled at her. Had she just used her power on me? After everything that had just happened, she was going to knock herself out again and leave me to deal with Sam and a million questions I couldn't begin to answer?

Instead of looking even a little sorry about what she'd just done, she beamed at me. Then, she leaned toward me, her intent to kiss me obvious. Annoyed or not, I wouldn't say no.

Our lips met softly, but she pulled back with a jerk. Her wide eyes stared at me. Her pulse leapt, and her scent changed subtly.

I eyed her warily, wondering what had happened now. Would this be another "catch me, Clay," moment?

Her fingers twitched in mine, and with speed I didn't know she possessed, she was out of her chair and straddling my lap. Shock didn't cover what I felt. Though it was completely unexpected, I loved the contact. In fact, I'd consider gnawing off my own arm to keep her there. But this physical contact wasn't like her. Especially not with the crowd around us.

She breathed in deeply as if scenting me. I shuddered in response and stared up at her, mesmerized. The room disappeared as she continued to study me with an intensity I'd never seen before. The green flecks in her hazel eyes seemed brighter, more alluring, as she leaned in until her cheek brushed mine. My lungs stopped working for a moment as she buried her nose in my hair. I held still, unsure what was happening but liking it. A lot.

She pulled back to press her lips to the tip of my nose, and my heart twisted painfully. She'd been so close to my neck. The skin there tingled with what might have been. I lifted my free hand and lightly rested it on her waist. Her skin felt warm beneath my fingers.

She sighed a little and closed her eyes. When she opened them again, she gave me a secret smile that made my blood boil.

She combed her fingers through my hair, brushing it back so she could lightly kiss my forehead. Her lips brushed a path to my cheek where she pressed another kiss. She moved lower, finding my lips. She nibbled at them until I opened my mouth for her. The aggressor, her tongue found mine. As much as I was spinning in my own heaven, I was starting to worry. This wasn't like Gabby. There were so many people watching us. It was as if she wasn't even aware of them.

She pulled back from me, gave me a quick frown, then leaned to nudge my jaw with her nose. My heart stopped and then tripled its efforts. She wanted my neck. Hope gripped me, warring with the worry. Should I let her? Was this really what she wanted?

My gut clenched as her lips skimmed my exposed skin, and my concern vanished. My pulse leapt higher. I let go of her hand so I could grip her, hold her in place. She had to keep going.

Her breathing hitched, and with one hand, she gripped my hair and tugged it hard. I tilted my head, willingly exposing my neck. She made a sound, almost a growl of satisfaction, before she set her lips on my neck once more. She kissed me, and I shuddered. Then her teeth sank into my skin.

There was no pain, only complete bliss. She'd done it. She'd Claimed me.

I closed my eyes with a sigh and opened myself for her. Her feelings flooded me. Desire consumed her. The unbridled need took me by surprise. Why hadn't I scented that? As fast as it filled me, it depleted, replaced with a stunned emotional silence.

She pulled back slightly and eyed my neck. I watched her expression, unsure of the silence over our connection. Behind her, someone moved and called attention to the fact that we still had an audience. Horror drifted over our new link. A Claiming typically occurred in private.

A deep blush stained her cheeks. Embarrassment battled horror. She wiped at her mouth with a shaky hand. Panic bloomed as she stared at me.

I couldn't take it anymore. Whether she'd intended to or not, she'd just given me the world. I reached up and gently touched her hair.

"I've been waiting for that since the moment I saw you," I said.

She scowled at me, and all the horror, embarrassment, and panic fled to be replaced by anger. I could guess why. She'd been after me about talking since she'd first seen me. I laughed and picked her up.

She wrapped her arms around my neck and hid her face as the room around us erupted in cheers. I didn't wait for congratulations but strode for the door. There was so much more I wanted to say to her. In private.

As soon as we were in our room, I closed the door and set her on her feet. I watched the play of emotions on her face and basked in each one I felt across our link.

"Why?" Her voice came out in a squeak. She cleared her throat and tried again. "Why wait until now to talk?"

I studied her and saw her hurt and confusion. I opened my arms. She didn't hesitate, but stepped right into them. Tucking her close, I spoke the truth.

"If I'd spoken, even just one word, I would have never been able to hold back what I felt for you. You would have run." And I would have chased you, scaring you even more, I thought to myself.

She pulled back and met my gaze.

"Can I finally get answers from you now? You'll keep talking?"

I smiled at her excitement and nodded.

"Do you think I'm right about the—"

"Now's not the time," I said, glancing at the door. "We'll talk later." I could smell Sam waiting out there. His heart beat steadily with his patience. If I could hear his heart, he was hearing every word we shared.

"No way. We're talking now. If not about that, then something else. I've waited over six months to hear your voice. You owe me. I bit you."

She made me want to keep smiling. This crazy, adorable, intelligent, and gifted person was mine. Thinking of her gift had me frowning. She'd just used it back there. I was sure of it. Yet, she seemed fine.

"How are you feeling?"

She frowned and seemed to do a self-assessment.

"Good, actually." Her gaze became unfocused, but she didn't wince or pale. "It's weird, but I don't feel sick." After a moment, she came back to me. "I think we need a safe place to talk."

I nodded and glanced at the door again. As soon as we left the room, Sam would want answers. Gabby had asked some pretty crazy questions. I had questions of my own, now.

She slipped from my arms and yanked the door open. Sam leaned against the wall opposite the door.

"Sam, since we don't have any privacy, we'd like to use the conference room. It's soundproofed, and there are a few things we need to discuss."

"I couldn't agree more," Sam said, motioning for her to lead.

"Clay and I, Sam," she said as she stepped from the room. "I don't have any answers for you."

"Gabby—"

"No. Now it's your turn to be bossed around and told what to do. I did what you wanted and Claimed one of you. Lay off."

I didn't need our link to know just how pissed she was. But she was also afraid. Of Sam. Still, she turned her back on him and started walking. Sam glanced at me. I arched a brow. He sighed and started to follow her. I followed him.

She opened the door to the conference room and turned to face Sam.

"Sam, I'm trying to do what's best for me, Clay, and the pack. There's a lot I haven't told you and things I haven't told Clay. Give me some time to sort everything out. I need to make sure your goals mesh with mine before I can fully confide in you."

I stood behind Sam as he considered what she'd said. Then, he stepped back and motioned me in with her.

"I'll be out here," he said.

She nodded, gently closed the door, then turned to me. She brushed a hand through her hair.

"I'm not sure where to start."

"Anywhere. I'll listen," I said as I pulled her into my arms.

I felt her smile. "I can see everything, Clay. Without pain." She pulled out of my arms so I could see her unfocused gaze. "Even without touching you, there's no pain. I can see so much more than before. Why?"

"It's our link."

"Wait. I thought the link happened when..."

Her immediate blush gave away her thoughts. I smiled.

"The full link happens after the Mating is completed. With the Claiming we have a more limited version of that connection." My smile faded, and I looked at her more closely. "It can still be broken, though. If there's another potential Mate out there...by biting him, you can break our bond and create one with him."

"Don't use up your word quota for the day," she said with a slight shake of her head.

I grinned at her sass, and she stuck out her tongue. Then she grew serious again.

"Clay, I won't be biting anyone else. Ever. But I do have

something to tell you. When those wolves attacked...the second one..."

Her hurt came back, and I nudged her, falling back on my quiet ways.

"I felt the same pull with him as I do with you. I don't understand why that would happen. Sam said just one. Experiencing that with someone else confused me and made me feel horrible, like I cheated on you."

I sighed, then gave her a reassuring smile.

"I saw what happened. It concerned me, but the kiss in the car helped me understand how you feel. Don't worry about it."

She gave me a radiant smile. Then I felt something over our link. It was warm and full and everything I'd dreamed of.

"I love you," she said.

In a blur, I wrapped my arms around her, picked her up, and spun her around. Now she was mine. My Mate in truth. My family. My place to belong.

She looked at me and laughed.

"Oh!" She squirmed to get down. "Please can we get rid of the beard?"

I set her on her feet, and she hopped from foot to foot in excitement.

I nodded and laughed.

"And I still want to get my degree. Can we stay where we are until then?"

I wanted to say yes, but two men had tried to take her, and she'd just hinted to an Elder that she thought they weren't werewolves but something else. Sam might try to change her mind about going back to school. I glanced at the door.

She saw the look and her resentment toward Sam drifted over our link. She stepped close to lay her head against my chest and wrap her arms around my waist.

"Everyone I've ever loved this way I've lost," she said, hugging me close. "Don't let me down."

She was talking about Sam. He'd shaken her trust. I would never do that to her.

"I won't. You're stuck with me forever," I said against her hair.

She pulled back and kissed me again. Her love wrapped around me, and I never wanted to let go. For as long as it took, I would wait patiently for the next step of our relationship. And the next phase, our Mating, wouldn't be decided by her gift or some other outside influence. It would be her choice, no matter how her sweet lips might tempt me.

Her phone chirped from her back pocket. She groaned and broke away from the kiss. But I saw promise in her eyes. I glanced at the number with her and recognized Luke's number.

As soon as she hit "talk," Luke spoke in a rush.

"Gabby, I have a problem," he shouted over the roar of an engine. Something popped loudly in the background, and Luke swore just before the phone went dead.

Gabby looked up at me with a frown. Then her gaze went vacant, and I knew she was using her special sight again.

"Clay, I don't think I have a choice anymore. Something's happening to Luke. The other werewolves are all around him. We need to get Sam." She turned to look at the door. "I don't know who to trust."

I didn't trust Sam either. As an Elder, he had to put the pack first. He would rush to help any potential Mate for our kind. But at what cost to those women? Charlene, Gabby, this new one who Luke had with him, and the one who Charlene's son had mentioned...Michelle. So many being found at once along with a new kind of werewolf; it all had to mean something. A shiver of trepidation ran through me.

I nodded and leaned my forehead against hers.

"I'll stand with you, always."

It's been more than a decade since I first started this series and a few years since I completed it. Did you know the Judgement series wasn't going to be a series at all but a standalone book? And not even for Clay and Gabby.

I dreamed of Michelle and Emmitt first. That scene where she's on the dance floor and sees him through the crowd. It was so vivid. I could feel her heart race and the complete yearning she had for him. I could see the way he watched her. Let me tell you…waking up from that was rough. I tried so hard to go back to sleep so the dream could keep going and I could find out what happened next. It wasn't meant to be, though. Back then, my kids were babies, and one of the two youngest started crying. (which is probably what ripped me from the dream in the first place!)

That dream wouldn't leave me alone for days. I thought of them constantly, wondering what they'd been doing there. Why they were apart and not dancing when I knew how she felt. I thought of it so much, I dreamed of them again. The next time, they weren't in the bar, but outside of it, and Emmitt was defending Michelle against two werewolves. Now, that didn't make it into the book, but it started a whole chain of thinking.

I'd dabbled with writing back then. Nothing serious, of course. But I started building a story around that dream and that story morphed from a standalone adult novel to the young adult Judgement series we have today.

Thank you to all the fans to stuck with me through the journey. I hope it was worthwhile!

If you happen to be reading this note and haven't yet completed the series, know that Clay and Gabby are the first of six couples in this interconnecting series. That means, even though you're going to meet some new people in the next book, we aren't done with Clay and Gabby yet!

Keep reading for deleted scenes from Hope(less)!

For more information regarding other titles, to sign up for my newsletter, or to read exclusive content, please visit my website at melissahaag.com.

I'd love to hear from you!

Melissa

DELETED SCENES

These scenes were written long before Hope(less) was first released in 2013 and no longer fit with the evolved story. But they're still fun to read. Enjoy!

Gabby meets Sam

My life hasn't exactly been what I would call normal, though I tried hard to keep it as normal as possible. At least, that's what I told myself as I walked down the hospital hall, passing under the buzzing fluorescent lights. The squeak of my white sneakers echoed around me as I pushed a supply cart across the waxed tiles. Nurses passed me, smiling, on their way to check on patients or to do paperwork.

Since as long as I could remember, I could see where people were without looking. It was as if my head came equipped with a giant fish finder, but it worked on people instead. When I focused my mind, a vast darkness filled with tiny sparks of light opened. The sparks I saw matched the locations of the people around me. Although the darkness stretched on forever, the lights only shone in the area immediately around me. I figured it meant my sight had limits.

Once, when I was younger, I'd made the mistake of telling my mom about my ability to find people. At first, she hadn't believed me, thinking it was a tall tale made up by an imaginative four-year-old. But when I found her unerringly no matter where she hid in the apartment, she'd looked at me differently afterward. I knew she still loved me, but she saw me as an oddity. Since then, I'd kept it to myself, using it discreetly, fearing someone might catch on and I'd be treated as a pariah.

For whatever reason, in addition to seeing life-sparks, I seemed to have a certain pull on men. It began affecting them as soon as they hit puberty and mellowed as they aged. I'm talking aged to the point of grey hair and a stooped walk. And it wasn't like there was anything significantly special about me physically that would explain it either.

I had straight, shoulder-length, ash-blonde hair, medium complexion, and hazel eyes. My nose fit my face well enough, I supposed, and my mouth wasn't so generous it'd give a guy dirty thoughts. So I didn't think it was my looks. No, there was something else that pulled at them. For some men, it was a strong attraction they couldn't seem to ignore. For other men, it was an odd puzzle they forgot as soon as I walked away.

Stopping the cart outside of a patient's partially opened door, I checked my chart and then my pale blue volunteer scrubs to make sure my name tag was clearly visible on my chest. The hard, white-plastic tag with 'Gabby' embossed in black hung from the fabric for everyone to see. Satisfied, I raised my hand to knock on the door, taking a deep breath. A male patient. This wouldn't be fun.

"Mr. Brandt," I called softly, peeking into the room.

Mr. Brandt, a sturdy man with blonde hair and blue eyes, who I estimated to be in his mid-thirties, was sitting up with the help of his inclined hospital bed. Wrapped in a white, green, and blue hospital gown, and covered by the bleached hospital blankets, he looked away from the T.V. he'd been watching. As soon as his eyes found me, they lit with pleasure.

"Come in," he said, motioning me into the room.

The room, decorated in the same green and blue tones as those on the hospital gowns, was a carbon copy of all of the hospital rooms. A green, fabric recliner, typically positioned close to the bed, and medical cabinets lining the walls to house many of the supplies and equipment needed for the room, were the only other furnishings.

I stepped just inside the door so he could see me. "Would it be all right if I checked some of the supplies in here?"

His blue eyes swept me from head to toe. "Sure thing," he answered with a flashy smile.

I struggled not to roll my eyes. Why couldn't there have been a woman in here? I could tell by his look that he felt my pull already. Nothing to do about it but hurry and get my job done.

Leaving my cart outside the door, I moved to the locked cabinet near the bed and opened it with the key around my neck to count supplies. The cabinet door opened toward the bed, blocking the supplies within from Mr. Brandt's view along with me. Sometimes, it helped to block their view of me.

Despite the door, he strained forward in an attempt to watch me and asked, "So, Gabby, how old are you?"

It was a typical question. At 5′ 5″ with a slight build and few curves to speak of, I looked pretty young. The freckles sprinkling my nose didn't help me look any older, either.

"Sixteen," I said, pausing so I wouldn't lose count.

When he was quiet for a few moments, I started counting again. Telling them my age usually confused them for a few minutes. This guy recovered pretty quickly, though.

"So you work here?"

The cabinet door moved a little, and I knew he'd reached over to try to open it a bit to get a better look at me. I pressed closer to the shelves to stay out of view.

No matter how hard I tried to convince myself that my life was normal, these incidents proved otherwise.

"No, I volunteer," I answered his question briefly, trying to finish my counting as quickly as possible.

"That's really cool. So when do you turn seventeen?" I could hear him shift on his bed.

"I just turned sixteen, so not for a while," I said, wishing he'd stop talking to me. As a rule, I avoided talking about myself because men usually took it as an invitation for a full conversation.

And that was what I was trying to avoid because, for some reason, when you had conversations with people, they took it as a sign you liked them. It wasn't a problem for most people. But for me, sending them any type of 'I like you' signal was not in my best interest.

He interrupted my thoughts and my count with another question. "So, you must still be in high school then. What grade?"

"Sophomore," I answered. Also, as a general rule, I tried not to be rude. It didn't pay to be rude. It tended to ruin a person's day. I mean since they were in the hospital, they might not be having the best day to start with.

"You dating anyone?"

Hidden behind the cabinet door, I rolled my eyes. He was a good-looking man but close to twice my age. What was he thinking? Who was I kidding? What did any of them ever think? It was apparent he was going to be one of the more persistent ones. Thankfully he was connected to an IV. It'd act like a tether if I needed a quick getaway.

"I'll be right back, Mr. Brandt." I left the room to grab the supplies for the cabinet without answering his question, hoping he would realize he'd crossed a line. In the hallway, I took my time collecting what I needed from the secured supply cart, in no rush to get back to his uncomfortable attempts at flirting. After a few minutes, I couldn't delay any longer.

"Hey," he smiled charmingly at me when I walked back in, "I'm being released tomorrow. Would you want to go out for a coffee or something?"

With difficulty, I refrained from rolling my eyes again. The man perceived no boundaries. When I ran into these types, safety in numbers was my best defense.

Using my sight, I checked the location of the charge nurse, who should have been at the scheduling desk now. No life-spark there. I was on my own until I finished restocking.

I placed the supplies in their appropriate containers and

relocked the cabinet before answering his question. "Thank you for asking, but I can't," I said, walking toward the door as I spoke, hurrying to leave before he could say anything further. "Have a good night, Mr. Brandt."

I left Mr. Brandt's room in a rush and collided with someone coming from my left. The force of our impact knocked me into the supply cart. I caught the edge of it, preventing a complete crash to the floor as a hand clasped around my arm. The cart rocked against the collision but held me up. I was glad I'd locked the wheels.

"I'm sorry about that, Gabby," a deep voice said from above me as the hand released its grip on my arm.

Straightening away from the cart, I looked up at an older man with kind brown eyes, a friendly smile, and grey hair. Grey hair was a good thing in my book. The odds were he'd been unaffected by me, unlike Mr. Brandt, who I could hear through the door, calling me back.

"I wasn't watching where I was going," the older man continued as he bent to pick up the coat he'd dropped.

How did he know my name? I tried placing his face but was sure I hadn't seen him before. Then, it hit me. Duh. My nametag.

I gave him a weak smile. "Sorry," I said. "Me, neither." I should have checked the hallway as I left Mr. Brandt's room, but I'd been too distracted trying to make a quick escape.

"Not at all," he said, looking at me intently. He seemed like he wanted to say something but then hesitated. Finally, he said, "You look familiar. Do I know you?"

"I'm sorry, but I don't think so."

"Hmm… Well, it was nice bumping into you." He laid his jacket over his arm, smiled, and walked away.

My eyes followed him as he made his way to the elevators. Dressed in jeans and a button-up shirt open to show a white t-shirt underneath, he looked like an older man who kept up with the times. He didn't look back. He was one of the reasons I was in the hospital. I liked working with older people.

Hearing movement in Mr. Brandt's room behind me, I quickly unlocked the wheels of the supply cart and moved on. I continued restocking supplies for the next hour before turning in my keys and heading for the elevator that led to the lobby. Exiting the elevator, I noted the dusky sky beyond the sliding glass doors. Waving goodnight to the receptionist at the admission's desk, I stepped out onto the sidewalk. It was a five-minute walk to the bus stop from the hospital.

Still dressed in my scrubs, I shouldered my messenger bag loaded with my homework, popped in my earbuds, and set out. It was an easy walk with very few pedestrians. Even though I wasn't in a dangerous area, I walked with my head up. I didn't want to look weak or like I'd be an easy target. Although I used my extra sense to check behind me occasionally, I continued casually looking around. The earbuds, clearly visible, were just a deterrent for conversation and worked really well once I was on the bus.

Late for the pick-up that would've gotten me home before dark, I stood next to the bus stop, waiting. Two people already sat on the long grey bench inside the bus stop shelter. Being under the matching protective awning had its benefits, but I didn't mind giving up the backless bench. As I stood waiting, I continued to look around, taking advantage of the structure's clear sidewalls. Recently replaced, they were once again smooth and shiny.

Glancing at the two people in the shelter, I did a double-take. In that brief look, I thought I saw the reflection of the old man from the hospital, but when I looked back, there was nothing there.

I stretched out my senses to identify the location of the people around me. The tiny lights were always the same color; a yellow center, with a dark-green green halo. I could see the two people sitting on the bus stop bench glowing gently. Other sparks moved nearby. One in particular, moving just out of my range, caught my attention. It was an odd shade I'd never seen before, not the typical yellow and green but a pale blue light with a bright green halo.

The squeal of the light grey city bus stopping beside me jarred me from my private world. For a moment, I stared at the ad for a local lawyer, which decorated the side of the bus, calming my racing heart. Stupid bus scared the crap out of me. I moved back, letting the other passengers board first. By being last, I could choose my seat, meaning I could sit alone.

Showing my pass, I climbed aboard. It wasn't late enough for drunks or punks, but I still sat close to the driver, a regular driver on this route, who had stopped trying to talk to me long ago. As soon as I sat, he pulled away from the stop.

I watched familiar buildings pass by the window, thinking about what waited for me at home. My foster home, actually. When I was a kid, I'd lost my mom first, followed by my grandma. The only two people I had in the world. It was because of my grandma that I wanted to work with the elderly. She'd been so sick at the end.

Gabby remembers Grandma

When I was eight, my mom had died in a car accident, leaving me to live with my grandma. I've always been quiet and serious. Being a product of a one-night stand that my mom couldn't recall, I had no father, absent or otherwise, to count on. My mom had done the best job she could do, but after telling her about what I could do, she'd distanced herself from me. She'd worked and put herself through school, graduating shortly before dying. She'd told me she was working so hard, trying to give us a better future. I went along with it, never questioning why I needed to get ready for school myself or why I had to walk home alone and let myself in with the key I wore on a necklace. Deep down, I knew it would have been different if I would have been normal.

Living with my grandma had been different. I never told her my secret. In her small two-bedroom white house with the standard tiny, city yard, I found the comfortable home life I hadn't had with my mom. Grandma had converted her tiny sewing room into a bedroom for me when I'd moved in. The soft, white, eyelet lace curtains, matching bedspread, and the old dolls sitting on the shelves lining the walls, had given me the stability that my world had needed.

At ten, I'd learned the only one I had left was going to die. I recalled sitting in my grandma's hospital room, studying the wallpaper border pattern while waiting for the nurse to bring grandma back from her tests. Just the pink and blue pattern in the border that repeated again and again. When they'd brought Grandma back in, pushing her in a wheelchair, she'd smiled at me, tears running down her soft, weathered cheeks and told me that we needed to talk.

Now, I volunteered at the same hospital and was glad they'd redone the décor to green and blue.